BEFORE WE HIT THE GROUND

SELALI FIAMANYA

THE BOROUGH PRESS

The Borough Press
An imprint of HarperCollins*Publishers* Ltd
1 London Bridge Street
London SE1 9GF

www.harpercollins.co.uk

HarperCollins *Publishers*
Macken House,
39/40 Mayor Street Upper,
Dublin 1
D01 C9W8

First published by HarperCollins*Publishers* 2025
1

A catalogue record for this book is available from the British Library

Hardback ISBN: 978-0-00-850956-9
Trade Paperback ISBN: 978-0-00-850957-6

This novel is entirely a work of fiction.
The names, characters and incidents portrayed in it are
the work of the author's imagination. Any resemblance to
actual persons, living or dead, events or localities is
entirely coincidental.

Set in Adobe Garamond by HarperCollins*Publishers* India

Printed and bound in the UK using 100% Renewable
Electricity by CPI Group (UK) Ltd

MIX
Paper | Supporting
responsible forestry
FSC™ C007454

This book contains FSC™ certified paper and other controlled
sources to ensure responsible forest management.

For more information visit: www.harpercollins.co.uk/green

To everyone still learning how to love, and be loved.

PART ONE

Chapter One

Abena – March 2019

Glasgow

'Look at this!' Kodzo called from the attic.

'Eh?' Abena lost her rhythm again as she replied. 'I beg, keep it and show me when we finish.' She picked up her cleaning cloth and started spraying, scrubbing, then spraying again. Kodzo had always been more nostalgic, but every wipe revealed another memory for her, too. The burn on the kitchen counter from her first attempt at sweet potato curry; the payday loan that bought the washing machine.

There was little left to pack: the glasses, lamps, rugs and books had already been boxed up. All that was left was to clean. As she passed her cloth across the patterned tiles above the sink, a gentle ripple underneath her fingers caught her by surprise. She had never noticed their texture before, in all the years she'd wiped them down.

They unpacked their Tupperware, napkins and forks and sat on the couch. 'Look at this,' Kodzo said again, turning to a pile of papers he had placed on the floor and producing a single, grubby photograph. It was a smiling six-year-old boy in a nylon Batman outfit, mask and all. Elom wore an oversized orange towel as a cape – the original had been lost on a day at the beach in Troon. Yet he was still beaming; his semi-toothed smile boasting a total confidence in his crime-fighting credentials.

She smiled, eyes fixed on the boy. 'So happy.' Then she handed the picture back suddenly, feeling another surge of grief. Kodzo carefully added the photo to a plastic wallet of documents and keepsakes while she wiped the corners of her eyes. They ate in silence, until he spoke again.

'I'm really grateful, you know.'

'Me too. So grateful. We've been blessed with this house,' Abena replied.

'And to you, too. It wasn't easy.'

'*Ho*, we both tried. And we did well.' She looked at him. 'I'm really proud of you.'

He sighed awkwardly. 'Well, that's just life.' He tried to hide his own welling tears behind another mouthful of rice.

They continued working into the night, with occasional rests and a fitful sleep on the airbed. Dzifa video-called the next morning on her way to work.

'Sorry I can't be there to help – the hospital's kinda hectic at the moment. Also, please don't throw out any of my old stuff! I'll pick it up from storage.'

'Okay, okay. And when will that be? Storage is expensive, young lady.'

'Yeah I know, Dad. I'll pay too, let me know how much it is.' Her eyes darted between the phone and the street as she navigated the rush-hour footfall. They gave her a digital tour of the house, now emptied of the things that had made it a home, while she stood outside work, dabbing her nose with her sleeve. Kodzo showed her the corner behind the green armchair that had once been her favourite hiding place, now an open expanse. 'All those times I had to pretend I couldn't find you. Crouching behind there is probably what gave you asthma, my dear.'

Dzifa laughed. 'So it's your fault for not finding me quicker.'

Abena saw Kodzo's smile falter, and she wanted to tell him that he had always left Dzifa long enough for her to be proud of her spot, but not so long that she ever got bored of hiding. The blue sky behind Dzifa's face jolted as she started moving again, eyes facing ahead. 'I've got to get in and changed before my boss starts the ward round. See you next week.' She gave her eyes another wipe and checked her face in the phone's camera.

'Bye.'

'Love you.'

Her face left the screen, and with it her sing-song voice and the gruff London soundscape. It suddenly felt very quiet in Abena and Kodzo's old house.

'I wish she was here,' Abena said.

'I know, but she's working hard. She can't take more leave.'

Abena softly kissed her teeth, almost tutting. 'We are all working hard. I don't like being here either.'

As they loaded the car with the final few boxes, Kodzo mused, 'I still can't believe he painted the living room yellow, you know?' Elom had moved back into the old family home less

than a year ago, just as Abena and Kodzo moved to a cottage in
the countryside in their retirement.

'Ochre,' Abena corrected. 'He just wanted some sun inside.
Something to make it his own.'

The funeral came and went. Elom was placed in the ground and
the minister's words, 'laid to rest', juddered in Abena's head long
after. Nothing had been laid to rest: not her, Kodzo's or Dzifa's
questions, neither their grief, and certainly not Elom, who lay
trapped under the black soil with whatever demons had always
troubled him.

They still spent their mornings together; in the early light
they pretended that the world outside their bedroom was
unchanged. They watched quiz shows, avoided the news, and
reached for each other quietly under the duvet, as if they still
risked a child bursting in to ask for breakfast. As the days
lengthened, Kodzo read less and walked more, and when
she was allowed, Abena returned to volunteer at the hospital
café. Her repertoire dwindled and she baked only oat cookies
and Empire biscuits for the dessert tray: those had been his
favourites. Now, each sliced cherry placed on the white icing
looked like a glazed wound. She couldn't eat them, but the
visitors did.

In the evenings they would call Dzifa and remember Elom
together, tears of sadness often mixing with tears of laughter.
They started with Dzifa and Elom as kids, but eventually Dzifa
wanted to delve deeper.

'Tell me more about Ghana,' she would ask. Abena had
intentionally avoided those years – she hadn't wanted to

trouble her children with her old pains – but knowing one of her children would never know her past loosened her tongue. She started simply – the canings at school, the times she got malaria. Kodzo joined in too, and with each month came a new revelation – of family royalty, famous cousins and alcoholic aunties; of long-forgotten travels; of boys kissed behind school sheds, and of mornings spent catching fish in the river at the edge of the family farm.

'What do you mean you grew cocoa?' Dzifa asked. 'How much?'

'But your dad's people are farmers – what do you mean you didn't know?' Abena added.

'Dad. No. I've never even seen you plant tomatoes in the garden!' Dzifa stared at the screen, incredulous.

'Oh, we had a few acres. The farm is still there.' Kodzo shrugged.

'Well,' Dzifa hesitated, 'I'm looking forward to seeing it, then.'

'Yes,' Abena nodded, 'You can take us there Kodzo.'

Dzifa spoke more confidently: 'We need to use the insurance vouchers soon. I'll check when's easiest for me to get leave.' She smiled.

Kodzo's voice floated over from the armchair a few feet away, interrupting Abena's response. 'I thought we were going to cancel.'

'How could we cancel?' Abena asked, confused. This was going to be their year of return. They had paid off the mortgage and moved to the countryside: the transition into retirement was complete.

Dzifa broke the silence. 'Dad, come on. I get it, but we have to go.' Kodzo didn't reply, and Dzifa persisted, filling her words with a quiet intensity: 'We're not sacking off the one thing he actually asked us to do.'

Abena was surprised at Dzifa's tone, but happy to see her commitment to Elom's wishes. Still, she tried not to side with the children in front of Kodzo, so she changed the conversation with a non-committal 'We'll see,' and waited until she and Kodzo climbed into bed.

'So you don't want to go?' Abena asked, remembering a similar conversation in the cold a few years earlier.

'And you do?'

'It's what he wanted for all of us.'

'Exactly – *all* of us, not just whoever's left,' Kodzo replied. 'We can go on holiday somewhere else, the three of us. But not this.'

'It's not just a holiday,' Abena said, curtly.

'Then what?'

There was a silence as Abena gathered her thoughts. She took a deep breath, then said, 'I want to go, yes. I want to go and, honestly, I don't want to come back.'

Kodzo paused before asking quietly, 'What do you mean?'

'What's here for me, Kodzo?' Abena shook her head as her eyes narrowed. 'What's here for me? My daughter is four hundred miles away. My friends from the café? They are not our people, Kodzo. Our people – the ones we came with, years ago – they are dying too. They are dying here and they never planned to. I don't plan to.'

'But what about Dzifa – you want to see her only once a year?'

'Dzifa is grown, Kodzo. Dzifa is grown, and I'm so proud of her. She is moving forward without us – the same way we left our parents back home. But the difference is, this is not our village. My children don't need me here anymore. Neither of them. I didn't come to this soil to set down my roots, I came here to plant seeds. Now I'm tired, and I need to go home. I need to see my people, speak my language.'

Kodzo spoke quietly: 'That village life is gone. This is where we chose.'

'That doesn't make it ours. I'm stranded, Kodzo. I'm stuck, you know? *Sankofa* – it's time.' Kodzo was staring at his folded arms across his belly. Abena took a calming breath, then continued.

'I went to the house last week. There was a blue Volvo in the drive. They've changed the curtains. I wanted to go inside and see what it looks like. I want their lives there to be as happy as ours were – but stepping on the driveway, I felt like a trespasser. How could I ring the doorbell to my own home?' She paused. 'I have nothing left here.'

Kodzo spoke slowly as he reached for his book on the bedside table. 'I walk to his grave every day. That's ours. That coffin is our root in this soil. I can't leave him.'

Abena called Dzifa and told her to book two tickets, and that Kodzo would not be joining them.

'He's gonna regret it. Sitting at home alone for three weeks isn't honouring Elom's memory,' Dzifa said through mouthfuls of dinner. 'I'll call him tomorrow. He can sit on the beach – he doesn't have to do the family rounds.'

'He's not ready,' said Abena.

'I know, but—'

'Please, leave it. This isn't the only time we can go.' Dzifa mostly did leave it, though Abena had to carry the conversation more on group phone calls in the following weeks.

As the departure approached, Abena packed her suitcases with the multi-dimensional magic of African women. Clothes, shoes, makeup; boxes of tea, tins of shortbread and bottles of olive oil; drinking-glass gift sets, old mobile phones and candles; a dusty PlayStation 3 from the attic. Presents that both satisfied her impulse of a mother's generosity, and maintained the illusion of a life of Western luxury, all in under 23 kilograms. Kodzo kept quiet when he noticed Abena packing her jewellery box alongside the second-hand cutlery, and her cherished handwritten recipe book between T-shirts.

Kodzo was out for most of the morning of the flight. Abena waited anxiously at home, portioning the last of a week's supply of home-cooked ready meals for the freezer. He arrived just as she had finished loading her suitcases into the car.

'Where have you been?' she asked, sliding into the passenger seat.

'I went for a walk.' He looked at Abena and smiled gently, then turned the key in the ignition and pulled out onto the unpaved village lane.

Dzifa would meet Abena in Amsterdam before transferring to the Accra flight. By the time Abena and Kodzo arrived at the airport, Abena had to head straight to security.

'I'm sorry you can't come,' she said, stopping before joining the queue.

'I know. Just call me when you land, okay? And I beg, keep the car window closed when you do. These people will just snatch your phone if you are not careful.' He chuckled, and Abena couldn't help but smile. 'I have something for you.' Kodzo reached into his jacket pocket and produced a small plastic sandwich bag. Inside was a handful of deep brown soil. It was dark and moist, like a rich chocolate sponge. Abena knew immediately where he had taken it from, and where he had walked that morning. She took it, feeling its cool, light softness in her palm.

'Don't be blinded by that red earth over there – keep this with you. It's yours . . . ours. *Sankofa*, yes, get what you need. When you've found it, we'll be waiting for you.' Abena thanked him, put the bag in her inside pocket and held him tightly. He was the same kind man that had asked her to marry him after three weeks of talking, and had stayed by her side for thirty years more. She loved him, and she knew he loved her, but if accepting his love meant accepting a life that wasn't hers, she had to make a decision.

'You can choose to mourn our son in the place where he died. I need to remember him in a place where I can live.'

She pulled away and turned towards the gates. Kodzo stayed until she was ushered to a queue out of sight, then slipped his hands in his pockets, and made his way home.

Chapter Two

Abena – April 1986

Accra

Abena lay in bed on Saturday morning, the first in weeks that she'd slept through the rooster's crow. The sun beat through the thin curtain; thankfully its heat had not yet matched its brightness, and Abena started to plan her day. She could doze for an hour and still have time to sweep the compound, wash her niece and nephew's uniforms, and make it to the market before the sun was at its hottest. Last night, Abena had joined her colleagues from the catering college for drinks. Only Fanta and Muscatella for her – Aunty Esther often stayed up to make sure Abena was home at a proper time, and in a proper state – but she still found her smile and hips loosening in line with the others' beer and schnapps, and even danced to a few songs, and with a few boys.

One had the neatest 'fro she had ever seen, with a sharp line shaved in from the corner of his forehead, like the Black Americans on TV. They sweated as they danced to Ebo Taylor's

'Love and Death', and her friends teased her when she returned to her seat. She got home too late to bathe before bed, and she wondered if last night her sweat had had the sweet-sharp musk that she could smell now. She wondered if he had liked it, the way she had liked smelling him. She closed her eyes and turned away from the window as she lowered her hand towards the waistband of her pants.

'*Hehn*, Abena, go and make breakfast for Ernest's friend.' Aunty Esther pushed Abena's door open and stood in the entryway in a faded wrapper, her hair running away from her face in six short, greying cornrows.

'Good morning, Aunty.'

'I said *now now*, you this idle girl. It's already eight o'clock.'

Abena sat up on her foam mattress, covering herself with her green and blue printed cloth.

'Aunty, please, what friend? I thought Ernest had travelled to the village?'

'Do you not have eyes? Ernest's friend, Kodzo, has been here for two days now in Ernest's room. He's visiting from UK. Go and fetch water for W.C. and cook for him before he leaves this morning.' Esther left the door open, leaving Abena to close it herself. She got as close to slamming it as she could get away with before changing into the wrapper she normally used for housework, her dress from the previous night hanging from the doorknob of her wooden cupboard. She slipped on her *chalewote*, picked up a large plastic bucket from the kitchen and headed to the tap outside, cursing Ernest as she walked.

Ernest was a distant relative, and like all of her relatives, his arrival had meant work for her. She remembered their introduction a year ago; how Aunty Esther had fawned the way she always did around educated men.

'If you want anything done, just come and ask Abena – she'll go to the market, cook for you,' Aunty Esther had said. Ernest didn't say 'thank you' in a way that meant 'but there will be no need', or ask Abena about her own life, so as not to interrupt it with his own errands. She was twenty-four, and for all he knew she might have been a graduate like him, maybe with a job in an important government department. Instead, he just smiled, shook her hand, and said, 'I appreciate that so much.'

Ernest's flat was on the third floor of the adjoining building in the compound, which meant no running water, and also that it was too far up to hear a knock on the front door. Abena stood outside, carrying the bucket of water on top of a small, coiled cloth-turned-cushion on her cornrowed head, with a loaf of sweet bread in her right hand. She looked up to the open window, took a deep breath and shouted.

'Kodzo!' Nothing. 'Kodzo!' Abena's jaw clenched at the irritation of being woken up to make breakfast for a man who was asleep. 'Kodzo!'

'Yes?' A voice came through the curtain. Abena sucked her teeth.

'Aunty Esther sent me. I'm coming up.' She spoke in English, assuming that, like Ernest, he wasn't a Fante speaker.

Abena climbed the stairs as she had done many times before; back straight, the water in the bucket frantically swirling, yet never spilling a drop. She knocked on the door to Ernest's flat and Kodzo opened almost immediately, his eyes exactly in front of hers. They were the same height, her slightly taller than average and him slightly shorter. His hair was flattened on one side and he still had lines on his cheek from his pillow.

'I've come to flush your toilet.'

He looked at her, cocked his head to the side and smiled with a grateful tut, then turned back into the house. Of course, there was no pretence of refusal. Abena rolled her eyes as she ducked into the living room, lifted the bucket from her head and lowered it onto the floor. He was skinny in his white singlet, though Abena noted the curve filling out his boxer shorts as he walked away.

The flat was spacious, with a terrazzo floor glinting in the increasingly hot sunlight. The only signs of habitation from the new tenant were a couple of heavy books and some records on the wooden coffee table – she recognised the face of Stevie Wonder poking from underneath a black one with a triangle and a rainbow. Abena carried the bucket straight through the door opposite and into the bathroom. She used half of the water to flush the toilet, and added the rest to the bucket in the shower for Kodzo to bathe with later.

'*Medaase*,' Kodzo thanked her as she re-entered the living room, and Abena confirmed from his attempt that he wasn't a Fante speaker.

'You're welcome. Aunty said I've to make breakfast,' she answered in English as she walked to the kitchen. The fridge and pantry had been stocked with eggs, rice, cornmeal, Tom Brown, a packet of cornflakes and several tins of Peak condensed milk. Abena wondered whether Aunty Esther actually made any money from her tenants when she spent it all on this, half of which they barely touched: Abena had yet to see Ernest cook a meal – if Abena wasn't around, he ate out with friends.

Kodzo joined her, leaning against the doorframe, now wearing a T-shirt and shorts. Abena didn't ask what he would prefer, deciding on Tom Brown, the easiest porridge to cook.

'So, what is your name?'

'Abena,' she replied, lighting the stove to boil the water.

'And, Abena, what do you do?' She paused, surprised: people rarely thought to ask her this question. 'I hope you're not a teacher, because everybody I've met here is a teacher.' He chuckled.

Abena looked at him directly. 'Well, I'm sorry for you, because me too, I am a teacher,' she replied, and Kodzo's chuckle faltered. 'I teach at the catering school by Mile 7.' She turned to the cupboard as Kodzo opened his mouth, not wanting to give his next insult the courtesy of meeting her face. It was typical, she thought, that rather than respect her work, this man visiting from abroad mocked it.

'Oh . . . well, I'm honoured to have you cook for me. Maybe you should teach me so I can stop wasting my money at the chop house.'

'Hm, maybe, oh.' Abena stirred the roasted cornmeal into the boiling water, still avoiding his gaze. 'Do you take it with milk?'

'Please, and just one sugar.'

'Okay. I'll serve you in the living room.' She kept her eyes on the pot, and felt his gaze for a few more seconds, before he shuffled away.

The next day, she found Kodzo already dressed in a T-shirt and shorts, his hair rounded out in a freshly combed 'fro. He stood in the doorway, asking more questions while she cooked, and Abena answered – at first because she couldn't maintain the rudeness required to ignore direct questioning, but then because she enjoyed the feeling of talking about herself, for once. Abena told him that she loved cooking, but she had only studied it – and ended up teaching it – because Aunty Esther didn't let her go to college to read books. Kodzo told her about his dad, who had been a goldsmith, and his childhood catching fish by the river, and his nursing studies in Glasgow. By day six, he had started eating whilst standing, chatting while she washed the dishes, and Abena started cooking more elaborate breakfasts. After a week she was taking up flour, yeast and nutmeg to make fresh bofloat to have with his koko.

'So, do you like music?' he asked as she washed the steel pot.

'Yes, of course.' Abena remembered her last night at the bar. Kodzo put his bowl down and turned to the living room. A wavering melody drifted through to the kitchen, with Kodzo following slowly behind. It sounded like the music at the churches where people didn't dance, and where the worship songs sound more like a funeral lament than rejoicing.

'Do you like classical music?'

Abena felt she should, that it was something listened to in universities and by people in films. 'Yes, I do.'

'Oh really?' He smiled. 'Who do you like?'

'Me . . . ?' Abena turned back to her washing, embarrassed. 'I like them all.'

Kodzo laughed, and Abena blushed. She looked at him again, whetting her tongue in retaliation, when she saw a brightness in his eyes, rather than the sharpness she usually saw when someone laughed at her. She smiled back.

That weekend Abena climbed the steps with a toddler on her back, wrapped close in a green patterned cloth.

'Who's this little one?'

'My sister, Abla.' She didn't clarify any further, checking his face to see if he had another, unanswered question about whether she had any children herself. She had noticed (and resented) how men changed when they confirmed she was unmarried and unburdened with a family of her own – their casual friendliness became something more insistent. But there was nothing from Kodzo; he looked just as excited as when she'd first walked through the door.

'But that's an Ewe name!'

'Her father is from Volta.' If Kodzo was working through the specifics – the age gap, the fathers from different tribes, and who may or may not have been legitimate – he didn't show it. Instead, he started babbling in Ewe to Abla, and Abena felt her nestling her head into her back in shyness. After cooking, Abena joined Kodzo in the living room, her back and Abla both tired of being swaddled. Abla tottered around the room in her cloth nappy, bumping into Kodzo's legs, her fear of him dissipated by a three-pack of coconut-flavoured biscuits. Kodzo put on some Stevie Wonder and spooned his koko, while Abena helped herself to a bofloat.

'Has your mother come to Newtown with Abla?'

'No, she's still with her people in Adabraka, but Abla will be here for a few days. Then maybe to Tema with Aunty Susan.' Abena smiled, watching Abla reach across the table, her stubby fingers reaching for a bofloat from the bowl in the middle. Kodzo had told Abena how he used to walk barefoot and laughing between compounds and villages with his friends and cousins, finding dinner and a bed at the closest aunty's house as night began to fall. She hoped he would think of Abla's itinerancy as similarly charmed, rather than chaotic.

'So you'll be busy with her for the weekend?'

'Yes, she will keep me very busy – won't you, Abla?' Abla looked over, nonplussed, her fingers mushy with wet dough, and Abena laughed.

'Well, then after she goes and you have some time, maybe we can go to see a film?' Kodzo was leaning towards her with one elbow on the sofa, his eyebrows raised in a question.

Abena felt herself being pulled back into the room, away from the cozy family daydream she had slipped into. She shook her head. 'No . . . no, thank you.'

'Oh, not even for some food?'

'Kodzo, thank you but I have to work. I won't have time. Anyway, I have to leave very early on Wednesday for Kumasi. That's why Abla can't stay here next weekend. I have some management training for work. Psychology or something.'

'But I'm leaving on Friday. You can't stay?' Abena had hoped Kodzo would be impressed, but he seemed uninterested in her course, and it left her smarting.

'Please, it's for work, I have to go. Anyway, I haven't been to Kumasi before.'

Kodzo looked like he didn't know what to say next, a first since she had met him, until Abla babbled, and he threw her his attention. Abena, grateful for the distraction, gathered the plates while Kodzo tickled Abla, her giggles filling the silence they had left behind.

Abena knew she liked Kodzo. When they talked about the news, he listened as much as he spoke. It seemed important to him to make her laugh, and he was good at it. His face and his thighs had started to infiltrate Abena's thoughts in the dark, when she was trying to get to sleep after she had showered and smoothed herself in cocoa butter. But he was another man visiting home from abroad, three weeks into a one-month holiday from Glasgow. She remembered friends like Yaa and Elizabeth; how their expectant smiles in the rainy season turned to cracked lips by the dry season, after the men they had latched on to had returned abroad without them. Even Aunty Esther's daughter, Sister Efua, seemed hollowed out by the burdens of her children Ayikaeley and Okaidja, despite her obvious love for them, despite their father being mostly present, and despite having Abena as a cousin and de facto maid helping to raise them. Abena's hope was fragile: she knew never to place it in something as risky as a handsome man.

On Wednesday morning she didn't make Kodzo breakfast. As she crossed the compound, she heard a call from the flats, and she turned to see Kodzo jogging towards her. She smiled in spite of herself. Though his hair was combed, his eyes were still bleary: clearly he was not used to waking up this early, Abena thought, putting down her suitcase.

'I'm disappointed you couldn't stay, you know.'

Abena sighed. 'I want to go to the training, Kodzo. Don't make me late.'

'Okay, I know. Listen. I was going to ask you something.' He took her right hand between both of his. It was the most they had touched since they had met. 'Will you marry me?'

Abena's face folded into a confused frown. 'Marry you? Marry you for what?'

'Ei, woman. I said will you marry me, what else for?'

Abena felt silly, standing in the almost empty compound, her suitcase by her side, late for the trotro into town, but she didn't let go of Kodzo's hand. She wondered what it might feel like to trust him. Abena had told herself she would never get married, or have children. She had only told *herself* this, and no one else, because she knew it was ridiculous: there were no better options for her, not really. She knew few old, unmarried women, fewer who were childless, fewer still with any money, and none who were happy.

She could stay under the thumb of Aunty Esther – who was annoyed that Abena had the gall to leave for a work trip for three days, and who demanded half of Abena's salary each month for homestead 'contributions' – or she could find safety in a man. And here was a man who had not laughed at her once, who had never sheepishly ushered out a half-dressed woman in the morning, and who was trying hard to make something of himself abroad. One who was kind to her, and made her laugh, and whose hands, still on hers, were gentle.

'I'll think about it.'

'You'll think about it?'

'Yes. I'll think.'

Kodzo looked calm, as if he had read ahead and already knew the answer. Abena wasn't sure if she was impressed or annoyed by his confidence.

'Okay. Well, have a good trip. I'll write to you from Glasgow.'

'Thanks.' Abena picked up her suitcase. 'I've enjoyed meeting you.'

'Me too. I'll miss your cooking, oh. You've spoiled bofloat for me now, nobody will match yours.'

Rushing for her bus, excited for the trip ahead, Abena laughed. 'I'll send you the recipe!'

Chapter Three

Abena – April 1989

Glasgow

Abena laid the shopping on the doormat and reached for her keys, pushing through the wet fabric of her raincoat pocket with numbed fingers. In the kitchen, rainwater trickled from the bags onto the counter-top, pooling underneath the plastic as she packed everything away. She topped up the heating meter, then sat down to watch the *One O'clock News*. At random intervals, her sodden hair released a few drops of water, which rolled down her forehead and stung her eyes, or landed with an unpleasant tingle in the folds of her nostrils. The poll tax was in, and people were chanting in the street. Abena respected their anger, and their hope. She turned the volume up when Princess Diana appeared on the screen: it was sunny, wherever she was, and she was sweating just enough for her skin to glow with a satin sheen, while her sallow-faced, red-cheeked husband looked on. She wore a choker, heavy with diamonds and sapphires, and Abena wondered how heavy it felt.

Abena didn't need to cook today – bricks of rice, stew and soup were stacked in the freezer in old ice-cream tubs and sandwich bags, but after the closing credits there was little else to do until Kodzo got home. She had been able to find some okro at the one-stop ethnic food shop in town, and started making banku and okro soup, one of Kodzo's favourites. Banku was the only thing he could cook on a par with her, somehow stirring it silky smooth every time, while Abena's had the occasional lump. She began chopping, deseeding, grating and blending onions, ginger, tomatoes, okro and chillies, and slicing, spicing and marinading fish and chicken, adding them all at the right times to the right pots until they were ready to be thrown together. The kitchen windows steamed and the tiles started to sweat as the room filled with familiar smells. She knew she should open them to release some of the moisture, but the humidity felt good.

Kodzo turned his key in the lock just as the stew began its final simmer. Abena's heart skipped slightly as she washed the remnants of diced vegetables off her hands. Kodzo walked into the kitchen, smiling and still in his scrub top, which fitted his chest and waist just enough to show the form of now softening muscles underneath. Abena smiled back, looking forward to sharing the evening with him, while also resenting that this was the most exciting moment of her day.

'Okro soup?' Kodzo asked, lifting the lid on the pot and letting out a billow of steam.

'Yeah, I was bored of rice.'

'And I guess now you need my services,' Kodzo said, clapping his hands together.

Abena laughed. 'Yes, please. The banku is all yours.'

Kodzo went to shower the ward off his skin before coming back and taking out the cornmeal. Before he started cooking, he turned to Abena and reminded her, 'We have to open the window or we'll get mould.' He leaned over the sink to push the window open, and Abena felt a rush of cold as the steamy air was sucked out of the kitchen.

The next day after church, Abena and Kodzo drove in convoy behind Maria and Mensah to Afi and Peter's house for lunch. Inside, Kodzo settled in the living room with a cold bottle of Supermalt. Abena joined the women in the kitchen, laying the yam she had brought on the counter while complimenting Afi's wig and Maria's dress.

'Abena, *medaase*. You too, you're looking nice,' Maria replied.

'Thank you.' Abena smiled. She had braided her hair simply, and wore a second-hand dress that she had taken in at the waist. Maria's dress was brand new and hugged her perfectly. They began cooking; chopping yam and onions, blending tomatoes and grilling chicken, all the while checking if the men needed more snacks or drinks.

As they cooked, the usual topics were picked off the shelves – which supermarket had a discount on rice, which shop had the best selection of winter jackets, and which family members in Ghana were asking for money. Abena thought these conversations always had the same rhythm and cadence, unlike those from the living room which seemed to alternate between explosive laughter, intense whispers and overlapping shouts as they weaved between the political and the personal.

'*Saa* Princess Diana *no*,' Afi started, coming back into the kitchen with a tray of empty bottles – she must have been on the television again next door. Abena's ears pricked; there was something about Diana that drew her in, more than her beauty or poise, and she wanted to know what the others thought of her. 'She is looking very skinny, oh. *Ondidi wɔ* Buckingham Palace *hɔ koraa*?' Afi continued, and the women laughed.

'They want to starve her!' Maria joked. 'Come and see a princess in Ghana looking like she can afford diamonds but not even simple gari soakings.'

'I'm telling you, she shouldn't be trusting those royals,' Afi continued. 'They will swallow her.'

'Hmm,' Maria agreed.

The conversation moved on to something else, and Abena kept stirring, frustrated. There were things Abena wanted to say about Diana – things about beauty, control, power, empire, freedom – but the thoughts floated high in her mind like clouds she couldn't grasp. Sometimes she talked with Kodzo about these things, and with time and the right nudges he could help her explain what she wanted to say.

Afi had graduated from Achimota Girls' School, and Maria had gone to nursing college. While they had benefited from books, homework and essays, Abena had been changing nappies and stirring pots. She had gone to a vocational school, but the only texts she'd read there were cookbooks. Yet when the chance presented itself for the others to use their knowledge, they shied away. It annoyed Abena that some essence emanating from the stove sapped their ability to talk in the same way as the men did on the other side of the kitchen wall.

Once the food was ready, the women dished it into matching serving bowls before setting the table – Afi and Peter were the only couple out of the three with a separate dining room. As the men served themselves, Afi poured beer into three glasses for Abena, Maria and herself in the kitchen. Abena and Afi clinked glasses and went to do the same to Maria.

'Actually, I'm not taking alcohol today.' Maria smiled.

'Ei!' Afi understood immediately. 'Congratulations, my dear! Eiii!' The shouts from the kitchen got the attention of the men, and Mensah called from the table, 'Ah ah, woman! What are you screaming about?'

'Oh, stop it, you.' Afi came through from the kitchen, fake-scowling. 'You can't be playing games anymore.' Mensah looked affronted, and Kodzo confused.

'I beg, what's going on?' Kodzo asked.

Mensah and Maria shared a smile before Mensah turned and said, 'We are expecting.'

The room broke out in renewed shouts of congratulations, with hugs, handshakes, clicks and a refilling of glasses. After hugging Maria, Abena stood by Kodzo, who held her close with his arm around her shoulders. He looked joyous as he congratulated Maria and Mensah again on their new baby. When he turned to her, Abena saw a question on his face – or maybe a hope – and it filled her with a wave of nerves and guilt, like a child about to tell her mother that she had broken her favourite pot.

While Kodzo was at work the following morning, Abena circled three job adverts in the newspaper: two for cleaners (no experience needed) and one for a cook at a local hotel restaurant (minimum

two years' experience). Then she planned the conversation she
would have with Kodzo later.

They had managed a year in Glasgow without getting
pregnant – Kodzo always pulled out, leaving a warm gel which
rapidly cooled into a shiny film on the bedsheets, or Abena's body.
He had done so religiously, even when a bit tipsy or tired. Abena
respected this about him, even more so as he became increasingly
exasperated. First, there had been the settling-in period, where
they enjoyed their young marriage and the freedom of life in a
new country – Abena allowed six months for this. When Kodzo
raised the idea of family, she explained that she wanted to study
first: she had come to Britain where she could finally pursue her
education, and she needed to be childless to focus.

Abena had no secondary school leaver's certificate, but she was
too old to enrol in the local school. Her primary school certificate,
on thick yellow paper with illegible cursive, was irrelevant to the
university, and no one seemed willing, or able, to help her bridge
the gap. She had tried calling, only to find the voice on the other
end as intelligible as the static from the radio. So she had gone
in person while Kodzo was at work, walking through another
downpour, and had been directed from marble-floored staircase
to wood-panelled office, and then from desk to desk until she
stood sodden in front of someone who gave her a prospectus and
told her she had missed the application deadlines for that year.
She reached out for the book, dripping water from her sleeve
onto the person's desk, and saw their tight lips twitch even tighter.
Abena took it and left as quickly as she could, too humiliated to
ask when the applications would reopen. The only courses she
found she could get onto were at one of the vocational colleges,

for catering (again) or to become a seamstress. After months of searching and failed applications, which Kodzo dutifully spell-checked, his questions had started again.

Abena remembered the last conversation, broached lightly whilst they were shopping together. 'We should get going,' he chuckled. 'I don't want to be an old man trying to play with my kids.'

'Mm-mm,' Abena had agreed. 'Soon. Maybe we should get a bigger place first, though.'

'We can move any time,' Kodzo replied, and Abena knew it was true, and that her excuses were getting weaker.

'Okay, let's talk about it.' She had delayed, and a week of late shifts followed by her period had brought her to today.

Abena rehearsed her speech in her mind: she had thrown herself into their mostly white church and knew her way round the jagged tones of the Glaswegian accent now. Kodzo was in the final year of his nursing diploma, and exams meant he was less able to use weekends picking up auxiliary shifts in the hospital. He would never tell her, but she knew from the amounts she got for the weekly shop that money was dwindling. His bursary had to cover her, as well as her family back home, who now expected allowances and school-fee payments from Sister Abena in *abrokyir*. Whatever he had saved must have been drained by his flights back to Ghana for their traditional wedding, her flight over, and the small Christian wedding they had had with friends here. Although they could live on less, a child would be expensive. In conclusion, Abena would say, she needed to work.

Abena could hear her heartbeat bouncing off the phone she pressed against her ear. She hadn't phoned a Glaswegian since her attempts to get into university, and hoped she could make it through the foggy accent without lip-reading as a guide.

'Hi, this is the Dundonald, how can I help?' The voice was deep, but intelligible.

'Hello, I'm phoning about the sous-chef job, please.'

'I'm sorry?'

Abena spoke more slowly. 'The sous-chef job, I'd like to apply.'

'Ah, right. I'll put you through to the kitchen manager.' Abena waited, noticing the coolness from the sweat under her armpit as she adjusted her arm.

'Hi, kitchen manager,' the voice started suddenly.

'Hello? My name is—'

'Hello?'

'Hi.' Abena hesitated before starting again. 'My name is Abena, I'd like to apply for the sous-chef job, please.'

'Wit wiz 'at?'

'Abena. I'd like to—'

'Abna? That's a lovely name, where ye fae?' He fell off the last syllable of her name rather than rising upwards in pitch.

'Ghana. I went to catering college there and have worked in hotels in the capital.'

'Oh have ye, aye?'

'Yes, one Western hotel called the Lotus Club.'

'Well we get folk here fae all over, but it's mostly British food wi' a bit of continental. Can you come in themorra for an interview?'

Abena put down the phone a few minutes later, as excited about the chance to open up her world as she was nervous about explaining herself to Kodzo. She worried that he saw her search for education, and now work, as a decision to set herself apart from him, and apart from their path to children. She didn't know how long she could convince him, or herself, that it was neither of those things.

It was still light when Kodzo got home. The expansion and contraction of the days in Scotland unsettled Abena, who had seen the sun rise and set at the same time each day for her whole life. They ate rice and stew and watched English men running around a hotel to eruptions of tinned laughter every few seconds. As the end credits rolled, Abena turned to Kodzo.

'So, I wanted to talk to you about something.'

'Oh, am I in trouble?' Kodzo smirked.

'Ho, stop it. It's just, I need your help.' Abena took another bite. 'I have an interview for a job tomorrow. At a hotel. The Dundonald. The one on Great Western Road?'

Kodzo took a few seconds to answer. 'An interview? For a job?'

'Yeah. I just think, you know I'm at home all the time and I'd like to meet people. And also I think we could do with more money.'

'We have enough money, we aren't struggling here.' Kodzo turned back to his food.

'No, I don't mean that . . .' Abena felt the conversation slipping from her. 'It's just, I think I can help. You have exams; Abla will be starting school soon.'

'I have one year left, then I'll be working full-time. We'll be fine until then.' Kodzo changed the channel on the television to the evening news. 'Do you see Afi and Maria working in this Glasgow? I'm telling you it can be very difficult here. We haven't even started our own family yet and you want to get stressed, running around all day.' Abena thought of Maria sitting in her kitchen getting steadily more swollen.

'I want to have children, Kodzo' – it was a vague enough statement for Abena not to feel like she had lied – 'but we need stability. I know what it's like when children grow up without stability.' It felt manipulative to use her past like that, but she was losing ground.

'So stability is you working night shift in a hotel kitchen while the baby is home? Or what?'

Kodzo looked angry, or hurt, and Abena didn't know what to say. Before she could think of an answer, he spoke: 'It's fine. If you want to work, it's fine.' He turned back to the television and Abena began stacking the plates, defeated despite achieving her goal.

In the morning Abena rose with Kodzo and made breakfast as usual. This time, however, she joined him in getting showered and dressed. Kodzo leaned against the counter eating a bowl of Weetabix while Abena sipped on a coffee, too nervous to eat.

'What time do you have to be there?'

'Eleven o'clock,' Abena replied. 'If the interview goes well, I'll join a trial shift for lunch.'

'You'll be fine, you've worked in hotels before.' Abena nodded her thanks, and kept sipping. She wished he looked more like he meant it. She wanted guidance – he had done it all before – and it irked her that despite her nerves, all he could give her was resignation, as if he was tolerating her stubbornly held ambition.

After he left, she read through her CV, letters of recommendation and a couple of old baking recipes, before catching the bus. The hotel was on a main road, set in one of the grander tenement buildings. The yellow sandstone glittered in the cold morning air, and the large bay windows gave view to a high-ceilinged dining room in which guests were finishing their breakfast.

The man at reception smiled when Abena greeted him, and directed her to the manager's office in the same deep voice she had heard on the phone. She stood in front of a black door in a hallway where the patterned tiles of the entrance had been swapped for a red linoleum with shiny bits of grit in it to make it anti-slip. She sat on the chair outside the door, listening to the clattering sounds of the kitchen across the hallway. A few people walked past as she waited, ignoring her, or offering a perfunctory 'Mornin'', and Abena wondered what it might be like to work with them.

At 10.55 a.m. Abena knocked on the door. It was opened almost immediately by an average-height man in a white shirt and black trousers.

'Abna, is it?' He smiled broadly as he held the door open, waving towards the chair opposite his desk.

'Yes. Thanks for inviting me to interview.' Abena sat as he shut the door behind her.

'No problem. I'm Rory, kitchen manager here.' There was a pause as Rory sat and looked at her, still grinning widely, and Abena was unsure if she should speak. It was her first interview in the UK, and maybe the respect shown by silence back home was different here. As she eventually opened her mouth, he began, 'So where are you from then?'

'Ghana – it's in West Africa.'

'Right, and how long ye been here?'

'Just under a year. I came with my husband. He's studying nursing.'

'Good on him. We moan a lot but I bet there's better for yous here than there is back there. Cold here though, I suppose!' He laughed, and Abena echoed him. 'And you said you worked as a cook back there – where was it again?'

'Accra, the capital.' Abena handed him her paperwork.

'And there are hotels and that over there, aye?'

'Yes, some very nice hotels. Western ones too.'

He nodded as he looked over her CV. 'Well, we don't ask for too much here to be honest. You just need to work when there's work to do. It can be quite busy, but nothing too fancy. Full Scottish breakfasts, standard lunches and dinners. I see you're a bit of a baker?'

Abena nodded. 'Yes, I was a pastry chef in my last hotel, before leaving to work at a catering school.'

'Well then, any suggestions for desserts here?' He put her papers on the desk and looked into Abena's face, his own placid and friendly.

'Oh. Sorry, I haven't actually seen the menu yet.' Abena felt her toes curl in her shoes while her face remained relaxed.

'Och, it's just the usual stuff. I'll tell you, I'm tired of crumble and custard – we could mibbie do with a new warm dessert. Anything come to mind?'

With part of her mind, Abena cursed herself for being foolish enough to sit outside Rory's office for twenty-five minutes without checking the restaurant menu. With the rest of it, she scanned her mental recipe library.

'Ehm . . .' Rory continued to gaze at her, his smile now accompanied by a slightly raised eyebrow. 'Well, for something warm, how about poached plums?'

'Poached plums?' Both of Rory's eyebrows were raised now.

'Yes,' Abena continued, visualising the recipe book from her classes years ago. 'Sliced in half, and poached in water, sugar, vanilla and cinnamon. With a butterscotch sauce.'

'Wouldn't they be a bit mushy?'

'Not if they aren't too ripe.'

'Okay. And what about the skins?'

'Oh, you would peel them, of course.'

'Peel plums? And halve them?'

Abena nodded, unsure what she had got wrong. It was a common dessert – she had learned about it in her first semester.

'And do ye remove the stones?'

Abena paused, her confusion mounting. She had never actually made this recipe before. Often in her classes they had substituted ingredients for the ones they had in Accra. Strawberries, grapes and butternut squash became guava, sisibi and sweet potatoes. They had used apples for this recipe. In a moment only slightly longer than the one it took Rory, she realised her mistake.

'Abna, you don't mean pears, do ye? Poached pears?' His smile had mostly faded.

'Yes, I mean poached pears. Sorry, I was just . . . Yes of course, I mean pears.' Abena tried to chuckle; to regain some of the joviality of the previous few minutes, but she felt the horror on her face despite her effort. Rory smiled again, but it was different. Abena wondered if he had found the answer to a different question he had been pondering – something about her, and her place in his world – but hadn't directly asked. It looked like whatever he had learned had helped make his decision.

Abena walked out of the hotel entrance ten minutes later, angry and humiliated. Rory had briefly shown her around the kitchen, but she had not been invited for a trial. Abena could lean into anger, even use it when she needed to, but humiliation was like a hot, itchy jumper she couldn't get off no matter how hard she tried. She started towards the bus stop when she heard a car horn beep. Kodzo was parked a few dozen yards away, and as he flashed his headlights at her, Abena felt the jumper grow tighter.

'So, how did it go?' he asked as she climbed into the passenger seat.

'Kodzo, you know how it went. And you too, I said I would have a trial this afternoon, so you came here now because what? You thought they wouldn't want me?' Abena didn't look at Kodzo as she spoke, aware that her anger was misdirected but comforted to have somewhere to put it.

'Abena, I didn't want to see you here.' Kodzo watched the road as he pulled out. 'I know you can cook, and I know you can work. I'm just telling you like I tried to tell you last night: this country, eh? It can be hard for us. Very hard.' Abena stayed silent, watching the passing cars blur as the itchy heat stung her eyes.

Kodzo dropped Abena off outside their flat before driving back to work. She changed into a green and blue wrapper, made herself some toast and washed up the previous night's dishes. She then put her CV and letters of recommendation back in her old suitcase, zipped it up and slid it under the bed. She remembered reading once that Princess Diana had left school without any O levels either, and she wondered if Maria had bothered to bring her nursing diploma over with her, or if it lay in a dusty box in a storeroom in Tema. That night, as Kodzo lay on top of her, she didn't respond when he said he was going to finish. When he said it again, she simply nodded and said, 'Okay,' and felt him pulse inside her for the first time.

Abena was unsurprised when, a month later, she started waking up sick. She was already two weeks late and this simply confirmed what she knew, but she had yet to tell Kodzo – there was a finality there she couldn't accept. It felt like Afi's kitchen with a locked door, or the pressure on her neck as she carried water up the steps to Ernest's flat. Though, trapped as she felt, it was at least familiar, unlike the rest of her life in Glasgow.

The surprise came with a phone call. Abena picked up the receiver tentatively, ready to say that Kodzo would be back later.

'Hi, izat Abna? Hi, it's Rory, from the Dundonald. Look, sorry for the delay in getting back tae ye. We've went with someone with more experience for the sous-chef job. But, eh, we're getting to the school holidays and we could do with a bit of general help in the kitchen. Not cheffing, but prepping, cleaning and that, maybe serving if numbers are tight. Would ye be able to work a cupla weeks over the summer?' Abena caught her breath as a wave came over her, somewhere between nausea, fear and joy: a door had opened in her locked room, letting in a rush of air. 'Mind you, we'd need ye workin' long days, but. You okay for—?'

'Yes. Definitely, sure.'

'Oh good!' Rory sounded pleased. 'Good, well we'd need ye from the start of next week.'

Abena hung up a few minutes later, unsure what the hot, heavy feeling was throbbing in her stomach. Kodzo had been more cheerful lately, and in a way, more caring, as if to encourage her that they were now on the right path. They were having more sex, and she could feel his anticipation growing.

She didn't know what to tell him: working was one thing, running around a hot kitchen while carrying his child was another entirely. She couldn't imagine telling him she didn't want a child now, or maybe ever: her childhood was scarred, and she didn't want to scar someone else's. Abena had friends in her position who had risked their lives with herbs, pills or worse to save themselves, and while there were safer options here, she didn't know if she could do that either. She sat as the television flashed brighter in the darkening afternoon, until she heard the key turn in the lock.

Chapter Four

Kodzo – February 1990

Kodzo rubbed his eyes as he sat on the toilet. Adrenaline had been replaced by caffeine, which now failed to mask his exhaustion. He had been at the hospital with Abena for six hours, and awake pacing their flat for ten hours before that. He rested briefly after he finished pushing, and awoke suddenly an unknown time later as his chin slipped from his hand. He wiped, pulled up his trousers and jog-walked back to the delivery suite.

The midwife had placed Abena's legs in stirrups during his absence. Abena maintained her focused breathing with long exhales, despite the sweat dripping into her eyes. The midwife spoke directly to the space underneath the drape covering her legs, 'Okay, we need you to keep pushing now, darlin'.'

Abena turned to Kodzo, her breathing broken, and Kodzo saw a look on her face he had never seen there before. He had seen it on the respiratory ward, with scared patients in fits of breathlessness, hungry for air. Kodzo reached over and held her hand, his excitement for the birth competing with an urge to protect her. The epidural had failed, leaving half of Abena numb while the other half felt every squeeze, stretch and tear, and Kodzo only felt a helpless guilt as she began to scream.

Later that day, Kodzo held their new baby Elom as Abena slept. His exhaustion had been replaced by a new emotion he had no name for, but which made the corners of his eyes prickle and reminded him of the worship songs his aunties used to sing in church. Abena faced away from Kodzo and Elom, breathing deeply once more, her eyes closed. They had not spoken much in the hours following the birth. The words they had exchanged had mostly been Kodzo saying a variation of 'thank you', 'well done' and 'I can't believe it'. Elom began to stir again, his gummy cry somewhere between a cough and a moan. Before it reached its peak, Abena was up, her eyes puffy and her hospital gown already half undone. She held her hands out to Kodzo, who passed Elom over and she placed his mouth on her nipple. Kodzo watched, smiling, as Abena lay her head back and yawned, while gently stroking the silky hairs on Elom's head.

The following day, when Kodzo stepped into the flat holding Elom in his carrier, he had the affronting sensation of stepping off a roundabout, or walking on land after being at sea. Away from the intensity of the hospital, back in their small, quiet home, they had a son. He had taken the rest of the week off so they could adjust to the new arrival together. He reheated meals from the stock Abena had piled in the freezer, picked up bits they had overlooked from the shops, and handed Abena whatever flannel, nappy or babygro she needed. At night he held

Abena while they could, before she was summoned by Elom's cries in the cot by their bed.

Kodzo started taking pictures of Elom, swaddled and peaceful, or wide-mouthed and tense. By the end of the first day he had finished a whole cylinder of film. He planned to send the pictures to his mother and sisters in Ho. Kodzo had written to them twice during the pregnancy – once after the twelve-week scan, and again a month or so before the due date – but he struggled to write now.

It seemed unnatural, writing to his family about a baby they should have been holding. It felt like a betrayal, too, having the secret of Elom's birth and knowing it wouldn't reach them for weeks. He thought of how his sisters Violet and Harmony had gathered for the births of his nieces, nephews and cousins, bringing food and sharing wisdom. Elom rooted him to a life in Glasgow, but made him feel untethered to his life back home.

On Kodzo's last day of leave, he picked Elom up in a brief moment of wakefulness without tears. He shook a red rattle in front of Elom's face, then held the handle out for him to reach, but Elom just flailed his arms and his eyes rolled.

Abena looked over from her side of the bed. 'Kodzo, he's less than a week old, he's not going to play with the rattle.' Elom started grumbling again, and Abena took him from Kodzo and sniffed his nappy before undressing him. Kodzo had known Elom was never going to grab the rattle, but he tried to ignore the feeling of dismissal as he tossed it into the cot.

'So, I'm on this weekend but on Monday morning I'll be free to come to the circumcision,' Kodzo said. Abena sighed whilst tossing a baby wipe smeared with brown into the dirty nappy.

'Kodzo, honestly. I really don't like this.'

'Don't like what?' Kodzo had tried to take as much time off as he could, but he was still on a starting salary, and needed to work extra shifts to afford the nappies he now realised were so expensive.

'This circumcision thing. Honestly, I thought it was something we could leave in Ghana.' Kodzo glimpsed Elom's penis as Abena wrapped him in a new nappy. It tapered to a wrinkly point, formless. The excess skin seemed superfluous and unclean, like the film on top of boiled milk.

'What do you mean? He has to be circumcised.'

'You know even in Africa not every tribe does it. And they don't do it here either. He'll be the only one.'

'He's an Ewe, that's what we do. Anyway, it's not your concern.' Abena knew more about babies, but Elom was his child too. In a week of Elom's constant need for her and her body, Kodzo was starting to feel more like an accessory than a father.

'"Not my concern" for what? Have you seen a baby after circumcision? It's not nice at all.'

Kodzo was irritated at the inanity of the conversation. 'Me too, I'm sure I cried when I had mine, but am I still sore?'

'I just don't know why you want to cut your son there.' Abena sat back on the couch now, with Elom lying chest to chest on her.

'He's my son, he should look like me.' It frustrated Kodzo that he should have to spell out something so basic – that mothers weren't the only ones who bonded with their babies through their bodies; that he would barely be a father if he left his son physically untethered to his history – but Abena looked at him as if he had asked to sell Elom at the market.

'You want his to look like yours.'

'Yes.'

'Hm.' Abena stood with Elom, walked to the kitchen and put on the kettle.

The circumcision happened on the eighth day as planned. Elom grumbled afterwards, but Kodzo knew he would settle. After the procedure – it was a procedure in Scotland, not a ceremony – he picked up his unfinished letter from the dresser and sat down to write. The words came easier now; the outline of the labour, birth and the first days of family life were clearer. He selected eight photos to send with the letter. Before heading to the post office, he asked Abena if she had something to send to her family.

'I've been too busy, Kodzo. I'll send something next week.'

'Don't you want to tell your people about your son? Write it today and I can send them both tomorrow.'

'Kodzo, I can't write it now, it's too much.' Abena had been up all night with Elom, and Kodzo admitted to himself that she looked tired.

'You can't have a baby and not tell your family. It's as if we aren't married, ei.' He laughed, hoping she would smile.

'It's not even like my mum reads well anyway. And as for Aunty Esther . . .' Abena didn't finish her thought out loud. Kodzo knew her family was disjointed, but he thought they would still be excited to hear about a new arrival. Babies brought families together: it seemed petty not to share the news.

'We have plenty of photos. Abla will like them.'

'Okay,' Abena sighed, 'maybe you can help me write it on your day off.'

Kodzo put on his jacket, glad for the compromise, but he still drove to work unsettled. Abena was a dedicated mother, and had been throughout her pregnancy. She had agreed to rest for the majority of it, aside from a few weeks of seasonal work (which Kodzo admitted had come in handy), and she always seemed to know what Elom needed. But that was where her involvement stopped – she didn't want to celebrate Elom the same way he did. Both in the traditional ways, like circumcision, and in these unexpected ways like letter-writing. It felt obscene to imply he loved Elom more, but it felt like something was missing: he wanted excitement where she seemed almost stoic. He posted his letter on the way to the hospital, imagining the glee on his sisters' faces as they saw the pictures, and on his mother's as they read her the words, and felt guilty for what Elom was missing.

In the next four months, Elom laughed as much as he cried, and began to grab the rattle when Kodzo shook it in front of him. Abena was also sleeping better as Elom learned the difference between night and day. Still, when Rory had called to ask for some seasonal cover over summer, Kodzo felt like Abena saw it as an escape. Despite this, he was easily won over; he understood Abena's need to leave the house, and the cash would help buy new baby clothes. Also, he was excited to spend time alone with his son, and to prove to Abena that he could.

On the night before Abena's first shift, Elom had been restless, but he quietened by morning. Kodzo dropped Abena off at 3 p.m. then picked up his most recently developed photos, before pushing Elom through the park in his pram, making sure he was well wrapped in a hat and blanket. Elom dozed as they strolled past palatial Victorian greenhouses and manicured lawns, and when he woke, Kodzo made faces and Elom smiled. He wished Abena could see him – she thought he was too tied to tradition, but here he was pushing his baby's pram, while his wife worked, and he was thrilled to be there. He wasn't old-fashioned, he just knew what was important.

Elom had woken earlier than usual, and Kodzo decided to feed him as soon as they got home, before his grunting developed into a cry. He heated the formula, but Elom started wailing as it cooled. It always surprised Kodzo, the ability of that scream to cloud his thoughts. Elom settled with the bottle, dozing off again shortly after, but within an hour he was up again, disgruntled. Kodzo checked his nappy and changed it with the same rehearsed precision he used to take blood or give intravenous medications. Soon after, Elom began again, this time skipping the early stages of his cry. Several nappy checks, attempts at feeding, and failed distraction with his favourite toys followed, but any respite was temporary and restless: the scream returned, Elom's face distorted and wet.

At 8 p.m. Kodzo called the hotel. He waited on the line, wondering if the receptionist could hear Elom in the background, until he heard Abena's voice.

'Hello?' She spoke in a hushed tone, her Ghanaian accent hidden behind an attempted Scottishness.

'Hi, Abena, sorry to disturb you. I can't get Elom to settle.'

'Kodzo, really? I'm at work.'

'I know, he just keeps crying.' He stopped himself from saying, 'I think he misses you.'

'Have you fed him?'

'Yes, twice now. And changed his nappy. He's slept since you went, too.'

'You fed him twice? Maybe he's overfull, or he's not taking to the formula. There's some antacid in the cupboard, try that.'

Kodzo dutifully mixed a sachet with water and fed it to Elom. He settled after a few minutes, and Kodzo gently rocked him as he walked around the room, feeling like Elom was on the edge of another outburst. He swaddled him – a technique he had learned from Abena – in the thick blanket and kept his hat on in case he was cold. The quiet didn't last, though, and soon Elom was crying again.

Kodzo watched the clock, but he felt like Elom's howl was holding back the minute hand. The sound boring into his head was all he could think about. He began to worry about this cry, which reached a pitch he hadn't heard before. He wondered if he had missed something; if it was more than indigestion. Elom hadn't been coughing, and his nappies were wet, though he hadn't pooed since before Abena had left. He even turned Elom's head to look in his ears and saw nothing. He thought of the parents he knew growing up who had 'lost' children, with no explanation. He looked at Elom and his tight, wet eyes and felt a sudden fear.

Kodzo immediately picked up the baby bag, slung it over his shoulder and went to the car. The nearest hospital was a few miles away, also on Great Western Road, just past the Dundonald. As Kodzo approached the hotel, he decided to stop and pick up Abena – her shift was almost done, and she would want to be with them at the hospital. He took the woollen bundle containing Elom, who had been calmed by the drive, and burst through the entrance into the hotel reception.

'I need to see Abena,' he told the receptionist.

'The kitchen porter? They finish at 12 a.m., sir. She'll just be half an hour.'

'No, our baby isn't well, I need to see her now.' Kodzo could hear the desperation in his voice, but he didn't care. He was taking action, and he was proud to be the kind of father who could embarrass himself for his son. The receptionist called the kitchen. In a few minutes Abena rose up the red-carpeted stairs, flushed from the kitchen or the situation, Kodzo couldn't tell.

'What's going on?' Abena took Elom from him and walked him towards the overstuffed armchair in the corner. She looked concerned, and Kodzo felt vindicated.

'He's been crying a lot. I'm worried – I'm taking him to A&E. I don't know if maybe it's his stomach or something. The antacid didn't work. Some children get blocked bowels, you know? Let's go, I can tell you in the car.' Abena looked at Kodzo, this time with a bit of confusion mixed into her concern. She looked back at Elom, who was already slightly more settled in her arms, and took off his hat. She held her hand to his forehead.

'Kodzo, he's too warm. Did you check his temperature?'

'No, I . . .' Before he could answer, she started removing the blanket. Once free, Elom's left hand went straight for his ear, his palm clumsily rubbing it as he whimpered.

'Hm.' Abena reached over to the receptionist's desk, where the receptionist was diligently squiggling over some paperwork and avoiding their scene. She took a single sheet of tissue from the hotel-branded box and folded it, before gently inserting the corner into Elom's left ear. When she pulled it out the tip was wet, the liquid tracking up the tissue.

'He doesn't need surgery, Kodzo. I think it's an ear infection.'

'An ear infection?'

'Yes. He needs paracetamol and maybe some antibiotics. We can call the GP.' She passed Elom back to Kodzo. 'I'm coming, let me just tell Rory.'

At 2 a.m., Abena paced around the flat with a calmed Elom wrapped on her back, his chest pressed against her body and his eyelids drooping after several mouthfuls of sickly sweet paracetamol syrup. Kodzo sat on the couch, having phoned the on-call GP, who said they could be seen when the surgery opened. Despite the silence, Kodzo could hear the echoes of Elom's crying bouncing off the walls, like tinnitus.

Abena looked through the photos that Kodzo had left on the coffee table, smiling at an Elom who was already so different from the baby on her back. Once she had seen them all, she squared the collection against the palms of her hands, slotted them back into the card photo-holder and handed them to Kodzo. She sighed and sat on the edge of the sofa, unable to lean back because of Elom behind her.

'You know, Kodzo, having children is not easy, oh.'

'I know.' Kodzo was only just starting to recover from an embarrassment that had begun on the drive home, and

deepened after Elom had calmed down following the first dose
of paracetamol.

'But do you? It's more than nice photos and toys and nappies,
I'm telling you.'

'Ah-ah, yes.'

'Elom's ear will be fine – do you know how I know? Do you
know how many children I've looked after?' Kodzo remained
silent, as it was clear Abena did not expect an answer.

'It's not just Abla. I was the oldest of all my cousins – Aunty
Esther's kids, her grand-kids Ayikaeley and Okaidja, even my
mum's friends' children. When I should have been playing, or
in school, my mum and Aunty Esther sent me here, there and
everywhere to look after children for some small money. Even
strangers' families. Hm . . .' She paused. 'I was a housegirl
for years before they let me go to catering school.' Abena
had never spoken so frankly about her childhood before, but
Kodzo had guessed as much. Growing up in the village, he
hadn't had a housegirl himself, but he knew girls from his
primary school who had been sent to the city to earn money
that way, in the summer before he started secondary school.
When they left, a cloud hung over the family who had sent
them: parents, guilty and ashamed; siblings, scared they
might be next. 'I know what it takes to raise a child, and raise
them well. I take it very seriously,' Abena finished.

'I know you take it seriously. You're a great mother.'

Abena smiled, and it looked to Kodzo like she was unsure.
'Thank you. And you're a great dad, too. I'm glad.' She paused.
'Maybe I should lighten up. Take more photos.'

'Maybe; but you're right, it's hard.' Kodzo felt like he had uncovered something underneath Abena's marble stoicism, and he wanted to apologise for doubting her, though he couldn't admit to her that he had. He felt a flash of anger, too, at Aunty Esther, and thought he understood a little of why Abena hadn't initially rushed to her with the good news. The anger was easier to feel than his shame at having accepted Aunty Esther's hospitality unquestioningly: of letting Abena act as his housegirl in Accra too, however briefly.

In the morning, Abena took Elom to the doctor's practice while Kodzo went to work. On his return, he insisted Abena go back for her late shift.

'Are you sure you'll be okay?' Abena asked. Elom had already given Kodzo a few smiles following the first doses of antibiotics.

'Of course. But before you go, can you do me a favour?'

'Sure.'

'Can you show me how to do the wrapper?' Kodzo looked to somewhere in the middle distance between the two of them as he asked.

Abena looked confused. 'The wrapper?'

'Yeah. When you do it, he always feels more relaxed. I even remember it myself, I loved it when I was small.'

Abena made a bemused-sounding half-cough, half-laugh. 'You want to carry him on your back?'

Kodzo nodded, and Abena smiled. She unfurled a length of fabric and showed him how to swing Elom on his back, before tightening the cloth around them both. Kodzo wondered how he looked to Abena, now with the silhouette of every mum, aunty and older sister in Ghana. Abena looked at Elom, whose head rested against Kodzo's back, then looked Kodzo in the eyes and smiled. It was a smile Kodzo remembered, from a time when he was still able to surprise her with the smallest things. He realised that what bound Abena's excitement wasn't indifference, but the fear of carrying another heavy load. He saw her breathe a little easier, knowing he could carry a bit of it too.

Chapter Five

Abena – February 1998

Abena woke to the *Batman* theme tune – Elom was watching his favourite cartoon again. She lifted her heavy eyes from her wet pillow and remembered the night before. The kitchen had been understaffed and she had stepped up, covering desserts and helping with the mains. She'd impressed Rory, and he had finally offered her a trial as sous-chef. She had been thrilled, and came home to tell Kodzo. She had found him stony-faced by the phone, the kids already asleep, and he told her that her mum had died.

She only had a few minutes left on her calling card, and it had been too late to go out and buy a new one, so she had called Aunty Esther and immediately asked to speak to Abla, unconcerned by her own rudeness.

'Sister, I'm so sorry, oh,' was all she could manage.

The line was silent for so long that Abena wondered if she had already run out of credit, then she heard a sniff. 'I'm okay. I'm okay.' Abena imagined Abla, surrounded by their extended family, yet totally alone. Thirteen years old, with both parents gone. The echo of her voice on the patchy line made her seem even more isolated, so Abena rationed her own sadness, as she had seen women older than her do. Before the line went dead, she did her best to comfort Abla, and promised she would call again the next day. Then she went upstairs and cried herself to sleep.

Abena had learned in her teens that her mother, Akosua, had been an alcoholic. It explained the feeling Abena had had as a girl, that Akosua's absence wasn't because of a lack of love, but because something stronger was pulling at her. Still, Akosua's addiction, and her repeated proximity to death, hadn't prepared Abena for the news. Instead, it had made Akosua extra-resilient in Abena's mind: like she existed outside life and death.

Now fully awake, Abena sat on the edge of the bed and listened. She could hear Dzifa's babbling and knew Kodzo was probably feeding her in her high chair. She was grateful for him, and the seconds of solitude she now had before having to leave her bedroom and be a mother. The seconds became minutes, though, as Abena sat until she heard *Batman*'s end credits, then the sound of bowls being dropped in the sink, and Kodzo shouting at Elom to get his socks on and put cream on his face.

For Abena, having one child had meant having two, and having them quickly. She had grown up alone, and when she eventually did get a sibling, Abena had had to be her caregiver rather than her peer – and then she had left for Glasgow. Dzifa was born a year and a half after Elom, and Abena hoped they would be close. She chose to think of Dzifa not as a companion made for Elom as if from one of his ribs, but as the final piece of their family, necessary and sufficient to complete it. They didn't have any other family here, and Akosua's death in Accra only emphasised their need to function as a self-sufficient unit in Glasgow. Akosua had never even met Elom, or Dzifa.

Abena stayed sitting until she heard a knock on the bedroom door, and she looked up – she had been staring at the floor all this time, she realised – and saw Kodzo peek his head through, attempting a smile.

'I'll drop them both off today. You just rest.'

'Thanks, Kodzo. Thanks.' She felt guilty. 'I'll pick them up before work.'

'Work?' Kodzo's face changed. 'Not today – just stay at home, we can sort something out.'

'No, I'll need to talk to Rory. I'll have to go to Ghana.'

'Just call him.' Kodzo was exasperated, and Elom was shouting from the hallway that they were going to be late for school.

'No, I need to go. I'll go.'

Kodzo shook his head and Abena stayed in the same position, listening to the sound of them leave.

Rory was understanding when Abena said she would have to go back to Ghana. 'Of course, Abna, that's awful. Go home and come back in a few weeks.'

'I'd like to do the trial first,' Abena replied.

Rory looked confused, and Abena realised he thought she was being callous. 'It's just, in Ghana funerals don't happen quickly. I'll leave in a month or so, but I'll need more than a few weeks off.'

Rory nodded, lips turned down thoughtfully. 'Aye, okay. Whatever works for you.'

Spending her days on her feet in a new, busy role did work for Abena. The stress of the kitchen distracted her while one month became two, then three; her mourning delayed by the bureaucracy of Ghanaian death. She had never known her own father, and Abla's had died shortly after she was born, so the responsibility of the funeral fell, as the eldest, on Abena's shoulders. She spent more and more money on international calling cards, speaking to Abla, Aunty Esther and myriad relatives, some familiar and some unknown. She cried often, but they were angry and unsatisfying tears: she cried because Akosua had been unwell with dizziness and vomiting for almost a week, and no one had taken her to hospital; because a doctor had initially denied her treatment unless she could pay upfront; because after the family had spent the day scraping together the cash to admit her, Akosua had died before they could contact Abena for more support; because the hospital were keeping her body in their morgue until the hospital bills (and increasing morgue bills) could be fully paid; because uncles and aunties were already squabbling over what little assets Akosua had; because friends and colleagues were already clawing for repayments on her debts; because the funeral costs were already rising, and it seemed her family wanted to use it as a self-promoting summer party, rather than a memorial.

Rory hadn't paid her extra for her 'trial', which Kodzo had warned her would happen. Despite this, Abena wired cash for the mounting bills, went gift shopping for the inevitable open hands on her arrival, and booked her flight once she had saved enough. Death was expensive, and since it involved her mother, there was no limit to the expectations on her to pay. She worked until the night before her flight, hoping to fill up her purse, but also, she could admit, savouring the feeling every time she told a junior chef or kitchen porter what to do, knowing they had to listen to her.

The main road to the compound had been covered in tarmac in the last decade, but it still had the children – slender, in baggy, faded T-shirts – hawking chewing gum, oranges, ice water, combs, extension cables, socks, pens, books and CDs from portable shopfronts carried on their heads to the cars inching along in near-gridlock. Their calls breezed in through the open window, and when Abena heard one for bofloat, she called back. A girl approached with a glass-panelled, wood-framed box balanced on her head, full of doughy brown balls.

'*Mmienu*,' Abena said, and the girl reached up and pulled out two pieces, placing them in a thin plastic bag. It was a Tuesday morning, and the girl looked no older than twelve – young enough that she was legally required to be in school. Abena handed her a note as she took the bag, indicating that she could keep the change. As Abena withdrew her hand, more children and some adults approached, touting their wares. They had seen her money, and perhaps her Western-ness, and clamoured for her attention.

'*Daabi, mepaakyεw.*' She shook her head, but they persisted, even when she rolled the window up. She could hear their muted calls until the traffic eased and they rolled further down the road, her heart beating fast in her chest. She looked at the family friend-cum-driver-cum-welcoming party, Gideon, in the rear-view mirror, and caught him watching her.

'These sellers, they can be very annoying, eh?' he said. Abena didn't reply: it was desperation she had seen, and it had made her sad and embarrassed, not annoyed. His comment had annoyed her, but she didn't know how to say that to this older man who had been sent to pick her up, so she ate her bofloat in silence, wobbling from side to side as they rolled down the potholed red-earth street leading to her old home. Gideon got out to open the gate, and Abena saw that the three whitewashed buildings were smaller and dirtier than she remembered, though she knew she hadn't grown any taller. Some local boys rushed to remove her luggage as she tipped Gideon, and people started trailing out of the middle building. Abena squinted as she walked over, readjusting to the light.

'Eiii! Look at you, big girl!' Aunty Esther pulled Abena into a hug.

'Hi, Aunty.' Abena hugged her back, comforted, in spite of herself, by her deep voice and her smell of coal, soap and sweat.

'You are welcome.'

'Thanks, Aunty. You are looking well, oh.' Abena noted she had gained weight, which was expertly reshaped by a tailored skirt and blouse.

'You too. You are looking fine.' Aunty Esther smiled, looking Abena up and down, making her feel self-conscious of her slimmer figure after years fitting her thighs into the straws that passed for jeans in Glasgow.

Abena greeted Aunty Esther's daughter Sister Efua, with her sleek black wig and her now teenage children Ayikaeley and

Okaidja, whose nappies Abena used to change – then she reached a
child, already her height, standing quietly at the edge of the group.

'Abla, you've grown, eh?'

'Good morning, Sister Abena, you are welcome.' Abla held
her hands behind her back and her gaze at Abena's feet.

'Come.' Abena held her arms open, and Abla looked up. Her
mouth wriggled as she bit her lip, as if her shyness were wrestling
her smile. She paused, as if trying to judge Abena's intentions,
and Abena felt like she could already see her mistrust of adults.
'It's okay, Abla, I'm here.'

Suddenly, Abla lurched forward and Abena felt her begin
to sob. She held her close and whispered, '*Eyi dzi yenkusε*. I'm
sorry.'

Abena woke the next morning to a knock on her door. 'Good
morning, please, breakfast is ready.' She looked up to see Aunty
Esther and smiled. 'Thanks, Aunty. Good morning.'

Aunty Esther watched for a moment, then chuckled. 'Hmm,
you too, you still like sleeping, eh?' she said before turning away
and letting the door close behind her.

Abena pursed her lips and got up, dragging her *chalewote*
across the floor with each step.

Over the next week she worked through the funeral task list. She
went where Aunty Esther told her to – to the hospital to settle
debts, to the market to buy fabrics, to the seamstress to sew the
mourning attire, and to family meetings where she sat quietly
and agreed with whoever Aunty Esther agreed with: deference
was the path of least resistance. She called Kodzo when she

could, and after two weeks she was able to tell him that they had finally agreed to hold the funeral in another two weeks' time.

'It's been a mission, eh?'

'Kodzo, I'm telling you.' Abena sighed. She couldn't speak frankly as there was always family around. Even in Glasgow, she avoided telling stories from her childhood, but since Akosua had died and she had been forced into regular contact with Aunty Esther, Kodzo had come to realise second-hand how difficult life had been growing up with her. 'How are the kids?'

'All good.' She could hear Dzifa and Elom squabbling. Kodzo passed them the phone and Elom asked when she was coming back because he wanted some Empire biscuits, while Dzifa told her, through some wet coughs, about the snake they had petted at nursery, before passing the phone back.

'Is Dzifa coughing again?' Abena asked as soon as she heard Kodzo's voice.

'Yeah, she—'

'Did you take her to the GP?'

'Not yet, we—'

'They said it could be asthma last time – you need to call them, Kodzo.' It was typical that Abena was trying to be present for her family in Ghana when her kids were falling ill alone back home. It was a helpless feeling.

'Abena, calm down. I called the GP, they'll see her tomorrow. Anyway, they said she's probably too young to diagnose anything. She's fine now, trust me.'

Abena paused. Kodzo was right, the kids weren't alone. He was no longer the panicked new father – he had shown that many times over the last few years.

'Sorry,' she conceded. 'Just let me know what they say.'

'Of course.'

Abena relaxed. She knew he would, and she was grateful for the peace of mind she had that Kodzo could handle things at home, and that he was on her side.

Since the date had been decided, Abena could begin arranging the funeral itself. There was no guest list – anyone who knew the deceased was welcome, as well as anyone who didn't – but catering, music and a marquee had to be organised. This meant more meetings with the elders where they decided how best to spend Abena's money. Kodzo was ever sympathetic, though she wondered if he knew how it felt to be here. His two sisters had died in quick succession while Abena was heavily pregnant with Dzifa. He had chosen to stay in Glasgow rather than fly over to help with the funeral, but his family ties were simpler, and they were able to send money to a trusted half-brother who took the reins. Kodzo had lived the hell of mourning from a distance, and Abena wouldn't wish that on anyone, but he hadn't lived the hell of organising a funeral with a pack of hyenas, and Abena wasn't sure which was worse.

'We need to order at least two hundred balls of kenkey. Minimum,' Uncle Kofi – Akosua's loud, grey-haired uncle – said, as they gathered in the living room. Abena wanted to slap the Guinness out of his hand.

'Do we really need two hundred just of kenkey? Will that many people be coming?' she asked with as much deference as she could manage.

'At least! And the other standard foodstuffs – waakye, fufu, jollof – and drinks. It has to be plenty. Akosua had many friends and we need to respect her,' Uncle Kofi replied, as Aunty Esther nodded along. He was active in local party politics and had dreams of breaking into the rank of state-level official. Abena knew that the food on display would not be for the eyes of Akosua, watching from above, but she, too, nodded and smiled.

Later, as they cleared the dishes, Abena asked Aunty Esther if they were going overboard. Aunty Esther looked at her, shocked. 'Ah ah, Abena, this one no be big ting, oh. You know your mother-sef loved kenkey anyway.'

The best part of the trip for Abena had been spending time with Abla. Abena walked with her to school every day and picked her up afterwards, with a stop for some fried yam and shitɔ. On her second weekend in Accra, Abena took her in a fifteen-minute taxi to the Kwame Nkrumah Memorial Park, and felt guilty when Abla beamed at the manicured lawns and water features; she had never been before.

They cooked together for the first time a month into the trip, after picking out fresh onions, peppers, chilli and tilapia at the market. Abena watched as Abla chopped – Akosua was there in the way her hands flicked at the end of each slice, how she banged the spoon against the pot to get every last drop in the pan before balancing it on the rim. Abla caught her looking and hesitated. 'Is it not correct, Sister Abena?'

'Oh no, it's fine. You're a good cook.'

'Sistah, in this house I have no choice.' She laughed, and Abena laughed too, happy that Abla could relax around her. Abena loved that Abla preferred to speak Fante, despite having better English than Abena had at fourteen. She was witty, and when she quipped in Fante, Abena was reminded of her mum on her good days. In Scotland, Abena spoke English, or Twi with other Ghanaians; Fante was delicate – her tongue had to soften to do it justice. She wished she had passed it on to Elom and Dzifa. English was her and Kodzo's only common language, and besides, they hadn't wanted them to slip behind in school. English was all they spoke at home, and all the kids could understand.

'Do you want to gut the fish?' Abena asked.

'I'm not so good with fish.'

'Here, I'll show you.' Abena used the knife to slice open the belly like Akosua had shown her, and she wondered what else Abla still had to learn, and who would teach her. When it was almost ready, Abla called Aunty Esther to eat, and Aunty Esther watched as Abena poured bubbling hot palm oil over the lightly grilled fish and vegetables, with a perfect static electricity sizzle.

Aunty Esther began to serve herself. 'So you are teaching this girl new tricks, eh?'

Abla and Abena shared a smile as Abena loaded Abla's plate, then her own. 'She's already an excellent cook.'

'Yes, I know.' Aunty Esther smiled with what looked like pride. 'We will send her to the same catering school.'

Abena cleared her throat and reached for her glass of ice water. 'Catering school?' She looked across the table at Abla. 'Do you want to be a cook?'

'Bɛɛ "want" mɔ,' Aunty Esther laughed, while Abla shrugged.

'Shouldn't she finish secondary school? Maybe she can go to university.'

'Ah-ah.' Aunty Esther stopped laughing. 'You too, we had this conversation many years ago, and wasn't I right?' Abena remembered well: she had been standing a few feet away in the same living room, while Aunty Esther spoke at her from the couch. Abena had returned to Newtown after a year as a housegirl for a wealthy family in Tema. They had promised Akosua that they would pay Abena's fees at the local state school, with crowded desks and torn textbooks, while their own children studied at a private international school. They worked Abena so hard that she was barely able to attend, so she left junior secondary school with failing grades and no certificate. Abena had asked for another chance, and Aunty Esther had asked her, 'With whose money?' Her mum was away on one of her trips, and the start of the school year had passed before she returned, with Abena already enrolled at the catering college.

'You wanted to go and read book, but it's the catering which got you to *abrokyir, meboa*?' Abena nodded, aware that Abla was watching her closely. 'And now you can even afford kenkey,' Aunty Esther laughed. Abena's anger settled in her jaw, stopping before it could become words. She wanted to tell Aunty Esther that she got to Glasgow in spite of her lack of education, and that life would have been easier for her and Kodzo if she had a degree. She wanted to shout at her, and stop her from taking so much away from Abla. She had felt the same almost two decades ago, standing in front of Aunty Esther in the living room, but had simply nodded, then cried in her room.

She tried to respond. 'Aunty, yes the catering school helped. But Abla is smart.' Abla smiled into her plate. 'She can go even further than—'

'Ei I beg, stop this now.' Aunty Esther dashed Abena before she could land. 'So she will go for five or six years in school, and then what? The same at university? Meanwhile, who is paying bills here?' Abena tried to respond, but was interrupted again. 'Please don't open your mouth to tell me any nonsense. *Your contributions are very welcome*' – she said this in a mocking English accent – 'but very soon I will be too old to work at my stall, and the money you send, whenever you send it, is not enough to keep us going.' Abena didn't try to respond this time, stuck between a sense of injustice and guilt that perhaps Aunty Esther was right.

'You are a very ungrateful girl, eh? I even thought when you had your own children it would change, but never never.' Aunty Esther brought her hands together as if clapping dust off them. 'You think this life is easy here, raising my sister's children – not one, but two of them' – she counted on her fingers for emphasis – 'because she cannot control her life, when me too, I have my own portion to deal with?' Her 'portion', Abena thought, was a son who she herself had paid through school despite him failing more exams than he passed, and a daughter Aunty Esther had pushed into an unhappy marriage. It was just Abena who had been expected to stick around at home, making money and flushing toilets for her.

She stayed mute, however, and her face burned where she felt Abla's stare. She was too ashamed to return it, worried she would see Abla's disappointment at her big sister failing to defend her.

'Anyway, that one is finished, please,' Aunty Esther ended the conversation. 'Thank you for dinner, it was very nice.' She began cleaning her teeth with a toothpick as Abena and Abla cleared the plates.

The funeral was held in the courtyard of their compound. It was loud and colourful and people danced and cried in equal measure. Abena welcomed her mourning dance – when she saw Akosua's corpse she had wailed and had to be carried to her seat, but when she danced, her grief felt focused and embodied, rather than wild and overwhelming. She had avoided seeing her mother's body at the morgue for this reason, despite knowing Aunty Esther thought her weak or callous for not paying respects sooner. They took the coffin to a local cemetery for the burial, then she spent the rest of the day accepting the condolences of friends, family and strangers, and barely noticed when Uncle Kofi introduced her to the gaggle of pot-bellied politicians who had arrived in jeeps.

Abena asked Abla to cook with her again a few days later. The two of them stood side by side plucking, chopping and stirring, and it felt comfortable. It was a feeling she had rarely felt in this kitchen, or this house.

'When will you be going?' Abla asked suddenly, breaking the silence as she lifted the lid off the pan. Abena sighed, feeling the weight of the question.

'A week or two.' Her mother had been buried and she was running out of cedis, though fortunately she still had some sterling left.

'Okay. Elom and Dzifa will be so happy to see you. And Uncle Kodzo.' Abla smiled, avoiding Abena's gaze.

'I can't wait to see them, too,' Abena said. There was another silence, and then Abena asked just as suddenly, 'What do you want to be when you grow up?'

'Oh . . . I don't know.' Abla shook her head, but smiled, as if she was thinking of something very specific – a thought she wanted to keep to herself.

'Tell me,' Abena said, then softer, 'you can tell me.'

Abla crumbled a stock cube into the nkatenkwan, 'I'd like to be a lawyer.' She laughed to herself, as if realising how silly it sounded. As she giggled, Abena remembered how young she was.

'You can do it,' Abena said. Abla shrugged and fanned the fire underneath the stove.

Abena took a deep breath. 'Don't listen to Aunty Esther. You can do it.' The words tumbled out rushed and hushed, and they both looked towards the closed door, as if she might overhear them.

'Maybe,' Abla replied, stirring once more before placing the lid back on the pot.

Abena walked to school with Abla the next morning. She laughed as Abla impersonated Uncle Kofi's verbose, sycophantic English, and they picked up a breakfast of Hausa koko and akara from a street stall. Abena felt increasingly nervous as they approached the school, and stopped a hundred yards or so from the gate. It was an okay government school, and Abena watched the kids trudge in, wondering which ones might be lucky enough to make it out. She looked at Abla and asked the question she had been waiting to ask all morning.

'Do you like living with Aunty Esther?'

Abla looked surprised, still slurping from the corner of the bag of koko. She simply made a sound through closed lips, like a vocal shrug, and kept sucking.

'Do you want to keep going to school? A good school?'

At this, Abla nodded, and smiled, though a sadness dimmed her eyes.

'Okay,' Abena sighed. 'Okay. Enjoy your day.' Abla hugged her and turned to join her friends, walking through the school gates with her closely cropped head bobbing above the others. Abena hailed a cab, wondering if her idea made any sense. Having Abla come to stay with them in Glasgow felt impossible. The flat was too small, and there was no guarantee of securing a visa. There was also a selfish part of herself, Abena admitted, that didn't want her there – that wanted to keep these lives separate; the one in which she was nobody, and the one in which she could become somebody.

The taxi pulled up in front of a high, whitewashed wall. Behind it was a blue and white two-storey building, and passing through the gates was a stream of young women in fitted blue and yellow uniforms, some on foot, and some seen through the windows of large, sleek cars. Abena found her way to the reception, and then some kind of shared office, where a friendly woman with an 'ADMISSIONS OFFICER' desk plaque seemed surprised but happy to see her.

'I'd like to enrol my sister, please. How much is tuition? For boarding. How much is tuition plus boarding?' The woman gave her a sheet of paper with various options. If Abena got the sous-chef job and spent every penny of the extra income, she would be able to cover the year – she could work out the rest later.

When she told Abla to come with her for an interview, she squealed in excitement, but almost immediately quietened, and Abena saw the same fear in her face that she felt herself.

'Don't worry. Let's just make sure you make a good impression for now. I'll talk to Aunty when we need to.'

Within a week, Abla had been accepted, and the new potential reality pounded in Abena's heart every time she saw Aunty Esther. She tried to tell her over lunch, while Abla was at school, but she could only use her mouth to eat. She saw Abla spend the evening on tenterhooks, clearly waiting for the bomb to drop, and Abena decided she had to tell Esther soon, for Abla's sake.

The next day, Abena went to the yard behind the house to pick a soursop when she saw her. Aunty Esther was sitting on a bench, elbow-deep in sudsy water, washing her underwear and bedclothes, the only items she did herself. Standing over her, Abena felt a sudden rush.

'Aunty, I've enrolled Abla at the girls' secondary school in Achimota.'

Aunty Esther stopped scrubbing and looked up at Abena, her forearms and hands glistening like shiny, skin-tight gloves. 'What do you mean?'

'I've enrolled her at the girls' secondary school. So she can read and learn and become what she wants to be.'

Aunty Esther laughed a long, spacious laugh that demanded to be heard. 'You this girl. You!' She pointed a finger, landing flecks of water on Abena's blouse. 'So she will go to this school, meanwhile I'll pay for her food and clothes and shelter.' She gave a short sigh and clicked with her throat at the audacity of the situation.

'No. She will be boarding, so you don't have to worry.'

Aunty Esther looked genuinely surprised. There was another feeling Abena couldn't place, like she was hurt, and it pleased Abena.

'Hmm. Good for her, you are her blessing.' She picked up her sodden, foamy pants and as she scrubbed the fabric against itself, it gave a thick squelch with each pass. 'Meanwhile, we are here.' She dunked them in the second tub of greying rinsing water, lifted them out and wrung them with a mighty twist of her hands, before throwing them in the weeping pile of clothes to be hung.

Sitting in the departure lounge, Abena felt small and weary. Abla had smiled and hugged her, and promised to send photos in her new uniform, but Abena felt like history was repeating itself. She was sending Abla to a stranger's house, but she hoped the books and sports and friends would make it different. As relieved as she was to be going home – because Glasgow was now home – and as excited as she was to see her family – because Kodzo and the kids were now her family, too – Abena was sad to leave Ghana. She resented that it still had a hold over her, despite her unhappiness growing up.

The airport staff announced first-class boarding and Abena watched as they lined up, self-assured and shiny. A woman stood directly in front of her, speaking on a mobile phone through strong white teeth. She seemed alone and unconcerned. She casually handed over her passport and boarding pass, and the staff handed them back with a smile, and when she walked towards the plane, Abena watched her deep green, wax-print dress shimmer as she moved. Abena passed her once more when she boarded herself, and the woman had already taken off her shoes and put her feet up, probably waiting for the parade to finish so she could sip some wine. As Abena sat in her seat in economy, she wondered what that woman's Ghana was like, tailored and air-con cool. It was so different from hers, and, she could admit with some sadness, even Aunty Esther's. Perhaps it could be Abla's, one day.

Chapter Six

Kodzo – July 2002

'*Scarabo popo, mika rabatatah!*'

'Amen!' Kodzo answered pastor Simon's call. His hands were raised with the congregation's, swaying to the music, full of bright, fuzzy cymbal rolls. He liked the Praise and Worship section of the service most. Long after the sermon had finished, his tired mind settled on a singular yearning to be close to God.

'*Kanta scalobim, parafaika batabolo!*' Simon interjected as the band started to fade out. Kodzo felt words pour over him, unconcerned with their specific meaning – to speak in Tongues was to rejoice in the Lord. Though he couldn't speak them himself, he felt like he understood.

'Praise God,' Simon signalled the end of the session in English.

'We bless you' and 'Amen' ricocheted around the room. 'We thank you for the week we are about to begin. For the blessings you will bring to us.' Kodzo kept his eyes closed and hands raised, willing God to receive his thanks. 'We thank you for your generosity, oh Lord, and gifting us with prosperity through working in your service. In Jesus' name—'

'Amen!' Kodzo replied, swallowed by the calls from the congregation. The music faded to nothing, leaving a heavy silence for people to sit with God. Kodzo heard the shuffles of people around him picking up their bags and babies. When he opened his eyes, he saw Abena with her handbag already on her shoulder.

After the service, Kodzo and Abena found Mensah and Maria in the hall, drinking instant coffee from Styrofoam cups. After a few minutes' catching up, Dzifa bounded over from Sunday school with a sheet of paper filled by a brightly drawn Bible scene, with glitter, glued-on string and balls of cotton wool for clouds. As usual, she accurately recounted their lesson that day – The Parable of the Sower – as Elom and Mawusi silently sidled into the group, hoping to avoid all conversation.

'Are you busy this afternoon?' Maria asked.

'Nothing major. Just going to the museum.' Kodzo replied.

'I wish we could take this one, but all she wants is TV and, *ɛyi*, "MSN messengah".'

'Mu-uh-um.' It was a full sentence in Mawusi's braced mouth, with at least three syllables. Maria shared a look with Abena and Kodzo, as if she had been chastised, and the parents laughed.

Kodzo shook Mensah and Maria's hands with a click and wished them a good week, then ushered his family through the milling congregation and to the car. He thought about when he had been Dzifa's age, where Sunday school was just a long sermon behind the church with the other children, and the hot afternoons were spent running, jumping or swimming around the village. It had been fun, but he was glad he could provide something more for his family.

When they got to the Kelvingrove Museum, Dzifa said she wanted to see the Ancient Egyptian collection, while Elom walked over to the natural history section to stare at the giant turtles, mammoths and wolves. When Kodzo had first come here as a student, fresh from Ghana, he had felt the need to scour every room and read the blurb of every artefact, until his feet hurt and his eyes blurred. He smiled now, proud that his children were familiar enough with the space to have their own favourite parts, and knew they could peruse the rest at their leisure.

Kodzo and Abena were both off that evening, which seldom happened, so she insisted they stop by the ethnic food shop and pick up ingredients for a new Indian recipe she had read about. An hour into her cooking, she shouted an 'Oh-oh!' and Kodzo rushed in, worried she had hurt herself. Instead, she was rubbing at a half-moon burn on the counter, and he could only laugh at her frustration.

The next morning, Kodzo got home from work while the children were still at school. He opened a letter from the school in the suburbs a few miles away.

'Thank you for your application, however we are sorry . . .'

Kodzo sighed and leaned back on the sofa to finish reading the letter, which had the same copy-and-pasted text as the year before, and the year before that. Another year with Elom at the local comprehensive – one with fights and drugs, and one that he worried was already casting a shadow over his son. The one that their home was in the catchment area for, because a house in the suburbs cost double what they could afford. He put the letter back in its envelope, folded it, and slid it into his pocket, then turned on the television, switching it to GOD TV. Creflo Dollar was on, preaching about the blessings of God and how to activate them in your life. Kodzo turned up the volume and listened to every word.

A job came up: sister in one of the surgical wards. These were rare, usually arising due to retirement, illness or death. Kodzo didn't know the outgoing nurse very well, but there had been no retirement party. He didn't have to think much about applying: it meant a pay rise, better hours, more responsibility; having the young doctors with puffed-out chests more likely to listen to him. Abena liked the idea of him working regular hours, as well as the extra cash. He was unsurprised when he was invited to interview: there were few nurses around with a decade of experience who hadn't been promoted. Despite that, he went to the church prayer group two days later to prepare.

They sat in a meeting room, with thin carpets and no window. Pastor Simon began by asking God to open His ears to the calls of His children, then members presented their problems so they could share the burden of praying together, like a religious microfinance scheme. Fiona's cousin was starting chemotherapy – breast cancer, young; Gary's sister was struggling with money after a divorce. Kodzo liked how everyone prayed with equal strength for each person. Still, when it came to his turn, he was embarrassed; his request was for himself rather than a sick or downtrodden relative.

'It's not a big problem as such, but . . . I'm up for a new job. One with more responsibility, where I could use my skills better.' It felt dishonest not to discuss money, but selfish to mention it.

'Congratulations, Samuel!' Pastor Simon smiled, using Kodzo's Christian name. He lowered his head and closed his eyes, with the rest of the group following. 'Our heavenly Father, thank You for blessing Samuel with this opportunity to step into his purpose: the purpose of serving You and Your will through healing others. Continue to anoint his path with the blood of Jesus, that he may have every professional success . . .'

A calm confidence settled over Kodzo as the pastor and the congregation prayed over him. It stayed with him on his drive home, and at work the next day, and then through to his interview. It was still with him when he answered the phone on Monday afternoon, and was told by his boss that she was sorry, but he had been 'unsuccessful this time'.

He felt cold as he put down the receiver – he had started sweating, and sat on the couch. He wondered which of the nurses he worked with had been given the job – nurses who had been years below him at nursing college, and were many years younger in age. This feeling was familiar, though it had been a while since he had felt it. It took him back to secondary school, when his above-average, but not exceptional grades had left him in Ghana whilst his schoolmates scored scholarships to Romania, France, Britain and the States. He had worked as a clerk in the civil service for half a decade while they'd made names for themselves abroad in business and medicine. He had prayed for change, and promised himself to God, fully, so that He could work His wonders in Kodzo's life.

Now, however, he still felt like he was behind – behind his friends, behind in his career, behind financially, and now his kids would fall behind too. Even Abena was forging ahead. He remembered consoling her after her first run-in with the capricious British interview system, and now she was practically running the kitchen. She still sent much of that extra money to Abla and other family, but Kodzo couldn't be bitter: extended family was family, and when he had needed to send money back, she had always encouraged him to be more generous. Besides, while the money she sent was enough to keep Abla in a good school in Ghana, it wouldn't have changed things for their own kids in Glasgow. The amount needed felt insurmountable.

Kodzo was still sitting when Elom came home. He wasn't wearing a jacket, despite the drizzle, and his school bag and trousers hung low on his slim frame.

'Hi, Dad,' he said as he dropped his bag and slumped onto the couch, reaching for the television remote.

'Hi, Elom, how was school?'

'Boring.'

'What do you mean "boring"? Did you not pay attention?'

'It was just boring, Dad, I dunno. It's school.'

'Don't give me that. We are not sending you there to be bored. Go and learn something.'

Elom pulled his eyes from the screen, unsure if he had missed something. The plainness of his stare made Kodzo angrier, as if he was demanding Kodzo explain himself.

'I said go and learn something – don't you have homework to do? And pull up those trousers, look like you respect yourself.' Elom stood silently, pulled at his waistband and stomped up the stairs to his bedroom, while Kodzo sank back into the sofa.

Kodzo didn't join the prayer group that week. On Sunday, when Fiona asked him how the interview had gone, he smiled and said, 'It didn't go my way this time.' She looked serious and said, 'What's for ye'll no' go by ye.' Kodzo was glad when the hall doors opened and the crowd began to shuffle in, so he could move away from her and her sincerity.

The sermon was to be delivered by the junior pastor, Michael. Kodzo knew people needed to learn, but he was not looking forward to a nervous presentation by a trainee. 'Today we're going to read from Psalm 66,' he announced, and there was a rustle as the congregation flicked through their wafer-thin Bible pages.

'Shout for joy to God, all the Earth! Sing the glory of His name; make His praise glorious,' he started. Kodzo was unfamiliar with this psalm, and wondered if the youth pastor was trying to be innovative. Regardless, the initial message was routine. Kodzo had sung the Lord's praises many times, in many ways, yet still didn't receive His bounty. He let his mind wander as Michael tried to impress upon the congregation the sheer power and benevolence of God.

'You let people ride over our heads; we went through fire and water, but You brought us to a place of abundance.' Michael paused, then repeated himself, pulling Kodzo back into the room. 'You let people ride over our heads; we went through fire and water, but You brought us to *a place of abundance*.' He lingered on the last phrase.

'What does that mean, "place of abundance"?' The congregation remained silent, and he answered himself: 'It's where God wants us to be. It may seem like other people get there before us, or that our journey is harder, but it's where He is leading us at all times.' There were a few 'Amen's around the room, and Kodzo nodded, as if making his body agree would make his mind follow.

'But what must we do to get there? It continues: "I will come to Your temple with burnt offerings and fulfil my vows to You. Vows my lips promised and my mouth spoke *when I was in trouble*."' Michael paused again. 'We've all been there: in crisis, praying to God and promising Him that we will work to serve Him, be better, more faithful, true to His word. But when He is gracious and delivers us, do we keep or break our promise?'

Kodzo remembered his near-desperation in a hot, cramped flat in Accra waiting for the results of another application, one to study nursing in Scotland, and his sincerity in devoting his life to the service of Jesus if he were to make it there. He felt shame as he thought of his life now, close to God in theory, but barely in practice.

Kodzo rose to his feet as soon as the band started the Praise and Worship section. He kept his eyes tightly shut and prayed again, this time repenting for his dishonesty in taking the job, but not offering himself, and asking for forgiveness. He made another promise to God and lifted his hands into the air in submission, feeling the presence of God descend through the ceiling of Styrofoam squares directly onto the palms of his hands as the cymbals crashed and guitars swelled around him. He began to pray out loud, praising God. He felt a heat in his stomach, rising to his mouth, where the words came fast; a pressure that needed release. When the music stopped, Kodzo realised the words he was speaking were not English, or Ewe.

'*Hintaraka, misamin!*' They flowed and flowed, and he didn't understand them, but knew them deeply. The feeling was almost overwhelming, but he relaxed into it and felt comforted: he hadn't spoken in Tongues since he was a child in his dad's village church. They spoke of love, glory and faith, and came from a blissful place, where his soul glimpsed the beauty of God.

Chapter Seven

Elom – May 2006

Dzifa suggested bringing the PlayStation 2 down from Elom's room, like when they were kids. They plugged it into the television, leaving a windscreen-wiper wedge in the dust from where they pivoted the TV on the stand then back again. Elom mostly had one-player arcade games, and they took turns on the controller. On difficult levels, she acted as strategist and he as infantry. The only game they competed on was *Tekken*. Dzifa chose Xiaoyu, meeting Eddie Gordo's forceful kicks and spins with more elegant evasions and twirls, and won two out of three. Before the next battle, Elom's Nokia sounded a nasal melody.

Hey bro, wuu2? Jade has an empty. Can u get drink n stuff?

Elom played a few more rounds before telling Dzifa he was heading out.

'Where?'

'Just seeing Chris.'

Abena was still sleeping off her late shift, so Elom showered as quietly as he could before putting on a baggy white T-shirt and jeans. He thought of the girls that might be there tonight, and the boys. He checked his reflection as he placed a gold chain around his neck, comparing it to the 50 Cent poster Blu-Tacked to the wall, its corners curling from having fallen down so many times. He thrust his chin up slightly and rapped Papoose's verse from 'Touch It (Remix)', believing for a second he really did run New York.

Elom reached underneath his bed and pulled out a shoebox. Inside one of the trainers was another package the size of a matchbox, wrapped in clingfilm and tied in a sandwich bag. He had last smoked a week ago at Kayleigh's, hoping it would help him relax, but his nerves had got worse. He hadn't spoken to her since, and neither seemed willing to correct their friends' assumptions about what they did.

He checked his wallet – a fiver and a few silver coins – and headed downstairs. He saw Dzifa put her phone away as he came into the living room.

'Can I borrow your MiniDisc?' Elom asked.

'Again, man?'

'I burn all your discs!'

'What if I need it?'

'I'll just grab it and give it back later.' Elom made for the door.

'No, don't go in my room. I'll get it.' As soon as Elom heard the creak of the seventh stair, he opened the old biscuit tin on the side table, which now held keys, letters and change. The coins were for Abena's bus fare, or for one of the kids to use when she sent them to the shop. He pocketed them quickly, feeling more guilt than the spirit of rebellion, but he had already promised Chris he would get booze and he couldn't show up empty handed – they were both sixteen, but Elom looked a hair older than Chris. A few seconds later, Dzifa handed Elom the player and he pocketed it too, pushing the headphone wires under the bottom of his shirt and pulling them out at the collar.

'Cheers, Dzifa. I'll do you a new disc tomorrow – let me know what you want.'

'Uh-huh.' She turned off the PlayStation as he opened the front door.

Elom arrived before Chris, opening his bottle of Buckfast as he entered the cramped main room. A flat-screen TV dominated the space, cycling through hectic dance hits, and a dozen or so folk sat chatting on the faux-leather couches. Elom perched on an armrest, sipping more than talking, and humming along to the tunes under his breath. By the time Chris and the others arrived, he had drunk a third of the bottle.

'Awrite, man!'

'Awrite, what's good, bro?' They clapped hands and pulled each other in for a tap on the back.

'Yeah, I'm good. Did you get the Bucky?'

'Aye.' Elom offered Chris the bottle and he took a swig. 'Sorry, man, could only get the one. Got some hash too, though.'

'Sound.'

By seven thirty the house was full. Elom followed Chris as he slipped through the crowd – it seemed like all the fifth and fourth years were there, and he even noticed some boys from Dzifa's year milling outside. American hip-hop blared as the boys and girls showed off – who could drink the most, be the funniest or dress the best, despite the fact they all bought their clothes from the same three chains in town.

'Here – comin' out for that smoke, then?' Chris asked as they finished the wine.

Elom was already buzzed, the alcohol and caffeine pulling him in opposite directions. He heard G-Unit on the speakers and nodded. 'Aye.'

They sat on some garden chairs outside. Elom unwrapped the hash, noticing people starting to notice. He felt their eyes, and the weight of the space shifted, like the garden's centre of gravity had moved closer to him. Eventually people would say 'hi', ask for a light or offer a beer; find some way to make it into his and Chris's orbit by the time the hash had been lit, so that they could casually accept a puff when Elom had to offer it round. As Elom burned, then crumbled the edges of the block, Chris picked up an empty bottle of Barr's ginger beer from the table and grinned.

'Here, mate. Bucket?'

Elom laughed and nodded again. Chris went inside and came back with a butter knife and some water inside the glass bottle. He shook it firmly, the knife cracking the bottom of the bottle cleanly away – a perfect design defect. He then went back inside and came out with the bottom half of a 2-litre plastic bottle, filled with water, and a roll of tinfoil. Elom looked at the small pile of hash crumbs on the clingfilm in front of him and remembered his teacher saying it was full of rubber and shit.

Elom set the bottomless glass bottle in the makeshift bucket and placed some tinfoil over the top, which Chris then poked with a toothpick. Elom sprinkled the hash on top of it, and lit it as people surrounded them. He slowly lifted the bottle, watching the milky smoke get pulled into the vacuum left by the receding water, then lifted the foil lid off. As he lowered his lips to the glass in the fading light, his gaze caught a familiar shape swinging through the gate.

He hesitated; she hadn't seen him yet. She was half turned, saying something to her friends behind her, all of them laughing, enthralled.

'Hurry up, ya mad pussy,' Chris goaded. Elom looked at the bucket. He felt alert, like he might be fine this time. He inhaled deeply just as Dzifa caught his eye.

Elom sunk into himself. The house and garden looked like a stage set. The big green bin looked more binny. He didn't look at Dzifa as he lowered the bottle, ready for Chris to relight.

'On yous go.' He exhaled. 'It's good shit, man.'

Chris took the bottle as Elom smiled, all of himself trying to stay focused.

'Gonnae move, mate?' Elom looked down; his fingers were still wrapped around the glass. He pulled his hand away, too quickly. He looked up at Chris and the others. They looked back, glee in their eyes. He smiled again, reaching for words that didn't come.

'Yeah, issmad bad my bad, innit?' Elom chuckled.

Chris screeched. 'Oh my God man, you're wrecked!' More laughter erupted, more noise and faces near his, and shouts of his name and pats, pats, pats on his back and rubbing of his hair. Elom tried to laugh, instead barely producing a series of heavy sighs. He was nervous. He left the bucket and slowly sat on a chair at the other end of the table. Dzifa wasn't in the garden anymore.

Where is she?

Chris refilled the bucket with smoke.

Has she told Mum?

The boys talked.

What are they saying? Do I look okay? Is Chris as high as me?

More laughter.

Who are they laughing at?

Elom felt on the verge of doing something utterly foolish. He watched the bodies in the fading light and stayed silent.

How long will this last?

Chris joined him, then the others – eyes reddening, but seemingly more capable, laughing at jokes Elom couldn't understand. There was movement and Elom followed, bumping through the crowds in the kitchen and on the stairs, mumbling apologies and hoping he hadn't spilled anyone's drink.

Don't look like the wasted guy at the party.

But you are the wasted guy at the party.

Where's Dzifa?

Elom sat on the floor in a bedroom, perched beside an extension lead and a wall. Jade sat laughing on Chris's lap on the single bed, while Del and Chloe danced to 'Shake That' on tinny mobile phone speakers. They passed around a half-bottle of vodka and Elom sipped, then repeatedly checked the floor in case he had spilled some on the extension lead, terrified he might cause a fire. Kelly sat next to him, asking him questions. He gave short answers, a hot sweat prickling his forehead and armpits as she leaned closer. The laughter quietened; Chris was kissing Jade, his hand awkwardly angled underneath her short denim skirt, between her black-tights-clad thighs.

'Whit you staring at, El?' Del called from across the room, standing behind Chloe as she pressed her bum into his crotch with the music. Kelly had her hand on Elom's leg.

'Nothin'. I'm just pure high, man.' He pulled his eyes away from Chris's hand, still moving slowly in the dark.

'Aye, mate.' Del smiled at Chris, who grinned back, and both returned to kissing, touching the girls with the confidence of inexperience. Chloe broke away, giggling, and hooked a chair under the door handle. Chris called to Elom, 'I hope you're no' leaving Kelly out.'

She laughed, eyes avoiding Elom's face. 'I hope not too!'

Wordlessly, Elom leaned forward and placed his lips on hers. The movements were familiar, though the sliding of tongues was nauseating in the hot dark. The song finished, leaving the sound of Velcro sucker kisses and the rustle of competing fabrics. Elom's actions were mechanical, but he moved at the right time – his hands on her waist, then her chest, over the top of her T-shirt, then under. The weed hit in waves, with him periodically coming to his senses, panicked that in the preceding seconds he had kissed too hard, squeezed an odd bit of her body, or was unknowingly kissing a lampshade.

Kelly moved her hand from his face to his chest, then his thigh, and began to slide it up. Elom kissed with more urgency, trying to take control. He pushed his hands down through the waistband of her skirt, scraping his fingers between denim and skin. He tried undoing the button at the top, then jammed his hand in again – the zip was still up but he didn't want to fiddle with it a second time, so he pushed on until the tips of his fingers felt moistness, then inched further, smearing and rubbing as he went. He saw Chloe sitting on the desk in the corner, Del standing between her legs. He felt Chris and Zoe through the rhythmic shaking of the bed. Elom pulled down Kelly's zip.

He slid one finger in. It felt like the inside of his cheek. He felt something in the base of his stomach. A good feeling, a feeling with potential, that he tried to push further down, into his pelvis and through his cock, but it stayed in his stomach and beyond it remained a stony nothingness. She moved her hand over his crotch, rubbing through his jeans, lightly at first, then more insistently. The room grew hotter and the noises louder. She stopped the kiss and looked at him, a question curving her brow.

The door was suddenly pushed open, clattering against the chair, and the room was flooded with laughter, shouts and light. Zoe hid under the cover, while Del quickly stood apart from Chloe, fiddling with his jeans as she snorted behind her hand.

'I need to piss.' Elom got up, glancing at Kelly as he left. He stood over the toilet and stared at his dick, shrivelled like it had been left out in the sun.

When he'd finished, he went straight downstairs and hovered over the dining table, looking for a drink. Dzifa tapped him on the shoulder.

'Hey, man!' She was smiling, a sweaty sheen glittering her face.

'What are you doing here?'

'You're not the only one who goes to parties.'

Elom took a sip from an abandoned mug and quickly wiped his lips, unsure if Kelly had been wearing lipstick. 'Aye, but you shouldn't be. Who're you with?' She was holding a half-finished Smirnoff. Elom wasn't sure how much she had been drinking, or who had bought it for her.

'Just my friends.' Dzifa's smile fell slightly. 'You been having fun?'

'Yeah. You should head back, though.'

Dzifa's smile left completely. 'We both should – I told Dad I'd be back soon. I just wanted my MiniDisc.'

'Here. It's running out of battery.'

'Well you owe me new ones then.'

'Fine.'

'Fine.' Dzifa paused. 'I didn't know you smoked.'

'Don't tell Mum and Dad.' The panic rose again.

'I obviously won't! I'm not an idiot.' Dzifa shook her head as she checked the earbuds for wax.

'Nooo! Where are you going?' Dzifa's friend Anna, cider in hand, rushed in and pulled the earbud out.

'Home. Can't stay out tonight,' Dzifa replied, reeling up the cord from the sticky floor.

'No no no, one more dance, pleaaaase.' She held on to Dzifa by the waist. 'You've got the moooves.' Elom had seen Anna and Dzifa act together in the school play, linking arms and bowing to applause from the whole school and the parents.

Dzifa laughed again, easily. 'Fine, fine, one more dance.' She shot Elom a glance. 'See you at home.'

Elom watched as they joined their group of friends in the living room, shout-singing the guitar riff from 'When the Sun

Goes Down' into each other's faces; how they held hands and raised their arms above their heads while they twisted their waists or jumped up and down. How they only looked at each other. How she tried to leave after the end of one song and they held on, hugging her and asking for one more dance.

He stood by the table sipping some sweet, was-fizzy-now-flat drink. Footsteps tumbled down the staircase behind him and out the back door. Elom turned to see Chris outside, lighting a cigarette or a joint – he still had Elom's hash. Chris caught Elom's eye and held up the lit tube, raising an eyebrow.

Kelly was nowhere to be seen. Elom wondered how close she was to Kayleigh.

Dzifa walked over, slightly breathless. 'Okay, I'm actually going this time.' She followed Elom's gaze and spotted Chris in the distance, then she turned to leave. Elom watched Chris say something to Del and they both guffawed, hands on stomachs, bending over.

'Hold on.'

'Huh?'

'Hold on, I'm coming.' Elom turned to Chris and Del and signalled with his thumb towards the front door. They shrugged, waved, and Chris took another toke. As he turned, he saw them laughing again. Elom and Dzifa walked into the cold, both jacketless, the threat of rain in the velvet clouds which darkened the sky.

'Shall we walk?' Dzifa handed Elom an earbud for his left ear, one already hanging from her right.

'It's baltic – let's get the bus.'

'I think a walk will do you good, man.'

Elom looked at Dzifa and slowed his pace as he worried his way through the events of the night, unsure if he had said something he shouldn't have, or if she had heard something from Kelly or someone else. 'What do you mean?'

Dzifa laughed. 'Honestly, your eyes are so red, man.' She turned on the MiniDisc. 'What are we listening to?'

Chapter Eight

Abena – March 2007

'Elom!' Abena climbed the stairs straight to his room, her shoes trailing wet footprints onto the carpet. Her face was still hot with embarrassment. She pushed the door open. 'Elom!' The room was empty.

Dzifa opened her bedroom door across the landing. 'What's wrong?' She was already in her pyjamas and satin bonnet.

'Where's Elom?'

'Out with Chris.' Dzifa shrugged, before asking, 'Why?' and Abena suspected she knew. Kodzo was on a night shift and had missed parents' evening, and Abena had sat by herself while three different subject teachers told her that their son was failing, or almost failing. She was tired.

'Text your brother. I'm going to bed. Tell him his father will meet him here.'

* * *

Elom wasn't home when Abena woke up. When Kodzo got home, she told him the news, and he shook his head, his night-shift-beaten eyes cast downwards.

'This boy, eh.' He drove Dzifa to her weekend theatre school, then he and Abena spoke, and then they waited.

The door clunked open just after 2 p.m., and Kodzo muted GOD TV.

'Sit down,' Kodzo said. Elom didn't argue, and Abena was grateful that the first battle was won. He walked forward in his baggy T-shirt and sat on the armchair in the corner, facing Abena; Kodzo sat on the two-seater along the wall. Elom's face was dry, as if he'd showered and not moisturised.

'Where have you been?' Kodzo asked, more calmly than Abena could have managed.

'Out.' It was the same word as always, though Abena thought Elom's voice was at least softer than usual.

'Where? With who?' Kodzo asked.

'Chris and Del.' Always the same. They were faceless to Abena – not like Dzifa's friends, who were always car-pooling between drama classes, sleepovers or the cinema; who would wave Dzifa goodbye and shout 'See you soon!' to Abena. Elom kept his friends separate. When Abena found out that Chris had dropped out of school after fifth year, she told Elom to let the friendship go, but he had refused. Now Abena feared where his loyalty was leading him.

'Hm.' Kodzo shook his head. 'And Chris and Del, do they know you're failing in school?' Elom sank into the chair. 'Or maybe you kept it from them, too?'

'It's just prelims, I've got time to study—'

'*Ho*,' Abena cut him off, 'it's been two months, and all you've done is go out or play PlayStation. Meanwhile your exams are around the corner.'

'You were lucky to get an offer.' Kodzo spoke again, and Abena let his voice cool the room. 'You need an A and two Bs for Glasgow. That's not going to happen with your current approach.'

Elom said nothing, and Abena felt like shaking him. He had been very lucky to get an offer for engineering, considering his previous year's results and his insistence on choosing Higher English. Abena had wanted him to focus on sciences to maximise his chances of getting a real degree, but Elom had gone against her, and now he was barely even passing that. He had loved reading as a child, but all of that had fallen away with secondary school and his new friends.

'Your mum and I have been talking,' Kodzo continued. 'You have two months until your exams. Number one: no PlayStation. Number two: you are grounded – school, home and church only. And number three: you are going to the Wednesday youth group every week.'

'I'll just study more, I don't need to be punished,' Elom started.

'We are not going through all that, Elom. If you want to show us you can do it, then do it. You'll get your PlayStation back after you sit your exams.'

'What do you mean "get it back"? Where is it?' Neither parent spoke, and Elom's eyes pinged between the two of them.

'This is so unfair! I'm gonna be stuck in here with nothing to do. We're going to a concert next month.'

Elom's audacity pulled Abena forward. 'Stuck here for what? You have important exams very soon. Don't tell me such nonsense.'

'How come Dzifa gets to do whatever she wants and I'm gonna be stuck at home?'

'Because Dzifa pays attention in school while you are foutering about with your friends.' Abena raised her voice. She was furious at his disregard for the opportunities that had been placed at his feet through their hard work, and terrified of where he might end up once those opportunities ran out. 'And those boys, you think you can be like them and live the lives they are living. But you can't, you are different, Elom.' Elom and Dzifa were one of two Black families at their school, and though the white kids were not well off, one thing they could afford was a lack of ambition.

Elom was breathing heavily, his arms tightly folded to his chest. He quickly untangled one to stop a tear falling past his eyelashes, before folding it back in.

'Elom, it's not long,' Kodzo said. 'Two months, and trust me, you'll see the bene—'

'This isn't fair.' Elom crossed the room in long strides, ran up the stairs and slammed his door with a grunt. Abena looked at Kodzo, surprised. She was used to shouting to be heard, but she couldn't remember Elom or Dzifa snapping at Kodzo like that. There was something hot buzzing underneath Elom's usual angst, and it felt dangerous.

Two Wednesdays later, Kodzo drove Elom to his second youth group. Abena knew he would cringe sitting amongst the earnest teenagers and listening to overly sincere pastors, but she still wanted him to spend some time outside of his room.

'What are you watching?' Abena asked Dzifa as she flicked through channels from the couch.

'Dunno, nothing really.' She settled on *My Wife and Kids*. They watched it so often that even Abena knew the episode already.

'How's the revision going?'

'Yeah, fine,' Dzifa replied, her eyes still on the television. 'I'm just having a break today.'

Abena smiled, worried that Dzifa thought she was speaking pointedly. 'You need to rest sometimes.'

Dzifa barely nodded, still focused on the onscreen family as the father and son fought over who was best at basketball. She didn't know whether Dzifa was tired, angry about Elom or just uninterested in her. She wanted to ask her something else, to use the rare time they had, just the two of them, but nothing came to mind. It was like she was trapped in a lift with a stranger, and it saddened her.

'What do you want for dinner?'

'I don't mind. Just maybe not rice and stew again.'

Abena got up to cook, digging past icy Tupperware in the freezer for something new. She found some fish, and remembered gutting tilapia side by side with a young Abla.

Soon after dinner, Abena and Kodzo went to bed, and she leaned in towards him.

'How was church?'

'Fine. I spoke to the youth group leader, Charles. He says Elom isn't engaging.'

'Has he been talking to you?'

'Not really.'

They lay in silence as Abena stroked Kodzo's stomach, sliding a finger through the buttons of his pyjama top to touch the smooth skin underneath.

'Charles recommended a camp,' he continued, 'a retreat for teenagers following God's path. Boys that age have so much confusion, you know?'

Abena just nodded. She wanted Elom to be under their watch more than ever, not sent away for strangers to deal with. Kodzo placed his hand on hers, gently flattening her fingers onto his stomach.

'What do you think?'

'Maybe . . . I just don't know if that's the best way to make him see.'

Kodzo turned to look at Abena. 'Is there a better way?'

'I don't know, oh.'

Kodzo sighed. 'We need to try. Me too, I've spoken to my boss. I'll be doing more early shifts, so I can be home in the evenings.' He didn't look at Abena as he said this, instead reaching to his bedside table to pick up his book as Abena's hand slid off his belly. 'This is more important than money. Dzifa only has a couple of years left too. We should be home more.'

It made sense, but Abena felt like she was being accused of something. 'You know it's hard for me – my hours at the restaurant are difficult.' Kodzo nodded, already reading under the glow of his bedside lamp, and Abena rolled over to her side of the bed.

She had been the one to find out Elom was failing, while Kodzo was at work. She was the one losing her temper over his behaviour, and still the one cooking for the kids between her shifts, while Kodzo sent him to church. She had done her best for Abla, and then her own two kids, with nothing in her favour. Abla had made it through university without the money to bribe her way along, or the connections to secure a high-paying job on graduation, but Abena knew she could now be self-sufficient at least, thanks to her. Abena knew what an absent mother looked like, and she didn't fit that shape: she was successful – a head pastry chef at a good restaurant – and it was unfair to be punished for that. She was still awake when she heard Kodzo shut his book, click off his light and tuck himself into bed.

With time, Elom's mood started to settle. He occasionally ate downstairs with the rest of the family instead of taking his plate up to his room. Abena admitted it was nice to see him and Kodzo in the living room together in the evenings, though whenever she asked how his studying was going, he shrugged a one-word answer. She was reassured, at least, when she went into his room to change his sheets and saw notebooks progressively filling with unintelligible equations.

A week before his first exam, Abena made kenkey. Elom sat with them all, and smiled as he ate with his hands. For dessert, they moved on to a Victoria sponge that Abena had lifted from work and Dzifa put on a film.

'By the way, Elom . . .' Kodzo started. Elom nodded with his eyes on the screen, and Dzifa turned the volume up. 'I spoke to Charles about the camp – you can go in July.'

Abena watched as Elom's eyes flicked to Kodzo's, then back to the TV. 'Uh-huh.' He took a bite of cake. 'How come?'

'What do you mean?'

'Just, how come you want me to go to a church camp?'

'Oh.' Kodzo shifted in his chair. 'It will just be fun. It's more for the activities – there'll be things in nature – walking, canoeing, that sort of thing. Dzifa did all that with Duke of Edinburgh, but you didn't want to. I think you'll enjoy it. You can meet other young people too.' He attempted some kind of conspiratorial smile.

Abena hadn't heard about the camp for a couple of weeks, and she didn't like Kodzo's sudden announcement.

'Kodzo, how much is it going to cost?'

'Not much. The church pay for most of it, so maybe £60 to £80 for transport and food.'

Dzifa turned the volume up even higher, seemingly in protest at the drawn-out conversation which was disturbing her film, and Elom locked his eyes on it again. Abena couldn't argue with the cost, nor with getting Elom out of the house with new people. It also didn't seem fair to say that she didn't like men she barely knew telling her son what to think, particularly now, when his peace seemed so fragile, so she just nodded.

'We can talk about it again with Charles next week,' Kodzo said.

Elom simply nodded. At midnight, when Abena cleared the dessert bowls after the film had finished, she tossed Elom's barely touched cake in the bin, shaking her head at the waste.

*　*　*

The next evening Abena called the kids for dinner, and after a few minutes Dzifa came downstairs, phone in hand. Abena decided not to disturb Elom's nap, or timed paper. They started eating without him, so Kodzo could make his now-rare night shift, which he had agreed to do when they offered double time.

The back door clattered open as Kodzo was putting on his shoes. Abena looked at Kodzo and sighed, and his shoulders dropped in resignation. The rules of the punishment had tacitly relaxed; Abena sent Elom out for errands, and occasionally he went to the library with Dzifa. He had even asked Abena if he could play football with family friends soon, and she'd said yes. But they were always to know where he was going.

'Elom,' Kodzo called him through to the living room. There was the sound of languid footsteps until he stood at the door. He looked flat, his eyes turned down. Kodzo shook his head as he put on his jacket. 'Where have you been?'

'Went out for a walk.'

A smell reached Abena's nose, sweet and musty. Her hands tightened on her fork, as Kodzo said slightly louder, 'Elom, look at me.' Elom looked up, his eyes puffy. 'Why are your eyes red?'

'It's nothing.' He looked down again.

'Were you with Chris and those boys? Elom, your exams are just coming and you're doing this now?'

'I wasn't with them!'

'Elom!' Abena was shouting. 'I can't believe you. Is something wrong with your head or what?' She wanted Kodzo's calm; to take a moment to tell Dzifa to go upstairs, but she was too hurt from Elom's betrayal. 'You are one week from your exams and you are smoking weed when you should be at home studying. Are you trying to . . . I don't even know. Do you have any respect for your life or what?'

'I wasn't smoking,' he replied quietly.

'Elom, we are not stupid,' Kodzo said.

'I wasn't! I—'

'Elom, stop it.' Abena cut him off. Elom's eyes were glassy, tears threatening to fall, and Abena was able to control her voice when she spoke again, trying to express the urgency she felt. 'These boys, the ones you will do anything for: they are not your friends. I'm telling you. You think all this fun will last your whole life, but it won't. Life will change and when you are looking for them to help, you'll find out that they've dropped you, because they are actually trying to get somewhere. And where will you be? They are not your friends, oh.'

Elom stood in the doorframe, silent. His jaw clenched and he wiped away the tears as quickly as they fell.

'I'm going to work. We'll talk when I get back.' Kodzo left through the front door. Abena watched Elom, tense and shaking, and remembered him as a child before a tantrum, bursting with emotions he couldn't name.

'Go to bed, we'll talk tomorrow,' Abena said.

Elom stomped up the stairs and she tried to think of what to say to Dzifa. They sat in silence until Dzifa said, 'He has been studying, Mum. I think he just needed some time out.'

'Dzifa, no.' Abena didn't want to hear a defence. Elom was treating his life – their efforts – like a joke. 'Finish your dinner and get ready for bed.'

'Mum.'

Abena ignored her and started eating again. The news droned from the television. As Abena scooped up some peas, she heard something hard sliding on the laminate floor above, then a crash. She dropped her fork and climbed the stairs to Elom's room, opening the door to find him standing over a broken mirror. A few bright dots had splattered onto the glass, and as she looked at his hand, she saw more drops falling, red and wet. She looked into his eyes, equally red and wet, and saw her own fear reflected back at her, as the tears started to fall.

Abena drove Elom to the hospital while Dzifa stayed at home. The nurse at the minor injuries unit asked Elom what had happened, and he mumbled something about pretending to be a boxer in the mirror. She cleaned Elom's hand and used tweezers to take out a shard of glass that Abena hadn't seen, and asked him, 'So you've no' been scrappin' then, son?'

Abena watched him shake his head. 'And there's nothin' else bothering you?' Again, Elom shook his head, and Abena felt smaller in her chair. He needed stitches, but his X-ray was clear and they were back home within a few hours. When Kodzo got home in the morning, he looked tired, and he sat with Abena in bed for an hour before they woke Elom up. He didn't argue when they reinstated the original rules of his punishment.

Elom was just finishing secondary school, and Dzifa had two years left. She had always done well, and had never had Elom's aloofness, but Abena knew that people could change. She wondered if she had missed something in Elom while she had been standing in a hotel kitchen.

She thought of Abla in Newtown, working now, but still walking the line between escape and failure. Abena worried she had missed something with her, or that there was more she could have given: perhaps the money hadn't been enough. Perhaps the time she had used to make that money should have been spent on Elom instead, or on both of them. She remembered being young and needing someone, and was ashamed that now she was the one who had disappeared.

Abena had had an eighteen-year career: eighteen years to be proud of, and eighteen years where she had earned respect for her work. She couldn't respect herself if her children were hurting. She knew it was time to let it go.

Chapter Nine

Dzifa – July 2007

Dzifa got home just after 7 p.m. Kodzo was at work, and Abena and Elom sat on opposite couches in the living room, eating the dinner Abena had cooked as a dozen people on the television failed to get along with each other whilst trapped in a huge house.

'Hi.' Dzifa spoke to the room, keeping her eyes on her shoes as she pulled them off. For the last few days, speaking with one person had felt like siding against the other.

'Hi. Were you at your friend's?' Abena asked. She had just started working day shifts at a local care home, and was now always around in the evenings, taking note of Dzifa's movements. Coming home late felt like a slight against Elom's lack of freedom, and Dzifa couldn't tell whether Abena's question was meant to highlight her favour, or if it was a warning shot that she was next.

'No, I was at a rehearsal.'

'Rehearsal for what?'

'Just a play I'm in.'

'Will you miss any classes?' Dzifa had already finished her exams for that year. Her classes had all but petered out, apart from half-hearted attempts to start next year's syllabus. Dzifa had gone for sciences, maths and English. She'd have loved to have chosen music, or art, but Abena and Kodzo had said there wasn't space to do them all, and that she should choose the subjects that would look best on a university application.

'No, Mum.' Dzifa became annoyed. 'Anyway, it's a good thing: it's learning Shakespeare – that's a good thing.' The obsession with exams and school had become feverish. Whilst Dzifa had avoided any direct heat, she resented the sentiment. It was her parents who insisted that she should keep these things as hobbies rather than school subjects, yet they were always so suspicious of them.

'Okay.' Abena nodded and silently continued eating. She didn't ask Dzifa any more questions. Dzifa looked at Elom, who had remained silent. She wanted to tell him she had been cast as one of the leads. Rather, she wanted him to ask, but he kept his eyes locked on the screen. She went through to the kitchen to get herself a plate of dinner, before heading to her room to learn lines.

Dzifa was late home every night that week. She spent her evenings running along the assembly hall's hardwood floor, collecting dust on the soles of her tights. She fumbled her lines in a run-through, and spent the next evening at her best friend Anna's house, highlighting difficult passages and imagining fanciful images for each other in order to remember them. Elom was usually in his room when she got back. Kodzo was often at work, while Abena sat alone in the living-room, on the phone to Aunty Abla with the TV on in the background, if she wasn't already in bed before an early shift. Dzifa would slide into place on the living-room sofa, or plug her headphones in and trawl MySpace until bed.

On Saturday she slept in, then packed a bag with a dress, some makeup and pyjamas.

'Just heading to Anna's for a sleepover, Mum,' Dzifa said to Abena as she dropped some bread into the toaster.

'Oh, okay,' Abena replied. Dzifa wanted, but didn't expect, her to ask what they would do; about Anna's hobbies and what they talked about. Abena must have seen them dozens of times, but Dzifa thought she would struggle to mention anything about them. She reckoned Abena probably knew more about Chris and Del, though she had never met them. 'When will you be back?'

'Tomorrow morning. I can get the train, or her mum might drop me off.'

'Do you want to eat before you go? It will be ready soon.' Abena was stirring a pot, and something bulky sat in blue polythene bags on the counter, suggesting Abena had been to the Asian and African shop that morning, but that whatever she was making was far from fully cooked.

'I'm already late, sorry. I'm just gonna have this toast and go.'

'No problem.' Abena turned back to the pot. 'Have fun, okay?'

'Yeah, thanks.'

*   *   *

Dzifa and Anna watched *Little Miss Sunshine* through fistfuls of chocolate and crisps in her television room (separate from her living room, which had no television, or their conservatory, which also had no television), and then were joined by two other friends to get ready for the party they would be heading to later. Anna's mum had allowed them one bottle of prosecco to share, but they had also all brought their own booze for the night itself.

The party was mostly people from fourth year, since the older years still had some exams. A few people ended up streaking on the golf course the house backed onto, and several glasses ended up broken. Dzifa had come in from the cold to play a game of table tennis with her friend Ritchie when the doorbell rang at about eleven and a few boys from the year above trickled into the basement, where most of the group were gathered. One of them made a beeline for Ritchie and handed him a four-pack of Stella.

Ritchie and the boy were brothers, with the same tuft of hair sticking up from the crown of their heads. They played as a team against Dzifa and another friend, jostling each other for the ball and cycling between shared congratulations or searing derision for won or lost points. They were so comfortably close, and laughed as if everything they said was buoyed by some inside joke. They played until Anna pulled Dzifa away – one of their friends had whitied, and they sat with her outside, forcing water into her until she was able to half walk, half be carried home.

The next morning Dzifa turned down the offer of a lift, choosing instead to walk to the train station with her tinny headphones playing *Alright, Still.* She got home just as the others were leaving for church, but said she wasn't feeling well enough to go, which wasn't a direct lie. She wanted to share a knowing look with Elom, but the line between looking conspiratorial and gloating was thin, so she kept her eyes to the ground as he passed her on the way to the car. There had been a time, before exams and before parties, when that line had never existed – when they were not best friends, but rather on the same team, in the simple way siblings can be, when the only teams are themselves and everyone else.

She slept until they got back and she heard Elom slink into his room. His last exam was in a few days, and her play was two days after, on the coming Friday. She still didn't know if anyone was able to make it – they hadn't asked much about it, and usually one of her parents was working whenever she had a show. She thought of Ritchie and his brother's ease around each other the night before, and got out of bed, picking up her script as she went to chap on Elom's door.

'Yeah?'

'It's me.'

Dzifa gingerly opened the door – Elom hadn't given her a clear invitation, and as she stood on the threshold, she sensed that she wasn't fully welcome to cross it. Elom sat at the desk in the corner, pen in one hand and chin in the other. There was a blank space on top of the squat chest of drawers where the television and PlayStation used to sit. Dzifa realised she hadn't been inside his room in a long time.

'I just wondered if you want to help me with my lines?' Dzifa asked, holding up her script. Elom looked at her, his palm still cupping his chin. His knuckles faced her, and she could see a partially healed scar stretching over one of them. His hand had been bandaged for a while, and Dzifa was surprised to see a cut on that side of it – Abena said the mirror had slid off the wall and Elom had cut himself picking it up.

'For the play?'

'Yeah. It's on Friday; I just need to run them a few times so it's in my head,' Dzifa said, still on the edge of the room.

Elom turned back to his equations. 'I've got to finish this off.'

'Cool. Maybe later?' She tried to keep her voice light.

'I don't think I can,' he replied.

'That's fine.' She answered too quickly, she thought, her upbeat voice revealing her disappointment.

'Just got a lot to do before Thursday.' He looked up and half shrugged.

'Yeah, no worries. Good luck.' Dzifa pulled his door shut and crossed the hall, shutting the bedroom door she'd left open.

Kodzo dropped Dzifa off at the theatre on Thursday evening for her dress rehearsal. Elom finishing his exams had both relieved and added some tension to the family; now they were all waiting to see if the last few months had paid off. It was like her parents had moved from a sinking ship onto a life-raft, but no one knew how strong a rower Elom was. Dzifa had barely seen him the last two days between school and rehearsal, but she hoped he was enjoying himself in the gap before results day.

Kodzo pulled up to the pavement as several teenagers hopped out of cars and into the building. He called out to Dzifa as she made to follow. 'Did you get us tickets, by the way? What time is it tomorrow?'

Dzifa's surprise made her hesitate. 'Ehm, seven thirty. I haven't got them yet, but I can.'

'Please. Your mum was asking too.'

It was like they had closed the exam chapter and looked up to see the neglected, dusty room around them. Frustration and appreciation grappled for Dzifa's attention.

'Yeah. I'll put a couple behind the box office for tomorrow.'

Dzifa's play was part of a local schools' festival, and her cast joined two other groups the following afternoon to preview each other's shows before the main performance. Dzifa, Anna and the others shuffled into a row of folding seats in their minimalist black leggings and tank tops to watch *Much Ado About Nothing* and *A Midsummer Night's Dream*, featuring a giant papier-mâché ass's head. Dzifa laughed out loud at the physical comedy, and the punchlines spun in fast iambic pentameter. She whispered to Anna, and nudged her after particularly poignant monologues. She enjoyed the plays, and she loved that she enjoyed them – that Shakespeare was something she understood and liked. When it was their group's turn, she felt a nervous exhilaration. The stage lights shone directly into her eyes, hiding the audience behind a haze, but she could hear their laughter as she bantered with Anna's Antonio, and she silently high-fived her friends between scenes backstage. Afterwards, their teacher Mr Buchanan got them a takeaway, and they each pulled a sweating paper bag of chips from the stuffed plastic bags and ate them on the green-room floor, waiting for the evening to begin.

As Dzifa heard the audience trudging in a few hours later, she wondered what her parents were thinking, and where they were sitting. Neither of them had watched a Shakespeare play before, that she knew of. She listened from the dressing room as muffled sounds of laughter and applause rolled in through the walls, as well as the occasional shout from an actor in a particularly dramatic scene. Eventually, Mr Buchanan came to get them and Dzifa waited in the wings as the previous cast took their bows.

Their own play moved quickly, and Dzifa felt a hot adrenaline pushing her forward. At the end of it, she couldn't tell if the audience's clapping was louder or more reserved than the applause for the other plays, but the elation of the actors in the dressing room afterwards, congratulating and commiserating over the many parts that had gone wrong, made it irrelevant.

'I can't believe I went on without my staff!'

'OMG, I totally skipped a line in my speech . . .'

'They couldn't stop laughing at your bits!'

Dzifa was still wearing her stage makeup when she went down to the lobby. She saw Kodzo and Abena grazing by the snack table amongst the rest of the families who were sipping from plastic wine glasses. She felt a jolt when she realised Elom stood beside them, hands in the pockets of his baggy jeans.

'Well done!' Kodzo reached out an arm to Dzifa, and they gripped each other in a sideways hug while she held her loaded tote bag under her other arm.

'That was really nice,' Abena said. 'All of you kids, I'm really impressed.'

'Thanks, guys.' Dzifa smiled. 'Elom, I didn't know you were coming.' She was apologetic. She had only left two tickets – she had assumed Elom didn't want to come.

'We had to buy another ticket. They almost didn't let us in,' Kodzo teased.

'What did you think?' she asked, mostly to Elom. There was laughter from the other clusters of families in the foyer. Some of her friends were holding flowers.

'I didn't quite get the horse thing,' Abena offered.

Dzifa chuckled. 'It's the head of an ass. The gods played a trick on him.'

'Why?'

'Just for fun, I guess.'

'He must have been so hot under there. Poor boy.'

Dzifa downed a glass of orange juice before they left. As they approached the exit, she saw Anna chatting with her mum and dad, and Dzifa split off from her family to give her a final, cheerful hug of congratulations. They lingered for a moment, arranging their next meet-up, and Dzifa casually accepted compliments from Anna's parents before walking back. Kodzo and Abena had left, but Elom was waiting by the exit, watching Dzifa.

'That was really cool,' he said as they stepped into the blustery street.

Dzifa was surprised, and slightly confused. 'What do you mean?'

'Just getting up there and doing all that. You were so funny, man.'

Dzifa blushed. 'Thanks. You should try it when you're at uni. There's never enough boys.'

'Nah. Everyone loved you. I could never do that.'

Dzifa wasn't sure whether he meant learn the lines, or stand on stage, or audition, or something else – or why it was that he couldn't do any of these things – but before she could ask, they were at the car and splitting off into different sides. She slid in and clicked in her seatbelt as Otis Redding began to play. Elom was already staring at his phone and punching buttons, pushing a black snake around the screen. When they were younger, he had been the funniest person she knew. He would make up the fantastical rules for their superhero games and play his role with total confidence. He was so quiet now, focused on his friends, and he didn't want to let her in. Dzifa turned to look back out of the window, and she whistled along to Otis as they drove home.

Chapter Ten

Kodzo – August 2007

Kodzo was eating soup on the couch when he heard the rustle and snap of the letterbox. The postwoman was late, burdened with the futures of a thousand teenagers. Abena was at work, catering at the care home, and before he could decide what to do, Dzifa had tumbled downstairs.

'Elom!' she shouted. Kodzo heard Elom's slower, heavier footsteps before he appeared. He wanted to say something right and wise, but he was too nervous to think of anything.

'Let's open them together?' Dzifa asked.

'Na, I'm gonna open mine upstairs.' The plastic window of the envelope crinkled as Elom took it from her.

'Let's do them at the same time. Or we can open each other's?' Dzifa smiled, almost pixie-ish.

'Eh, no,' Elom said, turning to the stairs.

'No, Elom, open it here.' Kodzo wanted to make sure everything was okay, but his fear made his voice harsher than planned. Elom's shoulders dropped. He didn't argue; he hadn't in a long while, and Kodzo missed the Elom that did.

Dzifa opened hers, her eyes darting around as she flicked through the sheets, before she looked up and smiled.

'What did you get?' She looked at Elom, who was still slowly pulling out the letters. The room stayed quiet as he read.

'What did *you* get?' he asked, and Kodzo felt his chest tighten.

'I got ones.' Dzifa was proud and bashful as she held out the sheet for Kodzo. The numbers fell down the right-hand side of the page like a line of Morse code.

'Well done, Dzifa!' Kodzo hugged her, proud but unsurprised.

Dzifa smiled. 'I thought I'd messed up the French exam, honestly. The speaking: I forgot so much of my speech and I had to make it up on the spot.'

'That's actually amazing.' Elom looked back at his own grades.

There was a pause before Dzifa asked, 'What did you get, then?'

'Ehm . . . I got an A in English, a B in Physics and a C in Maths.' He looked up, squinting, as if he was preparing himself for something bright, or loud.

Dzifa hugged him. 'That's so much better than prelims!'

'That's great! Elom, that's really, really great.' Elom had worked hard, but he was one grade short of Kodzo feeling any relief.

Elom sat on the couch as Kodzo waited on hold to the university admissions department a short while later. 'Hello, I'm calling on behalf of my son.' He looked over at Elom, who was tapping the letter against his thigh and staring at the coffee table, as the officer searched for Elom's application.

'Yes, so he needed an Advanced Higher A, an Advanced Higher B and a Higher B, but he got an Advanced A, an Advanced B and a Higher C. We're still very happy to give Elom a place.'

'Really?' Kodzo asked. Elom looked up, about to ask something, and Kodzo held out a finger, telling him to hold on.

'Absolutely. There are a few spaces with people choosing other offers or missing their grades.'

'That's great. Thank you.' Kodzo put down the phone a few moments later, after barely listening to some information about UCAS notifications. 'You're all good, Elom. University Boy!'

Elom grinned, the first wide-toothed smile Kodzo had seen in a while. 'Seriously?'

'Yeah, they said your results were great.'

Elom exhaled deeply as he sank into the sofa. Kodzo was surprised by how much he had been holding in. 'Thanks, Dad.'

Kodzo picked up the letter and put it back in its envelope. 'You are welcome, son. You're welcome.'

Abena was thrilled, and cooked jollof, chicken and plantain for dinner, while Kodzo picked up some Supermalt. They gave Elom back his PlayStation, with a new shoot-'em-up he had seen advertised.

'Thanks.' Elom took the machine and the game, and placed them on the coffee table. Kodzo was surprised he hadn't run upstairs to play immediately, and wondered if he had bought the wrong game.

'I heard that's a good one,' Kodzo said about the shoot-'em-up.

'Yeah, I think Del's got it, it sounds fun. Cheers.' Elom picked up his plate and spooned on seconds.

Kodzo and Abena were in bed by midnight, and Dzifa and Elom had gone out to celebrate (Elom presumably with his old friends, but Kodzo chose not to argue today). Abena drifted off while Kodzo read, but he was still up an hour later. He had cleared a hurdle he had been running towards for a decade – Elom had got into university, and Dzifa would be next. He wanted to exhale a long, deep breath like Elom had when he'd heard the news, but he couldn't. His chest stayed tight and his body restless, sprinting on. His faith and hard work had paid off – he was proud, and joyful, but as hard as he looked, there was still no relief.

By 5 p.m. the next day, Kodzo was tired. He had got a new job on the day ward, giving blood transfusions, iron infusions and draining fluid from livers. The slower pace and more regular hours were welcome, though monotonous. He stayed back to finish some paperwork after his shift, then drove alone to church for the men's group; Elom had asked to stop going as soon as his results had come through. Kodzo had imagined him growing into Christ with the group, and the camp, and even getting baptised; he had hoped a stronger faith in Elom might also pull Dzifa along. Abena said he couldn't force them.

In the church hall, the men gathered by the tea table, congratulated each other on their children's results, and lamented the pressure that kids were being put under these days. Kodzo nodded in agreement, but didn't mention the late nights chewing kola nut with his classmates, studying for O levels with the weight of responsibility of being the only boy in the family.

Simon called the room to prayer, and Kodzo bowed his head and closed his eyes, his tea still in one hand and the chocolate of his half-eaten digestive melting against his thumb in the other.

'Heavenly Father, we thank You for bringing us here today, and ask that You open our hearts and our minds to receive Your wisdom,' Simon continued, as Kodzo swallowed the mushy bite of biscuit in time to join the 'Amen'.

'Today's discussion will be about being a provider,' Simon started. 'Our reading will be two Corinthians, chapter eight, verse nine: "For you know the grace of our Lord Jesus Christ, that though He was rich, yet for your sakes He became poor, that you through His poverty might become rich."

'Jesus of course is the ultimate provider of all things good: forgiveness, and His eternal love. But all that came at a cost. It's important to keep that in mind for us, too, as fathers. Real fatherhood means making sacrifices; working hard so they can succeed. But remember we can always turn to Him when we are lacking.'

Simon opened the discussion up to the floor, and Kodzo was surprised to see Frank – who ran an import-export business and lived in Newton Mearns – speak. 'I had a wobble with the company a few years ago, and I couldn't be the provider my family needed me to be.' There were some sympathetic nods. 'With Celine . . . you can't take away her role like that: she's the carer. Don't get me wrong, I love my kids, and I hug them and that – my dad never did any of that' – some men grunted in solidarity – 'but she'll always be the mum just by being her. My ability to be the dad was taken away from me.'

'Thanks for sharing.' Simon nodded solemnly. 'There are differences between men and women. I'm sure most of the dads here have looked at the way our kids bond with their mums and felt left out.' Kodzo listened as John, then Fraser followed up with similar thoughts, then there were some more passages and prayers.

He struggled to untangle the threads that were knotted in his chest into a question. He felt like a carer and a provider – nursing had supported his family – but he also felt inadequate at both. He wondered if he could have been a better provider with a different line of work, or if he would have been a better nurse as a woman. He wondered if he had wasted his care on twenty years of patients instead of on his children, or if Abena's care had been enough. He wondered if he was being the right type of father for his children – the right type of man.

'Any other thoughts or questions before we wrap up today?' Simon asked, already closing his Bible. Kodzo shook his head, and placed his empty cup in the bin on the way out. The living room was empty when he got back. He showered before bed, quietly getting a towel and undressing as Abena slept. When he got into bed, the sheets were cool against his warmed, moisturised skin. Abena stirred and moved closer, her foot nudging his.

'How was church?'

'It was good.'

She leaned in closer, bringing her right hand to his nipple and gently flicking it. Kodzo turned towards her and ran a hand up her thigh, realising she wasn't wearing any underwear. She opened her legs slightly, and Kodzo moved his hand a little further. She was wet, and his finger slid in easily. With his thumb he found her clit, and gently moved in and out, flicking her nipples with his tongue until she told him she was going to cum, and he picked up speed just enough.

When she rolled away, he didn't move towards her side of the bed, or climb between her legs as he usually would. Instead, he told her how tired he was, and rolled over before she could reach below and feel that he was soft. He closed his eyes and said the Lord's Prayer, and listened to the sounds of Abena falling asleep.

The Praise and Worship section was still Kodzo's favourite part of the service: for a moment every Sunday, he was reminded what God felt like. As the 'Amen's started and the band died down, Kodzo lowered his hands and felt the energy leaving him quicker than it used to, until he sat down and noticed the cobwebs in the corner of the window behind the pastor. At the end of the service, Simon reminded the congregation that the church council was still looking for a new treasurer, and as soon as they left the hall, Kodzo sought him out.

He told Abena on the way back to the car, while Elom and Dzifa trailed behind.

'Good for you.' Abena smiled. 'How often do they meet?'

'Monthly. Second Sunday of the month.'

'And you'll still be going to the men's group?'

'Of course,' Kodzo replied as he and Abena slid into their seats.

'Okay. Well, good. Will we have to get home after church ourselves?'

Kodzo paused with his key in the ignition. 'I think so. I'm not sure, we have to figure out the details.'

Abena nodded, and Kodzo rolled down his window to let some of the summer heat escape the car. Dzifa was singing along to the radio and Elom had tilted his head back and closed his eyes to catch up on missed sleep. As they were lifted up above the city on the Kingston bridge, Kodzo suddenly found it difficult to breathe, like the knot of loose threads had tightened. He squeezed tighter on the steering wheel and his jaw clenched. He knew something awful was going to happen, if it wasn't happening already.

'Woah!' Dzifa shouted as Kodzo swerved left, crossing a lane of traffic.

'Kodzo!' Abena gripped the door handle. Kodzo saw Elom wake in the mirror as he stopped on the hard shoulder. 'Kodzo, what's going on? Are you okay?'

'Dad?'

Kodzo opened the door and stepped out, breathing deep. His heart was beating so hard it was painful, and he leaned against the car, as he wasn't sure his legs would hold him.

'Kodzo.'

'I'm fine.' He breathed again, smelling the exhaust fumes of the cars rushing past.

'Kodzo, get in the car!' Kodzo surreptitiously felt his pulse – fast, but at least strong – as he turned and sat in the driver's seat, still with one leg out of the car.

'Dad, are you okay?' Dzifa asked, her face looking fragile, like the wrong answer would crack it.

'Yeah, I'm fine. I think I just felt a bit sick. Maybe I ate something off after the service.'

'Are you sure?' Abena asked.

'Yeah. Maybe it was the sausage rolls.' He relaxed back into the seat, feeling his heart calming down. The sweat under his collar was clammy and cold, and he felt himself starting to shake slightly. 'I'm okay, Abena. Sorry, everyone.' He looked into the back seat. Elom was staring silently, and Dzifa still looked concerned.

'Do you want me to drive?' Abena asked.

'Eh, please, yeah. I think that would be a good idea.' Kodzo flashed Abena a smile before she stepped out of the passenger side. They swapped places and Kodzo rolled down the window, letting the wind whip his face on the drive home.

Abena, Dzifa and Elom asked him if he felt okay, and he said yes, and then they stopped asking. But he had never felt as scared as he had in that moment, and the next day he drove to the hospital and cannulated patients with his mind constantly scanning for signs of a repeat. Abena called him on his break and he put down his fried-rice packed lunch to answer.

'How are you feeling?'

'I'm fine, I'm fine,' Kodzo replied, slightly irritated at being mollycoddled.

'Good. Sorry to bother you, but someone has called in sick tonight and two other staff are on leave. They're asking me to work late tonight for time-and-a-half, till after ten.'

'Sure. I'll be home around six.' Kodzo was happy for her to take the shift, though a contrary part of him now felt miffed that Abena had only checked in to ask a favour.

'Okay, so for dinner I took some chicken out from the freezer. Can you cook it for me?'

'No problem.'

'Just add some salt, pepper, garlic and onion powder and chilli flakes.'

'Mm-hmm.'

'Pre-heat the oven first, not too hot. And put some rice in the rice cooker. There's some frozen stew in the freezer. You can just defrost it in the microwave, and Elom or Dzifa can make a salad. Okay?'

'Ah-ah, yes, okay. It will be fine.'

'Okay, thank you.' Abena sounded reassured.

Kodzo got home late that evening to find the chicken thawing in a plastic mixing bowl on the counter, pale and bloated. He tried to remember what Abena had said. Salt, pepper, spices. It was already twenty to seven. He still had to pre-heat the oven, wash the rice and season the chicken. He couldn't remember how hot the oven was supposed to be. He looked around from chicken, to oven, to sink, to cupboard, to rice cooker, to clock, holding his jacket in his hand, and felt the whisper of the metallic fear he had felt on the bridge, like a vapour seeking him out. He immediately turned back to the living room and popped his head through the door.

'Do you guys want a takeaway?'

Kodzo was in bed when Abena got home just after midnight. 'How was the shift?'

'It was fine.' She took off her work clothes and went to the bathroom, and Kodzo listened to the calming, fuzzy sound of the shower, then the scratching of her toothbrush through the wall, until she came back into the room. She didn't say anything as she moisturised and changed, and neither did Kodzo.

Finally, she climbed into bed and asked, 'Kodzo, why was the chicken still out there?'

Kodzo sunk into the mattress, picturing the lukewarm, sweating meat. He had completely forgotten to put the chicken back in the fridge.

'Sorry, I got the kids a takeaway. I got home late.'

'So you spent how much on takeaway? Meanwhile I had to throw away that chicken.'

'It was already out for a long time when I got back.'

'When did you get home?'

'About seven.' Kodzo couldn't lie outright to Abena, but he could exaggerate. Still, he cringed at the weakness of his answer.

'It would have been ready in half an hour.'

'Look, Abena, I'm sorry, oh.' His tone was harsh. It would have taken him longer than thirty minutes, and he was tired, and the kids needed to eat. And they never had takeaways.

'It's just annoying. Simple thing I asked you to cook.'

'Ah, Abena, I don't need to be cooking too.' Kodzo was angry; he just wanted to close his eyes, rest, and not have this conversation.

'So is it always me who should be cooking after work? Okay, and you can just keep going to church, church, church.'

'Ah-ah?' Kodzo turned, surprised at the attack, and ready to release his building frustration. 'What are you on about? I didn't cook, so what? I'm looking after this family. I'm paying the mortgage. I'm driving everybody around town, making sure Elom got into university.'

'Ho!' Abena's eyes were wide with shock, and Kodzo saw hurt, too. He turned away, facing the wardrobe. He had always earned more than her, though he had worked more hours while she juggled childcare and sent a bigger percentage of her earnings back home. He had never wanted her to before, but he wondered now what might have happened if she had committed to working more and sending less to Ghana – what type of house they might have had, or schools the kids might have gone to.

'And me too, what am I doing? Is my small money a waste of time? Is my cooking a waste of time?' Kodzo didn't reply, knowing there was no answer that would end the argument.

'Remember this,' Abena continued, 'your father was a big man. He built a nice compound. But was it not your mother who raised three children and sold peanut' – Kodzo still had his back turned, but he could see Abena in his head, listing on her fingers – 'palm oil, dzowe, tomatoes, smoked fish, cloth at the market to feed you? Was it not your sisters at home who sewed your school uniforms so you could read books?' Still, Kodzo stayed silent, weary. 'I never asked you to look after me. As for that one, you know it's true.'

He heard the click of her bedside lamp and felt her shuffle into her side of the bed. There was quiet for a moment, then she added, 'And these kids need a dad, not a manager – and not a priest.'

Something about the dark – about not seeing Abena's hurt, or her anger – made it easier for Kodzo to lean into his. 'You're the one who told me to stop being Mr Fun Fun for the kids. You're the one who said we need to get serious.'

'Kodzo, I said being a parent is not a game. You were right, we need to spend more time with them. I don't know why you're now running away.'

*   *   *

Kodzo didn't sleep until after 4 a.m. that night, or the next. He phoned his GP to ask for a sleeping tablet. Fortunately, he had never taken any before, and knew to say it would be for short-term use. Annoyingly, they called him in for an assessment first. He had hoped with him being a nurse they might have spared him the hassle, and wondered if they might have trusted his judgement without dragging him in if he'd had 'Dr' in front of his name.

The waiting room smelled like something green and syrupy from a dark glass bottle, and he watched as a little boy pushed colourful wooden beads along squiggly wires.

'Hi, Kodzo, I'm Dr Qureshi. What can I do for you?'

'I was just looking for a few days' worth of sleeping tablets. My sleeping pattern is a mess and it's affecting my work.'

The doctor scribbled as she listened and talked.

'When are you getting to sleep?'

'About 4 a.m.'

'And what's keeping you up?'

'Mm . . .' Kodzo shrugged. 'Just not getting to sleep.'

'Uh-huh. And have you tried cutting out coffee? And no caffeine – even tea – after 4 p.m.? No screens after nine or ten, that sort of thing?'

'Yeah,' Kodzo lied. 'I just need to settle my pattern, then I'll be okay.'

Dr Qureshi put down her pen. 'Are you kept up by any thoughts in particular?' Kodzo didn't answer. He thought of the motorway, and of the scriptures, and of buying Elom's new mirror, and Abena angry and warm next to him, and of trying to keep the threads together, neat and strong.

'Kodzo, are you coping okay at home?'

He pulled harder, keeping them tight, but the silence stretched until he looked up at her face, sympathetic and patient. He pulled tighter – too tight. The threads snapped, and he unravelled in front of a stranger.

When Kodzo got home, Abena was cooking dinner, Elom was in his room and Dzifa was out. He sat on the couch and picked up the remote, typing in the number for GOD TV, then stopped: he didn't want to hear the shouting tonight; couldn't bear being told to rejoice. He went upstairs to have a shower, keeping his new tablets in his jacket pocket. While drying off he looked at the small bookshelf in his and Abena's room. He lowered his eyes below the Bibles, the books on scripture and the prophets, and found an old paperback – *Things Fall Apart*, one that had stayed with him since secondary school – and lay down to read.

Chapter Eleven

Elom – April 2008

Elom arrived fifteen minutes late to meet Chris, Del and Nico at a bar on Sauchiehall Street that did two-for-one spirit-mixers. He wrapped up his headphones – he went for the subtler sounds of Mos Def over 50 these days – and scanned the room of excited, barely post-adolescent faces drinking from brightly coloured plastic cups. He couldn't see the others, and considered either finding a seat, but looking like a loner, or walking round the block to kill time, but getting caught in the drizzle.

He wondered what Dzifa might have done. She might sit silently and comfortably alone, or maybe she would bump into someone she knew from drama or athletics, or a tipsy student would tell her how much they liked her dress and sit with her a while. She had been invited to two parties that night, but had stayed home instead to practise her guitar – she was going to another party tomorrow anyway. Elom thought her sense of adventure was both smarter, and calmer, than his.

After checking Facebook Messenger to make sure he had the right time and place, Elom walked to the bar and shouted his order. He was halfway through his cider when Del, Chris and Nico walked in, a triptych of shirts, jeans and black leather shoes. Jackets and umbrellas were never an option, so their hands were shoved in their pockets to brace themselves against the cold, and their gelled hair had been flattened by the rain. Elom wasn't sure whether to wave them over, or act like he hadn't been checking the door every few seconds, but they saw him before he had made up his mind, and they tumbled into the booth.

'All right, mate?' Chris called across the table.

'Elom, man!' Nico, still tall and gangly, leaned in for a handshake and pulled Elom into an embrace, while Del went for a fist bump, all smiles. He saw them less frequently since they had left school. Del was doing an electrician's apprenticeship, Nico worked in a restaurant, and Chris was studying to be a physical trainer, and had bulked out accordingly. Elom was the only one at university, and some things had changed – he read the *Guardian* now, and had even gone to a couple of guest lectures. But he couldn't abide talking ideas like the soft kids from the suburbs, always showing off how smart they were. He was glad he spent his time with these friends – rowdy, down to earth, coarse.

They brought the usual Friday night excitement, talking about how much fun (or more specifically, how drunk) they were going to get. They already seemed tipsy, and Elom wondered if they had started drinking without him. As Nico touched down the second round of drinks, he shouted over the cheesy-pop remix, 'Here, so, are we doing Zante then? Or Shagaluf?'

'Aye, defo mate.' Del giggled, already imagining the chaos. 'I'm off from the beginning of June.'

'I can get a week aff nae bother,' Chris replied.

They looked to Elom, who realised he must have missed a previous conversation. 'What's the plan?'

'I reckon just us four get a wee villa. It's heavy cheap,' Nico said. Elom's gratitude at being invited competed with the feeling that he had been an afterthought.

'You in, then?' Chris asked, his eyebrows raised with expectation.

His gratitude won. 'Sounds great. I just need to check money, though. I'll let you know ASAP.' Elom had enough cash saved from his maintenance grant, since he lived at home, but he didn't want to say that he was still nervous about what Kodzo and Abena would say about him going on a trip like this, with these people. The thought of going stirred up excitement, but also fear. He had never gone on holiday without his family, apart from the week at church camp.

Chris smiled as if Elom's attendance was secure, and Elom felt pleased that he seemed to care. Nico reminded them that if they wanted to get free entry at the club, they would need to leave soon. They finished their drinks and Elom shuffled out of his corner seat and headed to the loo. He was peeing at the trough urinal, aiming at one of the yellow urinal balls when he heard Chris's voice to his left.

'Here, you better come on holiday, it's gonna be amazin'.' Elom looked straight ahead as he heard Chris unzip, then pull his cock out. He stared ahead, counting the seconds until he heard the splash of piss in the metal trough.

'Yeah, I want to. I think Mum and Dad wanted to go to Portugal or something, but I don't know when.'

'Oh, come on, man, sack that off and come wi' us!'

Elom turned his head and saw that Chris was smiling at him, and he relented and smiled back. There was something scary in the planning, flying, the week of drinking and of sharing rooms with these guys. In spite of himself, he had liked his quiet summer the previous year – he had still been grounded when holiday plans were being made. Now he felt safe, if a little bored, in his routine of lectures with posh kids and nights in with Abena's home cooking. But there was also something alluring about being bold, and about being asked to join the adventure.

'Yeah, okay. I'm down.'

The plane landed to claps and cheers. The boys had started with pints at the airport bar and continued with vodka Cokes during the flight. Elom was already woozy when he stepped into the heavy heat of Magaluf airport. They rushed for the bus to their resort – a huge, white building with balconies unevenly jutting out, holding groups of tipsy and hungover travellers – despite Del's demands to use the airport toilets.

'No' bad, is it?' Nico said as they entered their suite. Del farted in reply, barging past the rest of them and locking himself into the loo.

'Bagsie this room.' Nico picked up Del's discarded duffel bag and rolled his suitcase into the first bedroom, with sliding doors to a balcony overlooking the swimming pool.

Elom took the other, which had a double bed and one small window facing another building. The mattress was a thin foam,

and he lay back on it for a moment as he heard the unzipping of
bags and the opening and closing of drawers and cupboards. He
sat up as Chris came in.

'How come we got the shite room?'

Elom shrugged and chuckled.

'Doubt there'll be much sleeping anyway.' Chris smiled. The
bathroom door clicked open, and Chris kicked off his shoes on
the way to use the loo. Elom rested his sweaty socked feet on the
cool, cream tiles, waiting for the night to begin.

'Fuck me.'

Elom moaned in response, his eyes still closed, barely able to
peel his tongue from the roof of his mouth.

'I feel fucking rough as fuck.'

Elom felt the mattress shift as Chris stood to go to the
bathroom, and he heard the heavy bubbling of water hitting
water for at least a minute through the open door. The night
before had been a lot – of alcohol, and some coke Nico had
sourced – but also of laughter, silliness and dancing.

'Balcony beers?' Del popped his head around Elom's door,
his freckled face made redder by the Spanish sun.

'Hmm.' Elom stretched into semi-wakefulness. 'Yeah, I'll be
two secs.'

Elom waited a moment for his hard-on to deflate, then slid
on his flip-flops. Del and Nico were sitting on loungers in their
shorts, and Nico passed Elom a cold bottle of beer as he sat. He
sipped it hesitantly, feeling the bubbles burst over his dry tongue
and fuzzy teeth.

'That was some night,' Nico said.

'Aye, man. Mind that guy outside the tattoo shop?' Del asked, and they all laughed. As they had left the club, a sunburnt man had stumbled onto the pavement, his shirtless chest showing the outline of a half-finished tattoo. He leaned against a lamp post, cocked his head like a rooster crowing, and let out a volley of vomit to a chorus of cheers from the promenade. He managed three more waves, each one followed by applause, before stumbling back into the shop, presumably to get his tattoo finished.

'You enjoy the club then, Elom?' Del shared a look with Nico. They had all danced with girls, but Elom had been the only one to kiss one; a drunken collision of faces, but it had still been fun. Before he could answer, Chris crashed into a chair, reaching forward for the last beer.

'I'm actually dying, boys.'

''Mon, let's get lunch then head to the beach,' Del suggested. The others finished their beers, while Elom just gulped a few more mouthfuls. It was a short walk, and the strip felt fake in the full light of day, without fights and inflatable sex dolls, as if it was hiding its true self from the sun.

From their spot in the sand on the crowded beach, Elom could hear three different sets of music: some beach house from a bar on the street behind, pop tunes from the speakers of a man selling beers from a cool box, and up-tempo dance remixes from a group of girls a few yards over. They took turns napping and playing catch with a tennis ball and Velcro disc, until Del suggested they swim out to the floating platform. Elom looked out with his hands over his eyebrows: it must have been a hundred or so metres from the shoreline. There was a handful of people on it, sunbathing or diving into the calm water.

'Yeah, sure.' Chris sat up, and he and Del led the way, with Nico loping behind. Elom followed, watching both Del's stocky bottom half and Chris's sturdy top half. Elom wasn't a strong swimmer, but it didn't seem too far, and he was learning to be bold. As he stepped into the water, he breathed deep and slow. At waist height, the others dived forward – Del and Nico emerging to a breaststroke, and Chris to a front crawl. Elom walked until he ran out of ground, then kicked off the seabed to begin a mixture of the two strokes, unsure which one would be the most efficient. He settled on a breaststroke, keeping his head above water as he focused on his breathing. His eyes stung with the saltwater, and he kept interrupting his stroke to wipe his face.

The others were now several metres ahead, and Elom quickly flicked his head back to see how far he had come. He guessed about 20 metres, and his shoulders were starting to burn. The world sounded different, as if someone had changed the settings on the audio-mixer. He could hear his breath, loud and harsh, and the slap and splash of the water as he pushed through it. The sounds of fun – of people shouting and laughing on the beach and the platform – were turned down, fading into the background.

He was tiring. Chris, Nico and Del were on the platform now, facing out towards the horizon. Del had briefly looked back to wave, and Elom hadn't known what to do. He was too exhausted to wave back, yet shouting for help seemed like an embarrassing overreaction. In any case, his body was telling him to save whatever breath he had. As he eked his way forward, he realised that if he died, he would die quietly.

Ten metres from the platform he could make out the rust on the ladder as it bobbed in and out of the water. He switched to an erratic front crawl, reaching out with each stroke, begging to feel something solid. Eventually, his hands touched metal and he gripped on tight, pulling himself out as quickly as he could. His biceps were shaking and he felt nauseated, his stomach full of salt and air. Chris looked over and smiled, and Elom smiled back as he lay down on the painted wood. He didn't move for half an hour as the others jumped in and out of the water, instead fretting about how he would make the swim to shore.

The sun had started to cool when Nico suggested they get some dinner. Elom nodded and Del climbed down the ladder while Nico dived in. Chris was part-way down the ladder, facing Elom, who was still and lying on the platform, when he asked, 'You coming?'

'Eh.' Elom felt a wave of nervous nausea and let out a little burp. He was grateful for the excuse, and took it. 'I'm fine, just feel a bit sick – probably the hangover.' He forced a laugh. It was embarrassing to be the only holidaymaker on the island unable to swim.

'You good?'

'Yeah, I might just be a bit slow coming back.'

'Come with me, then. Just don't whitey when am beside ye.' Chris climbed down the rest of the ladder. Elom stood, the weakness in his legs compounded by the moving platform, and climbed into the sea where Chris was treading water, waiting for him. They swam side by side to the shore, Chris with long, slow strokes – he had spent summers as a lifeguard at the local pool – and Elom trying to emulate his calm.

Elom's feet met sand a dozen metres from shore and he stood immediately, breathless and relieved. 'Cheers, man.' He forced another burp. 'Feel a bit better now, too.'

'Nae bother.' Chris strode forward to Nico and Del, who were already packing up, and Elom followed behind, watching the seawater sparkle on Chris's back.

The second night was a repeat of the first. Cheap drinks and loud music, and this time Chris had potentially fingered a girl in the club, but he couldn't quite remember the details. They had ended up on the beach in the early morning, and when they eventually made it back to their rooms, Del fell asleep in the bathroom, hugging the toilet bowl. On the balcony the next afternoon, Elom couldn't bring himself to drink the beer Nico handed him. When Del came through, there was a round of applause.

'Wayyyy!'

He slumped into a chair, silently holding his head in his hand.

'You were a fucking riot last night, mate,' Nico laughed.

'I actually can't remember.' It was one of the first times Elom had seen him without a laugh on his lips, or a hair's breadth away from a giggle.

'Aye – you kept shouting at strangers to go skinny-dipping, and ran into the sea with your hairy arse out like a mad weirdo,' Chris said. Del just shook his head, and Elom couldn't tell how deep his embarrassment went. He remembered Del running headlong into the water, and watching Chris and Nico laughing mirthfully as he went.

'You were absolutely steaming,' Nico added. Del said nothing and Chris handed him a beer.

'I actually can't, man.'

'It'll make you feel better,' Chris insisted. Del brought it to his mouth for a sip, then retched.

'Oh, man.' He paused, pressing his fist against his lips. 'Oh, man.' He suddenly stood up and marched to the bathroom, to guffaws and shrieks from Nico and Chris. Elom laughed too, aware that his beer sat open and untouched between his thighs. On his return, Del wearily suggested they spend the afternoon by the hotel pool. By the time they were setting up on the loungers, he was spinning his own stories from what he could remember of the previous night, laughing at his shenanigans, his embarrassment left behind in the toilet bowl.

Chris started teaching Nico how to backflip, and Elom watched them leap and splash into the alcopop-blue water. They looked joyful to Elom, the two boys – one tall, one short – jumping, splashing and laughing, and he wanted to learn too.

Chris stood with him side by side as they placed the balls of their feet at the edge of the pool. 'You have to get low, then jump straight back-the-way.' Chris demonstrated. Elom tried a few times, launching himself backwards and to the side slightly as he built up the momentum for a full flip.

'You just have to go for it, mate,' Chris advised after Elom climbed out of the pool again. Elom set himself up at the edge of the diving board, aware of Chris, Nico and Del watching. He bent down deep, kicked back with his legs and hurled himself backwards. Looking directly up at the sky, he quickly realised he was falling, with no chance of flipping his legs over. He landed with a splash, flat-backed, feeling the sting as he twisted underwater and reached for the surface. Low-pitched grumbles dialled up into screeches as his head broke through the water to see the others pointing and laughing at his back-flop. Elom joined in, embarrassed, but not overwhelmed, as he pulled himself out.

'Oh my God, man, that was so shit,' Chris said breathlessly. Elom laughed at himself in response, seeing the silliness of it all.

On the third night, Chris decided he would finally pull, and warned Elom he would have to sleep on the balcony. The four of them danced together, with the occasional joking grind on each other, or serious attempt at grinding with a girl. Half an hour before closing, Chris finally kissed one. When the lights came on, her friend grabbed her hand, saying something about the cloakroom as the drunken crowd filtered out of the building.

'Meet yous outside then? Wantae come back to ours?' Chris asked.

'Maybe next time.' The girl smiled and her friend giggled, already pulling her back through the crowd. 'We might be going to another club though.'

'I'll get yous outside,' Chris called. He looked torn between the girls going back into the club, and his friends heading out of it. He turned to follow Elom, Nico and Del out, and asked if they wanted to go on to the next place.

'No, mate, I'm shagged,' Nico said. Del nodded in agreement, swaying slightly.

'Elom?' Chris asked.

'Nah, man, I'm gonna bagsie the bed while I can.'

Chris scanned the crowd for the girls. 'Fuck's sake, man.' He turned. 'Fuck it.'

It was slow progress walking back to the hotel, fielding groups singing Beatles songs or accosting them to play drunken games. When Elom got into the room his head was already flickering with the beginnings of tomorrow's throbbing hangover. He turned the light off and climbed into bed under the orange glow of streetlights falling through the window.

Chris came in, taking his T-shirt off as the door shut behind him. 'Can't believe that girl, man.'

'You were so close!'

'Aye, mate. In fucking Shagaluf and canny even get a shag. One of us shoulda pulled her friend.'

'Nico tried.'

'What about you?'

Elom laughed. 'I'll try harder next time, mate.' At the bar, Del had told Elom that he was maybe-sorta-kinda seeing someone in Glasgow, and so didn't actually feel like trying to pull. Elom had enjoyed the opportunity to keep him company, and just dance, drink and chat without constantly scanning the room for a potential target. Chris climbed into bed as a slight breeze lifted the thin cotton curtain in front of the window, and Elom closed his eyes.

'Canny even have a wank in here, man. Need separate rooms next time.'

Elom opened his eyes. Chris was lying on top of the sheet in his boxers, his hand resting on what looked like the outline of his hard cock. He suddenly became aware of his breath, and the exact position of his body in the bed. He wasn't sure if Chris had seen him open his eyes, or seen him staring; if he was too close, or too far, or if he should move. He knew that his heart was a kick-drum. He watched as Chris gently squeezed his cock.

'Fuck it,' Chris breathed. He reached under the waistband of his baggy boxers and pulled at his dick.

Elom was caught between elation and panic, but he knew he wanted this to continue. He took a deep breath and stretched slightly, as if he was turning in his sleep. Instead of pulling his hand away, Chris reached deeper, then pulled his dick out above his waistband. It stuck up towards his belly, pushing against the elastic of his boxers as he slowly stroked. Elom watched the foreskin slide over the head with each pull in the orange semi-darkness.

Gently, almost breathlessly, Elom closed his eyes and rolled onto his back, bringing his own hand to his crotch under the covers. He could still hear Chris, his rhythm speeding up with Elom's heartbeat. He was still drunk, and scared, but he wanted to dive head first into the water; to be bold enough to take what he wanted. With another fake stretch-sigh he opened his eyes, and kept them on Chris's fist. He knew Chris could see his face, and his hand kept sliding up and down, faster to the sounds of rustling fabric, and wetness on wetness. Elom began jacking himself off underneath the blanket.

''Mon, then.' The two words were almost a whisper, with the slightest hint of bass. But they were full of something – desire, command, lust – that gripped Elom. He slid up to lean against the headrest, side by side with Chris, and pushed down the covers. He looked up from Chris's cock to his face, which was staring at Elom's cock. They sat like that, the bed trembling with their joint rhythm for a minute or so until Chris turned back to his own dick and grunted as his fist pumped slower. He slid his hand down to the base of his cock as it pulsed, shooting a string of cum into his belly button, then another, and another, each pulse weaker, until the last dribble over his thumb. Elom came almost immediately, his toes curling as he stared at Chris's hand, still slowly, gently covering and uncovering his head. Chris, still looking at his own mess, sighed as Elom finished.

They both slowed down to a stop, then Chris turned to Elom with a smile. 'Nice one, mate.' He reached down to the floor to pick up his T-shirt and clean himself up, and Elom did the same. Chris tucked himself into his boxers and got under the thin blanket, turning away from Elom before Elom had finished wiping.

Elom wiped and tucked himself into bed. He turned to the window, feeling the warm, orange glow soaking gently through his eyelids, confused, jittery, but more content than he could ever remember being.

Elom woke sweaty and hot, with a throb in his head. The streetlights had been replaced by the yellow sun shining on the empty space beside him. Its glare cleared away the hazy contentment of last night and all he felt was worry. He heard laughter from the balcony and panicked: what were they laughing about, and why hadn't they woken him up to join them for a beer? He sat quietly, straining to hear any snippets of conversation – it sounded like Nico was talking the most, thankfully, unless Chris had already told his story.

'Morning, mate,' Del said as Elom slid open the glass door. He had his sunglasses on, and Elom couldn't tell what his eyes were saying. The others said hi and Elom sat down and reached for a beer, and they looked out over the pool to the sea beyond. Elom frantically assessed the situation – what did they know? Who had told them? And most importantly, how did Chris feel about last night?

'Do you guys wanna go to the beach or the pool today?' Del asked.

'Beach?' Chris replied.

'Aye, beach. Let's get tickets for that boat thing,' Nico said.

Elom nodded. 'Sounds good.' Chris had barely looked at him.

'You guys sleep all right?' he asked, nervous again – was that a weird question?

'Aye, okay, but I'm really, really tired – it just gets hot so early,' Del replied.

'Yeah, me too, man. And my piss was like, so dark this morning, man, I'm dehydrated as fuck,' said Nico. Elom realised he was drinking an orange juice, rather than beer. 'Let's do the boat, but I might not go out-out tonight. Save myself for themorra.'

'Sounds good,' Chris said, and Elom nodded, allowing himself to believe that the mood that morning was calm because they were exhausted after three days of partying, and not because Chris had revealed his secret, and the others were horrified, or disgusted, and didn't want to speak to him.

The 'booze cruise', as Del insisted on calling it, was two dozen travellers on a boat, drinking to tepid beach house music with a stop to jump in the ocean. They all perked up after a few drinks, and nothing seemed different to the day before. Still, Elom's attempts to catch Chris's eye were either missed, or met with such casual friendship that Elom wondered if his friend had been too drunk to remember what they had done together.

Elom jumped into the ocean, but stayed close to the boat while the others swam out. He climbed back in before long and sat under the shade of the canopy. Behind him the noisy crowd continued, but ahead was perfectly peaceful and inviting. It was ironic that as free as it felt, sailing on this boat, they were still essentially trapped – there was no getting off, unless he wanted to drown.

He replied to the text Kodzo had sent him yesterday, checking in. He sent a couple of photos of the sea and said he was having a lot of fun, though his swimming skills were lacking.

I need to take you to the village. When i was a kid the river was our playground man!

Elom said he'd love to go. He had never been to Ghana, and this taste of adventure had him wondering about it. The captain announced through the tannoy that across the water was Algeria. Elom could almost see it, just at the horizon. He imagined placing his fingers in the invisible line where translucent blue sky met gemstone blue water, peeling them apart, and going exploring.

'All right?' Chris clapped him on the shoulder and sat on one of the blue plastic chairs opposite, with Nico and Del joining.

'Yeah, man, I'm good,' Elom replied. 'View is amazing.' They nodded in agreement.

'Aye, not looking forward to getting back home,' Nico said.

'Yeah,' Elom agreed, 'me neither.' Drinking with his friends, with the sparkling sea behind them, he realised rules might be different here, though he hadn't grasped exactly how, yet. But he knew he wanted to keep exploring; keep playing in this playground.

After dinner they stayed at the hotel's poolside bar until it closed at midnight, then they went back to their suite to finish off a crate of beers Chris had bought. Elom was drunk, but he kept his mind on Chris as they tenpin bowled with empty cans, trying to decide if he should go to bed before, after, or at the same time as him. By 3 a.m., Del had already fallen asleep on the couch when Nico called it.

'I'm gonna go to bed, guys.'

'Aye, me too,' Chris said.

'Yeah,' Elom agreed, as if the decision hadn't already been made for both of them. Lying on the thin foam mattress, under the soft orange blanket of the streetlight, Elom listened to Chris's breath. It was slow and deep, like he had fallen asleep within minutes of getting into bed. Elom moved closer, hoping for a reciprocal movement from Chris, but there was nothing.

Chris hadn't brought it up all day, which was to be expected. This was their drunken secret, it didn't need to be announced. Elom told himself he could be bold, and he slid his hand onto Chris's waist. As the sound of the blood rushing in his ears subsided, he realised that he still had no new information. Chris was still asleep, as far as he could tell. Once more, he summoned the bravery to move. Chris was lying on his back, and Elom placed his hand flat on Chris's stomach, feeling it rise and fall with each breath.

Chris stayed still. His mouth was slightly open, and Elom could smell his stale, beery breath. A minute passed, and Elom wanted to believe that Chris was the nervous one this time. He slid his hand down a few inches towards the waistband of Chris's boxers. Then Chris laid his hand on Elom's, stopping him. He moved his hand away again, but his eyes were still closed. There was no turning, no moving, no signal as to what Elom should do. They lay there like that for a while longer, the chaotic sounds of the strip filtering through the window, until Elom gently slid his hand away, drained from the effort and the anxiety. He woke some time later – minutes or hours, he wasn't sure – and Chris had rolled away on his side, facing the door, with Elom's hand on an empty patch of bed.

Elom squinted his eyes open against the light, which had scraped everything bright and clean like a Brillo pad. He replayed his memories from the previous night, picking apart the moments that had been real, and those that had had alcohol poured into them, causing him to misunderstand, or fill in gaps with fear.

'Mornin'.' Elom wondered how long Chris had been awake. He heard the click of the cable landing on the tiles as Chris took his phone off the charger. Elom did the same, and they lay scrolling side by side. He replied to Dzifa's requests for travel updates, all the while waiting for Chris to speak. His silence was inscrutable. Elom didn't know if he had crossed a line, or if he was supposed to have gone further. Thinking it through, it wasn't clear if Chris's hand had been stopping him, or saying something else. He didn't know if Chris only wanted Elom when he was drunk, or if he even wanted him at all. He didn't know if Chris was angry, embarrassed, disgusted, or maybe even hurt. He didn't know how Chris felt at all.

Elom heard the balcony door slide open. 'Shall we head out?' he asked.

'Aye, sure.' Chris nodded. He swung his legs over the bed and slid them into his flip-flops. Elom followed, and they walked to the balcony with a lazy scrape-slap-gallop of skin, plastic and ceramic. The mood was relaxed. Nico and Del were drinking orange juice, and Elom poured himself a glass.

'I slept so much better last night, man,' Del said. 'It was just that wee bit cooler.'

'Aye, but then I had to hear your snoring all night,' Nico replied.

Elom and Chris laughed, and their eyes met, and Elom thought that maybe things were okay between them.

'At least you didn't have Elom snuggling up to you all night,' Chris said, his eyes still folded with laughter lines.

'Ohh, some hanky-panky in the other room, then?' Nico goaded.

Elom suddenly felt like his body had fallen through the balcony and left his organs sitting in the chair. His face burned and his back was itchy with sweat, but he laughed as loudly and as freely as the others while his brain hunted for a way to make this okay.

'I must have thought you were that girl from the other night,' Elom said.

'Oh, that's no' fair on her!' Del laughed. Elom hated his stupidity – he had sounded too earnest, taking Chris's bait and showing his own fear. He should have made a joke about Chris wanting to be the little spoon. If he had been really smart, he would have called back to Del's liking the cooler weather and joked that cuddling was the only way to stay warm. He looked at Chris but then thought he looked like he cared too much, so he looked away again and then thought he looked like he was avoiding his gaze.

'We might as well, boys, with our hit rate this trip,' Nico said.

'Speak for yourselves – we've both pulled,' Chris replied.

'Aye, each other!' Nico fought back.

'We should go back to the club tonight, then,' Del suggested.

'Let's go out with our stuff and just head straight to the airport after. Be pished for the 6 a.m. flight.' Nico let out a burst of laughter at his own plan. Elom watched as the conversation continued, like a ghost watching his family move on without him. His heart was pounding, but the others seemed deaf to it. He wanted to casually but emphatically deny what had just happened. Instead, he laughed and gave suggestions for dinner.

He packed and changed while Chris showered, then waited on the balcony for the others. Nico and Del continued with inane chatter while Elom finished the warm orange juice. When Chris came through about twenty minutes later, damp-haired and fresh-faced, the air filled with the sweet, cocky smell of Black XS, it clogged up Elom's nose and made him angry. Chris made him angry. The way he bumped fists with Nico and Del filled him with the same frustration as untying a knot of a thousand pocketed headphones.

'Shall we head out?' Chris asked, sticking his hand into the open packet of crisps on the table.

'Yeah, ready when you are.' Elom rose. Chris had either been vindictive, or totally careless, and Elom had been a fool. As they sat on the beach, and then went for dinner, then drinks, Elom's anger cooled and thickened like cement. He felt jealousy run through it like a crack: it had been so easy for Chris to make that joke, or revelation – whichever it had been. Elom wanted that confidence, and had no idea how to access it. Instead, he stood terrified and humiliated at what his friends thought of him.

In the end, they'd left their suitcases at reception, and so the journey home involved taxis from the club to the hotel, then to the airport, where they had one final drink before boarding. It had been a long day to end a long week, burning the last of Elom's energy.

'I'm so tired, man,' he said, sipping his pint. 'What time do we get in?'

'About eight,' Del said. 'But don't worry, El, you can rest your wee head on my shoulder.' He giggled, catching the eyes of the others, who all joined in. Their gate was displayed, and they finished their pints and picked up their luggage. Elom's exhaustion was almost total, and the thought of landing in Glasgow, hugging the boys, and seeing them in a week or two weeks' time in a pub back home made him feel heavy.

He needed a way out: life here, with them, forever, felt like a cage. He was always quietly drowning in this group, while they watched and laughed. As he boarded the plane he wondered if there were other places, other people. He wondered if he could be a different person there too, carefree and brave and honest.

He stayed awake the whole flight, watching brown become blue, become brown, become green, become grey, with the thin margin of the horizon always in view. When they hit the tarmac back in Glasgow, he waited for a cheer, but all he saw were red-eyed travellers, not quite ready to return home.

Chapter Twelve

Dzifa – November 2010

'He's going to break up with her,' Clem said as they passed a young couple. Dzifa followed them with her eyes. The couple were holding hands, his fingers slightly splayed and pointing downwards, hers curled up and resting on his knuckles.

'Really?'

'Definitely. You can just tell. I saw them at dinner last night and they barely spoke to each other.' Clem's voice had a depth that gave her statements gravitas. Dzifa imagined her fully growing into it in her mid-forties, wrapped in a deep blue shawl and with grey-streaked hair. She seemed excited rather than malicious about her revelation. Dzifa was appropriately scandalised, though she couldn't actually place a name to either of the faces in the couple. It was sufficient that Oxford was small, and they were in her college, so the ripples of any drama wouldn't have far to go before they touched her. She had remained a reasonably big fish in this pond, a transition that happened to few undergraduates after the freshers' mix-up.

It also didn't really matter if Clem was right or not. Dzifa thought Clem lived in a heightened reality, where the world was constructed by her conversations – dramatic and hyperbolic. Dzifa had regularly heard her debrief nights out at brunch, when debates became 'shouting matches', tipsy friends were 'wasted', the walk home became a 'trek', heading to bed was 'passing out', and the hangover was – without fail – the worst she had ever had. Dzifa often wondered whether this was how things had actually happened, and if she had simply been missing the excitement everyone else had felt. Her own stories would end in a few sentences; everyone else had been there, of course, and she never quite mastered the art of telling someone something they already knew. Instead, she often found herself filling the space after she had finished with 'It was *so* funny . . .' to chuckles and nods. Nevertheless, she enjoyed the nights out themselves. She danced the most and argued the least amongst her friends. While she never struggled for boys if she wanted one, she found most eighteen-year-olds were too intimidated by her to make the first move, which suited her perfectly.

Dzifa's lectures at the medical school had finished for the day, and she had met Clem outside the English faculty to walk to their college. She found her classes interesting, but not thrilling. Science had been easy at school, and medicine had been given to her by her parents, teachers, and that one weird 'careers aptitude quiz' they had done as the logical next step. A competitive streak had pushed her to apply to Oxford rather than stay in Scotland. She hadn't been nervous until after the interviews – hanging out with the other applicants in the ancient, stone-walled bar, she realised how much she wanted to be in that world, and she surprised herself by getting in. It was harder here – her lectures and the social dynamics were more complicated than things had ever been at school – but she coped, though she found much more joy in her extra-curricular pursuits than in her tutorials.

Their feet kicked up the orange leaves that lined the left of the pavement, while cyclists trailed past on their right. Clem's phone rang and she swiped right to accept the call.

'Hi, Mum . . . Good, thanks. Just walking home from lectures with Dzifa.' Dzifa took her own phone out to pass the time for the rest of the walk, but Clem took the phone from her ear and put it on loudspeaker.

'Hi, Dzifa, nice to finally meet you. I hope you're keeping Clem on track.'

'Don't worry, Mum, she's too busy with her play to distract me,' Clem replied, playfully taking the bait.

'Fantaaastic.' Clem's mum Helen drew out the middle syllable. 'Which one?'

Dzifa entered the conversation: 'Oh, *The Importance of Being Earnest*. Opening night's next week.'

'How wonderful! I spent far too much time doing drama instead of history when I was there. Best of luck.'

They spoke all the way home, with Helen as interested in Dzifa's week as she was in Clem's. She was nice, and Dzifa was happy to oblige – charming parents had always come easily to her. Clem hung up as they arrived at hall for lunch, and as she updated her mum on her weekend plans, Dzifa reminded herself to call home that night.

*   *   *

Dzifa hadn't spoken to her parents or Elom for a couple of weeks. That night after dinner, she opened Whatsapp and saw her family's three profile pictures listed by their numbers: Elom's picture was still the grey default, Kodzo's was a picture of Dzifa from her prom, and her mum's was a smiling, middle-aged woman — some friend of a friend who must have had a recent birthday. She amused herself with the Ghanaian expectation to show off friends and family, rather than oneself, on this specific platform. She called Elom, then Kodzo, both of whom rang out, so she opened Abena's chat, which mostly contained videos forwarded from unspecified sources questioning all manner of medicines and headlines. The unknown, friendly-looking woman filled the whole screen.

'Hi, Dzifa, long time.' Abena answered. 'What's up?'

'All good. Just had lectures and hung out with a friend.'

'That's nice. Lectures go okay?'

'Yep, thanks.'

'And are you eating well? You sound tired.'

'Yeah I am, I just went to the canteen today for dinner.'

'Good. Make sure you take your vitamins.'

'Yep.'

'And are you okay for money?'

'Yeah, the rest of the loan came through.'

'Good.'

They talked a little about the news, and a little about *The X Factor*, and Dzifa asked about Elom, who was working hard on his dissertation.

Dzifa felt the conversation petering out, her tiredness growing. 'I'm off to bed, got an early rehearsal tomorrow.'

'What for?'

'Just another play.'

'Oh, okay. But what about your lectures?'

'I'll be fine, Mum – they're recorded anyway.'

'Just be careful, don't take on too much.'

'I won't.'

'Okay. Bye, love you.'

That week, Dzifa had written two essays and got a first on one of them, been clubbing three times, had lacklustre sex once, attended a guest lecture given by a Nobel laureate and spent ten hours in rehearsals for a play where she was one of the leads. She had cried twice (once as part of a scene), and laughed more times than she could count. Scrolling her feed before falling asleep, she got a notification from Elom.

Sorry I missed your call! Been a bit hectic. Can I talk to you tomorrow?

Sure. hope dissertation going well too!

She plugged in her phone and went to sleep.

On the way home from the club that weekend, Dzifa and her friends stopped by a late-night Caribbean place for food. The smells and sights were familiar, but the rice and peas of her Jamaican cousins wasn't quite as homely as Abena's earthy waakye. She spotted the curry goat and felt a drunken hunger which wasn't quite hunger, but rather an urge to fill her mouth, regardless of how full she actually was. She paused though, imagining asking for goat meat in front of her friends – three white girls from London.

'Can I get the curry goat, please?' Clem stepped forward, all smiles.

'Yeah, salad?' asked the man behind the till.

'Yes, please.'

Dzifa stood silently, caught off guard as the others ordered, then stepped forward herself.

'Another goat curry, please. I mean, curry goat.' She looked to see if her mistake had been spotted. She had her excuse ready – they don't have 'curry goat' in Ghana, though they do put goat in stews, and just call it goat-meat stew, that's all – but no one was interested in her amateur mistake. They were already dissecting the night and complaining about the work they had to do tomorrow. Dzifa sat down to eat the food with her friends, remembering between mouthfuls the ham sandwiches and fish fingers that, as a child, she had begged of Abena when friends had come to play.

The following afternoon Clem sat cross-legged on Dzifa's unmade bed, typing rhythmically while Dzifa sat at her desk, the sounds from her keyboard somewhat more stunted as she paused to check facts. Plates with the remnants of beans on wholemeal toast lay on the carpet tiles. The piano intro to 'Limit to Your Love' thumped in on their shared study playlist, playing from Clem's phone. Dzifa instinctively started humming to James Blake's wounded voice.

'How's it going?' Clem asked, breaking fifteen minutes of silence.

'Yeah, okay. Just one more paragraph comparing how influenza and herpes bind to cell membranes and I'll be done. You?'

'I mean, I literally just wrote "The stake in the hands of Buffy is therefore a gendered object, disrupting the male-female, hunter-hunted, penetrator-penetrated dialectic. A Foucaultian analysis thus reveals the contemporary gothic graveyard as a site of production of sexual discourse, as well as of sovereign power relations: a mortal, and sexual battlefield." So, not good. I'm supposed to be writing about *Dracula*.'

Dzifa snorted. 'That sounds a million times more interesting than my chat about herpes.'

Clem's phone rang, cutting off Blake's overlapping laments. Helen's voice filled the room, offering generic advice about study breaks and specific advice about Mary Shelley's superiority to Bram Stoker. Dzifa joined them on the bed.

'Hi, Helen.'

'Hi, Dzifa. How are the rehearsals going?'

'Yeah, really good, thanks.' Dzifa nodded. 'It's tech tonight, then the dress on Monday.'

'I hope it doesn't run on too late tonight. Techs were always the worst.' Dzifa agreed, then Clem asked how the rest of her family were doing before ushering Helen off the call and reopening her essay.

'What're you cooking tomorrow, by the way?' Clem asked as Dzifa packed her bag to leave.

Their house Come Dine With Me was always fun. Two of the four housemates were good cooks, and two were average, so it rotated between slap-up meals and casual boozing. Dzifa always cooked pasta, while Clem charred something while parboiling something else. Dzifa remembered how the group had relished the plantain sides the night before. 'I was thinking of cooking something from Ghana?'

'Awesome. Jollof?' She pronounced it *jo*-lof rather than jo-*lof*. 'I've had it once before, it's so good.'

'No, actually, a plantain thing. Just for the starter.'

'Can't wait!'

Dzifa scrolled through WhatsApp as she walked across cobbles, the Rad Cam to her left domed at the top like a big brick tit. She saw the last message from Elom, and remembered that she had forgotten to call him, or that he had forgotten to call her. She held down on the chat and tapped 'Mark as Unread'. She'd get back in touch with him later. She scrolled further down, then tapped on the row with the picture of a middle-aged Ghanaian stranger, and typed:

Hey mum. How do you cook kelewele?

Over the next twenty-four hours, Abena called Dzifa twice, and sent pictures of every ingredient and its alternatives she needed for her starter. Dzifa left the limestone-walled, oak-panelled city centre and walked to a multi-ethnic food shop in Cowley, where garam masala rubbed shoulders with palm oil, ghee, black-eyed beans and misshapen onions with green spots. She sent Abena a picture of the plantain before she bought it.

No it's not good, not that one. It took a few more messages before she understood this particular 'not good' to mean 'not ripe enough'. Back home, she set her laptop down on a pile of textbooks on the kitchen counter as she readied her ingredients: three ripe plantains, fresh ginger, onion, nutmeg, cloves, cinnamon, fresh chilli, salt and pepper. She started peeling the plantain. Their skins were mottled yellow and black; a blackness that would mean rotting in a banana, but on these skins promised a soft sweetness. She wondered how many people had walked past those boxes of plantains sitting outside those untidy shops with brown people inside and wondered to themselves, *why are they selling such putrid bananas?*

Holding the peeled plantain in the palm of her hand, she tried to slice it into oblongs the size of the tip of her thumb, the way Abena did. They came out like irregular wedges: she knew the thin ends would burn while the thick edges cooked. She couldn't recreate the image of her mum – couldn't visualise exactly what her hands were doing – though she must have seen it a hundred times.

Her laptop lit up with a video call from Abena. Dzifa answered as she slid the last of the plantain from the chopping board into the bowl. Her finger left a slimy streak of plantain across the mouse pad.

'How's it going? Let's see.' Abena looked on excitedly as Dzifa showed her. She gave some encouragement ('the chopping takes practice') and some critique ('no, you need more ginger'). As she grated the onion, Dzifa asked how hot the oil needed to be before adding the plantain.

'You know, you should know all this by now. You never wanted to learn from me,' Abena admonished.

'You never wanted to teach me. You got snappy when I came into the kitchen.'

'What do you mean? You were never there. You were always going to your friends' or your evening clubs. And when you were in, I didn't have time to take you through everything.' Dzifa remembered those days, asking Abena to hurry up so she could eat before Kodzo drove her to drama. 'It takes time . . .

me and Abla, we learned from our mum – we were just always there.'

Abena remembered seeing Aunty Abla and her mum in the kitchen together when she visited Glasgow for the summer the first time. How they'd moved in sync between chopping boards and pans, with no instruction, as if they'd been cooking together for years. They seemed to understand exactly what was needed of each other.

'I wish I'd stayed,' she said, blinking through the onion vapour. She mixed the ingredients together in the bowl, her hands coated in the sticky fruit and spice mix. 'I'm ready to fry now. How long for?'

'You'll know when it's brown enough. Just don't stir it up too soon. You have to let the spices stick to the plantain before you break them up, or else they get lost in the oil and it will taste plain.'

Dzifa spooned the plantain into the oil and it started to bubble and froth. She let it settle for a minute, watching the pan silently, as Abena watched her.

'Right, that will be ready now. You can turn it.'

Dzifa flipped over the golden pieces, allowing them to cook evenly. The edges started to brown, first at the sharp ends, then slowly spreading across each piece. When they were ready, she scooped them out and drained them on a bowl lined with kitchen paper. She pierced a piece with a fork and brought it to her mouth. Beautifully sweet, chewy, caramelised, spicy warmth briefly hit her taste buds before they were blunted by the burn of the just-fried morsel. She smiled, remembering how many times this exact sequence of events had occurred when she was a girl.

'Let's see . . . Well done, that's perfect! Just don't have it too often because it's a lot of oil.'

'I remember when we were wee, I used to get so annoyed that we couldn't have this every day for dinner. I'd be like, "But Mum, it's a vegetable!"'

'I know. We could have had it more, but it was just a hassle.'

'It's not too tricky though, is it?' Dzifa was pleased with her success.

'No, it's so easy. But it was the travel. Back then I had to take two buses to the other side of Glasgow to the Asian shop just to find plantain. Sometimes you go all the way-aah, after a late shift the night before and you find the plantain left is not good, or the shipment hasn't arrived.'

'Wait, really?' Dzifa looked at her mum's onscreen face, slightly out of shot as she lay on the couch in her pyjamas. Abena nodded with the corners of her mouth turned downwards, emphasising the truth of the story, though clearly not wishing to dwell on a distant memory.

'Oh, man.' Dzifa put down her fork. 'Well, thanks.'

'Ho, it's no problem. Anyway, it's better now. So you can get plantain whenever you want.'

'Yeah. I'll bring you some next time I visit. You can show me how to cut it properly.'

Abena smiled as Dzifa began boiling pasta, to which she would add a store-bought tomato sauce. As Abena asked Dzifa what time she would be up for lectures tomorrow, she heard the fire door open, then slam shut down the hall. She felt her attention split in two – one side timing how long it would be until her friends entered the kitchen, and another still focused on talking to her mum.

She imagined introducing them as they walked in, and the inevitable awkwardness when it became clear that Dzifa had never told Abena their names, even after almost two months of living together. Dzifa pictured them listening to her explaining the rudiments of her weekly timetable to her mother, as if she had just started her first week of classes.

'Hey, Mum, my housemates are back. I've got to go but I'll tell you how it goes later, okay?'

'Okay. Enjoy dinner, love you.'

Dzifa had switched back to Spotify by the time the kitchen door was pushed open.

The next morning, Dzifa's phone buzzed as she walked with Clem towards their respective faculties, both late for lectures. Abena's new profile picture filled the screen, this time one of herself, her hair falling in curls round her smiling face. A paper plate laden with jollof, chicken, salad and a boiled egg sat on the table in front of her, narrowing the event to an uncle or aunt's wedding, christening, funeral, birthday party, graduation party, New Year's Eve celebration, wedding anniversary or Easter Sunday.

'Oh, my mum's calling – you go ahead and I'll catch up?'

'You sure?'

'Yeah, won't be long.' Clem strolled off while Dzifa picked up the call. 'Hi, Mum, sorry I didn't call last night, we got a bit carried away,' Dzifa explained, stopping short of saying, *We got drunk.* 'The kelewele was a hit! Thanks so much.'

'Oh, I'm so glad. Next time it will be even better. Are you going to lectures today?'

Dzifa watched Clem texting in the distance as she climbed the steps of the English fac. She so desperately wanted to tell Abena how dull her lectures were, but how fascinating her last tutorial on neurotransmission had been. She wanted to talk to her about *The Bell Jar* and her first time on mushrooms. She wanted her to understand how proud and nervous she was about her play tomorrow. She wanted all these things, but with her mum on the other end of the phone, she just couldn't find the words. What was an essay crisis to someone who hadn't been allowed to finish secondary school? Other than her own school plays, Dzifa wasn't sure Abena had ever been to the theatre in her life.

'Yeah. I was just walking with my housemate, Clem. She's really lovely – hopefully you'll get to meet her soon. She cooks a lot, I think you'll like her.'

'E-eh? What does she cook?' Abena asked.

'Loads of stuff. She really likes curry.'

'Oh, that's nice.'

'Yeah, we cook for each other quite a bit. I was thinking next time I might try red-red if you can help me out?' And suddenly Abena was already deep into the recipe, including a ranking of palm oil alternatives, before Dzifa was able to remind her that she was already late.

'Sorry, oh. And please, message Elom too. Have you heard from him?'

Dzifa remembered his text and kicked herself. 'No, I'll message him today.' They said goodbye as Dzifa rushed through the faculty gates. She crept into the lecture hall, silently perching on a seat near the back. Once it was clear the lecturer wasn't going to acknowledge her in any way, she got out her phone and texted Elom a picture.

I made kelewele last night!!

Chapter Thirteen

Abena – May 2013

Abena scooped some boiled potatoes onto a plate and handed it to one of the carers.

'Macaroni cheese and chips.' Another carer placed an order for a resident. Abena stuck the serving spoon into the tray with a squelch and scooped out some more. Everything was bloated and off-yellow: macaroni cheese, chips, garlic bread, boiled potatoes, apple crumble, custard, even the 'roast chicken' which came ready sliced in packages that they placed in the industrial oven.

Dinner was served by 6 p.m., and she had cleaned up the kitchen by eight. Her feet hurt on the walk to the bus stop, and she was home by nine. Kodzo was reading a book in the living room – these days he leaned towards books from 'spiritual teachers', with words like 'manifest' and 'power' in the title; the kind of thing he probably would have called demonic twenty years earlier. In the past few years his world had become smaller. He went to church less, listened to music and read more. He had lowered the dose on his tablets and started laughing again like he used to. The old brightness had returned to his eyes. He had always been stoical about his mood, or 'stress', as he called it, the rare times he mentioned it. Abena didn't pry, nor did she reveal any of his secrets to the kids, and she was happy that things were now much better.

Abena's world had become smaller too. She had given up her career so she could spend more time at home. First for Elom, then for Dzifa, and then again for Elom as he approached the end of his degree, fearful of where the stress might take him. She considered going back, but with the kids growing up, money wasn't as tight. And – she was embarrassed to admit – she was scared to go back to the time pressure, the heat and the noise of the restaurant kitchen which she used to love; used to control. Catering in a care home was easy, if boring.

'Elom, are you still working?' Elom was typing on his laptop, his eyes occasionally flicking up to watch the news.

'Yeah, just finishing one wee thing.' He was interning at an engineering firm, but not doing any engineering. Instead he was writing reports, or newsletters, or press releases – Abena wasn't totally sure. He had explained that interning wasn't quite a job, but when she asked how much he was being paid it was almost as much as she made at the care home. She was glad that four years of university had moved the starting line so far forward.

'Have you guys eaten?'

'Yeah, we had the waakye,' Kodzo said. 'I left some in the bowl for you in the kitchen.'

Abena had a shower before heating up her dinner; although she never ate the food at work, the smell of it was so thick that she felt the need to wash it off before she could feel hungry again. She checked her phone before eating – she had called

Dzifa earlier, and Dzifa had texted that she would call her back. She often said this, but rarely called. Abena joined the others in the living room and sat down to eat.

That weekend, Abena and Kodzo drove across town to Maria and Mensah's for the day. They did this less often than they used to, and now there was no thunderous footfall of children playing in the bedrooms or shrieking in the garden. Abena didn't mind – she liked sitting in their conservatory drinking beer and eating salted peanuts before the dinner Maria cooked; reminiscing, debating, laughing.

'So when will you be going?' Abena asked. Maria and Mensah had been spending more time in Ghana the last few years, sometimes together, and sometimes apart. Mensah was older, and had retired with an NHS doctor's pension, though he worked as a locum consultant when he was in Scotland. Maria had never worked, and seemed to be doing just fine travelling back and forth.

'Sistah, I'm not sure, oh.' Maria looked at Mensah. 'It just depends.'

'There are some things not quite finished with the house,' Mensah added.

'Eh, so did you stay there last time, or somewhere else?' Kodzo asked.

'When I was in Accra, I stayed there,' Mensah replied. 'But I spent some time in Ada Foah, anyway.'

'Abena, you heard correct. We spent a lot of time and big money building a nice house in Accra, so that when we go to Ghana we can still be renting apartments in some *nyama-nyama* towns.' Maria burst out laughing, and Abena and Kodzo joined in while Mensah pretended to be shocked.

'Anyway,' she continued, her words still punctuated with her fading chuckle, 'in answer to your question: Mawusi is off this summer – she's at college now, you know – so I might wait until she finishes, then we can go together. If the house is finished we can stay there, or if not we will stay with my people.'

'That would be so nice. When was she last in Ghana?' Abena asked.

'Like, eight years or more. She only remembers coconut and Fan Yogo but she wants to come. She's been asking me to teach her Ga.'

'That will be a good trip,' Kodzo said, shuffling peanuts into his mouth.

'Really,' Abena agreed, nodding sincerely.

Abena waited until she and Maria were alone in the kitchen before updating her. Abla was pregnant again. Maria stopped stirring the huge silver pot of jollof to hug Abena in congratulations, before turning the conversation to the important questions.

'You too, you don't like that man, eh?'

'Hmm.' Abena sighed, peeling baked fish from the foil it sat on without leaving any skin behind. 'It doesn't matter if I like him or not. I just don't understand Abla.' They spoke in Ga now that they were away from their non-Accra husbands.

'Eeh?'

'She wants a sibling for Ama – fine. But she too, one minute she's done with the man, the next she's pregnant.'

'And is he still in Lagos?'

'He works there mostly. And Abla stays in the house in Accra.'

'And he provides?'

'Mm-mm.' Abena nodded. It had been years since Abla had called needing money. The expensive education Abena had paid for had got her out of Newtown, but instead of Abla stepping into a boardroom or operating theatre, she had stepped into the car of a businessman's son that she had met at university.

'Listen, sistah,' Maria said as she slid freshly chopped tomatoes into the blender, 'not every man – especially not every Ghanaian man – is like Kodzo. You are blessed.'

Abena nodded, acknowledging the truth they both knew, and the younger, possibly prettier reason Mensah sometimes stayed at Ada Foah without Maria. It was true – she loved Kodzo, and he was devoted to their family in a way she had never doubted. Her only competition had been the church, and even that was fading. Still, as they carried the pots and trays loaded with banku, okro soup, grilled fish and fresh pepper into the conservatory, she felt uneasy about the fact that, regardless of education, or work, or children, her happiness and that of the women around her depended on a man not being cruel – or more often, on how a woman managed it when they were.

Dzifa phoned Abena when they got home late that evening, over a week after their initial call. She told Dzifa about Maria and Mensah's plan to visit Ghana soon.

'For good?'

'No, no, not yet. Just for holiday. Mawusi might go with them.'

'Oh, sick. I'd love to go at some point but I'm at the Fringe again this summer.'

'Of course.' Abena smoothed her pyjama top. 'It's just a thought. Maybe next year.'

'By the way, Mum, I went to this dinner at college last night and the dessert was amazing. It was a French thing with cherries? Really creamy. I can find a recipe to send you, it was called a clafoutis.' She said the word delicately, enunciating the syllables to make it extra clear for Abena.

'Yeah, clafoutis. I used to make that when I worked at the Dundonald. Sometimes you can make it with raspberries or peaches, too.'

'Oh, well maybe next time I'm up you could teach me how to make it? I'm a bit obsessed.'

'Of course – it's really simple.'

They spoke until Dzifa arrived at wherever it was that she was walking to and she said goodbye, and Abena promised she would look over any clafoutis recipe Dzifa sent to make sure it was a good one. She was pleased for Dzifa – whilst she wasn't as focused on university as Abena might have liked, she was living, and living for herself, as much as that sometimes made Abena feel left out, or even a little jealous.

If she was honest with herself, she was jealous of Maria too. Abena was proud of her choices – she had no education, but had worked hard, and soon she would have two graduate children from good universities with professional degrees, while Mawusi had only just started a course in business administration at the local college. Still, she would like to go to Ghana with Dzifa, maybe lounge on a beach with her and Abla, all sunglasses and green coconuts and sugar cane. More than that, she wanted Dzifa to really want to, and part of her wondered if Dzifa would want to if Abena had done something different – had been at home more, like Maria. Perhaps she might still, one day, but until then Abena didn't know how her pride would fare against Maria's Facebook pictures of her and Mawusi in Accra.

A few months later, Elom came downstairs and found Abena and Kodzo in the kitchen, putting away the shopping. He joined in without being asked, and Abena watched gratefully as he put tins on the wrong side of the shelf.

'Ehm . . . can I say something?' He took some more tins, not looking at either of them as he continued to stack.

'Yeah, of course, son,' Abena said.

'So this comms internship finishes in August, and they might actually like to keep me on, which is cool.' Abena looked at Kodzo, and they both smiled. Elom's heat had cooled in the last few years, and they were proud of him.

'That's great,' Abena told him.

'Yeah, it's cool, and I've learned loads, but I don't think it's what I actually wanna do.' He slid his finger around the lid of a can of sweetcorn, avoiding their eyes. 'Remember I did the communications courses in the last bit of uni? That's kinda how I got this job. Anyway. I don't know why I'm being weird. It's good news. I got into a master's in journalism. In London. It starts after summer.' Elom rushed the last few sentences, and only when he had finished did he look up from the floor.

'Well done!' Kodzo's smile was wide, and he shook Elom's hand with a click.

Abena was as happy as she was surprised. Once she had been reassured that he would be able to afford it – he had saved just enough to get by, he said, from living at home these last two years (his only real expense being driving lessons) – she was able to tell Elom how proud she was. She was so pleased that he finally felt ready to step out on his own. Since university, he had spent most of his time indoors (she understood, now, his constant watching of the news) or listening to music. He didn't seem to go to those parties anymore, and she'd heard less and less about the boys he used to hang out with. She didn't mention that the idea of him alone in London also made her nervous – he was never as easy-going as Dzifa.

It wasn't until she was getting ready for bed after dinner and a family group phone call with Dzifa that Abena thought about what Elom's news meant for her. She had given up her career so she could spend more time at home. But now she no longer needed to be home every night for dinner – she'd done her job. For the first time in a long time – perhaps since Kodzo had held her hand under the dusty heat of the Newtown compound – it seemed like a choice had opened up before her. She could continue her life working in the care home, bloated and beige, or she could try the restaurant life again, hot and loud and late. At this point, neither seemed attractive. As she lay in bed with Kodzo already asleep beside her, the image that filled her mind like ink spreading across tissue paper was warm, with sandy toes, and the spicy gristle of suya in her teeth. She wondered if she really had done her job, and if it might be time to leave.

PART TWO

Chapter Fourteen

Elom – September 2013

'So, what's your favourite band?'

Elom paused to think, remembering the Bob Marley poster on the wall behind him. 'I don't listen to a lot of bands, I guess, but I like a lot of hip-hop . . . underground stuff, like J Dilla, MF Doom . . .' It had been a long time since he had hammered his eardrums with G-Unit, imagining himself on the streets of Compton, and he cringed at the memory of the ill-fitting T-shirts and accents he and his friends had worn. 'Band-wise, the Fugees are definitely up there.'

'Yeah, I like them too.' Dimitris nodded. 'The Fugees, man . . . *Ooh la, la la!*' He laughed.

'Cool,' Yianni said. 'Do you have any more questions?' The 'h' on 'have' was scratchy, like the sound of the last straw-suck of an icy drink. 'The room is £450 a month but bills will probably be another hundred.' It was the cheapest rent Elom had found in London within an hour's commute to university. The bedroom itself was so small that the chest of drawers couldn't be fully opened without them bumping into the single bed. The living room they were sitting in had the same nondescript faux-leather sofas Elom had seen in every other flat he had visited. The smell of tobacco and weed rose from the full ashtray on the wooden veneer coffee table.

'Sounds good to me. When will I hear back?'

Elom moved in the next day, lugging his overstuffed suitcase and a bunch of almost bursting plastic bags along the Underground from his hostel to the flat in Willesden Green. The text from Yianni welcoming him to the flat had arrived before he had even made it back to the hostel after the viewing. The feeling of being chosen wasn't familiar, and he was as excited as he was confused.

The text had come just after another from Chris, asking him how the move had gone, which he had ignored. They had never spoken about what happened in Magaluf. Elom had seen less of him since then, and was happy for a clean break. He told Chris and the others it was just that uni, and then his internship, were busier than expected. He told himself it was because of a gulf opening up between the teenager he was, and the professional he was becoming – something to do with class, or diversifying interests. But whenever he heard from Chris, the truth struck him in a flash – he felt less like he was being chosen, and more like he was being marked, or condemned, and the fear and humiliation was what made him ignore the notification.

Dimitris cooked a curry and they ate it with a few cans of lager. The conversation was easy – the others were so comfortable with each other that Elom could relax as they led the discussion. After eating, Stelios asked, 'So, what should we watch?'

'A classic?' Dimitris answered.

'I still haven't seen *This is England*,' Yianni added.

'I could do that,' Stelios said, picking up his laptop. 'Elom, what do you think?'

The three men worked in film, as gaffers and occasional camera crew for small projects, and Elom trusted their judgement. 'Yeah, sounds great to me, I haven't seen it either.'

'Cool.' Dimitris illegally downloaded it while Stelios brought out a plastic tray with papers, a small jar full of weed, a grinder and some tobacco from underneath the coffee table. Elom watched closely as he rolled a joint, checking how much weed Stelios put in and feeling his chest tighten. He hadn't smoked since his second year of university. Yianni took the dirty plates to the kitchen and brought some more beers, while Dimitris went to the bathroom and pissed with the door open.

Stelios lit the joint as Dimitris plugged his laptop into the widescreen television. He took a long drag, and Elom heard the sound of Velcro being softly pulled as the end burned orange. Elom made calculations based on the size of the joint, the amount of weed in it, the number of people it would pass through (Elom was directly on Stelios's right) and the length of Stelios's drag. He concluded he would be getting higher than he wanted to – which, really, was not at all.

As the film started, the joint passed left to Dimitris, who held on to it for a few more puffs before passing it to Yianni. The smell reminded Elom of embarrassment and panic – no particular memory stood out, just a swirl of images and feelings he only seemed to remember when he smoked, which he had avoided for years. Yianni passed it to Elom and he brought it to his lips, making sure to inhale so that they knew that he knew how to smoke. As he brought the smoke in deeper, it caught in his throat and he coughed loudly. He didn't have an open beer, and his embarrassment intensified as he tried to clear his throat as quickly as possible, still holding the joint.

'Here, man.' Dimitris passed him a can. He barely looked at Elom, still focused on the film. As Elom took a sip, Stelios said, 'Sorry, bro, the tobacco's a bit dry – I usually just smoke it without.' Elom looked around the room once more as he sipped the beer and cleared his throat; the others were totally unconcerned. At school – with Chris and the others – anyone who coughed would be the joke of the group, until someone else did something deserving.

'It's fine, sorry, just haven't smoked in a while.' Elom took another puff, carefully this time, showing his deep inhale, though he realised that the others weren't watching. He passed the joint to Stelios, who held the filter in the tips of his fingers as he sucked in the last of the hot air. The familiar weight of the drug fell on Elom – he always wondered why it was called 'getting high' when all he felt was heavy, as if the air in the room was pressurised, pushing him into the chair. Before long, Stelios started rolling a second joint. The film was intense, and Elom felt a bleakness clouding his thoughts. The thought of more smoking scared him. The joint made its way left again until it reached Yianni. After his puffs he turned to ask Elom, 'Do you want more?'

He looked Elom directly in the eye as he held the lit joint between them. Elom was caught off guard by his sincerity, and realised he might be able to answer truthfully. 'Eh, I think I'm okay, actually.' Wordlessly, Yianni leaned past Elom to pass it on to Stelios, who finished it off again. Elom sat back to watch the rest of the film. He was already too high and the violence on screen made him anxious, but the room itself – unusually for him – didn't. They spoke about the film after it finished – Dimitris wasn't a huge fan but Stelios loved it. Then they all went upstairs, Stelios rolled himself a third joint to help him drift off, and Yianni taught him how to say 'Kalinychta'. Elom went to sleep in his new bed for the first time, too high, exhausted, but calm, and hopeful for the start of a life outside Glasgow.

A week later, Elom woke up from a post-wank nap and got the Tube into town to meet his new coursemates for drinks. The first week of classes had been exciting and nerve-wracking. He had never had to discuss ideas publicly, with expert interrogation. His undergraduate degree had been about numbers and problem-solving, but now he was asked to opine on how the digitisation of music was changing the industry. It felt like the job of a journalist was to have an opinion on everything, yet somehow remain objective, and it was overwhelming. His coursemates – now, possibly, his friends – didn't seem to worry. Pippy, Josh, Luc and Freya spoke boldly, enjoying the chance to share their knowledge, while Elom hoped he wouldn't be picked to speak at all.

They met outside Elephant and Castle Underground station and walked to Wetherspoons, where they planned to pre-drink before the larger freshers' night. The short walk was a mix of suits, schoolkids with oversized tie knots, and women laden with shopping bags. There were a lot of Black people – more than Elom would see in a year in Glasgow. He had to train himself not to give the nod as he passed, in case they confused his recognition of their Blackness with recognition of them.

The bar was busy, but Pippy found a high, sticky table that they could stand at. Josh offered the first round, and the others requested gin and tonics and lagers. Elom hesitated – there were five of them, and he was already in his overdraft after the final student fee instalment. 'I'll have a pint, please, ta.' They stayed for the full five rounds, laughing more and raising their voices in line with the volume of the room.

They shared stories from their lives pre-master's, mostly tailored to present themselves as fun-loving, adventurous and talented. Freya had taken a year out after university where she 'just travelled around South America' and then volunteered in 'a local NGO in Colombia for three months'. Luc had gone to several international schools, following his parents around Europe and some of the Middle East – though it was unclear to Elom what their professions might be – and he spoke four languages. The dynamic was totally different to his friends back home: the laughter was less pointed, and there were a lot more questions. He didn't fear he was about to be made fun of, but he couldn't totally relax either; they were heightened versions of the people he'd avoided at university, who always had something smart to say, when Elom felt like he was barely understanding. But he was more confident now, and he could see that they were nice, and welcoming. Still, he felt he didn't have much to add, but their eyes widened simply from the fact that he'd grown up in Glasgow.

'Wasn't it, like, really rough?'

'But you don't really sound Scottish . . . I met someone from Glasgow a few years ago and I could barely understand them!'

'I've heard it's sick for like, art and stuff, but I've only ever been to Edinburgh.'

Elom appreciated their approval, despite himself. Pippy said that one of her tutors was from Glasgow, and she loved his 'tutes' on hungover days because of his accent. Josh immediately asked her what university she'd gone to.

'Oxford?' The single-word sentence rose at the end, as if she was unsure the others had heard of it.

'Oh, sick,' Josh replied. 'Which college were you at?'

Pippy looked relaxed. 'Um, LMH. Do you know Oxford?'

'Yeah, I was at Keble.'

'Oh my God,' Freya interrupted, 'you must be geniuses, then. Like, Oxford Oxford?'

Pippy and Josh laughed coyly. Elom saw a route for connection and took it. 'My sister's at Oxford. She's going into fourth year. Medicine.'

'Nice, what college?'

Elom couldn't remember its name. 'I need to double-check. I haven't visited yet.'

'It's like an hour on the train from here, so you'll definitely be able to.'

Elom nodded, making a mental note to arrange a date with Dzifa. 'Yeah, it'd be good to see her, definitely.'

They finished their drinks before walking out. It was warm enough that Elom could carry his jacket in his hand, and it surprised him how many ways London was different to home. The street was still busy, with artificial light falling down from the streetlamps and chicken-shop windows. There were Black faces waiting at bus stops, travelling to or from graveyard-shift jobs, or in groups talking, some stony-faced, some laughing, slight frames drowning in baggy clothes. Elom found himself avoiding their eyes and walking straighter, closer to his new white friends, a guilty part of him wanting to be recognised as a different kind of Black.

The club was packed. Elom and his group found the other master's students, who formed a slightly calmer island amongst the sea of undergraduates. It was a noughties night, playing the types of songs you could sing along to in drunken euphoria, and Elom bopped with one arm around his friends and a plastic cup of vodka cranberry in his other hand. When 'Song 4 Mutya (Out of Control)' came on, he belted the chorus then mumbled through the verses, and he almost ran back from the toilet when 'Heartbroken' dropped. The others were there with him, singing along and spilling their drinks, and he didn't have to rein it in, or pretend the music wasn't for him.

As the night went on, Elom noticed people were pairing off, often briefly and clumsily before returning to dance, and sometimes intensely and messily, drawing looks from the people around them. It happened less so with his group, he supposed because fewer of them were single, and some were already engaged or married. Pippy danced closer to him, turning her back on the circle, in a routine Elom had felt before. Part of his reason for moving to London had been to avoid this situation, or to open up the possibility of getting into other situations. In the last few days, he had scrutinised every conversation in real time, looking for an opportunity to say what he needed to say: 'I'm bi?' 'I'm gay?' Something direct or something allusive? He hadn't been able to, and now Pippy was looking into his eyes as she moved her hips.

On autopilot, Elom half-heartedly matched her movements. He caught himself, finished his drink and put it on the shelf by the wall. When he turned back, he said the easiest thing he was able to say: 'I'm gonna grab a smoke.' Elom hadn't smoked cigarettes in years either, but he started walking as Pippy said, 'Sweet, I'll come too.'

The smoking area was a patch of concrete behind velvet ropes by the front door. After an awkward moment of Elom patting his pockets, Pippy knowingly brought a packet of straights from her bag and passed him one. They stood slightly apart, making small talk as the wicking sweat cooled their bodies. A boy – probably an undergrad, Elom thought, with his smooth face and happy confidence – approached them and asked Elom for a cigarette. Pippy handed him one, lighting it as he pinched it between his lips. He thanked them profusely and started a friendly conversation none of them really wanted to have, in order to justify his having interrupted them to steal a fag. When Elom spoke, his eyes widened, and he made another fuss over him being Glaswegian.

When he left to find his friends, Pippy and Elom dropped their stubs and went back in. 'I think that guy fancied you!' she said as they walked downstairs.

'What?'

'He barely looked at me, and *I* gave him the fucking fag.'

Elom laughed. 'I didn't really notice. Bit rude of him, I guess.' He honestly hadn't noticed – his mind had been too occupied by thoughts of what would happen when he and Pippy went back downstairs. Regardless, he wasn't even sure what to look out for; flirting with a man had never been in the realm of possibility. He wasn't sure if Pippy was making a joke, and if she was, he wasn't sure who was the butt of it. He remembered Chris and the sweaty shame of Magaluf, and feared that the feeling would follow him wherever he went.

They rejoined the group and continued to dance, Elom slightly lightheaded from the nicotine. He saw the boy and his friend through the crowd. Pippy followed his gaze, then looked back at Elom and leaned into his ear.

'Give him your number!' Elom pulled back to look at her. She was grinning, her eyes slightly glazed. 'Oh my God, just do it.' She pushed him playfully in the ribs.

Elom shook his head. 'Nah . . .' he laughed. 'Eh . . .' Pippy rolled her eyes and twirled to the music. When she faced him again, she shook her head and let out a giggle. She was laughing, but not at him – well, yes, at him, but not like he'd experienced before. Elom smiled back and felt his heart humming in his chest, more hopeful than fearful. Crashing cymbals and a wailing police siren cut through the air, and everyone in the club seemed to simultaneously inhale and widen their eyes in anticipation. Dizzee kicked in forcefully, and Elom and Pippy joined in and jumped up and down, rapping each line word for word.

Elom scrolled through the Facebook Messenger group chat the next morning as people shared photos and stories from the night before. He found himself in a few of them, smiling and dancing, lankier than he had imagined, but happy. Pippy sent him a direct message:

So fun! Hope ur not too hungover
just thinking, ask ur sis if she knows Lou Weston
a medic mate of mine a couple years above, shes lovely!

Dzifa was moving back to Oxford from Glasgow that
weekend, after her summer holidays. They hadn't spoken since
Elom had arrived in London a couple of weeks earlier, apart
from a phone call he'd had with Abena where Dzifa was briefly
in the background before heading out. Elom thought about the
chance that Dzifa knew Lou, and imagined them and him and
Pippy all hanging out together in London, talking about ideas
over colourful drinks.

He messaged her with the name, and she replied a few days
later:

Yooo, no don't know her unforch. Sorry for delay, had start of
term exams. Hope the course is good. U enjoying it?

Yeh all good. Would be good to see you soon here or in Oxford.

Defooo. Lets work out a date. Next month?

Sounds good

Neither of them followed up in the weeks that followed.
Time was moving quicker for Elom; university intensified and
his weekends were fuller. He went to dinners at his friends' flats
in north London and helped them cook, chopping fresh garlic
and tearing basil from pots by the sink. Occasionally he had a
few puffs of a joint whilst watching another film and the panic
was duller each time.

London gave him autonomy, and anonymity, and he decided
to use it. He googled the local cruising ground, then went, only
to watch. It was busy, and he gorged himself on the thrill of
bodies. Watching quickly became an adrenaline-fuelled fumble.

After the first time, he zipped himself back up and headed out of the treeline, amazed at the simplicity of it all.

He cruised more, sneaking into parks after nights out, then began finding men online, meeting them at their flats around London. Riding on the Tube towards someone's place, or another cruising ground, he felt like he was a spring being pulled taut along the tracks. He was packed with the energy of anticipation and fear, which was discharged suddenly, and completely, on contact. Initially, he would leave the memory behind when he left the men. But slowly, he began to admit to his own desires in the daylight: he didn't have a name for what he was, but he knew what he wanted. The white-hot release of sex gained more colour: he had good sex, bad sex, intimate and wild sex. Eventually he brought men back to his, scooting them past his housemates, then later walking downstairs with a bashful pride. Now when he went out and saw other boys, he was more concerned with communicating his interest than with hiding it. He stressed out about uni, and money, and getting enough sleep, and sex: normal things.

A week into December, after Dzifa shared a link to 'You Know You Like It' by AlunaGeorge, Elom asked about meeting up before the holidays. He picked an affordable Thai restaurant in Camden and tidied up his living room in case Dzifa needed to stay. He felt like he was to blame for their lack of contact: he had tried to distance himself from her as a teenager, saying to himself that it was because he hung out with the cool kids, and she was a drama geek. He could admit to himself now that he had always seen that she was special – smart, confident, liked – and he had felt like he would infect her with his mediocrity. As they got older, she'd only become more perfect, and he'd been too embarrassed to let her in. But things were different now: he was in London, in a new world, and at the very least he was treading water. On the Jubilee line eastbound, he thought about the different ways he could tell her the truth about himself, and imagined her hugging him and saying she had always known, or shrugging it off as if it didn't matter to her in the slightest, or turning sombre and asking whether he had told their mum and dad.

He arrived first and was seated at a table for two. He took the chair, leaving the sofa-like bench for her. Dzifa arrived ten minutes later. Her hair was in the same braids she'd had done in Glasgow before the start of term, now slightly woollier at the roots. She shared a laugh with the waiter at the door before he turned to bring her to the table. Elom watched people watch her as she walked through the restaurant – she had such presence.

'Hey, Elom!' Elom stood to meet her, arms outstretched for a hug. It was odd – they had rarely hung out alone outside of home, and certainly had never had dinner together in a restaurant without their parents. But Elom was happy to see her, even if it felt comically formal, like they were playing at being grown-ups.

'Hey, Dzifa, lovely to finally see you.'

'You too. Sorry I'm a bit late, thanks for picking the restaurant.'

Elom had first tried Thai a month previously, and was looking forward to showing it to Dzifa. She asked him about his life in London, his course and his coursemates. It felt good to have something in common again – this new life they shared away from Glasgow.

'How was the train?'

'I just came up from south London today, it was a bit delayed as usual.'

Elom nodded, noting that she didn't have any bags. 'Were you in London last night?'

'Yeah,' Dzifa nodded, looking at the menu, 'staying with a friend then I need to leave in a couple of hours for another mate's birthday thing in Dulwich.'

The waiter came to take their order, and Elom asked for a prawn pad Thai. Dzifa paused for a moment, then said partly to Elom and partly to the waiter, 'Oh, I reckon we should do a sharing thing. Like a curry, a noodle and a salad between us?'

Elom looked at his menu, feeling the awkwardness creep up his neck. 'Erm, yeah sure.'

The waiter nodded. 'Sharing's good, we'd recommend that and a side of rice for the curry.'

'Do you mind, Elom? My friend told me that's how to do Thai properly.' Elom nodded, and Dzifa ordered for the two of them, looking at Elom with each suggestion, who nodded in response. They spoke about Christmas plans – they would both go back home – and the music they were listening to. Dzifa was loving Solange's EP *True* while Elom had been rinsing Dizzee's *Boy In Da Corner*.

Elom was happy, but the dinner table set-up made him nervous; they couldn't just *be*. He ran through topics in his head, worried there would be a lull in conversation. The food arrived and Elom tried to find an opening to talk about his sexuality, but the conversation didn't seem to dip deep enough to justify it. As three o'clock approached, he started to feel more pressured, and slightly annoyed that Dzifa had imposed a time limit. As they walked to the Tube stop, Elom wondered how many times she had been in London in the last few months without telling him.

'I hope the party's fun. Is it gonna be a big one?'

'Eurgh, yeah,' Dzifa half sighed, 'it'll be fine.'

Elom nudged her. 'Too cool for house parties. I remember you used to sneak into them.'

Dzifa laughed. 'No, it's not that. I just don't know if I can be bothered tonight.'

'What do you mean?'

'It's literally nothing . . . sometimes it can just be a bit . . . like it's fine, just cba, you know?' For the first time all afternoon, Elom felt the conversation open up between them, with the same calmness he used to feel watching *Dragon Ball Z* with her in the living room in Glasgow. 'You doing okay?'

'Oh my God, yeah totally. Maybe just a bit stressed with uni or whatever.' Elom thought about her friends that he hadn't met, and about the smile she wore when she walked into a room, and wondered if he had missed something. For a moment, he felt pride, almost triumph – he was doing well for once, and Dzifa was on the back foot. But as soon as the feeling came, it left again, washed out by an embarrassed guilt.

He wanted to push her further: they could talk about music, and their courses, and laugh about their parents, but he struggled to ask how she was feeling. He didn't have the practice – just like he didn't have the practice, he realised, to tell her what was happening with him. He knew her humour exactly, and what food she might like, but he knew so little of the details of her life that he wouldn't know where to start questioning.

Dzifa leaned in for a hug at the ticket barriers. 'So nice to see you. Really glad uni's going well. Maybe we should get the same train back to Glasgow?'

'Yeah, let's figure it out. Have fun tonight.'

She tapped in. Elom watched, feeling the weight of what he hadn't said tensing his jaw. He waited until she passed through the gate, but she didn't turn to wave before heading down the escalator.

Chapter Fifteen

Kodzo – January 2014

Kodzo got back to an empty house after dropping Elom off at the station: Dzifa had left for London a few days before, and Abena was working a half-day. Elom said he was doing okay on his own, but the worry never left Kodzo, even though it now seemed unfounded: He had seemed relaxed over the Christmas holidays. He had slept in most days and eaten loaded plates of leftovers. While Dzifa had dotted in and out, catching up with schoolmates, he had joined Abena and Kodzo to visit family friends. Elom deciding to move away to study journalism had surprised Kodzo, but not as much as the fact that it seemed to be working for him.

The kids had slid back into their old rooms when they arrived and had left them as messy as when they were children. Kodzo took two mugs from Dzifa's room, half full of brackish leftover tea. He was pleased that they had left for bigger things, but the silence felt so empty, and so final.

As Kodzo put the second cup on the drying rack, he heard the mechanical clunk of the front door, and he was relieved. He found Abena sorting through the mail in the living room – mostly bills, since the time of handwritten letters from Ghana, or wedding invites from friends nearby, had long passed.

'Did Elom take the food from the freezer?'

'Yeah, he packed it and some Supermalt too.'

Abena let the letters fall onto the side table. 'It felt so short. Maybe we should visit them in London.'

'I still have some leave.' They were both still working full-time. There were a few years left on the mortgage, a steady trickle of requests for money from relatives in Ghana, and neither of the kids were earning yet. Abena went upstairs to shower, and the silence returned. Kodzo didn't feel like turning on the television, but he also didn't have much else to do. Nobody needed him to fix something, or drop them off, or make sure they had eaten. There was nobody to take care of.

He heard Abena's feet on the floor upstairs and lifted himself off the couch. In the bedroom, Abena was running a thick cream through her hair while a few dribbles of water escaped it and ran down her forehead.

'Are you busy?'

'I need to go to Rana's to buy some smoked fish. Do you need me to get something?'

'I can drive you. Then let's go and get some coffee or something. There's some places near there I've seen for years but we've never gone.'

'Right now?'

'Yeah.'

Abena turned down the corners of her mouth and nodded casually, as if to say, 'Why not?' but when she came downstairs thirty minutes later, she was wearing her newest wig, and had matched her eyeshadow to her flowing green blouse. Abena smiled, less casually this time, and Kodzo smiled back as she passed, picking up his car keys from the table.

Kodzo and Abena fell into a new routine over the months that followed. They now had a favourite coffee shop, in Woodlands, with soft couches and reasonably priced traybakes. They also had favourite coffees – Abena had a flat white, and Kodzo a cappuccino, decaf. They went for walks in the parks in the West End, and Kodzo looked up day trips, for the first time based on what they would find most interesting, rather than what the kids would find the most educational. Kodzo started taking pictures again, and getting them developed like when he'd first moved to Glasgow.

On a cold, sunny Saturday, Kodzo drove them to Loch Lomond, where they shared a lemon drizzle cake overlooking the water. A grey-haired pair of hikers were talking about who had got them lost on a previous holiday. They were interrupting each other between mouthfuls of scone, laughing and shaking heads with sly little glances.

Kodzo's previously comfortable silence with Abena suddenly became very uncomfortable, as he tried to think of something to talk about. She was looking out of the window as a group of teenagers stepped into kayaks which wobbled on the surface of the loch as their instructor watched. Kodzo could think of nothing interesting, or funny, and he felt the way he did when he had to make small talk with a colleague from another ward before a meeting.

Even with the kids gone, they spoke about them often, in present, past and future tenses. Kodzo desperately wanted to speak of something else, and he was scared by the possibility that without them as a guide, he had little else to hold Abena's interest. Abena was still looking out of the window, unconcerned. Before he risked her growing bored, Kodzo lurched for a topic from a book he was reading.

'I was reading more about meditation today.'

'E-eh?' Abena had always accepted Kodzo's Christianity, but had seemed ambivalent to his new learnings, though never discouraging. Now though, she turned towards him. 'What's it saying?'

'It's just talking about different ways of communicating with God.' Kodzo was nervous; so far, he had only played with these ideas in his own head. 'In some religions, meditation is about reaching heaven,' Abena nodded, 'and they might chant or say or imagine certain things. This is saying that those methods don't belong to a particular religion: you can bring meditation to Christianity, or whatever, to build a relationship with God, rather than just asking for things, or worshipping Him.' The thought of sitting cross-legged and chanting om for Jesus could easily be met with ridicule, or even accusations of blasphemy from many Ghanaians, and though Kodzo knew Abena wouldn't be so extreme, he wasn't sure what she would say.

Abena sipped her coffee. 'But that's already in the Bible anyway, isn't it?' She nodded, as if she was answering herself.

'All those times Jesus went away to pray by himself, he wasn't shouting praise and worship, he was talking with God. Moses and the older prophets, too.'

Kodzo relaxed a little. 'Yeah, exactly.'

'In Fante, *mpaebɔ* means meditation, but also prayer. I wouldn't be surprised if things got lost in translation in the Hebrew Bible too.'

Kodzo was surprised, both at the fact, but also at her interest. 'I didn't know that.'

'Mm-mm. You can say it's because our language is not as complicated, or doesn't have as many words, but traditionally I don't think there was really a difference between the prayer and the meditation. I mean long ago, before Christianity came.'

'True. And we've forgotten the knowledge they had about how to do it in an African way.'

'It's a shame. Having that peace would be helpful, I'll tell you. That's what religion should be about, really. Something that actually serves people, rather than stresses them out.'

Kodzo understood the implication. He was pleased, but also embarrassed. He was back in the third-floor guest room in Accra, chatting with the young woman who was so brash, yet so meek, and so bright, but who had never been told so by those around her. It was embarrassing to have forgotten those conversations in the thirty years of discussing mortgage bills and school runs. They both turned to watch the kayakers paddling steadily across the loch as they finished their coffee. The silence returned, but this time Kodzo felt hopeful.

* * *

The next day they joined Maria and Mensah for lunch after the service. This, rather than the Praise and Worship section, had become Kodzo's favourite part of the church day. He felt like he could now see the scaffolding behind the service, and it made it mundane and trite. The cheerful introductions, where everyone carried a genuine friendliness but a false righteousness; a sermon where he was told in what new way he was spiritually failing; a worship section designed to whip them all into a frenzy, followed, conveniently, by the offering. Deviation from the formula was rarely permitted; there was no space for voicing doubts or confusion. Still, the routine was comforting, and the sermons often had a nugget of usefulness, but he mostly went to be among friends.

Maria and Mensah's conservatory windows concentrated the thin light coming through them, and the warmth made Kodzo feel like he was outside a chop house in Accra. Abena had told them about their trip to Loch Lomond, and they had all remembered going with their children for a picnic decades ago.

'At least now when you go you don't have to fill your car full of nappies,' Mensah laughed. 'Though, to be honest, maybe we don't have long until we need them ourselves.'

'Me?' Maria interjected. 'Never in this life. God forbid.'

'Hmm, we shall see,' Mensah replied. 'So, you are both enjoying your freedom?'

'Oh yeah,' Kodzo replied. 'Although I feel guilty, like I've forgotten to do something.'

'Ei, my brother, guilty for what? The second Mawusi moved out, Maria was already looking at cruises in the Mediterranean.' They all laughed, and Maria shrugged as if to say, 'And so what?'

'Will you move? There are some very nice houses you can buy now, in some residential estates – you don't have to have all the *wahala* of building from scratch,' Maria said.

Abena nodded. 'Abla has even sent me some. But Kodzo still has a while before he can retire. Though maybe we can start going for longer holidays before then.'

'Yeah,' Kodzo agreed, surprised. It seemed Abena had thought about it more than he had, though they hadn't discussed it in any detail. The thought of starting again in Ghana, away from the children, filled him with more unease than excitement: life was easier in Glasgow than in Accra.

'Of course,' Mensah agreed, crunching a handful of crisps. 'Me too, I don't think now I'll move fully to Ghana anyway. After paying tax here for thirty years I want to use the NHS in my old age. The health sector there is just unreliable.'

'As for that one, it's always been the case.' Kodzo shook his head.

'It's a real shame,' Maria said. 'My cousin *ankasa*, she has – *ɛyi*, what's it called?' She clicked her fingers until it came to her. 'MS. Yes, and when I tell you how hard it was to get MRI scan in Cape Coast. We had to take her up and down until we found one private hospital which could do it for her in Accra.'

'Ho . . .' Abena clicked her throat and shook her head in sympathy. 'Such simple things, oh.'

'And to be honest,' Maria continued, 'one thing we don't take seriously at all, at all, is the mental thing, too. Every time I go there are just mad people walking all over the street. It wasn't like that before.'

Kodzo felt his skin prickle.

'The stress over there is just too much for some people. Life can be really hard,' Mensah said.

'Yes, it's stress, but also, sometimes it's some small juju in there too.' Maria laughed and winked.

'That's what people used to say about even malaria,' Abena replied, 'and then we got sewage systems and anti-malarials.' Kodzo was grateful, though he still wasn't sure where to place himself in the conversation.

'I'm serious, oh!' Maria said, though her wide eyes and puckered lips still glinted with humour. 'You can take anti-depressants and anti-psychotics for some of them, of course, but for some you need prayer. The health of Ghanaians is a mess: physical – yes, mental – yes, but spiritual too. People will go to church on Sunday and visit fetish priests on Monday.'

Kodzo agreed that the health of Ghanaians was in crisis, though he thought it was too much, rather than too little, church that was to blame. 'There are some ways to combine healing for the mind, body and soul,' he said, popping peanuts into his mouth as casually as he could. 'Like yoga and meditation, and mindfulness. They're saying now it's the way forward.'

'Ei, no thank you!' Maria laughed. 'All that chanting to their gods – that one is just an Asian juju.'

Kodzo didn't reply, instead taking a sip of beer to wash down the peanut paste that was coating his mouth. He thought about telling Maria and Mensah that he still took tablets for his mood every morning. He wondered what advice he would be given if he told the leaders of their church. The books he read now told him that the world was not made as a test, and that he was allowed to enjoy it here and now. That the rules were few, and simple, and that choosing the right path should feel rewarding rather than punishing. He didn't add anything else, and Abena changed the conversation to something about Ghanaian public transport. They stayed until the sun set. The glass that had trapped the heat before was now too thin to keep it in, and Kodzo had to pull on his jacket to dampen the shiver.

The following Sunday, Kodzo woke before his 7 a.m. alarm. Abena was still asleep, and he went downstairs to put the kettle on. He was grateful for her. He thought about the week before: how she had changed the subject when he'd needed it. How she was always playing on his team, even though there were times, particularly with Elom, that he hadn't initially thought so. He remembered when he had asked her to marry him, and she had told him she would think about it. She hadn't been being coy; she had been deciding whether a life with him would give her what she needed. He had told himself he would make sure it did, and now he wondered if he had actually managed it. Abena had never lingered on it with him, and so he had realised too late how cruel life had been under Aunty Esther's control; by then, they were already embroiled in raising their own family. Life had been hard for her, but she'd worked harder. By the time he had carried the two mugs of milky tea upstairs, Abena was up and in the shower. He slid open the wardrobe while sipping his tea and looked at his Sunday clothes, starchy and pre-ironed. He put his cup down on the dresser and made for the bathroom.

'Abena,' he called, opening the door.

'Yes?' Her response was muffled by the sound of her washing her face.

'Should we skip church today?'

'Why?' She leaned around the curtain, her face shiny and wet but her hair still dry and fluffy. 'Are you feeling okay?'

'Yeah. Do you want to go? Let's go to Troon. Or the cinema or something.' Kodzo tried to keep his voice confident and casual.

'Yeah?' Abena said. 'Are you sure?' Kodzo nodded. 'Why don't you want to go?'

Kodzo wasn't sure. He just knew he wanted to spend the day doing something that made them both happy, and he no longer felt guilty admitting that church was not one of those things. Abena's head disappeared back behind the curtain as she rinsed soap from her face. All Kodzo could say was, 'Let's just do something different.'

Chapter Sixteen

Elom – March 2015

Elom scooped a salad onto his plate. It had a yellowish grain, sultanas, toasted nuts and torn leaves – coriander, or maybe mint. It sat beside three others in a rainbow of vitality, next to some homemade dips and grilled halloumi. Pippy and Freya had moved in with one of Pippy's undergraduate mates, and Elom had joined them for a housewarming dinner. It turned out that Pippy and Freya had mutual friends from growing up in north London, so over the last year and a half, Elom had found himself included in a patchwork of their home crew and their master's coursemates. The ten guests ate buffet style, picking from the bowls on the kitchen counter and small dining table, but sitting in the living room on a sofa and some chairs brought in from bedrooms, as the dinner party aspirations clashed with London rental realities.

'Mmmm, so good. Where did you find the recipe for this one?' Ben asked. Elom was continually surprised by how many ways a salad could be complimented – so far they'd been individually praised for their presentation, colour, smells, crunch and 'mouthfeel'.

'It's a modified Ottolenghi recipe,' Pippy smiled.

'I love Ottolenghi,' Ben said, 'but who has the time or money to find blue carrots grown in an angel's arse.' Everyone laughed. Elom had only met Ben a couple of times, and he admired and envied his easy openness. He always charmed the room, and did it with a smile.

'Ottolenghi is great, but the real secret to any salad is a vegetable, a nut, a fruit and a leaf. All you need is a dressing and then . . .' Ben kissed his fingers, and the others agreed. His fancy-yet-no-frills approach to salads was in keeping with his general vibe. His accent was as posh as the others', but where they carried neat leather satchels, or Fjällräven Kånken, he had a worn black rucksack Elom imagined he used to use for his PE kit at school.

Elom continued his conversation with Freya's friends on either side of him, a management consultant and a TV script editor. Both were frustrated with work for similar reasons – a combination of long hours, uncompromising bosses and difficult clients. Elom wanted to ask how much money they made, but instead asked about their commutes and indulged their laments about entry-level jobs that were more administrative than creative or technical, despite their education.

When they asked what Elom did, he said he was a journalist, like Pippy and Freya. They'd had a similar number of bylines, but Elom had got them whilst working a full-time job, most recently as an editorial assistant for an engineering industry monthly. The others had managed to 'work freelance' whilst living with their parents, before getting full-time journalism jobs and moving here.

The dinner ended with the midnight rush of coat-grabbing and hugging before the last Tube, and Elom left full, smiling and slightly tipsy. Ben had suggested he stay, and offered to share a taxi later. Ben was already jolly and drunk, and his short black hair stuck to his face, wetted by a lick of sweat. Elom considered it, but he lived much further west and couldn't afford the fare. He walked down the flat's shared staircase and was met by the wet pavement of Bethnal Green. Pippy and Freya said they had moved there because it was 'cheap' and 'cool', with 'lots of nice bars and stuff'. Elom went into one of the still-open corner shops with rain-splashed fruit and veg on display, and impulsively bought three plantain for a pound. He carried them in a blue polythene bag on the Tube back to Willesden, where they sat blackening for a week before he fried them.

A few weeks later, Elom arrived at another friend's birthday party. He walked into the kitchen at 10 p.m., sober against the room's loud drunkenness, and was glad to see Ben there. He saw Elom, and immediately left the group he was with, bounding over with a wide smile to pull him into a hug.

'Eloooooom! How are you?'

'Hey man, you good?' Elom spoke to the air behind Ben's shoulder. Ben hadn't shaved in a few days, and when they pulled apart, Elom followed his stubble down the open neck of his shirt, merging with his chest hair.

'Yeah, nice to see you. You want a drink?' He turned to find a cup from the table beside them.

'I've got some, actually.' Elom held up his blue plastic bag full of cans of cider. 'I'll see you in a bit, lemme just stick these in the fridge and head to the loo.' He walked away quickly, putting in three of the cans before stepping into the hallway. He had brushed his teeth just before leaving but his breath had that dry, dehydrated smell he got when he didn't drink enough water. He was still wearing his jacket and had the hot, humid feeling he got from speed-walking from the Tube in the drizzle, and wanted to take it off before he sweated too much in the crowded flat. He could still feel the fuzz of Ben's beard on his cheek, and his heavy, hot hand on his shoulder as they spoke. He left his jacket on the pile of coats in the spare room, then rinsed his mouth with mouthwash in the bathroom, fanning the sweat patch on his back and cursing himself for wearing such a light-coloured shirt.

The music – pop-rock and R'n'B from their schooldays, or more recent alternative electronic music, depending on whose phone was plugged in – was so loud that everyone in the living room had to shout to be heard. When 'In Da Club' came on, Elom remembered every lyric. He wasn't alone, but while the others rapped along with a sense of irony, he remembered the baggy-jeaned Elom of a decade earlier who'd wanted it to be so sincere, and he was happy to have escaped him.

He swung through the night, moving between groups of friends he had been introduced to by Pippy, Freya and their other coursemates. He felt like the outermost node on the chart – he knew many people there, but they all knew each other from past lives, and Elom himself had brought nobody new to the circle. But the more he drank, the less he felt like an outsider, and the more he believed that their questions and laughs were genuine, and that they liked him.

He kept noticing Ben, and wondered if he was queer, but didn't know how to ask. Over the previous year and a half, Elom had moved from cruising the Heath to occasionally going for a public drink with the men he had met online before slinking to a bedroom for a hookup. He didn't have a gay circle and had only gone to a couple of queer nights, where he had been too nervous to try to pull while his friends watched, imagining their shocked or goading faces. He didn't know how to flirt; he wasn't comfortable being seen to flirt.

He watched Ben swim through the room, as agile, speedy and cheeky as a dolphin. Where Elom would slowly edge into, or be accidentally enveloped by a group, Ben would come crashing in, hands on shoulders, offering tequila or compliments. The focus would shift to him, and he wore it well, like a welcome guest rather than an intruder.

They ran into each other by the drinks table, and waiting for the loo, and while Elom's nerves made him compulsively reach for crisps, or sip his drink instead of speaking, Ben found no difficulty in small talk. When Ben joined Elom and Freya on the couch, sitting on the armrest beside him, Elom wanted to rest his arm on Ben's thigh, or for Ben to place his hand on his neck, like a boy and girl were doing on the other side of the living room.

As the door shut behind the last of the Tube travellers at midnight, Ben roamed the living room with a shot glass and a half-full bottle of tequila. The glass was quickly abandoned in favour of waterfalls from a few inches above mouths, or swigs directly from the bottle. He approached Elom, who had finished his ciders and drunk a few glasses of wine from unmanned bottles on the kitchen counter.

'Your turn!' Ben held the bottle above Elom's mouth, expecting him to tip his head back.

'I'm okay, thanks, I need to be up early tomorrow,' Elom replied, already woozy.

'One shot! What time do you need to be up?' Elom didn't have to be up early, he was just more drunk than he would have been if Ben hadn't been there that evening, spurring his body into a constant state of action, and being drunk made him more nervous.

'Open up!' Ben smiled his smile, and Elom relented, choosing to trust him and wanting to please him. The smoky liquid spilled into his mouth and dribbled down his chin. Ben cheered and moved on to the rest of the guests as Elom wiped his face with his sleeve.

Elom and Ben left together at 4.30 a.m. The few people they saw on the street or at bus stops seemed to be heading to work and home in equal numbers. Elom wanted Ben to suggest a cab: if he did, Elom felt like he would have permission to ask to go home with him. But he didn't, and they started walking towards King's Cross. It was the first time they had been alone together. Their arms occasionally bumped into each other, sending jolts into Elom's side. Ben was still talkative, and held the conversation for the short walk. When they arrived, Ben suggested they get a coffee while they waited for the first train. They sat on a bench, facing each other, with one foot on the ground and one leg bent on the seat, so their knees touched.

Ben asked Elom about his family. He ended his questions with a confident silence, and didn't interject until Elom had finished speaking. The space was unnerving at first – with Elom's group of friends, people were always on the alert for a launchpad to their own anecdote, joke or cultural reference. But eventually, Elom found himself filling the space with more of his thoughts, tumbling out half formed, and Ben was listening.

'And are you guys close?' Ben sipped his coffee, and Elom noticed how he first licked, then rolled his lips together, taking in every last drop.

'Yeah. Like . . . I mean, yeah, we don't talk on the phone every day, but we get on. We don't fight and stuff, not anymore at least.' Elom thought Ben seemed like the type of person who would call his sister every day after work, just to check in.

'Are you out to them?'

Elom hesitated at the directness. He still hadn't actually spoken to Ben about his sexuality, and he was unsure who knew other than Pippy and Freya. Despite meeting men on his own, he had been living in an ambiguous space with the wider friendship group. Nobody spoke to him directly about romance and sex, and he alternated between dropping hints and avoiding certain topics of conversation. The smile Ben flashed Elom was different now – knowing, and slightly cheeky.

'No. To be honest, I'm still figuring stuff out and that.' Ben nodded, leaving more silence for Elom to fill, still listening. 'I think, like, I'm happy to talk about my sexuality if it comes up? Maybe I'd talk to them if I had a serious boyfriend.'

'How would they take it?'

Elom gazed across the square. 'I think Dzifa would be fine. My mum and dad, I'm not so sure.' Elom looked at his phone. It was just after six. The sun and the streetlights now both offered the same amount of light.

'God, today is going to be such a write-off,' Ben said, watching commuters trail out of the Tube station and disperse across the plaza.

'What're you gonna do?'

'Probably watch a lot of YouTube and have a few wanks,' Ben laughed, his knee still touching Elom's. Elom didn't move, despite the pain in his hip from the awkward position he was sitting in. He felt the cold on the back of his neck as his sweat dried in the morning air.

'I mean . . .' Elom thumbed the underside of the lid of his coffee cup, feigning nonchalance. He had tried to be bold only once before, and he had regretted it. It had felt dangerous, like running across a motorway. But now he felt like he had a pistol in his hand as the engines revved in front of him, ready to fire the race's starting shot. 'I'm probably gonna do similar. You could just come and do that at mine?'

An hour later they tiptoed into Elom's room. He shut the door and drew the curtains, but the daylight had already crept in. Ben kissed Elom. With girls it had felt mechanical, and with the men from websites and parks, Elom had given tight-lipped pecks, avoiding their searching, darting tongues. This felt different: Ben's lips – still cold from outside – were soft, and his tongue gentle, and Elom opened up. He ran his hands up Ben's back, feeling the cool skin underneath his shirt, pulling him closer, until they broke apart to kick off their shoes and lay side by side on his single bed. When they finished, Elom used his boxers to wipe both loads from his stomach, and they lay down, stuck together by sweat and drying cum. Ben pushed off the duvet as the day grew hotter, and turned to face the wall, while Elom fell asleep with his arms wrapped around someone else for the first time.

Elom spent most of his free time over the following month with Ben, holed up at one or other of their flats. Whole days passed moving between bed and kitchen, learning about each other (he was a secondary school teacher at a massive sixth-form college in Ealing, though the first time he had stepped into a state school, it was the one he had trained in). One weekend when Ben's flatmate was away, he cooked them breakfast, naked apart from his slippers. His easy confidence made Elom want to be near him; to learn what it looked like to move so freely. He pulled open cupboards, dashing ingredients and spices into a creamy sauce, and whisked a pot of hot water before dropping eggs in. He looked like he had done this so many times before – not the recipe, but the scene: cooking for a man he was sleeping with. It seemed the most normal thing in the world to him.

Afterwards, they went back to bed. 'Lie back for a sec . . .' Ben took the lead as usual, tugging off Elom's boxers and taking hold of his cock, already hard. Elom loved the firmness of his grip; how he told Elom what to do, or what he was going to do to Elom. At times Elom felt guilty for being too passive, or not playing the role he had been expected to by the men he had met online, but it was a relief to relax into the care of someone who knew so much.

'I wanna see how many times I can make you shoot.' Ben started sucking, stroking as he did, and it wasn't long before Elom came for the second time that day. Ben joined him at the pillow and they kissed, before Elom loaded his favourite Tiny Desk on his phone. He had been swept up by the heavenly strings and brass of Laura Mvula's 'Sing to the Moon' the first time he had heard it, and every time since. This stripped back concert was more quietly mesmerising. He wasn't a great cook, but he hoped Ben liked this instead. Before the third song, 'She', Ben's hand cupped his crotch, and stroked him hard again. Hand-jobs always left him a little tender – he blamed his circumcision, and wished he still had a foreskin to smooth things over. It was embarrassing and mechanical always to have to interrupt the moment to ask for lube, or a break.

This time though, Elom just chuckled, still watching his phone. 'I don't think I can go again yet.'

'That's not what this is saying.' Ben squeezed slightly, and Elom looked away from the screen to see him smiling back.

'You really want another go, don't you?' Elom asked as surprised as he was flattered.

'Yeah. And I don't think many guys complain about getting too *many* blowjobs.'

'No,' Elom laughed, 'you're right. Elom five years ago wouldn't believe it was possible.'

'So?' Elom nodded his agreement, locking his phone, and Ben went to work, thankfully with his mouth.

After a nap and dinner, Elom loaded up *Human Traffic* on Dimitris's recommendation. Ben had never seen it either, but agreed to watch on the basis of seeing a young Danny Dyer.

They watched side by side in Ben's double bed, moving the laptop between their laps as their joints got sore. Elom alternated between mirth at the perfectly captured drug-fuelled kitchen conversations, and deep awkwardness as Jip struggled to stay hard in bed with Lulu. The film felt like a mirror of his own teenage parties, and he felt the heat creep up on him, like he was back in one of those bedrooms, smothered with anxiety, shame, horniness and intoxication.

Ben pushed the laptop to the side as the end credits rolled. 'That was so good.'

'I know, right?' Elom replied, though he was still calming down from watching some of his biggest fears replayed to him as a big weekender in Cardiff. 'That scene in the house party: the way people chat when you're off your face and everything seems like the best idea ever.'

'And then three hours later you can barely speak and you know for a fact you will never text them about your plan to make an EP together,' Ben finished, and they both laughed.

Elom wondered what else Ben had found relatable. 'And that stuff with Jip and Lulu.'

'Yeah?'

Elom felt his heart thump against his chest. 'Yeah, just, it reminded me of when I was younger.'

'What do you mean?' Ben looked at him, once again leaving so much space that Elom had no option but to fill it.

'Just, there were a few times where I was sleeping with girls and I was a bit drunk, or high or whatever. And it just . . . it wasn't happening, and I'd get really stressed about it.' Elom pulled the duvet up over his belly and crossed his arms, thinking. 'The way they were in his head there, I just remember that feeling so well.'

'I totally get that,' Ben said, getting out of bed to turn the knob on the radiator up. 'I've not had it so much with girls 'cos I didn't really do that, but staying hard can be stressy. I reckon that's a bit of why I got more into bottoming.' Ben sat on the foot of the bed, facing Elom.

'Really?'

Ben thought for a second, biting his lip, then nodded. 'Yeah, I think so.'

'Hm,' Elom replied. He was getting more used to finding the words he wanted to say with Ben, though he now felt on the edge of his ability as his adrenaline rose. 'Yeah. I think it all sort of happened when I was a bit confused about who I was or who I wanted . . . it definitely added to all that confusion.'

'I can imagine.'

Elom nodded, staying silent as he scanned the conversation they had just had. He wanted to make sure he remembered how he had phrased these thoughts that he had never before said out loud. Ben was scrolling on his phone when he looked up and caught Elom's eye.

'Are you okay?' Ben asked.

'Eh, yeah. Just thinking.' Ben kept watching. 'It's just, I've never told anyone that before.'

'Oh, Elom, were you like, proper stressed?' Ben put down his phone.

Elom smiled, trying to lift the tone. 'No, no . . . nah.'

Ben leaned over and kissed Elom's forehead. 'I'm really glad you told me. But, El, not staying hard when you're wasted is not that big a deal.' He laughed, and Elom realised Ben might be right: Ben had gone through similar and seemed completely unfazed by it.

'You don't have to worry about telling me stuff like that, you know.'

Elom put his arms around him and pulled him close. 'Yeah, I know.'

'Do you, though?' Ben pulled back slightly, planting his palm on the bed. 'Let's just be honest with each other. I can be myself around you, I want you to feel the same.'

Elom cleared his throat before answering, 'Yeah. I really do, babe.' And for the first time, with anyone, he did.

Chapter Seventeen

Dzifa – May 2015

Dzifa's neck hurt, and she wondered how she could forget her travel pillow every time she got the train to Glasgow. Courtesy of the train's Wi-Fi, her phone was hot with the guitars, drums and shouts of Arctic Monkeys' *Favourite Worst Nightmare*, plus all the WhatsApping she was doing and the articles she was reading, while her uni revision stayed stowed away underneath the seat in front.

'Old Yellow Bricks' stomped in and Dzifa was suddenly fourteen again, huddled against the rain in the entryway of the science block at break-time with Anna and the rest of their friends. She opened their last WhatsApp chat, surprised to see it had been months since they last spoke.

Hey Anna, I'm back in Glasgow this week, are you around?

Dzifa hadn't planned much for her short time home, and hadn't yet messaged any of her home friends to say she was coming. Part of her was looking forward to being away from the chatter of university students, always so keen to make some kind of noise. Anna replied almost immediately.

YAS! When are you free till? Im about tomorrow, and monday weds and possibly thurs nights. West end drinks?

Aye sure. I'm off to the lake district on thursday for a uni mates birthday thing but free till then. Lets do tomorrow?

'Hey! So good to see you.' Anna threw her arms wide, and Dzifa lunged in for a hug. It had been almost a year since they'd last met, but as ever, she felt so familiar in her dungarees and tortoiseshell glasses.

'You too, it's been ages. Do you want a drink?' Anna shook her head and pointed to her almost full pint, and Dzifa went to the polished copper bar and ordered a lager, returning to sit opposite Anna at a table in a corner booth.

'Here, this place is so nice,' Dzifa said. It was an old stone church with vaulted ceilings, now full of twenty-somethings eating and drinking by candlelight. They clinked their glasses and made a show of staring into each other's eyes as they gulped, both remembering the line about seven years' bad sex.

'Mmm – so,' Anna pursed her lips as she finished the mouthful, 'how's it all going down there?'

'Good. Fifth year now, one more to go.'

'Jesus. It's a slog, isn't it?'

Dzifa laughed. 'This year we have exams every eight weeks.'

'But I saw on Insta you're still doing drama stuff?'

'Yeah. Like, I'll do a play or two a year. It's nice to not think about abdominal pain all the time.'

'I don't know where you find the time to study medicine and still do all that other stuff.'

People often said this to her, as if she was particularly talented or impressive, and she never knew how to take the compliment. 'We'll see how the rest of the exams go – maybe I'll regret learning all those lines instead of any rheumatology.'

The waiter came to take their orders, and both made a show of apologetically reaching for a menu, and asked him to give them five minutes.

'So what's happening with you?' Dzifa asked as she read through the vegetarian options.

'I'm good, actually. Work's all right, feel like I've got a handle on most of the classes. The third years are still wee pricks but I guess we all were at that age.'

'Mate, we were absolutely not.' Dzifa cocked her eyebrow. 'We were fucking angels. My God, we just loved learning.'

'Hahaha. Okay, fair, *we* weren't. But did we love English or just love Mr Buchanan?'

'I still would.' Dzifa smiled and sipped her beer, feeling the comfort of easy conversation. 'Have you heard much from the others?' Dzifa hadn't been good at keeping in touch since she'd left for university, and she always felt guilty, like she had abandoned her friends, or been distracted by newer, shinier ones.

'We were all together for Jess's birthday last month. Aiden and his fiancée Sarah are moving in with each other. Jess is working a lot but hoping to go travelling again next summer. Eh . . . Mhari's doing a master's now, so back in with family to save money. They all miss you and send their best, it's just a bit rubbish they weren't all around tonight.'

Dzifa felt a pang of jealousy, or perhaps of rejection. She often wondered how much time they spent together without her, but it was an impotent fear, since it was also her fault for not being present.

The waiter came by again and took their orders, and they had both finished another drink by the time the food arrived. Dzifa leaned over to take a chip from Anna, who then plunged a fork into Dzifa's mac and cheese.

'So this school's in the southside, right? But you were working west before, or did I make that up?' Dzifa feared it was a detail she should have remembered, but the laughs and alcohol had relaxed her.

'Yeah, I was west for a while, but had a bit of a mare at my last school.'

'What do you mean?' Dzifa asked, biting into a slice of cucumber.

'Did I not tell you?' Anna asked, and again, Dzifa worried she had forgotten something. 'I was just out of training and the school had shitty management. People kept leaving, so I was like, teaching English, my supervisor was barely around, and I was also supposed to cover a few history classes and they wanted me to be a form tutor.'

'That's a lot. Were you okay?'

'Yeah, it was just so busy. And eventually my anxiety just took on a life of its own. I basically got signed off a few weeks before the summer holidays.'

'Oh man, I'm really sorry.'

'It's fine, like I had a good summer break and got my head right. Sertraline's good stuff, man. And eventually got some CBT.'

Dzifa nodded, and asked what she thought were the right questions. She was sorry that her friend had suffered, but happy that she seemed to be past it. She also felt more guilty that she hadn't texted, or called, while this was happening. The others must have known, and she wondered how they had helped, and whether they had chosen not to tell Dzifa, or if they hadn't even thought to.

Dzifa was drunk when they hugged each other goodbye later on Hyndland Road. 'Please just message me if you ever need to.'

'Aww, thanks,' Anna replied. Dzifa felt like she was playing catch-up with the friendship, but Anna looked genuinely touched, which surprised her.

'Honestly. And I'm sorry I haven't been around more – I'll let you know next time I'm coming up and we can plan something.'

'Och, don't worry about it, you've been busy. But please do let me know – we should go up to Loch Lomond, or Arran or something.' They hugged again, and Dzifa felt warmed and confused by Anna's sincerity as she walked to the bus stop. Dzifa didn't feel like a good friend, and she wondered if Anna had actually felt supported by her.

She got on the bus and pressed play on *Oumou* by Oumou Sangaré as she sat down under the bright fluorescent lights. The unison calls of the women's chorus cut through her drunkenness, at once shrill and comforting, and Dzifa hummed along as the bus rolled through the night.

Dzifa left for Clem's birthday at her family's holiday home in the Lake District a couple of days later. She got the train to Oxenholme and watched as the landscape opened up into a rolling expanse, like an enormous green playground parachute. Two of Clem's friends from home, Frankie and Phil, picked her up at the station on their way from London, and drove them down country roads until they arrived at an old stone building, set off the road and surrounded by fields. For five years, Clem had described it as 'a little cottage thing' but it looked more like a manor house to Dzifa.

As they added their bits of the food shop to the bags on the hardwood table in the kitchen, Dzifa heard Clem tumble down the stairs.

'Hey!' She wrapped her arms around Dzifa, Frankie and Phil in turn. 'So good to see you. How was the drive?' She walked them through to the living room. The ceilings were low and cosy, and everything looked like it had been there since the seventies – thin rugs, mismatched chairs, black-and-white lino in the kitchen, and books and board games behind the glass in the sideboard which looked like they hadn't been touched in decades.

'This is so cute,' Dzifa said, sitting down on a weathered armchair. 'Do you come a lot?'

'We used to loads when I was younger, but now I'm just up once a year. Pick a room to dump your stuff upstairs, I'll make some tea and we can go for a quick walk before dinner?'

Dzifa left her bag on the last empty bed in a room of two singles and a double, and quickly changed into her walking gear. Other friends emerged from bathrooms, bedrooms and the drawing room, and when they set off there were thirteen of them in total. Most of them were Clem's friends from home, most of whom had also gone to Oxford. Dzifa counted two others including herself who were friends she had only met at university, and then there were a few partners.

Clem pointed out through the drizzle the field where she picked magic mushrooms with her cousins. Dzifa caught up with university friends who had moved to London while she was finishing clinical school, and by the time they got back to the house she had a warm, excited feeling from hearing about their joys and dramas, and sharing her own.

They had all volunteered to help with a meal, and Dzifa's was tomorrow, so she went upstairs to shower before dinner and to mentally prepare for what would be a loud and boozy night. She moisturised and changed into a comfortable shirt before heading downstairs to set the table.

'Nice shirt, Dzifa,' Sonali, one of Clem's home friends who had been at uni with them, said as they laid down cutlery.

'Thanks, it's my dad's. From the eighties, I think?' It was a piece of multicoloured, baggy polyester she had rummaged from Kodzo's wardrobe.

'It looks great on you. But everything looks great on you, doesn't it?' Sonali playfully rolled her eyes.

'Literally!' Clem called over her shoulder from the stove, where she was stirring an enormous pot of pesto pasta. 'I used to think she was a fashion icon until I realised she literally throws on whatever she finds in her wardrobe ten minutes before leaving and it's always just fucking impeccable. Horrid behaviour.' Dzifa laughed and continued to set the table, again unsure what the expected response to the compliment was supposed to be.

Dinner was warm and jovial. Dzifa felt the push and pull of multiple conversations moving between the serious and the silly among friends. Afterwards they played games – chaotic Murder in the Dark, then a quiz written by Loz, one of Clem's schoolfriends. Most of them were still in the living room after 1 a.m., drinking warm wine in front of the fire.

'Okay, so what animal am I?' Clem asked. They had agreed Loz was a bear cub, Phil an otter, and Frankie a panda.

'You're, like . . . a gazelle maybe? Or a doe. I don't know – something graceful but, like, also a bit of a lad,' Frankie replied.

Clem laughed. 'Okay, a laddy doe . . . so . . . like a stag, then?'

'Yes,' Loz agreed, 'a stag. Who said the animals have to be gender-conforming?'

'Sweet, I'll take a stag.'

'I see it,' Dzifa said, sipping her wine and leaning back on the rug.

'What are you then?' Clem asked. Dzifa's skin prickled in the silence that followed, which seemed to last marginally longer than it had for the others.

'Hmm,' Loz said.

'A seahorse!' said Sonali from the couch.

'Ohh . . .' Clem replied, nodding.

'A seahorse?' Dzifa leaned forward, remembering just in time to feign the 'mock' part of her outrage.

'Yeah, like . . .' Sonali looked as though she was trying to pick her words carefully. 'Elegant. Good posture. Social, but kind of elusive? I dunno. Ultimately unknowable.'

Dzifa laughed. 'Oh my God, that's so deep.'

'Okay, unknowable is strong. Enigmatic! You're not like a puppy, craving attention like Loz.' Sonali giggled.

'Bear cub.' Loz acted as the stern teacher. 'But the point still stands.'

'Can I suggest that I can have those traits as a normal horse, running in fields, and not a seahorse in the depths of the ocean, or a six-year-old's tank?' Dzifa asked, still reining in her indignation.

'That's way better. Regal, thoroughbred horse vibes,' Clem said, nodding seriously. 'I see it.'

Dzifa smiled. 'Never actually been horse riding though – they kinda scare me.'

The conversation moved on until Frankie looked at Phil and suggested they head to bed loud enough for the rest of the group to answer that they would too. Dzifa picked up some wine glasses and set them in the kitchen while the others took some plates. They put out the fire, then she made her way upstairs, brushed her teeth, and eventually fell asleep.

Dzifa woke earlier than the others in her room – Clem, Sonali and another of Clem's friends from school – and went downstairs to make a coffee. She sat on a window seat in a small lounge downstairs with *So Long a Letter* by Mariama Bâ. The fields were wet, calm, still, but breathing. She enjoyed the tranquillity, and as she thought back to the previous night, she saw the irony. It was hard to be annoyed at the choice – a fucking seahorse – when the very next morning she was sitting downstairs, alone, hoping the others would stay asleep for a little longer. It wasn't that she didn't like people. There was just an 'on-ness' to these sorts of trips – a constant excitement and talkativeness – which she needed to balance. Sometimes she wondered if the others' exuberance was a little fake, but it was more that she had to mine the energy from somewhere, whereas for them it simply poured out, thick and shiny, by the barrel.

After breakfast they walked to a lake through a valley and over two small hills. They ate pitta breads filled with grated cheese and Branston pickle at the top of the second one. Dzifa loved the feeling of sweat under her jumper, the way no one washed their hands after a wee behind a tree. She loved how, even for her, conversation seemed to flow for the hours of a walk in the country, but how easy it was to slow down, or speed up, and walk by herself in silence for half an hour. She wanted to take her family hillwalking. She wished it hadn't taken a degree at a fancy university to feel at home in the countryside.

She walked alongside Clem, Sonali and Phil on the final stretch to the lake. Her shoes fell heavily on the rocks underfoot and they paused between sentences to crouch and lean a hand against an outcrop as they jumped down the bigger steps. The others were talking about a mutual friend's wedding.

'I love how close you guys are with your mates from school,' Dzifa said. She had an impulse to be more open – a little less unknowable – though she wasn't sure how deeply to lean into it.

'What do you mean?' Sonali asked.

'You're all so in touch, you can just tell you get each other.'

'I do love our crew. We don't see each other as much as we used to, though,' Phil said.

'How often do you?' There was an insecurity in Dzifa's question that she tried to hide – she knew that whatever the answer, it would be more than she saw Anna and her friends from home, and would probably be more than she saw Clem and her friends from university, too.

'Like . . .' Clem answered as she peeled apart a grass stalk, 'I guess now a lot of us are back in London, I see a couple of people every week or so . . . and then there's an actual big meet-up every couple of months? Not that often, to be honest.'

'It's nice, though. I think I have lots of different friends from home, or my course, or drama stuff, but not one set group,' Dzifa said.

'Yeah, that's your fault for being so talented,' Sonali laughed. 'Everyone wanted to be your mate in college, and you were always dotting about with your fingers in so many pies. I was just hanging about with these losers.'

'Yeah, I suppose.' Dzifa hopped down a ledge. 'You ever heard that song "Everybody's Free to Wear Sunscreen"? Baz Luhrmann.'

'Is that the nineties old man talk-rapping one?' Clem asked.

'It's like, an essay put to music. This woman Mary Schmich actually wrote the article, then it got made into a song. There's this line in it, something about working to keep in touch with old friends because when you get older, you need people around you who remember what you were like when you were young.'

'It's nice for sure to have history,' Clem said. 'But do you think you're super different now to how you were when you were at school?'

Dzifa thought about how she had looked in three cupboards for the cafetiere that morning, and the Waitrose date and Stilton wafers she had munched through whilst playing cards. She thought, too, about sharing bottles of Lambrini with Anna at dingy house parties and playing PlayStation with Elom. 'A bit, yeah. And it's not just the past. Think how much we got to know each other getting pissed on a Thursday night at uni. You can't do that with colleagues you meet in your thirties, can you?'

'Wait till you have your first work Christmas party, it's tragic,' Sonali said as the land levelled out and they approached the shore of the lake.

'So, who knows you from when you were really young?' Clem asked, turning to Dzifa.

Dzifa thought for a moment. 'I guess Elom? My brother.' She paused. 'Him, and a few friends from school I'm still in touch with.'

'And how often do you see them?' Clem asked. They were almost with the others, who had started to take off their boots and jackets.

'Not enough.' She thought of Anna, who had already sent her a text with an article she hadn't read yet. And Elom, who was living a life in London she knew almost nothing about. She didn't know what held her back from making the time, which other people seemed so capable of doing.

'Okay, bums out and line up!' Loz's call interrupted Dzifa's thoughts as he became circus master. Everyone stripped – some kept their bras and pants, some their boxers, but they were mostly nude. On Loz's shout, they sprinted forward, and Dzifa's laughs and shrieks caught up with the others' before their bodies dived into the cool water. She looked around as she walked back to the shore naked and refreshed. She felt connected, and free, and joyful, surrounded by friends, and like a version of Dzifa she wanted to keep.

* * *

Dzifa next saw Clem a few months later – Clem had a spare ticket to a play at the Globe, and Dzifa skipped classes to get the bus into London to stay with her for the night. She had missed a couple of other meet-ups in London because of uni work, but she was glad she could squeeze this in. They met early and snuck their overpriced gin and tonics from the venue bar to the riverside to drink in the golden-hour light.

'Have you been before?' Clem asked, pressing herself into the wall so a cyclist could roll past.

'No – I can't wait. Though not looking forward to three hours of standing.'

'It flies by. Anyway, the seats are just wood, and I'd rather have my feet hurt than my arse hurt.' Clem gave Dzifa a look and Dzifa snorted, choking on her drink.

They caught up on the previous few months. As Clem updated her on the others, Dzifa felt the same sad mix of jealousy and rejection she'd felt with Anna, but this time she was embarrassed. She remembered the commitment she'd felt the last time they were together, but she must have lost it on the train to Oxford, or unpacking at home, or forced it out of her brain with revision. Her desire to be included was sincere, even a little bit desperate, but she didn't know why she failed to follow through.

Macbeth was surprisingly funny; the actors occasionally moved through the crowd and they both agreed standing was better than sitting. They walked along the river afterwards, laughing about the Lake District.

'Loz must have spent days on that quiz, right? Just finding those photos is hours of Facebook deep diving,' Dzifa said.

'Dedication. Our little bear cub, hunting for the honey.'

'Oh my God, yeah. Thanks. And I'm a bloody seahorse.' Dzifa said it casually, with a mock outrage she felt was more honest now there had been some distance.

Clem rolled her eyes. 'Nah, you got horse, that's legit.'

They shared Clem's double bed in her flat in Clapton. Dzifa remembered doing the same many times at university, and she felt the need to apologise. 'Sorry I've been shit at replying to messages. I'm glad I came through tonight. I'll make sure I come down next month, we can check out the open mic in Peckham.'

'Yeah, babes, just give me a date,' Clem said, plugging in her phone.

'I'll have a look tomorrow and let you know.'

'You're going to disappear off the face of WhatsApp for weeks as soon as you get home,' Clem laughed.

'No, I won't!' Dzifa was stung, but felt justified in her determination.

'Dzifa, I love you, but you just have so much initial charisma, and so little follow-through.'

'What does that mean?' Dzifa asked, but she knew exactly what Clem meant, and hearing the thought that had been bubbling in her head put into words chilled her.

'Everyone loves you, literally everyone. But then you're just shit at texting back,' she ribbed. Then Dzifa thought she sounded more serious, though Clem's smile barely changed: 'Or like, just making time.'

'I'll do better, I promise.' She tried to keep her tone light-hearted, and didn't make excuses about exams, or plays, because they both knew she had always been like that, regardless of how busy she might have been.

'Okay, mate, I'm looking forward to hearing the dates for the open mic,' Clem said, still smiling. She turned the lights out and they got comfortable under the feather duvet. Dzifa felt exposed, like she'd walked in on someone reading her diary. The phrase 'initial charisma' sank deeper into her chest and scraped at the core of something.

Dzifa knew that people had always liked her. Accepting it had felt conceited, but when she saw people who stood at the edge of things – the ones who nobody texted to double-check they'd still make the party – it felt dishonest to pretend otherwise. She wondered if it had made her shallow; if she had just never learned how to be a good friend because she could get away with it. And that now, underneath her charisma – whatever hand of personality, looks or intelligence she had been dealt – there was heartlessness. Anyone could imagine someone being less beautiful underneath their makeup, or less smart behind an inflated vocabulary. She feared that her fraud was more vulgar, or more ruthless: that she insinuated compassion when there was only indifference. That she only loved in theory, and not in practice.

Chapter Eighteen

Elom – August 2015

Elom and Ben met in secret for a couple of months before relaxing enough to leave the pub together when meeting friends. Eventually Pippy asked Elom at brunch, 'What's happening with you and Ben, then?'

Elom shrugged and smiled. 'We've been hanging out since Raj's birthday. We went back to mine after.'

'Oh my God, I love it!' She tipped her head back and laughed. 'Is it like, a *thing*?'

'I dunno, just casual at the moment.' Elom didn't say that Ben was always on his mind, or that he still felt static electricity in his chest when Ben was near, or that he got a hard-on every time Ben texted asking him to come round.

'So who came on to who?'

'Eh . . .' It was new to Elom, being the one to share the exploits. He had always thought of himself as a private person, but now he considered how much of it was because he hadn't been ready to share anything before. 'I guess both of us? But I

definitely asked him to come round – that was me.' It felt good
to be the one telling his story.

'And so have you just been hooking up ever since?'

'Yeah.' Elom smiled. 'Honestly, it's pretty hot. Like . . . the
sex is really good.'

They both laughed. 'Oh good, Elom. I'm happy for you.'

'Thanks.'

A couple of weeks later, Elom and Ben went to Soho on their
first date. Elom had gained a new feeling of normality around
Ben. He felt like he was a regular person: someone who was
liked, and who had interesting thoughts. Ben held Elom's hand
as they walked towards the restaurant, slightly ungainly as
a pair, forcing others to move around them. Elom liked how
Ben focused on him, unconcerned by the eyes of others, and
uninterested in making himself or his voice smaller. His self-
assurance was enthralling.

Following their chat after *Human Traffic*, Elom felt like they
were on a mission to share themselves. Elom was ready to put
the things he was scared of into words, and each time he did,
he was a little more reassured by Ben's response. At dinner, Ben
ordered a whole roasted garlic bulb – somehow a standalone
starter – and asked Elom when he planned to come out to his
parents.

'I'm not sure. I still need a reason, I guess.'

'What kind of reason?'

'I mean, the obvious one would be a relationship.' Elom
smiled awkwardly.

'Interesting, that.' Ben smiled back playfully.

Elom took a bite of oil-soaked bread before responding, 'Obviously I'd like to tell them about you. I think you're *just* enough of a reason,' Ben made a face of mock offence, 'but it's hard not really knowing how they'll take it.'

'Yeah, I guess it's difficult coming from your background.' Elom appreciated the consolation whilst being slightly irked by the implied assumption. 'Are they really religious?'

'Kinda. We've never really talked about it, so I don't really know what they think, to be honest. They grew up in Ghana and went to church, though they don't go so much these days. They sent me to a Christian camp once.'

'What, like a conversion thing?' Ben looked alarmed.

'No,' Elom answered hastily – he felt the need to defend his parents, like he had exposed them to an unfair attack. 'No, not at all. It was just a week away with the church.' He didn't add that he had been terrified that they knew something, and wanted to fix him. That night he had run to his friends; they were smoking, there were girls, and Elom's fear only rose, and he had left immediately. He'd cried on his walk home: it was the loneliest he had ever felt. His parents had mistaken the cause of his red eyes, but he couldn't tell them the truth. He couldn't control his feelings either, and they had erupted onto a mirror.

Ben nodded. 'It sounds tough. I support you whatever you decide, but I think you should just tell them.'

'What do you mean?'

'You should push back. There's no ambiguity here: you're right, and if they have a problem with it, they're wrong.'

Elom pursed his lips and turned his head to the side as if to say, 'Yeah, but . . .'

'Obviously they love you and they're good parents, so you just have to let them know that if they want you in their life, they'll have to put in the work to come round.'

Elom felt like it should make sense. He aspired to the confidence that came with moral certainty, and wanted to engage with his parents as equals, but he still felt a duty to them.

'It's different with African parents. I don't know how to explain it, but it's not as simple as saying, "Accept me or I'm out." My parents have done a lot for me.' Elom thought about Kodzo and Abena, bleary-eyed after night shifts, and him and Dzifa watching TV with subtitles on so as not to wake them. 'Keeping this from them, or at least not throwing it in their faces, is the least I can do.'

'Like I say, I obviously support you . . . I just think they're adults, and you are too. You should treat each other like adults, you know?'

'I get you. But they're still my parents . . . That doesn't change because I'm grown up.'

Ben smiled and held his calves on either side of Elom's under the table. It was gentle and reassuring, and Elom felt like he did understand.

'What was it like for you?' Elom asked.

'It was a while ago. It's fine.' Ben smeared some goat's cheese onto a cracker. Elom left space for him to fill, but he stayed quiet. Elom wanted to ask more. It was unusual for Ben not to tell a story, and he thought it may be one he wasn't yet ready to share. He knew that Ben and his parents were close – they spoke on the phone more often than Elom and his parents, even though they only lived an hour away. If Ben had successfully brought his family round, Elom thought maybe he could too.

'Maybe you're right.' He refilled their wine glasses, and they cleaned their plates before heading out to dance.

The next few times they spoke, Elom toyed with the idea of telling his parents. The chats were semi-scheduled, instigated by Dzifa, who said they ought to keep in touch more regularly. On a call in early November, Abena asked when they would be up over the holidays. Dzifa said she would be there for most of December, prepping for finals, which delighted their parents. Ben had invited Elom to his yearly New Year's Eve countryside getaway with friends. He wanted to go, but if he went, it would be the first time he didn't bring in the bells with family.

Dzifa left the call after she had given her dates as she was late for dinner. There were overlapping 'Bye's as her square blooped away, and then silence as the screen rearranged itself from a three-way to a two-way split. Elom saw mostly wall, straddled by the right side of Kodzo's head, and the left side of Abena's.

'So when are you coming, Elom?' Kodzo asked.

'I'm off from the twenty-third.'

'You should book your train soon otherwise it will be really expensive,' Kodzo advised.

'Yeah, I will.' Elom always booked at the very last minute. 'Ehm, I was thinking though, I might come up for the week over Christmas, then come back down here for New Year's.'

'Oh, okay,' Kodzo said. Elom still couldn't see most of his face, and thought he sounded more confused than disappointed.

'Are you working?' Abena asked.

'No.' Elom tried to remind himself that it wasn't that big a deal: he hadn't changed as a person, and all that was different was that there was someone special in his life he wanted to share with his parents. He decided to focus the conversation on that. 'It's just that a few friends – and my boyfriend, actually – are having a weekend away thing, and I thought I might join them for New Year.' The words came quickly and quietly, and were followed by silence. He saw Abena's head turn towards Kodzo and back, still never fully entering the frame. He couldn't tell what they were thinking, but asking them to show their faces fully now felt like an escalation of something he hoped could remain casual.

'What boyfriend? Did you mean girlfriend?' Abena eventually asked. There was a nervous edge to her voice, like she was speaking to a wild animal, or a man with a weapon, rather than her son.

'No, eh . . . I mean my boyfriend. Ben.' Elom smiled weakly at the screen.

'Okay,' Kodzo said. Abena remained quiet. 'So, are you . . . gay, or . . . ?' Kodzo asked, almost casually.

'I dunno, maybe. I don't know if it really matters. Maybe, yeah.'

'What do you mean you don't know? Is everything okay?' Abena asked.

'Yes,' Elom replied. The conversation already felt too messy, and he wanted to close any doors to more confusion. 'Yeah, I'm gay.' Abena nodded.

'Well, okay,' Kodzo said again. 'Okay. If you want to go away for New Year's, that's fine. We can have Christmas together.'

Elom didn't know what he wanted, but he knew it wasn't going back to making Christmas plans. 'Are you guys okay?'

'Yes,' Kodzo answered. 'We'll figure it out.' He spoke like he had been told that his car had failed its MOT. Elom was unsurprised by the implication that his sexuality was a problem to be fixed, but he was also irked by the seemingly minor magnitude of it, like it was just an inconvenience.

'What do you mean, "figure it out"?' Fear, confusion, anger and love jostled one another in his mind. The last time his sexuality had been this close to his parents' knowledge, when Kodzo had just told him he would be sent away to church camp, he'd been terrified and angry. He was older now, reassured by his move, and his friends, but anger still slipped out – less because he really felt annoyed, and more because confrontation was a tangible thread to pull him out of the haze he was in. 'I can't really see you – can you move the camera or something?'

'It's just a bit of a shock.' The onscreen world tumbled around as Abena moved the laptop. 'We had no idea.' Guilt was added to his flurry of emotions as Elom saw from Abena's face that she actually was shocked. He had always thought that they must have known, somehow.

'You're still our son,' Abena said. 'Of course we love you.' Her words clashed with the stunned look in her eyes.

'Thanks,' Elom said. 'I love you too.' There was a brief pause. 'I'm gonna go, I've got an article to finish.'

'Good luck,' Kodzo said, his face inscrutable. 'Let's not tell Dzifa for now, okay?'

'Why?' Elom asked, the annoyance returning.

'She's busy with her exams and everything. She doesn't need to know yet.'

'Fine.' Elom chose not to argue. 'Talk soon. I'll let you know when I book my tickets. Bye.' Elom hit the red button. Even though he had worked endlessly over the last decade to keep his sexuality from them, he still felt wounded that they hadn't realised. It was as if they hadn't been looking closely enough. In a way, their surprise seemed more hurtful than anything else. Elom closed the laptop and ran the conversation over in his head, parsing it for a feeling other than disappointment. He didn't move from his bed until Dimitris called him down for dinner.

Ben comforted Elom the next day as they walked around Regent's Park, though Elom's overwhelming feeling now was relief: he had finally said it, and he was still a part of the family.

'They were proper shocked. Of all the reactions, that wasn't one I expected.'

'They say a mother always knows, but I guess not,' Ben laughed. Elom shrugged and sipped his already cold coffee. 'Well done though, it's not easy.'

'Thanks. And credit to them, compared to how they grew up, they've come a long way.'

Ben nodded. 'How do you feel about Christmas with them? And with Dzifa not knowing?'

'I don't know, man. It's obviously a lot for them to deal with. Maybe I don't tell her. But that just feels so weird. She has gay friends, she won't care.'

'I think it's kind of fucked, to be honest.'

'They think it's gonna turn her world upside down before her exams. It makes it sound like I've got cancer.' They walked in silence as a drizzle fell. A couple drifted past on a pedalo, cutting a trail through the algae-covered lake.

'You could maybe just come to ours for Christmas.' Ben looked at Elom and nodded with his eyebrows scrunched, as if he was only just considering the suggestion. 'It could be really nice. My parents would like to meet you.'

'Have you told them about me?'

'I mentioned I was seeing someone.' Ben shrugged, coyly.

Elom smiled. 'Thanks for the offer.' He put his arm around Ben's waist. 'I've never spent Christmas without my family. I dunno, maybe that would be stranger – just not going.'

'Have a think. It would be nice to have you at home over the holidays. My flatmate's away for ages too, so you could stay at mine for a bit, and we could be as loud as we want.' Elom laughed and pulled him closer, kissing his cheek as the rain started falling in earnest.

No one mentioned their conversation again, and it was clear Dzifa hadn't been told. On a call a couple of weeks later, when Elom mentioned that he wouldn't be around for New Year's, she was disappointed, but said she hoped his weekend away would be fun. After the call, he immediately messaged her.

Heyyyy. Just wanted to let you know, part of the reason I'm not doing new years in glasgow is cos im spending it with my boyfriend. I told mum and dad a few weeks ago and they're okay but I think a bit freaked out. They said not to mention but I wanted to tell you.

He stared at the phone for a few minutes until the header burst from 'Online' to 'Typing . . .'

Yooo! Thats huge. Whats his name? Happy for u big bro. She added a yellow face with a party blower, and Elom exhaled the breath he hadn't realised he'd been holding.

Thanks!! His name is Ben, he's really nice. Looking forward to you meeting him maybe.

Yes please. Is he in London? Tbh I had some thoughts but wasn't sure. Annoyingly cant talk now but I can call later?

Of course. Thanks thanks thanks.

<3<3

When they spoke the next day, Dzifa treated the news like gossip. It felt light and scandalous, and Elom regretted not telling her sooner. He mentioned that Ben had invited him to Christmas in Surrey, and she asked him if he wanted to go.

'It would be nice. Though I do just want to be at home with you guys, eating kenkey on Boxing Day.'

Dzifa laughed. 'Christmas in Surrey will be carol services in some village church and an absolutely baltic walk on Christmas morning. I know so many of those people.' Elom chuckled, happy that they understood each other. 'Just come home. It's a lot for Mum and Dad to take on but they just need time.'

Elom texted his parents a few days later: *Hey mum and dad, I know we havent talked about what I said. If you have any questions, I'd like to talk to you about it.* They didn't respond, and a couple of days later he sent an article about queer Black families. Kodzo responded, *Thanks, will read.* Another couple of Skypes passed with conspicuous silence. Dzifa didn't bring anything up either. Elom hadn't told his parents that she knew, and he wasn't sure if he wanted to anymore. They were acting as if nothing had happened, and it left him yearning. He had been striving to learn how to open up, but their silence was shutting him down.

'Maybe they need space, yes, but maybe you need space too,' Ben told him as they walked home after a night in Camden.

'What do you mean?'

'You've told them this thing and asked them to be there for you, and they haven't been.'

Elom spoke with his mouth full of doner meat and chips: 'They haven't, like, *not* been there, they've just not been there, I guess.'

'Yeah, well maybe if you're not there they can properly think about making an effort.'

'Hmm.' Elom considered this.

'Also, I mentioned Christmas to my parents and my mum's absolutely gagging to meet you.'

'Really? And your dad?'

'Of course. Though he might be disappointed if you tell him your opinion on *The Times*.'

Elom smiled. It was an enticing prospect, being welcomed into Ben's picture-perfect holiday. The thought of home was looking increasingly tense, and besides, it would be an excuse not to see Chris and the others, who had texted asking if he was around.

'Obviously I have an ulterior motive.' Ben grinned suggestively, breaking the tension. 'I'm still thinking about sucking you off in my childhood bed.'

Elom choked on his kebab. 'Fuck's sake. Terrible.'

*   *   *

Elom lay in bed after Ben fell asleep. Once he could no longer ignore his bladder, he sat on the loo and drafted a text to Kodzo and Abena.

Hey, nice talking the other day. I know its short notice but I think I might stay in england for Christmas this year with Ben. I was really looking forward to seeing you an dstill hoping to see you early next year or maybe Easter, but maybe its all a bit complicated now and we need to figure things out. Love you both.

In the morning he re-read it, corrected the typos and hit send. They asked him if he was sure, and said they were hoping to see him. When he said he was, they jovially wished him a good time, as if he was going on a weekend away to Mallorca. When they next spoke on the phone, Abena asked what address they should send his presents to. Nobody mentioned Elom's relationship, or named Ben, or alluded to his sexuality. Elom felt like he had come out of the closet only to find that he was invisible. He wished he had the words to make his parents see him, but since those were lacking, he chose to side with someone who did.

On the twenty-third of December, Elom got on a train with Ben to a commuter town south-west of London, and met Ben's parents for the first time on the salt-gritted paving stones of the station entrance. Their winter jackets were so well fitting they looked tailored. Agneta linked arms with him as they walked to the car. John lifted his bag into the boot and joked about how lightly he had packed. In the evening they ate homemade mince pies and drank 'proper mulled wine', bobbing with cinnamon sticks and pulpy orange. John asked Elom if he knew the harmonies to any carols and he shook his head, realising that he wasn't supposed to improvise any old lines when they handed him a hymn book with written-out parts, while Ben played the piano from memory. Ben and Elom climbed into bed after midnight – it felt immodest to Elom, sleeping with his boyfriend with his parents metres away – but also freeing.

'I'm glad you could make it.' Ben kissed his lips, cheek and neck as he moved to rest his head on Elom's chest. 'They like you already.'

Elom smiled. 'Really?'

'Yeah, you're so charming.'

'I'm glad I could make it too.' He squeezed Ben closer and they kissed, deeper, before Ben turned round to be little spoon and tucked his feet between Elom's legs. Elom closed his eyes and thought of home: Dzifa and Kodzo watching a film, wrapped in the fluffy blue blanket they had had since they were kids, while Abena slept on the couch. He wanted to be there, but also, he wanted to be here. Importantly, he was wanted here.

Chapter Nineteen

Abena – December 2015

Abena watched with a glass of wine in one hand and a Stilton-loaded cracker in the other as a man played the pipes on BBC Scotland.

'Ten!' the voiceover began. Scottish landmarks – mostly bridges – flashed by with each second, and Abena joined in the chant with Dzifa and Kodzo.

' . . . two . . . one . . . Happy New Year!' They clinked and hugged as fireworks erupted onscreen. Abena's phone vibrated on the coffee table, followed by Kodzo's which was charging on the couch. Dzifa had hers in her hand, and quickly accepted the call.

'Hey, bro!'

'Happy New Year!' Elom called out. He looked happy, and maybe a little drunk. Abena could only see his head floating on the deep red wallpaper behind him. The room was quiet, and she wondered who he had left to make the call. She was glad he had phoned, and so soon after midnight – it seemed they were still on his mind. 'You guys having a good night?'

'All good, son. Did you see *Still Game?*' Kodzo asked.

'They don't have it here! We just had dinner and played charades, it was fun.'

'Aww. We miss you. I'm glad you're having a good time, though,' Dzifa said. Elom smiled, and Abena could see that he was happy, and despite the circumstances, that made her happy too.

'Are you guys going to Muhammad's?' Elom asked. Muhammad was one of the first wave of Ghanaians in Glasgow, and every year they went to his party to see the growing fold, after bringing in the bells together as a family.

'Yeah, we're leaving soon,' Kodzo replied.

'Give him my best and send pictures please!'

'We will, son,' Abena said. She wanted to ask him to send pictures too, but she also didn't want to see the home and the family he was with. It was an odd jealousy, like meeting your ex's new partner.

'Okay, I should get back, but I'll talk to you soon.'

Kodzo suggested they drive over to the party, and they headed to the car. He had been calm these last few weeks. He felt clarity would come with time, and that they needed just to take each day as it came. Abena followed his advice, but the questions bubbled in her stomach. She had been getting heartburn in the last few weeks, and she placed a hand under her ribs now as a wave of pain arrived. She grimaced, crunching an antacid from her purse as they drove down country lanes, annoyed at herself for eating all that cheese.

She still didn't know how to deal with Elom's news. She missed him – Christmas dinner had been lopsided with just the three of them. She was uncomfortable with him spending Christmas

with people she didn't know, and with the realisation that a
world of unknowns had opened up between her and her son. It
felt like he was blaming her; or punishing her with his absence.
She didn't know why he was distancing himself when they had
tried their hardest not to overreact. She wanted to ask him how
long this had been going on – if it was a new confusion or an old
one; if it was something she could have foreseen, or prevented;
if he was safe. But Elom was already pushing them away, despite
their attempt at calm. She worried how much further (and how
much more permanently) he would push if she stepped out of
bounds. She hoped time would be enough to fix things.

The frost on the leaves and the grass of Muhammad's driveway
glittered like crushed diamonds. The fizz of steps on the
gravel met the bassy thud of music from the house, and eager
anticipation was added to the mix of emotions Abena felt: she
loved Muhammad's New Year's parties. She opened the front
door – nobody would hear the doorbell now – to a glut of light
and noise. Friends were shouting, laughing, drinking from
plastic cups and eating from paper plates. Kodzo and Dzifa
followed her inside and they shared a look which seemed to say,
'It's good to be back.'

'You are welcome! You are welcome!' Muhammad called
out to them as they entered the kitchen. Abena put her
contribution of chicken thighs on the dining table as she saw
him approaching, tall and wide – wide eyes, wide smile, wide
with his arms outstretched, a beer in one of his giant hands.

'Happy New Year, my brother!' Kodzo and Muhammad
clapped and clicked their right hands in total sync.

'Happy New Year,' Muhammad replied, leaning down towards Abena to kiss her on each cheek. 'You are looking well.' He turned to Dzifa. 'And you! You used to be this small girl, asking for extra biscuits.'

Dzifa laughed. 'Yeah. I'll still take some if they're going.'

'Are you a doctor yet? Or we are still waiting?'

'I'll finish next year,' Dzifa said, 'then I'm not sure – maybe stay down south, maybe come back up here.'

'Oh, this one be book-long *koraaa*.' Muhammad laughed again, and Dzifa rolled her eyes. Abena liked that now, Dzifa stayed with them in the kitchen instead of tugging her sleeve for permission to head upstairs with the kids.

'*Afehyia pa!*' Abena hugged Aunty Mary, who took a break from stirring a pot of stew to embrace Abena fully.

'Ei, long time, sister! How are you?'

Abena's stomach had settled, and she fixed herself a plate of jollof, goat meat and coleslaw. 'We are well, oh, we are well. How is Kilsyth?' Aunty Mary had moved to a village outside of Glasgow when her daughter Kafui left for university. She was the type of Ghanaian who had never lost a hint of her accent, despite working here for thirty years. The thought of her living in a cottage out in the countryside, pottering in her garden wearing just a wrapper, next door to Joan and Jeremy, filled Abena with fear, envy and respect – she'd struck out on her own, again, after so many years.

'It's nice. Quiet. I can just do my own thing, you know?'

'Mm-hmm.' Abena nodded. 'I'll make sure I come and visit soon.'

'Please. And please, *brɛ mɛ* yam when you do.' Abena laughed. 'It's been long. Dzifa is looking fine!' She looked over at Dzifa talking to Mensah with her dad, calmly sipping from a wine glass.

'She's doing well. She's in her final year. How is Kafui?' Abena wanted to know, but she also wanted to ask before Mary mentioned Elom.

'She finally broke up with that boy Adam, so she's better now. Still in the southside.'

'Good.' Abena could feel the pain again, coming in waves from her full belly, and she put down her food. Drums filled the air in five sharp hits, followed by a groovy synth guitar.

'Oh my God!' Dzifa downed the rest of her glass and rushed towards the living room, and DJ Kwabena's decks. Kodzo was laughing, and Abena tried to smile through the churning in her side.

'And how's Elom?' Mary asked, raising her voice over the singing from next door.

'Oh, he's fine,' Abena answered, louder still. The music was blaring, and a few more people left the kitchen to join the dancing. 'Still in London.' Abena paused, not sure what to say next. The pain worsened, as if the muscles in her stomach were squeezing themselves around a fistful of nails. The noise of the room beating her ears wasn't helping.

'Is he with friends now?'

The music cut out as the crowd next door roared the chorus line to 'Premier Gaou' in unison, then DJ Kwabena brought the beat back in.

'Yes, he's with friends,' Abena shouted. The pain seemed to have shifted. A sharp wave of it pulled at her right-hand side, just under her ribs. She looked towards Kodzo, who looked serious as he spoke to Mensah, and she wondered what he had been asked, and how he had answered.

'Abena, are you okay?' Abena glanced back at Aunty Mary, who looked concerned. She pulled a chair over from the dining table and ushered Abena into it. She tried to say she was fine, but something else threatened to leave her mouth. She ran to the bathroom and lifted the lid of the toilet seat before heaving the chicken and cheese that had been swirling inside her.

Three days later, Abena lay in an uncomfortable hospital bed, one gallbladder lighter. She now knew her heartburn hadn't been stress-, or even stomach-related, and felt silly for not getting help before. Morphine helped her post-op pain, and earplugs helped her sleep through the overnight scurrying of nurses, but the unavoidable hospital food was even worse than at the care home. She wasn't sure if her reaction to the gungy mince and tatties she had just been served was post-operative nausea or disgust.

She looked at Dzifa, who looked at the plate with a grimace before looking back up at Abena. The two of them broke into giggles, Abena's belly tearing slightly with each squeeze of laughter.

'Stop, I can't laugh!'

Kodzo was at work – Abena didn't want him to miss his shifts now that she was feeling better. Elom had been asleep when Kodzo had called from the hospital waiting room early on New Year's Day, and had phoned back in the afternoon, panicked. Abena had told him not to try travelling from Cornwall to Glasgow by public transport, late on a bank holiday, but she was glad that he'd called when she was out of surgery. Dzifa kept her company while she recovered. The visiting hours were the longest time the two of them had spent together in one room, alone, since long before Dzifa had gone to university. Abena liked that she was choosing to sit with her.

There was a chap on the door and a doctor came in wearing an unironed shirt tucked into chinos. 'Your blood tests are back and they look much better, so we can keep you on the tablet antibiotics and send you home.'

'Great,' Abena said, then smiled, knowing what she was about to do. 'This is my daughter, Dzifa.'

'Oh yeah, the med student?'

Dzifa looked at Abena and Abena felt the weight of her disapproval, but she didn't care – at this point, sitting in a hospital bed, she got to brag. They spoke to each other about the job, and about Abena, in medical jargon, and Abena smiled, imagining Dzifa in a year's time.

'Anyway, it'll just take a few hours to sort out the paperwork, so I'd say you can go some time before five-ish.'

'Thanks,' Abena said, but he had already rushed out, crossing off another job on his list.

'Mum, come on,' Dzifa chided.

'I can't wait for you to be a doctor.'

'Did you see how stressed he looked?'

'I felt bad for him following the consultant around this morning,' Abena agreed. 'But please, at least iron your shirt when you start, okay?'

Dzifa laughed and hugged her goodbye, promising to pick her up that afternoon.

                              *   *   *

Abena took the rest of the week off to recover. She lay on the couch, gossiping on the phone with Abla – she could spin a story like their mum, and more than once Abena worried she might have ruptured a stitch from laughing. Her daughter Ama could already understand Fante and English, and Abena promised she would visit one day soon. By Friday she had the energy to bake again – something she hadn't had the time to do for fun in years. She made two banana cakes, and when Dzifa came home from the cinema she plunged a knife straight into the loaf as it cooled on the rack, and Abena smiled as she chomped it down.

On Sunday night they all watched a film together – Dzifa looking up sporadically as her thumbs skittered across her phone screen – and Abena thought about the kitchen at the care home with the colour-coded chopping boards and laminated notices about the different consistencies of solid food for residents with eating difficulties. When she woke early the next morning, she dropped a slice of banana cake in the toaster and called her boss.

'Hi,' she felt nervous, and her planned words flitted around her head, out of reach, 'I'm so sorry, I'm still just not feeling right. Pain. Just, yeah, I think I need some more time off.' The toaster popped as Abena hung up the phone, and she burned her fingers on a caramelised edge as she pulled out the slice.

Abena felt guilty, though her colleagues had done the same many times, sometimes leaving her totally alone on Saturday mornings. She was dreading calling her practice for a sickline. She ran her script through her head as she redialled almost thirty times, waiting for the receptionist to pick up her call. Her GP sounded tired when Abena sat in front of her the next day.

'I had my gallbladder out last week and I'm still in a bit of pain, and tired too.' The latter was true – she had missed Denzel saving the day as she had fallen asleep on the couch.

'Okay. Any fever or issues with your bladder or bowel?'

'No, no problems.'

'Right, and is the pain coming in waves or with nausea?'

'No, no, it's not like the old pain. I think it's just from the operation. I just need some more time off work.'

'Oh sure.' The doctor looked relieved and turned towards her computer. 'You'll be knocked out for a while, and you don't come here often so it's probably pretty bad.' She looked at Abena with an understanding smile. Abena kept her head still, feeling like nodding in agreement would be closer to lying. 'Is two weeks okay?'

It was that easy. Over the next two weeks Abena cleared out the cupboards, baked a red velvet cake, called Abla almost every day, and realised she was a fan of *Location, Location, Location.*

Her sickline ran out too soon and she went back to work. The lifting, scrubbing, stirring was more effort than she remembered, and she almost missed her stop on the bus home after falling asleep. More than that, the featureless building, the nosy staff, the thick smells – boiled vegetables, soiled sheets and disinfectant – were more oppressive now than she had remembered. On February mornings, Abena chided herself again for believing, even after twenty-eight years in Scotland, that the worst of winter ended after December. She dragged herself through the work day, slamming cupboard and oven doors to a relentless pulse. This job, in this kitchen, with these people who mispronounced her name, was so boring.

Abena took the bins out into the yard – the home was down a cleaner, and they seemed in no hurry to hire a new one – and instead of rushing back in through the back door, she paused, breathed, and took out her phone. Her colleagues got away with smoking breaks at any time of day, so she tried to feel less guilty as she opened WhatsApp.

'Abena.'

She turned, putting her phone in her pocket, knowing she looked silly for trying to hide it. 'Yeah, I'm just coming, sorry.'

Her manager Linda was at the open door, leaning out into the cold. 'It's fine. Can I talk to you after you're done today?'

'Sure,' she responded, but Linda had already turned into the kitchen. She knocked on Linda's door a few hours later, still in her work clothes and aware that this conversation would make her miss her bus home.

'Come in.' The office was small, with two desks on opposite sides – one for Linda, and one for the nursing manager. 'It's been good to have you back – I hope you're feeling better.'

'I'm good. A little more tired than usual, but good.' Small talk with bosses made Abena's skin prickle. She just wanted to skip to the point where Linda made her life harder with a few choice words.

Fortunately, Linda readjusted herself, clearly having barely registered Abena's response and having deemed enough conversation to have taken place to get down to business. 'So, you know there's some restructuring going on with the company.' Abena nodded. 'It's looking like we'll keep this home open, close Rutherglen and merge some services with another in Knightswood.'

'Okay,' Abena replied. Knightswood was much closer – she would be able to walk to work if they moved her there.

'There's going to be some changes as we re-allocate staff. You've been a great colleague here for so long, and we'd love to keep you,' Abena smiled, unexpectedly grateful, 'but if you'd like to consider early retirement, we can facilitate that with a redundancy payout.'

Abena was planning her walking route to the Knightswood home, and how she could fit in a food shop along the way, when her head suddenly went blank.

'Redundancy?'

'Or probably more like early retirement. You'll get some cash, and you can access your work pension. I'd need to confirm details with management, but I thought I'd ask you if it's something you'd be interested in early on.'

The offer was a surprise, and Abena didn't want to interrogate whether or not it was complimentary, or whether it was related to her recent illness. She asked questions she knew she should, about timing and cash amounts, but her imagination couldn't get beyond walking past the fishmongers on the way home from work in Knightswood.

'Thank you, I'll think about it.'

Early retirement would mean Abena wouldn't have to work if she didn't want to. She had worked at the care home for nine years, and as a chef for eighteen prior. Before that, she had taught at the catering college in Accra. But she had never really wanted to do any of those things. She tried to remember what she'd wanted to be as a girl, and she couldn't. She couldn't remember anyone ever asking her. She remembered being young, and wanting to leave Newtown; and being older, and wanting to be more than a mother, or a wife; but there was nothing specific to hold on to. She had never been allowed to dream, and now she wondered if she could. All the way home to Kodzo, she struggled to see what her life could look like without waking up cold every morning, falling asleep on a bus in the evening, and spending nights washing cooking oil out of her skin. She couldn't yet see it, but she knew she wanted it.

On her last day at the care home, Kodzo surprised her by picking her up. He sounded the horn, windscreen wipers on, and she let out a short laugh. They drove to a pub by the canal, and Kodzo ordered a glass of red wine for her and a cola for him, which they clinked with a 'cheers'. It was a sweet way to end her day, and she hoped it might signal something for the way she'd be spending her future – though she would have liked to have showered and changed into something nicer. She felt like she was bringing the stench of her past into her present.

Abena knew Kodzo would be paying, and the thought fell like a stroke of paint on the blank canvas where her imagined future was supposed to be.

'I was just thinking, with the lump sum I'm getting, maybe I pay off the rest of the mortgage?' she suggested. They only had a couple of years left, and her payout would cover most of it.

Kodzo raised his eyebrows. 'Is that what you want to do?'

They had considered investing it in Ghana, or saving it, or getting a new car, or using it for the kids' future deposits. 'Yeah,' Abena said. 'Then maybe you can cut your hours down too.' Kodzo had always paid the mortgage. Abena now had the means to help significantly, and looking at him now, it was exactly what she wanted to do.

They stayed for another drink and Abena was tipsy on the short drive home – she hadn't drunk more than one glass of wine in months, and the time before that had been months again. The house and overgrown garden were damp from the rain. The house was so square, and narrow, and squat; the angles perfect and rigid. She turned her head as she opened the car door, and instantly felt like she couldn't turn back to look at the house. Something had spilled in her mind – another splash of colour on the canvas, showing her what she wanted. The thought of spending all her money on this terraced house, and living here – dying here – under a grey sky, still smelling of cabbage, was so bleak it made her eyes water.

Inside, Kodzo had set up a couple of silvery helium balloons with '*Congratulations*' written across them in bright red, and he handed Abena a card. Abena hugged Kodzo in thanks, unable to speak for a moment as tears of gratitude now filled her eyes.

It was a cosy, joyful evening, but all the while, Abena was conflicted. For the first time in her life, she was not working: she could focus on pleasure. She knew she had this patch to call home, and she was proud to be able to pay the last bit to secure it. She was proud of her children, but she missed them. They were changing, and the future of their bond scared her. She knew leaving – perhaps to return to Ghana – might only make things worse. But she also knew that the canvas was filling, and the picture of her future was starting to look very different to her present.

Chapter Twenty

Elom – November 2016

Elom pulled his trousers over his odd socks, then put on his freshly ironed shirt. It was Ben's, made of thicker cotton than any of Elom's, and it came in at the waist to give his body some form. Ben had insisted Elom wear a suit, so he had pulled his only one, which he had last worn at his graduation, from a suitcase under the bed and had it dry cleaned. He poured a coffee from the pot Ben had made and added an equal volume of milk – he didn't like the taste of coffee, nor how anxious it made him, but it helped him get into character.

'You're gonna do great, El,' Ben said. School was out for half term, their housemate was away, and Elom's job interview with the *New Statesman* was in a couple of hours.

'Thanks, B.' Elom sat at the table in the living room-cum-kitchen-cum-dining room and opened his laptop to re-read his CV, which Ben had also helped re-format. He tried to remember some bylines from his freelance gigs but the more nervous he got, the faster he read and the less he seemed to remember.

'I spoke to someone at work yesterday who recommended this curry place in Kilburn,' Ben said. Elom nodded, half listening and half thinking about how he would describe his reporting style. 'I might try and book a table for tonight.'

'Sweet,' Elom replied, distracted and a little annoyed, and Ben squeezed his shoulder.

'Stop stressing! You're great and your writing's great and you'll be great in the interview. You won't remember the stuff you read now, honestly.'

Elom had never seen Ben before an exam, but he imagined he was the person at university who said things like 'I never study after 8 p.m.,' and who chatted with mates in the foyer before the examination hall doors opened. Elom would always be reading lecture notes until the last minute outside, before reluctantly stuffing them in his bag and rushing into the hall with a handful of pens and a ruler.

'Let me know if you're up for a celebratory dinner tonight? We don't have other plans, do we?' Ben asked.

'Yeah, sounds good. Celebration or commiseration.' Elom chuckled and stood. 'I'm just gonna go next door and do a bit more reading before I leave. Thanks for the coffee.'

'Seriously?'

Elom's frustration flared; he didn't have the bandwidth to cope with Ben's emotions and prepare for the interview. 'I just need to focus for a bit.'

Ben sighed. 'Uh-huh, fine.'

Elom sat on the bed, his suit trousers too tight to cross his legs properly. After half an hour he opened the bedroom door and put on his shoes, hoping Ben would appreciate that he had taken his advice to get there early. Ben rose from the couch to give him a hug.

'Good luck.'

'Thanks.' He walked out and Ben shut the door behind him.

Elom got the job, and Ben seemed even more excited than him. 'Well done! Check you out, Mr Reporter.' They toasted his success with a glass of wine at home and danced to Robyn. Elom felt relieved and surprised, and laughed when Ben told him that his bum looked good in a suit.

'I'd have given you the job based on that alone,' Ben said, sitting on the couch. 'Like in a *Men at Play* video.' Elom lifted up his untucked shirt and wiggled his hips playfully, and Ben rolled his eyes. 'Oh, don't tease me.' Elom joined Ben on the couch and kissed him. Neither had mentioned the tension from the morning, and Elom hoped they could play it away.

'Thanks for the support, and the shirt,' Elom said.

'No problem. Honestly, though, I wish you wouldn't stress so much. You're smarter and have more substance than half the journalists out there.'

'Hmm.' Elom pursed his lips and shrugged with his eyebrows, brushing off the compliment.

'Stop it! The *New Statesman* knows that, and you should too.' Elom bashfully picked up the wine bottle to refill their glasses. They drank more, then kissed on the couch, with Elom eventually pulling out Ben's cock.

'Wait,' Ben said after a few strokes, 'we still haven't had any dinner.' Rebuffed, Elom let him put it back. 'We could still go to that curry place?'

It was eight thirty, and Elom was tired after the exertion of the interview and the wine. 'Yeah, I don't mind. Could also just have the leftover pasta in the fridge.'

'We should have a proper meal to celebrate,' Ben said.

'Okay.' Elom felt guilty about dismissing Ben that morning. 'Let's do it.'

The restaurant just off Kilburn High Road was small, and they were seated at an empty table for four with faux-leather chairs and laminated menus. Ben did the bulk of the ordering and updated Elom on his mum's birthday plans as they waited for the food. Elom drank water to dilute the chalky dryness the wine had left in his mouth while Ben continued with beer. The curries arrived as Ben laughed about one of his students who'd tried to impress his mates by acting silly with a Bunsen burner, and instead ended up with no left eyebrow. Elom gave a soft chuckle as he moved the glasses out of the way to make room for the hot plates and bowls.

'Don't laugh too hard,' Ben said, annoyance breaking through his sarcasm. Elom kept his eyes on the table, awkwardly aware of the waiter still leaning over them.

'Sorry,' Elom said as the waiter left the table, 'I'm listening, I was just sorting the plates out. It's a lot of food.'

'I know, but we can just take back what we don't eat,' Ben said, and Elom realised he thought he was being accused of over-ordering.

'It looks good.' Elom tried to keep it jovial.

'Uh-huh.' Ben started spooning saag paneer onto his plate. 'Are you in a mood with me or something?'

'No.' Elom shrugged, trying to imply he didn't know why Ben might think that.

'You just haven't said much since we left the flat. I'm doing all the talking, again.' On the walk down they had held hands, but Elom had been preoccupied with the thought of telling his parents about the job offer – he wanted to call, but they still hadn't met Ben, and he hated hiding in another room to talk to them with Ben next door.

'Sorry, I'm just tired.'

'Yeah, me too, I've been lesson planning all week, and helping you prepare for the interview.'

'I already said thanks for that.'

'I don't want you to say thanks, I just want to actually spend time with you and for you to want to spend time with me that doesn't involve either sex or sitting in our living room. Instead, I have to fight to take you out for dinner.'

'You didn't have to fight to get me out – I'm happy to come.' Elom's words came out more pointed than he had wanted, sharpened by resentment that he was expected to feel grateful for a meal he hadn't asked for.

'Yeah, except when I've had a long day, I actually look forward to hanging out with you rather than finding it draining.'

The waiter came to drop off the last of the naan, and asked how they were finding the food so far. They both smiled broadly and said it was delicious, though Elom had barely eaten three mouthfuls. When he left, Elom used the interruption as a chance to reset the conversation.

'Sorry, Ben,' he said.

'Yeah, me too.'

'This daal is great, by the way.'

'Pass me some, I haven't tried it yet.'

They ate until they were full, then asked for the rest to be packed up to take home. The walk back was quiet, and Elom ran over the argument in his head. Once again, he confirmed that the phrase or action that had turned an evening from fun to tense seemed as normal as any other. They had had more arguments since moving in together a few months earlier, often triggered by Elom's quietness. It wasn't until they shared a bedroom that Elom realised how much time he spent silently facing a screen in bed; or staring into space, organising his thoughts about the previous few days, or a minor grievance from years before. He loved their friends, and was excited to see them when they could, but it hurt Ben that Elom could be engaged and talkative when out with them, but would dim when they were alone. It frustrated Elom that whenever they were together, he felt like he had to be on, no matter how tired he was, or if he had run out of things to say.

After a weekend seeing other friends and running errands, Ben would, in turn, become frustrated that they hadn't spent any time together, and it took a while for Elom to learn that 'time together' meant something different for him. Elom thought about the past few days, where they had spent each night at home. Ben had cooked on Wednesday and Elom had reheated the leftovers on Thursday, and both nights they had watched a bit of television with dinner. Before Ben had gone to sleep the previous night, he'd made Elom try on a couple of shirts, and found some polish for his scuffed shoes. Just being in each other's company wasn't enough for Ben, and Elom admitted that he was justified in wanting more than microwaved dinners and Netflix.

As always, Elom's guilt made him grow even quieter. Ben always seemed to be looking out for him, and Elom didn't want to seem like he took him for granted. He looked at Ben, who was scrolling on his phone, and tried to resist the urge to retreat.

'Ben, I am really sorry. I was just feeling tired but I'm really grateful for the help and I had a lovely night.'

'It's fine.'

'No, you're right, we didn't get to spend much proper time together this weekend, and dinner was a nice idea.'

'Yeah, we didn't,' Ben said. 'Look, I get that you can get tired or whatever sometimes, but you need to actually communicate better. If it was going to be a problem, you could have said and, like, actually suggested another time, or organised a takeaway or something. Instead of it being me doing all the legwork.'

Elom nodded, the guilt weighing on his tongue. 'You're right,' he said again, 'and I don't want it to seem like I'm taking you for granted. I do want to spend time with you. Now this interview's out the way I'll have a look at some fun bits this weekend. Maybe a show?'

'You don't have to. But thanks.'

'I want to,' Elom said, and took Ben's hand. Ben smiled, unclasped his hand and put it around Elom's shoulder, and they continued the walk home.

*   *   *

They kissed in bed with the lights off but the curtains open, so they could see out into the night. Elom liked the sense of exhibitionism without any actual risk of being seen through their third-floor window. Ben went between Elom's legs and started to suck him off whilst stroking with long, slow movements, and Elom relaxed enough to allow himself to moan. Encouraged, Ben took him deeper and squeezed tighter, then after a few more seconds, he paused, and Elom felt him slide off the bed. Ben pulled Elom towards him before pushing his legs back by his thighs and resting his feet on his shoulders.

'Not tonight, I'd need to have a shower,' Elom said before Ben moved any closer.

'You sure? I don't really mind.'

'Eww,' Elom laughed, 'yes, I'm sure.'

'No worries,' Ben said, unconcerned, and joined Elom on the bed again and slowly stroked him as he talked. 'Your arse did look amazing in those trousers today.'

'Thanks,' Elom said lightly, as if Ben had complimented his choice of aftershave.

'You're welcome. So, when am I gonna get to fuck it?'

Elom laughed again. 'Ah, I don't know. I want to, I mean I admit it looks really fun' – Ben nodded as if to confirm this as true – 'but last time we tried it was just sore.'

'You like the rimming though, right?'

'Yeah, definitely.' Elom loved it.

'Maybe I could just try fingering you then?'

Elom thought for a moment – it had been a year and a half of him topping. Ben had said from the start that he was versatile, and whilst he was happy to bottom, Elom knew it was frustrating for him. Elom also wanted to bottom, but it never seemed to work. He didn't answer at first, but kissed Ben again slowly, his hand on Ben's cheek, and rearranged himself so they were side by side. Ben took hold of Elom's thigh and pulled his leg across his own, then slid his hand over Elom's arse. Elom liked the feel of his hands, and thought it might be worth trying. As he thought of their discussion a few hours prior, his guilt resurfaced, and he pulled away slightly to face Ben.

'Okay, let's try it.'

'Really?'

'Yeah, sure. Let me just go to the loo first.'

Elom came back from the toilet and lay face down on the towel Ben had put down for him. Ben lubed up a finger and kissed Elom's neck as he circled his hole before gently pushing in. It was tight, and Elom felt a hot, searing sensation as Ben's finger advanced. He caught his breath and Ben pulled his face back.

'Just breathe,' Ben said. 'Maybe next time we can get some poppers.'

Elom nodded and exhaled, aware that this discomfort ought to pass soon. As he let out the breath, Ben pushed in further.

'Hold on,' Elom said. He could feel himself involuntarily clenching against the finger, giving a painful, scalding throb each time. Ben paused and kissed Elom's neck again. It was supposed to be reassuring, but it just felt too hot and too close. He felt a sweat breaking out on his forehead as if he'd taken a shot of vinegar.

'You're almost there, just a bit more,' Ben said, and slowly pushed in the final length of his finger. Ben's sliding finger felt like tearing, like a plaster being pulled from a still-wet wound. Elom screwed up his face and let out a grunt.

'It's really sore.'

Ben kissed Elom again. 'Relax. It's not supposed to be painful, you're supposed to enjoy it.' He didn't move his finger and Elom continued to try to find the pleasure. After a few moments, Ben started to gently move the tip of his finger, curling it towards Elom's stomach. On top of the pain, it just made Elom want to wee.

'Stop that,' Elom said, and Ben paused. 'I think take it out? It just hurts.'

'Wait a bit longer, it'll get better. I want you to enjoy it.'

Elom took another breath and tried to relax, but his whole body felt tense. There were other sensations alongside the pain – feelings of stretching, fullness, pressure. He wasn't sure if these would make way for something else, and if he should be focusing on them. Regardless, he still felt like he wanted the finger out. As more time passed, Ben began to move his finger rhythmically again, each time making Elom wince.

'Look at me,' Ben said, and Elom opened his eyes. 'It's just the two of us here. I love you. Do you trust me?' He had the same look in his eyes as he did when he was listening to Elom tell a story, giving him all the space he needed to say what was on his mind. Looking at him now, though, Elom wasn't sure how to answer the question. He nodded mutely and closed his eyes again. Ben continued to wiggle his finger inside him for a few more minutes, as Elom tried and failed to identify the pleasure.

*   *   *

Elom shut the curtains at about 1 a.m. and climbed back into bed. They had both cum and cleaned up, and Elom was ready for sleep. Ben seemed much happier than before, and he pulled Elom close to his back, with Ben as little spoon. He asked Elom what his parents had said about the job, and Elom said he had yet to tell them.

'They didn't know the final interview was today actually. I told them I was applying but it was too much pressure to let them know the date.' Elom was talking to his parents more. He was glad to see them enjoying their free time now that Kodzo had cut his hours too. Last week they had excitedly told him about their upcoming trip to Ghana – they hadn't been there together since before they were married. While they didn't talk about his relationship, he felt fortunate to still have them in his life.

'I'm sure they'll be chuffed when you tell them.' Elom wasn't sure if there was a hint of discontentment in Ben's voice. Ben had met Dzifa for the first time the year before, and they had casually bonded over life in the public sector. But Elom still hadn't felt able to fully involve Ben in his family, preferring to answer calls when Ben wasn't around, and visiting home without him. He felt like Ben blamed him for not pushing hard enough.

'Maybe we can call them together tomorrow to give them the news,' Elom said.

'No, I get it, it's hard. Parents are parents.' Elom felt relieved. 'Did they have any gay friends when you were growing up?'

'None. They were big into the church.'

'Fair. Mine did, though honestly it just made them so cringe.'

'What do you mean?' Elom asked.

'I remember my parents sat me down after a sleepover with a friend when I was like, fourteen, and definitely too old to just be curious.' Elom felt Ben's back vibrate on his chest as he giggled, 'Oh my God, it was so peak! We must have been louder than we thought. My parents thought they were being so cool. They think they're bohemian because Mum lived in a squat for like three months after uni.'

'So then what happened?' He tried to stay casual, but Ben hadn't ever gone into detail about his coming out.

'Yeah, I dunno. It was pretty open, which was cool, but maybe a bit smothering? They met my boyfriends when I was at school, then uni. Tried to give me condoms once but that was too weird, and I said I'd get free ones myself from the pharmacy.' He kissed Elom's hand. 'I'm looking forward to meeting your parents one day. Just tell them we're okay for condoms.'

'I'm looking forward to it too,' Elom said. His eyes were still closed, though he knew he wouldn't sleep for a while, despite his exhaustion. Ben's coming out had never been a thing of tension. He sat with this fact, tossed it up and spun it round on the end of his finger like a basketball. He remembered Ben's advice to him: that it was his parents' problem, and they had to come round to keep Elom in their lives. He had said it so confidently, and so supportively. Elom thought of the fear he had had before he told Kodzo and Abena – a fear that hadn't left – that he might lose his parents forever, or at least lose the way they were together. He now knew Ben had never felt that fear. Yet he had smiled and urged Elom to plunge into the deep, perhaps never understanding how real the risk was that he'd never come back up.

It unsettled Elom, and he sifted through his and Ben's previous chats to see if he had missed something Ben had said. They had promised to be honest with each other, but now Elom felt foolish for having tried, when Ben had either purposefully or accidentally omitted his painless coming of age.

He wondered if he was at fault. He never understood the rules of social games. Relationships weren't like they were in films, and smarter people knew which promises were real and which were romantic aspirations. Perhaps he'd taken things too literally in his eagerness to connect: it wouldn't have been the first time he had misread the signals from someone. Or perhaps Ben just hadn't tried to correct him.

Elom opened his eyes – Ben had fallen asleep, his chest slowly pressing into Elom's forearms then easing off again. Elom gently pulled out his right arm, which had gone numb from the weight of Ben's body. He looked at Ben, following the long arc from his shoulder, up his neck to his ear. He did love looking at him, and felt comforted with Ben's back pressed against his chest. He had trusted Ben, from the moment they'd met, but he fell asleep wondering for the first time if Ben had his best interests at heart.

Chapter Twenty-One

Kodzo – February 2017

Kodzo's heart raced as he stood to collect his and Abena's hand luggage from the overhead compartment. He heard Twi and Ga on either side of him as phones reconnected and passengers asked each other for help carrying their bags down. Abena was staring out of the aeroplane window. The aisle was packed, and there was little to be gained by standing, but Kodzo felt giddy and couldn't sit. It was his first time in Ghana for thirty years.

The air outside was thick: full of water and heavy, bright sunlight. The queue for immigration was long and ordinary, and in the humidity Kodzo wasn't sure if his shirt was wet from his own sweat or from the moisture in the air. He handed over his burgundy passport to the sullen, smooth-faced officer, who flicked through to the visa. Kodzo was embarrassed – his Ghanaian passport had expired fifteen years earlier, and he hadn't bothered to renew it. It seemed silly coming home with a travel visa, and he wanted to tell the man in front of him that he was a Ghanaian, that he still spoke Ewe, and that life had just got in the way.

'Welcome to Ghana.' The man stamped the page, barely looking at Kodzo. Kodzo took his passport silently and walked through to baggage claim, where Abena was already waiting.

'Do you remember what colour Prince's car was?' Abena asked. Prince was Abla's driver.

'No, but he'll be waiting in the foyer.'

'You can't always rely on people here.'

'Relax,' Kodzo said.

'I'm serious, oh. Ghana has changed.'

Kodzo saw the suitcases bumping along the carousel, threatening to tip over the edge, and he pulled them off. They passed through the door that said 'Nothing to declare' – ignoring the hundreds of pounds' worth of gifts stuffed into the suitcases stacked on their trolley – and into a tunnel of people shouting, taking photographs and holding balloons or A4 paper with names written on them. Kodzo looked for the round face of Prince that he had seen in a photo Abla had sent to Abena.

'Did you see him?' Abena asked as they approached the end of the tunnel.

'Why would I still be looking if I'd seen him?' Kodzo teased. They turned back, craning their necks but only seeing the backs of welcomers and the tired faces of new arrivals.

'Taxi, sah?'

'Huh?' Kodzo turned to see a young man in a football top, jeans and sandals.

'Where you dey go?' The man had a hand on Kodzo's trolley and turned it towards the exit.

'No, no we are waiting.'

'I dey go to Accra, very good price.'

'Ah-ah.' Abena told him in Twi that they had a driver and
that he should go. Still he lingered, his hand on the trolley.

'Accra, Tema, I can drive for your holiday if your driver no
dey come.'

Kodzo was embarrassed to realise that he was intimidated
by this slender young man, a third his age. Again, he wanted to
say that this wasn't a holiday, this was his home, but the man's
persistence pushed Kodzo's words back into his mouth.

Abena took control of the trolley. 'Please, driver *no wɔ ha.*'
She walked back to the arrivals gate where Kodzo could now
see Prince near the back, holding a small sign. The man turned
immediately and silently, as if he had already forgotten their
interaction in pursuit of his next customer.

Prince drove them to Abla's house in a gated compound in
Legon. The buildings were painted in pastels, each one a unique
arrangement of squares and rectangles flanked by outsize cars
parked freestyle in the large concrete driveways, so different
from the neatly arranged terraced houses of Glasgow.

'Ohhh, you are welcome!' Abla burst through the front door
to greet them in the driveway, wrapping her arms around Abena
then Kodzo. 'Uncle Kodzo, you are looking well.' Abla stepped
back to take him in, and Kodzo smiled.

'You too. It's good to see you.' They had last seen each other
almost a decade earlier, when Abla had stayed in Glasgow
for the summer. He had liked how she was always laughing,
openly and generously, and though he never mentioned it to

Abena, how she treated him with the respect older Ghanaian men usually get just by being older and men. It was odd seeing her grown, with the trappings of a life they could never have afforded in Glasgow, and which she had used a sizeable portion of Abena's salary for several years to reach. He didn't begrudge her – sending money home had never been up for negotiation, and she had always shown gratitude – but it was interesting that convention only allowed the flow in one direction: from older siblings to younger, and from Western to Ghanaian. He had status from living in Glasgow, despite living in a three-bed terrace.

Abla led them into the house, signalling to Prince to carry the luggage with a 'Please,' and a nod at the suitcases scattered on the floor. The air con chilled the sweat on his shirt as Abla showed them their en-suite room. They had time to shower and change before dinner with her kids when they got back from school and nursery. Kodzo lay down while Abena took her shower, a nudge from her waking him up a few hours later.

'Dinner is almost ready.'

The lights were on and the sky outside the windows was a deep orange. Kodzo felt heavy and hot, but rose quickly.

'Why did you let me sleep so long?'

'You were tired.' Abena shrugged. She was putting in her earrings and looked at home in her *chalewote* and painted nails.

'What have you been doing?'

'Just chatting with Abla. We cooked. I'm going to set the table – we'll be eating in fifteen minutes.'

Kodzo pulled himself up, quickly showered and dressed, and walked through to the dining room where Abena and the children were already sitting. Abla's husband, Kwame, was working in Lagos, and then Dubai, while they were visiting. Abla came in holding a ceramic bowl with a cloth to protect her from its heat just as Kodzo pulled out a chair.

'Hi, Uncle, how did you sleep?'

'Fine, thanks. I forgot what the Ghana heat is like,' Kodzo laughed.

Abla nodded. 'I'm telling you.' She put down the bowl. 'Osei, Ama, this is your Uncle Kodzo – say hello.'

'Hi, Uncle,' Ama mumbled, her legs swinging from her chair and her eyes avoiding Kodzo's.

'Hello, princess,' Kodzo said, reaching out a hand. She took it gently and he shook it. At his touch she looked up and, seeing Kodzo's smiling face, she blushed again and looked away. 'Did you have a nice day at school?'

Ama nodded, her eyes still fixed on the tablecloth. 'Stop pretending you are shy!' Abla laughed as she arranged the dishes, making space for another brought by Abena. 'And this is Osei.' She picked the toddler up from his high chair and put on a baby voice, 'Say hi,' taking his hand to wave at Kodzo. He giggled, then wriggled towards the high chair with the confidence of a baby used to being caught, and Abla placed him down as he started reaching for the food in front of him.

Kodzo looked at the spread: jollof, grilled fish, boiled yam, *shito*, boiled eggs, waakye. The reds were redder and the browns browner than he had ever seen in Glasgow. They blessed the food and he took his first bite. He could taste the saltwater in the fish, whereas in Scotland he had only tasted cargo ships and ice. He ate his fill, and Abla kept their glasses full of Star beer and

7 per cent Guinness until he and Abena fell into bed at 2 a.m., sweaty, sleepy and smiling.

The first week of the trip was a rediscovery for Kodzo. They spent some time with Abena's family in Newtown – Abena felt she had to, rather than wanted to, and Kodzo complied. He made it clear he was happy for them to skip that part of the holiday, though: Abena had only given glimpses of her childhood, but it was enough for him to feel no obligations towards Aunty Esther and her minions. He had thought her obsequious but harmless when he'd met her thirty years prior, but now he cringed at his naivety. As soon as they could – after Abena's family had accepted her gifts and they had all shared a meal – Abena and Kodzo left to explore Accra. It was a new city, full of bars and beaches where everyone looked like him, and spoke to him like they wanted him to be there. His Twi had never been great, but his Britain-loosened English marked him as someone of note. It felt nice in those moments, when he could order something lavish for him and Abena.

Being a marked man sometimes worked against him, though. Abena argued with a taxi driver on their way to visit Ernest, making him pull over and dragging Kodzo out of the car because they were being charged something outrageous (though this time Abena had also made clear she didn't want to see Ernest anyway – apparently he had been a demanding houseguest, which was news to Kodzo). He often felt like a tourist, but he reassured himself: Accra had never been his city. He was a bush-boy from Volta, and they would be heading there the following week.

The Sunday before they left for the village, Abla took Abena and Kodzo to church. They wore their newly sewn outfits, fresh from Abla's seamstress. The roads were stuffed; most of the city seemed to be en route to worship. Kodzo, Abena and Ama sat in the back of Abla's car, while Osei sat on Abla's lap in the passenger seat, all of them bumping along the uneven road together.

'I hope we can get to park,' Abla said as they approached the church. It was long before 9 a.m., but cars flooded the venue. The building must have been able to fit thousands of worshippers, and Kodzo watched as people poured down the rivulets between cars to the front doors. They were talking, laughing, pulling on the arms of over- or under-excited children, and Kodzo realised he missed the ritual of the Sunday pilgrimage.

Inside there was music, fervour and a commitment to the spirit, shown through shouting, sweating and singing. Kodzo enjoyed the intensity of it all, and the feeling close to euphoria he got by singing his favourite hymns. Still, he and Abena shared a glance when the pastor insisted on the importance of paying 15 per cent tithes.

After an hour of preaching and an hour of praise, the time for blessings came. People lined up for the pastor to hear their woes and bestow the grace of Jesus upon them. Kodzo noticed the collection buckets passing up and down the aisles. He felt uneasy – the link wasn't as direct as payment for prayers, but there was a connection, and he wondered what sacrifices the people lined up in front of the pastor had made.

The pastor called out their whispered troubles through his microphone – people were sick, or had sick parents, wanted children or visas, or help finding work or getting into university.

He commanded that demons leave and afflictions be banished by the blood of Jesus, slipping between Tongues, English and Twi as he anointed foreheads with holy oil. Kodzo missed simply knowing that all of your problems could be fixed by praying hard enough, rather than fixing society – the underfunded schools, potholed roads and corrupt police that kept people in precarity. He wondered how much the pastor – his voice still strong despite three hours of non-stop speech – really believed in what he was doing. Kodzo had once believed it himself, and he didn't want to assume the pastor was a swindler, like Abena surely did.

After the sermon, the sun was at its fiercest, and it took a while for the car to cool to a tolerable temperature. Congregants drove slowly along the clogged side street to the main road. Kodzo watched as a pair of children passed along the traffic in front of him towards their car. They were light-skinned, with brownish, wavy hair – beggars from Niger. They threw themselves at the windscreens of each car they passed, soaping, wiping and rinsing in under twenty seconds, then holding their hands out in front of the passenger window. After the sermon's pressure to be charitable, and its message of bounty and blessing, Kodzo was disappointed by the small number of hands that reached out of their cars to join those outstretched by the children.

Accra was full of excitement and energy, but it was also hard in a way Kodzo was no longer used to. He pulled some notes from his pocket and slid down the window, letting in the heat that the air con had tried so hard to counter. The girl smiled as she took the money, and Kodzo nodded as the traffic eased slightly, rolling them forward. He pushed the button to raise the window and leaned back in his seat, looking forward to the next day's drive to the village, and to something greener, older and softer.

The Adomi Bridge was a border between worlds. As they drove over the calm water towards the green hills in the distance, Kodzo felt himself leaving Accra's confusion and noise behind, like he was approaching a slice of Eden.

Abena and Kodzo broke up the journey from Accra with a couple of days in Ho with Kodzo's cousin and her family. They turned off the main road – still full of stalls selling plantain, coconuts and biscuits, though more relaxed than the roads in Accra – and turned onto a bumpier, earthier one. The tyres squelched as they rolled along wet earth made dark by the morning rain. Eventually they stopped in front of a house along the street, and the driver beeped his horn. A scraping noise came from behind the 8-foot-tall gates, and they clunked apart, pulled open by a young man, his abs rippling and shiny as he held on to the huge sheets of metal. The house was more modest than Abla's, painted pink, but with more flowers and fruit trees crowding the soil lining the wall around the small compound.

'Oh, brother!' Sister Grace rushed out of the house, her deep-blue, wax-printed skirt trailing behind her. The scene was similar to the one at Abla's, except this time Kodzo heard Ewe rather than Fante, flowing treacle like Grace's dress. There were also more people – second cousins, husbands and wives, children, all streaming out of the door to meet Kodzo and Abena. He had only ever spoken to them over the phone, but they welcomed him earnestly. He hadn't heard this much Ewe in decades, and it felt like he'd found his favourite childhood record.

'*Woezɔ!*' welcomed Grace.

'*Yoo, efɔa?*' Kodzo replied. The words were pushed, rather than flowing out, and Kodzo suddenly felt childish and embarrassed, but persisted. 'Abena *yenye ya.*'

Grace switched to English and greeted Abena, who she hadn't seen since she had been to Ghana for her mum's funeral. They hugged like sisters, and Grace held Abena by the hand as she led her to the house, laughing in a way that reminded Kodzo so much of his mum. The afternoon was full of food and reminiscing – stories of sisters getting swindled at marketplaces and uncles who grew the best yams – as well as updates on the extended family that Kodzo hadn't been able to keep track of. Grace knew it all, like the family bookkeeper.

'So is nobody else really in the village?' The conversation was mostly in English now, which Kodzo told himself was for Abena's benefit, though he admitted he had lost his stamina in Ewe.

'Yes. Some of the houses have even fallen down, or are just empty. We go for holidays or to do some small-small jobs, but the farming has mostly stopped,' Grace said.

'Honestly, one afternoon is all you need. There isn't much there,' added Senom, Grace's husband.

'Everyone left for Ho, or Accra, or *abrokyire* if they could!' Grace winked.

Kodzo didn't know what to say – it was impossible to comment on the abandonment of his home when he had left it behind himself, but he still wanted it to be home.

'But there's good land there – the government should be investing in jobs in those areas,' he said.

'Uncle, nobody wants to stay in some small villages anymore. All the work is away from those places,' Senom replied.

Kodzo and Abena stayed in Ho for a couple more days. Kodzo laid flowers on the graves of his parents and sisters while the older family members took turns in prayer. Later, Abena organised the transport to the village while Kodzo remained quiet for the rest of the day.

As the time came to leave, the excitement he had felt to see his old home became nerves, fluttering just below his belly button. It deepened as they rode in Senom's car, the driver dodging potholes which got more numerous as they travelled further away from the city and closer to Wutevi. There were more than he remembered, and he felt self-conscious.

'Sorry, the road is so bad,' he said to Abena.

'It's fine,' she said, looking ahead unfazed, her head wobbling freely. 'That's just village roads for you.'

The closer they got, the more Kodzo wanted to turn back. He flashed through the images he had of the streets, trees, houses and stalls of thirty years before. The sounds and smells of the blacksmith and goldsmiths, the traditional priests and the women pounding fufu. The shrieks and splashes of children filtering up from the river. It seemed at once so real, and too perfect, and he didn't want whatever was at the end of the road to spoil it.

Eventually the forest on the sides of the road opened up, with buildings replacing the trees. They were short and stout, with cinderblock walls and corrugated-metal roofs. The driver turned right, down a smaller side road, and Kodzo hoped that the area closer to his own home would feel more familiar. After a few minutes' drive, they arrived at another compound house, hidden behind a cream-coloured wall. A few other houses were dotted further along the path, with the treeline restarting just beyond.

'We are here,' the driver said, getting out of the car to open the gate with the keys Grace had left. He then climbed back into the car and drove Abena and Kodzo up the driveway as Atsu came out of the front door of the main house.

'Welcome,' he said, heading straight to the boot of the car to take their luggage. He was a distant cousin who was paid to look after the house when the others were away. Kodzo thanked the driver, who declined the offer of a drink or some food, and then followed Atsu into the house. He showed them where they would be sleeping, how to use the air con, and where to get water from. He didn't speak much English, and generally didn't speak much at all. After the tour, he returned to the kitchen where he had left a pot of something cooking.

Kodzo had listened in a slight daze. When his family had asked for money to build a new house in the village, Kodzo had sent it. He had known that he wouldn't come back to a hut with no indoor plumbing and a coal stove perched outside the back door. Still, seeing this flashy new building on the ground he used to graze his knee on, and sit on to share abolo with his sister after school, was unsettling.

'It's so nice here. Peaceful,' Abena said. She had washed her face and changed out of her jeans and into a wrapper to sit out on the verandah as the sun began to set. Kodzo joined her and Atsu brought them their dinner to eat outside. Everything felt familiar and unfamiliar at the same time: the deep blue of the sky was diluted by the electric lights from the house. In bed that night, the balmy air carried both the buzz of generators and the calls of crickets that once used to send Kodzo to sleep, and he stayed up listening to both, unsure which was louder.

They woke early to a breakfast of Keta school boys, cooked by Atsu. Kodzo wanted to relax, but he was restless at home. He left Abena reclining with a book and some freshly sliced pineapple and went for a walk. Few of the buildings were familiar, but he walked to the treeline, and then down towards the river. He was less sure-footed than he was as a child, and the heat bothered him more, but after a few minutes' walk he found the bend of clear water where he and his friends, siblings and cousins – there had been little distinction at the time, really – used to play. To his left was the tree they used to swing from. It still stood, sturdy, with a fat, mossy branch leaning over the water. He saw a white rope hanging down and remembered swinging from it into the water below.

There were no children around now, even though it was a weekend. He looked back at the rope for a second and realised that it really might be the same rope that had given him friction burns fifty-odd years earlier. There was no way it could have lasted all that time with the way they used it, he thought – unless at some point it had stopped being used.

He looked at the still tree, with the rope hanging below it, straight as a compass, to the smooth surface of the water curving round the bend. There were no laughs, and no splashes, but the sound of a generator still made it through the trees to where he stood. He was suddenly overcome with sadness, like mourning a lost child, and the feeling pushed him back through the forest and to the house, where Abena had fallen asleep on the couch. He let her rest a while, before suggesting when she woke that they head back to Accra, to get an early start at the beach resort they had earmarked for the end of their trip.

Abena handed Kodzo a cut of suya wrapped in oily paper and joined him on the sun loungers. It was their penultimate day in Ghana, and Kodzo agreed: the sun, sea and suya combo was a winner. Afrobeats played through the speakers from the bar on the waterfront. Children tumbled in and out of the water alone, carrying boogie boards or using the fishing boats along the shore as props, whilst teenagers played beach volleyball or football, or just lounged around playing it cool. The resort had been Abla's recommendation, and there were other couples nearby lying on fluffy towels or wearing expensive sandals and sleek sunglasses.

'This is the life, right?' Abena said as she sipped on a yellow and pink cocktail.

Kodzo nodded, his mouth still full of tender, fatty, spicy meat. 'I could get used to this.'

'Me too,' Abena said.

Abla joined them for the afternoon, and Kodzo took the kids for a paddle in the sea while she relaxed with Abena. He knew they would miss each other, and they had already been discussing plans to meet soon, either in Glasgow or in Accra. Kodzo looked around again and wondered what 'getting used to it' would look like. He could see himself here, on the beach, for a time. But once the holiday was over, he would have to go home. Did home look like Accra, with its noise and hunger?

It no longer looked like Wutevi. He knew he wasn't one of the people beside them on the sand, who had inherited wealth, or taken it, and whose lives in Accra looked like an episode of *Made in Chelsea* or *The Real Housewives of Atlanta*.

They all squeezed into Abla's car, and her driver took them straight to the airport after a late checkout. It was going to be a long, overnight journey, but Kodzo was exhausted and ready for sleep. They hugged Abla and the kids goodbye, Kodzo giving them each a final bag of sweets – Starburst and Skittles – that he'd brought over from Glasgow.

As they settled into their seats a few hours later, Abena sighed. 'That was such a nice trip. I'm missing Ghana already.'

'Me too.'

It was mostly true. For so long, Ghana had been a mixture of grainy memories and second-hand stories, and neither seemed to align with Kodzo's experience of it now. His old life there was gone, and he didn't know if he could build a new one. Dzifa, with her hip London ways, wouldn't fit there, and he didn't want to dig too deep imagining how Elom might find village life. His wife, his friends, his only house, were in Glasgow. He had lived there longer than he had ever lived in Ghana, and it was familiar in a way Ghana no longer was. He realised as the plane angled upwards, pushing him down into his seat as they took off, that he was relieved to be heading home.

Chapter Twenty-Two

Elom – April 2017

'Do you want a tea?'

Elom opened his eyes. 'Yeah, thanks.'

Ben smiled. 'Sure.' Elom caught his eye as he left their bedroom, and remembered how handsome he was. He looked Ben in the eyes less often now than he used to. He wasn't sure why, but it was easier to avoid whatever it was that they asked of him. They didn't argue much anymore either. Instead, they chose a conflict-free life, watching prestige TV or sitcom reruns in the evening. They still had sex a few times a week; unlike everything else, that part was mostly easy.

Ben remained chatty – Elom would leave the spaces for him to fill, and Ben would fill them more and more, sometimes endlessly, with stories about friends, family, the news, or house admin. Elom felt more tired around Ben these days, and the more he talked, the more withdrawn Elom became, and the more Elom withdrew, the more Ben talked to get a response. But Elom couldn't let go of what Ben had told him about his family. He thought about it often, and wondered what else Ben had hidden. He thought about how he had allowed Ben to convince him to talk to his parents, believing it was for his own good, when maybe, it had just been for Ben's. More than that, Elom had spent so much of his life keeping himself hidden, or pretending to be someone else. He had told Ben his secrets, but Ben hadn't shared his. It made him feel embarrassed, and stupid, and reminded him of other boys he had trusted who were never really on his side. It made him close off a part of himself to Ben, and all they had left was small talk, or silence.

Elom joined Ben in the living room when he heard the kettle click and the rumble die down.

'What time should we leave today?' The previous night, Ben had made a vague suggestion that they see an exhibition together.

'Eleven? We can check out the Tate then get lunch after?'

'Sounds good.'

Elom checked his phone and noticed a new message from his rugby coach. *Hey elom, are you free today? Severely lacking in backs and no wingers! Message back asap if able to play with the IIIs.*

He had signed up to an inclusive rugby team after a dinner with Pippy and other friends. Ostensibly it was to stay fit, but also to meet some new people outside of their glossy circle. They were his friends, and they were sincere, but there was something about the food, the holidays, the plays and the ever-zeitgeisty conversation that left him wanting something a bit more artless, or uncurated. Still, like him, many of the players on the team were new to the sport, and at times he felt like the whole team was a performance – of gayboys trying to prove their secondary school bullies wrong, or maybe just trying to sleep with them. But when he played with them he felt validated in a way he hadn't before – as a man who could shout, run, tackle, get hit, and drink beers after.

Elom thought about how to mention the text to Ben. He felt a sense of duty to his team, but a part of him simply felt it would be a more fun afternoon. He unlocked his phone and typed, *Should be able to make it, will let you know shortly,* then picked up the cups and plate from the coffee table. As he started washing up, he said, 'Eh, Ben, do you think we could go to the gallery later this afternoon maybe?'

'Why?' Ben looked up from his phone.

'I just got a message from Graham. They're down for the game at twelve and need some more players.'

'Uh-huh.' Ben did not like Elom's signing up for the team. He said it was because of how little quality time they spent together, but Elom thought it was more to do with the changing rooms, communal showers and alcohol. Ben had said they should have talked it over first, but Elom felt like he shouldn't need to ask permission. Ben's distrust had only hardened Elom's resolve to play.

'I'm really sorry. They'll have to forfeit otherwise.'

'I mean, it's twenty past ten and you're telling me now. This is the only day we've had to ourselves in ages.' Ben sighed. 'So when do you want to go to the Tate?'

'Well, I'd finish at about three, so could get there for four?'

'I mean, you're not going to get there for four, are you . . . and what am I supposed to do all day?'

Elom's phone vibrated in his pocket and he took it out, making an apologetic face. 'They really need me, they want me to confirm now.'

'Just do what you want. I don't even know if I want to go anyway. Might just stay in.'

'Ben.' He didn't like seeing Ben sullen, but his passive-aggressiveness made it easier.

'It's fine.'

It was the answer Elom wanted to hear, and he chose to accept it. He texted Graham to let him know he could join. 'Okay, I'm going. I've finished washing up, but I need to leave in, like, five.'

'I thought you said it started at twelve.'

'Yeah, the match, but we need to be there at eleven for warm-up. I'm going to be a bit late already.'

'Jesus.' Ben turned back to his phone and started scrolling.

'Sorry, Ben.' He was sorry, and he knew Ben's anger was justified. But he also wanted to be out on the field, shouting and tackling and being loud, rather than the constant walking on eggshells.

'You will do literally anything to not hang out with me.' Ben didn't look up.

'We can go this afternoon. Or we can just stay at home, and I'll make some dinner?'

'Yeah, maybe. I'll see what my friends are up to – maybe I'll hang with them.'

Ben didn't reply when Elom texted him after the game, so he went straight home, skipping drinks in the clubhouse. His stress rose as he changed Tube lines, and he wondered why it took so long for the doors to open and close at each station as the platform clocks ticked past 4 p.m. He thought of the best way to apologise to salvage the evening, but he also resented that he had to: he wanted the freedom to play rugby whenever he chose, and he didn't like how doing what he wanted increasingly seemed to be a transgression to Ben. His love was starting to feel like pressure, and Elom saw the irony in that the more upset Ben became about his playing, the more vindicated he felt in going.

'Hey, Ben,' Elom called, trying to clear the air with cheerfulness as he walked in.

'Hey.' The response came from the bedroom. Elom didn't go in immediately, taking his shoes off and dumping his rugby gear straight into the washing machine, hoping to stay on Ben's good side. He noticed a parcel on the dining table: square and flat, in thick wrapping paper. It had his name on it, and his heart dropped as he ran through birthdays, anniversaries and Hallmark holidays.

'What's this?' he called. Ben didn't respond and Elom walked through to the bedroom, where he was lying in bed watching a video on his phone. There was a damp, scrunched-up pair of boxer shorts on the floor. Elom pointed at them and attempted a chuckle. 'Been having fun?'

'Yeah, there was nothing else to do.' Ben kept his eyes on the screen. 'How was the match?'

'Good, ta.' They had lost, but Elom felt like it sounded worse to say he had left for a game that they hadn't even won.

'What's this then?'

Ben looked up from his phone. 'It's no big deal, just open it.'

Elom pulled at the wrapping paper and it tore in unpredictable directions, which felt like an affront to the careful folds and tape.

Inside was a record, and as Elom pulled away the paper he saw cheekbones, a buzzcut and impossibly smooth skin.

'Oh my God. *Sing to the Moon*?' Ben nodded, still watching his video on YouTube. Elom saw a scrawl on the bottom right. 'You got it signed?'

Ben looked up and nodded. Elom remembered waiting for Ben outside the concert as people left the building, smiling, laughing and singing their favourite snatches of song. He remembered being annoyed at having to wait so long, and wondering why Ben couldn't have waited to use the toilet at home. 'I was gonna give you it today. Thought we could've listened to it after the gallery.'

An increasingly familiar guilt – from being ungrateful and unempathetic, of taking Ben for granted – crept over Elom. 'Thanks. Thanks so much, Ben, this is so nice.'

'No worries. Glad you like it.'

Elom leaned in for a kiss, and Ben let him plant one on his cheek before looking up at him and smiling a formal, tight-lipped smile, like a repair person before they ask where the boiler is.

'Honestly, it's great. Shall I put it on now? I can cook?'

'Yeah, if you want.'

Ben took off his headphones but went back on his phone as Elom put the record on the player in the living room. A choir of Lauras blasted the opening line, '*Our love feels like the morning clouds . . .*' as Elom rummaged through the cupboards, deciding what to make.

The evening slowly unwound over dinner and two episodes of *Black Mirror*. Elom did the washing up and Ben suggested they finish off a bottle of white from the fridge before it went off. The mood was heavy, but Elom was glad they were talking. Before they went to sleep, they caught up on messages, sharing the odd tweet with each other, or confirming dates for meet-ups with friends.

In bed, Elom turned to face Ben's back and shuffled forward, unsure about how close he should get. Ben immediately sidled into Elom, who wrapped his arm around Ben's chest and spooned him. Ben relaxed, and it confused Elom. He didn't understand why Ben still wanted to be held by him, despite the way Elom had treated him today.

'Thanks again for the record, Ben. And sorry about the rugby, and being late.'

'It's fine. I just wish you were sorry because you actually cared about my feelings and not just because you feel awkward when I get upset.'

Elom didn't reply as he thought about the comment, and realised he hadn't appreciated the difference before. This frightened him, and he looked at the back of Ben's head and wondered what it would mean to understand Ben's thoughts in the way Ben wanted. Missing this basic element of empathy was embarrassing, like being found out for not knowing his twelve times table. Instead of answering, he held Ben tighter, and Ben put his arm over Elom's, as if he just wanted to be held with no further discussion.

When Elom had been hurt by Ben, he held on to it. It clouded his thoughts and grew through his feelings like a fungus. He wanted to ask Ben why he had encouraged him to come out, but he still hadn't; rather, he had grown bitter and guarded. Instead of trying to enjoy their time together, like Ben seemed to do, he increasingly resented it.

Elom looked at Ben again, who had already fallen asleep in his arms, and realised how simply Ben enjoyed Elom's company. Ben wanted to be around Elom enough to put pain or disappointment aside, at least momentarily, and this was something Elom couldn't do. Elom tried to think if there was anyone he felt like that with – anyone whose presence made him smile enough to forget his anxieties or frustrations and take him out of his own head; he realised that there wasn't.

At some point in the twilight, Ben drifted back into wakefulness as Elom was drifting asleep. Ben pushed back onto Elom's crotch as Elom pushed forward, and his hands travelled downwards. Ben turned and they started kissing. It was easy again, and Elom didn't know who was leading whom. He took off Ben's boxer shorts and Ben wrapped his legs around Elom's waist as Elom lay on top of him and kissed his neck. Eventually Elom reached for some lube and Ben nodded.

Elom slid in gently as Ben held his legs from behind his knees and gave a few long exhales, then nodded to signal Elom could begin. Elom always found this moment extraordinary. He looked Ben directly in his eyes as he built up the pace of his thrusts, and felt something close to awe in Ben's ability to lie back, spread his legs and let another man fuck him. It wasn't just the physical act, but the social act too: the ownership of a masculinity that Elom felt was in jeopardy every time he tried bending over. He looked Ben in the eyes, and thought how handsome he was, and felt grateful that he got to be the man to fuck him. Ben smiled up at Elom with his hands on either side of his face and said, 'I love it when you look at me like that. You only ever look at me like that when you're fucking me.'

Elom came shortly afterwards, followed by Ben, and Elom was glad. In the moments after – the slowing down, the pull in for a hug and a kiss, and the pull away to get cleaned up, he was able to hide the tears that had gathered in his eyes and threatened to slip down his nose. It was guilt again, but deeper than from skipping out on a date. He thought of all the times he had avoided Ben's gaze, or looked at him and saw his own grievances rather than seeing Ben as a person. Elom wondered if he would ever know how much he had hurt Ben, and if he could meet his need to be loved, like Ben loved him. He checked his eyes for redness in the mirror before going back to bed.

Elom's guilt overpowered him; he felt deficient in love and didn't know how to be better. He withdrew suddenly and totally, so that they barely spoke over the subsequent week. On a silent walk home from the Co-op, Ben suggested that Elom move out. Elom nodded, his sadness and guilt now compounded by shame: he was a coward, too. He got his keys out to open the front door, Ben picked up the post from the table in the common hallway, leaving behind the junk mail, and they put away the shopping together.

They agreed to keep living together until Elom found a place. The eggshells had finally broken, and in those two weeks he tried to enjoy slipping on the yolks. They finished off the miniseries they'd had on the back-burner, went to see some live music, and had sex a few more times, with Elom trying bottoming once more. The certainty of the ending seemed to relax them both,

and they handled each other lightly, without the weight of the
previous two years. On the day he left, after the movers had
picked up his boxes, Elom made two cups of peppermint tea
and they sat at the Ikea dining table. Their hands met on top of
the stained wood, and Elom gently squeezed Ben's fingers. Ben
started to cry, and Elom continued to hold his hand; neither
of them drank their tea, which grew tepid and stewed. Elom
emptied the murky water down the sink, then picked up his bag.
He hugged Ben and told him he was sorry, then left his key on
the table. As he walked past on the street under the high sun, he
looked up at the window, but he couldn't see beyond the glare
on the glass.

PART THREE

Chapter Twenty-Three

Dzifa – August 2017

'Next up is Flora Stiller, a seventy-eight-year-old woman admitted with shortness of breath and fever.' Dzifa took the medical receiving unit handover from Rajiv and jotted down the tasks left over from the night shift. 'Background of COPD, quite frail. Being treated for pneumonia. Her X-ray also showed a possible mass in the right lung so she's due a CT scan this morning, then I guess it'll be palliative care if it is anything serious.' He stifled a yawn.

'Did you tell her the CT scan is for cancer?' Dzifa asked. She was only in her second year post medical school, but she was already tired of the way shit trickled down in the NHS. Everyone was always too busy to dot the 'i's and cross the 't's.

'We just said we wanted a closer look at her lungs. It was 3 a.m. and she was a bit confused. She'll also need a DNACPR discussion,' Rajiv added. He spelled it out like it was an inconsequential word of its own – *dee-enay-see-piah* – rather than an acronym whose words meant something important.

Dzifa looked over Flora's medical history – COPD, diabetes, two heart attacks, barely mobile with carers four times a day – and wondered why they'd bothered ordering the scan in the first place. 'Over-investigation', they called it: why look for something you won't be able to fix?

'Can you sort that, Dzifa?' her consultant asked, and she nodded as Rajiv moved on to the next patient. She wrote, underlined and circled the letters. It was one thing to tell someone they might die; it was another to ask them if they wanted to be brought back or not.

The shift was busy: helping her F1 who was incapable of taking blood, ordering every manner of X-ray and scan, checking blood results, and discharging patients wherever possible, to make room for the endless stream arriving from A & E. The CT scan didn't show cancer, and the circled 'DNACPR' written on her list stared back at her every time she opened it. Sometime after 12 p.m., Dzifa walked to Flora's bay. Hospital policy stated patients were not to be disturbed during lunch, but Dzifa's to-do list was growing.

A younger man was with Flora, trying to feed her. He held the fork of mashed something in front of her as she grimaced, streaks of food around her mouth. Her oxygen tubes poked out from her nostrils as she turned away from the fork.

'Hi, I'm Dzifa, one of the doctors. Is it Flora?' The woman nodded in response. 'Can we have a quick chat?'

'Finally,' the man started. 'I've been here all morning and no doctor's come to see us. She got her antibiotics an hour late because of that scan, which no one's bothered to give us the results for.'

Dzifa readied herself. 'Sorry about that,' she said, drawing the half-plastic, half-paper curtains around the bed. She found if she continued to talk loudly, it affirmed the illusion that they were indeed soundproof. 'Sorry, what was your name?'

'Harry. I'm her son,' the man replied quickly, as if trying to push the conversation forward.

'Flora, do you mind if Harry sits in with us?' Flora nodded again, keeping her lips pursed as she inhaled through her nostrils.

'I've got lasting power of attorney anyway,' Harry said.

'Is she normally a bit confused?' Dzifa rearranged Flora's oxygen prongs.

'I live in Manchester, but the last time I saw her she was fine.'

'How long ago was that?'

'Five or six months? Just at the start of the year.' Harry shrugged and put the bowl on the bedside table. Dzifa nodded and smiled, understanding this man a little more. He was the man who moved from home, and promised to call once a week, then didn't. He was the man who visited every month, then every two months, then just the big holidays, and now that he lives far enough away, he pops in once a year on Boxing Day or New Year's Day (spending Christmas and New Year's Eve with more interesting people). He's the man who will question every decision Dzifa makes as she cares for his mother in the last weeks of her life, rather than question every decision he made in the last few decades of it.

Dzifa explained the scan results just confirmed the pneumonia, and no cancer, and Harry looked relieved. She hoped to take advantage of his improved mood as she addressed Flora.

'Hopefully you'll improve with a course of antibiotics, but I'd like to talk about what we would do if you became more unwell.'

'What do you mean?' Harry asked.

Dzifa liked having difficult conversations with patients. It was sometimes a dance, sometimes a fencing match: it depended on her skill, her empathy and her knowledge.

'Have you heard of a DNACPR decision?'

Harry simultaneously sat up straighter and became perfectly still. 'The GP tried to do one and she said no. We want you to try everything.'

'This isn't about withholding treatment – we would treat her—' she caught herself, remembering to always address the patient, 'we would treat you exactly the same regardless. But in the case that your heart stopped, CPR can be intense both for the patient and the family. The chances of someone "coming back" are extremely low.'

'I don't care, we don't just write her off because she's old.' Dzifa wondered if it was love, or maybe religion driving him.

'We just want to make sure she maintains as much dignity as possible.'

'Letting her die isn't dignified.'

She wanted to tell him it wasn't dignified to spend forty minutes cracking Flora's ribs for a 1 per cent chance her heart would start beating again. And that if it did, it wasn't dignified to spend days, weeks or months in intensive care, in pain and delirious with a tube down her throat. Or that she'd inevitably die following that, too.

'I don't want to hear this anymore. Particularly from some kid doctor. She's been in twenty-four hours and already you can't wait to put her down.'

Dzifa stopped, aware she was not going to convince him.

'Flora, have you got any particular thoughts?'

Flora shook her head. 'I want you to bring me back.'

Dzifa accepted it hadn't gone to plan. Legally, she could still sign the form, as resuscitation would be futile. But hospital culture said it was best to keep the family on board. Fortunately, as Flora was currently stable, Dzifa decided to let the consultant sort it on Monday.

'Okay, we can continue this conversation another time.'

Dzifa scrolled through Twitter on the loo before the end of her shift, and saw an article from the *New Statesman* about a by-election. She tapped it and found Elom's page on the website, full of articles, some of which she had read and most of which she hadn't. She had tried to keep up with them when he first started, but life had got in the way. The most recent one was from a few days before. She switched back to WhatsApp and opened their chat. She had last sent him a link to 'Turiya & Ramakrishna' by Alice Coltrane almost three weeks ago, but he hadn't replied.

She didn't know the details of the relationship, or the split, and she didn't know how to feel about it. She had seen him once since his breakup. He had seemed sad, but hopeful. She was happy if Elom was happy, but she didn't know if he was. She had liked Ben's cheerfulness and had hoped it would rub off on Elom. She'd liked how he had pushed Elom out of his comfort zone, and, she admitted selfishly, into a world a bit closer to the one she now lived in.

She also knew something was making Elom unhappy, but she didn't know if that was because of, or in spite of the relationship. He was getting on with their parents, as far as she knew – they had never met Ben, but were sympathetic about the breakup – and work was evidently going well. She remembered him as a teenager, and how she had looked up to him – he was so calm, and cool, and dared to break the rules, while she was always pleasing teachers and parents. Something about him now reminded Dzifa of him then, and she wondered if what she had perceived as a calm aloofness was an indication of something murkier.

Looking at the last text, Dzifa wasn't sure what to do. She had tried to reach out, but he'd ignored her, and it annoyed her, despite herself. It was close to the feeling of a patient not showing up for an appointment. She had also just started a new job, and had exams to think about, and friends to deal with too. Dzifa and Elom had got used to long stretches of little contact, and though Dzifa now realised she wanted more, she resented that he rarely seemed to be the one to make the effort.

As Dzifa pulled up her pants, the crash bleep went off, a high-pitched ping stabbing the air. She stopped, waiting for the location alert from the switchboard. A walkie-talkie voice crackled through '. . . room 16, ward 8.'

'Fuck.'

Dzifa sped across the length of the Victorian hospital corridor. She arrived to the familiar chaos of a crash call. The curtains had been half pulled around the bed, leaving two sides open to the eight or so responders. A screen was erected to block the views of people walking by, and the curtains pulled around the other patients' beds, leaving them in a confused darkness. The red crash trolley had been opened and one of Dzifa's juniors was diligently sticking a cannula into Flora's left arm.

Sarah, a nurse, was standing over Flora, her hands clasped together, one over the other. Like a clockwork toy she pushed deep into her chest, a dutiful hundred times per minute. Dzifa watched as Flora's chest collapsed with each push of the heel of Sarah's hand. A trickle of reddish spittle frothed out of the corners of her mouth just as someone else covered it with an oxygen mask connected to a bag of air.

'Rhythm check!' Rose, a colleague at her grade from another ward, signalled for the compressions to stop so they could see if her heart had restarted on the defibrillator. 'Asystole, back on!'

Sarah dived back onto her chest with renewed vigour, as if she could beat the life back into Flora. Dzifa turned to Rose, who was now reading from a folder of medical notes in her hand.

'This is Flora Stiller, a seventy-eight-year-old woman being investigated for lung ca—' Rose started.

'I know, we need to stop compressions,' Dzifa cut her off. 'She shouldn't be for resuscitation.'

Rose looked unsure about stepping off track. 'There's no DNACPR form.'

Time was ticking on, and Flora's chest caved with each second. Dzifa turned to the rest of the team. 'This lady is too frail. Diabetes, heart disease, age. She should have had a form, her consultant agrees.' She embellished his passing comment from the handover that morning. Several pairs of eyes looked back at her, some confused, some relieved. Rose was hesitant.

Before she could respond, Miri, the medical registrar, arrived, followed by the anaesthetist. Rose immediately turned to her and explained the story, and Miri read the notes as she listened.

'We've only finished one cycle. We haven't given adrenaline yet,' Rose finished.

'She seems pretty frail,' Miri said, to Dzifa's relief. 'But we've started now. Let's give her a couple more rounds with adrenaline then stop.'

Dzifa gritted her teeth. A crash call was not a place for argument, and she wasn't bold enough to try with a senior.

'Dzifa, can you take over compressions? Sarah looks tired,' Miri added. Dzifa dutifully took Sarah's place and plunged her hands down onto Flora's chest.

Dzifa sat in a small plastic chair, facing Harry in an oversized, hospital-blue faux-leather armchair beside the bed. She ran her tongue over her teeth, aware of the fact she hadn't eaten or drunk anything in six hours. She was long past her finishing time, but she wanted to be the one to talk to him. The room was too small, with furniture facing them at odd angles so Dzifa was too close to Harry, but still unable to look him fully in the face unless they both contorted their necks. Still, she figured he was too far away to smell her breath. He had come back from a cigarette break to find his mum surrounded by noise and people, and had been guided to this room, where he sat alone, waiting. Dzifa was surprised he had stayed in the hospital at all, this late into the night. His leg was shaking, sending the waves into Dzifa's feet.

'I'm afraid it's not good news,' Dzifa began.

Before she could finish, he turned his head, hiding his eyes behind his hand. He coughed out a sob, flicking the tiniest spray of spittle down his lip. She explained the events leading up to Flora's crash as she had been told them. She explained that they weren't sure what had caused it, but that it was probably a pulmonary embolism, or maybe another heart attack, and it couldn't have been predicted. He nodded occasionally. After she had asked about support for him – his partner was at home and would be looking after him – he turned to look at her directly. His eyes were pink and wet, small red squiggles reaching across the whites.

'You did CPR then, after all?'

Dzifa hesitated. 'Yes, we did for a few minutes.'

'Thanks. Thanks for trying.'

On her way home, Dzifa caught her reflection in the windows of the Tube train as it rattled from station to station, and saw an image of herself pushing into Flora's chest. At first, Harry had made her angry – by his stubbornness, and his obvious projection of guilt about his own lack of care. She still thought he'd been brash, and rude, but she pitied him now, too. Anyone could relate to the feeling of not having done enough. Still, she didn't think that had given him the right to expect her to breathe life into a corpse. Dzifa's main regret was not pushing for the DNACPR sooner – they had only delayed the inevitable.

She pulled out her phone as soon as the train surfaced at Finsbury Park. She wanted to offload, and thought of calling Elom. She missed him, but she didn't think it was fair to have their first conversation in weeks be a rant about a dead patient. She also didn't know if he would pick up. She rang Clem instead, and decided to text him again later.

Chapter Twenty-Four

Elom – September 2017

Dirt and blood, carried by too-hot water, curved around naked feet on the way to the drain. The shower washed away the last of the adrenaline and uncovered the beating Elom's body had taken. Soap stung hidden cuts into being, and every bend of a joint voiced a new bruise. Each jolt of pain was like a flash of light on his skin, reminding him of the shape of himself; he took stock of the damage before dulling the pain once more in the club bar.

His team had lost, which they were used to. The spirit was celebratory, and they sang the club song and laughed over fumbles and yellow cards through the steam. Elom's eyes flicked towards the drain, as usual. A first surge of red-streaked muddy browns, a longer wave of foamy whites, then a wash of pure, clear water. At this point he looked up and saw the only other team mate still showering. Guy's back was facing Elom, and he watched the water soak his dark body hair as it was funnelled between the curves of his arse on the way to his thighs. His toenails were neatly trimmed and there was a blister on his right heel. He had scored a conversion earlier with that foot. Their eyes brushed as Guy turned around, and both reached for their respective shower gels and re-lathered, though they had fully cleaned themselves at least twice already.

'You heading to the bar?' asked Guy.

'Sure,' Elom replied.

The wet warmth from the shower followed them into the crowded bar upstairs, so there was a thickness in the air and Elom didn't feel quite dry. The club logo was drawn in the condensation on the windows facing the pitches, along with a few cocks and rugby balls.

Elom found it hard not to touch Guy. They spoke in different groups for most of the evening, though as if connected by a steel rod they kept their distance while moving in sync, each having perfect knowledge of the other's position. By the time they came together they were both tipsy. The room was loud, and Guy put his hand on Elom's neck to draw him close to speak. A touch like that was supposed to feel electric, but these days, Elom always felt electric: jolting, vibrating, formless. Instead, there was a firmness to Guy's touch, helping Elom feel grounded in his own body again.

'Drink?' asked Guy. Elom breathed in cheap shower gel, grass and beer.

Guy returned a few minutes later with a Belgian lager in a plastic pint glass. As Elom reached over to meet his outstretched arm he glanced at the gold band hugging Guy's ring finger, tickled by a few coarse hairs – the team's token straight. He had been here before with Guy, and what had seemed like a harmless flirtation a few months ago had become overwhelming.

'All right, boys – Soho?' Alex asked.

Guy glanced at Elom over his drink. 'I have work tomorrow,' Elom replied. Alex was always three drinks and a bump ahead.

Guy had almost finished his pint. 'Come on, Elom. A cheeky half?'

'We got fucked enough today, I don't need seconds. Have fun, guys.' He hugged Alex and Guy goodbye and made his way to the overground station.

Elom opened Grindr automatically, then closed it just as quickly, barely remembering the faces he'd scrolled past, as if he'd checked his watch only to immediately forget the time. Since Ben, men had become a habit, rather than a passion, or even a hobby.

As he scrolled through the news, a text popped up from Guy. It was a selfie with an exaggerated sad face – it looked like he was sitting on the loo.

Defo not coming??

Lol, sorry pal, not tonight. Guy was intoxicating, but Elom knew better than to be the stereotype of a gay, fixated on a married man.

'Online' changed to 'Last Seen'. A minute passed, then he saw Guy was typing again.

all ok with your dad btw? Kodzo had spent a night in hospital the previous week with a kidney infection.

oh yeah, thanks man. He's much better now. Milking it if anything lol

Brill. Lemmy know if you need to chat x

Online . . . Last Seen . . . Online . . . Typing . . .

Lol alex is too far gone. You defs not up for a nightcap? I'm probs 10 mins behind you.

Elom relented – Guy was still his friend. He stepped off at the next stop, Hampstead Heath, and was ready with two pints by the time Guy arrived. They both felt a bit too lively for the quiet weekday pub, and were conspiratorial in their hushed laughter in the corner over the drunken videos Carlos was sending.

'Are you still thinking of moving?' Guy eventually asked.

'Maybe,' Elom replied. He had been living in a cramped, shared flat again after breaking up with Ben, and was thinking of making the well-trodden migration back out of London. His friends had started to put deposits down, helped by partners and parents. Dzifa was renting a nicer place than him on her doctor's salary. He didn't feel like a small fish in a big pond so much as a puppy, frantically paddling amongst sleek dolphins who were speeding off into the distance.

'We're gonna miss you.' Elom could feel Guy's thigh resting against his own, grounding him again. He remembered the water running down Guy's back and thighs in the shower.

'Okay, guys, five minutes, yeah?' the bartender said faux-politely, as he placed chairs on tables beside the pair. Elom excused himself to the loo as Guy emptied his glass.

Elom had been lonely since Ben, and under-prepared for how much he would miss someone with kindness and wanting in his touch. Despite himself, he missed having someone who knew his secrets, and had felt the effort of having to reintroduce his real self to every new person he met. He felt comfortable with Guy, though, and felt light in his chest as he turned back to their seats.

Guy looked up from his phone as Elom sat down. 'Mine's three minutes away.' He left his phone on the table as he stood and put on his jacket. Elom saw the little black car juddering back and forth around a corner, one second moving towards the dot that was them, the next moving away. Guy was heading home, evidently without Elom.

Elom watched Guy get into the cab after they hugged goodbye. Not tonight, then. He turned right and walked up the hill, a heaviness in the space that hope had left behind. First, it had been the hope that he could be strong enough not to want Guy, and when that passed, it was the hope that Guy would want him too. Once again, he had misread the signs of desire. He hated the insecurity that came with being single – he had hoped it would make him feel in control, but instead it put him at the whim of whoever was nearest.

His feet trod familiar ground up the Heath, first concrete, then grass. A gentle breeze shook the trees, and he saw the dark outline of a man. He seemed half drawn; partly shaded in or partly rubbed out, Elom couldn't quite tell. Elom approached, craving the man's body, as much as the danger of the encounter itself. They touched each other's crotches through their jeans, and he reached around to feel Elom's arse. Cruising was direct, and simple. Even he could understand the signs here. Elom acquiesced as the man turned him around and lowered his waistband. The air was cold on his skin, but the man's tongue was warm, and Elom bent his knees instinctively, steadying himself on a tree.

The tongue stopped after a minute, and he felt the cold air on his exposed hole, then something thick and blunt pushing against him. He breathed in sharply with the pain, unsure what to say, or if he should say anything. He hadn't had anyone try since Ben, and the memory made him tense. Suddenly he felt air again. 'Are you all right?'

'Yeah,' Elom said, turning to look over his shoulder. 'Yeah, just a bit sore. I'm quite tight.' The stranger looked at him for a moment, his hand resting on Elom's ass. Elom could see more of his face as his vision acclimatised to the dark. The man's eyes darted back and forth as they looked at his. Elom mentally prepared himself to continue getting fucked, knowing that the man would want his desire sated. Instead, he just grabbed Elom's hand and put it on his cock. Elom started stroking him until he heard cum splattering on the leaves on the ground, then the man patted him on his still nude cheeks, said thanks, and walked off with a smile.

An hour later Elom slowly opened the door to his flat, took off his shoes and made his way to the toilet with a quiet urgency. He exhaled as he sat, squinting his eyes against the halogen light bouncing off the faux-marble tiles. He rested his face in his hands and breathed in the fading scent of tree bark, slowly mingling with his own shit and sickly synthetic oils from an overpriced diffuser, while the extractor fan made a white-noise whirr. His right elbow rested on the edge of a bruise on his thigh from the match. Gently – almost absentmindedly – he rolled his elbow across to the right, feeling the skin pull taut as the muscle rippled underneath. He stopped just at the point where the flesh became most tender; the almost-pain wrapped in sweetness. When he wiped, he felt a sting. He checked the white paper – a red-streaked brown – before letting it drop. He stood to watch as the flush emptied the bowl, leaving only still, clear water.

Chapter Twenty-Five

Abena – October 2017

'This one looks good. It won't need much work either; the kitchen was renovated in 2012.' Kodzo passed Abena the laptop, and she slid her glasses on to look at the house listing. It was another bungalow in another village an hour north of Glasgow, on winding roads. Abena looked over photographs of thick mauve carpets and doily-covered sideboards that hadn't been changed for as long as she had lived in this country. 'Yeah, it's nice,' she said. 'The living room will need updating, though.'

'That's easy,' Kodzo said, taking back the laptop. 'The garden's a good size, too.'

The thought of a house in the country excited Kodzo. When he had learned how much of his pension he could take as a lump sum, Abena hoped it would mean they could finally build or buy a home in Accra, like the ones they had seen on their trip. But Kodzo had other plans. Somehow, she instead found herself browsing worn-looking cottages in the Scottish countryside. Kodzo's plan – to buy a smaller house in

Scotland, move, rent out the family home and use that cash to travel – seemed like too many steps in the wrong direction. He was concerned with investing in British property and the kids' future, but Abena didn't want to think about the future anymore. She also didn't want to keep giving up her present for her kids.

She wanted to argue, but didn't know how: it was Kodzo's money, after all. Still, she remembered how easily he had accepted her redundancy lump sum to pay off the mortgage. Things to do with money and obligation were messy, and it was easier to shrug it off than to challenge. She stood up to start cooking when her phone, and then Kodzo's, started ringing.

'Long time no see.' Abena picked up Elom's call. They rarely spoke these days – it felt like he only remembered the family on occasion; that whatever work or social life he had in London seemed more important.

Kodzo put his laptop down on the coffee table and leaned into the phone screen. 'What's up, young man?'

'I'm good, yeah.' Abena noted it was 2 p.m. as Elom shuffled up in bed and quickly rubbed his left eye. 'Yeah, fine,' he said more briskly, 'just been working loads.'

'Son, you look tired.' Abena couldn't help herself.

'Yeah, just work and stuff.'

Abena was undeterred. 'If you're working a lot, you can get some healthy ready meals at M & S. You need to get some nutrients or you'll exhaust yourself.' She couldn't understand how at twenty-seven he still needed to be reminded to take care of himself.

'Okay. I'm eating fine, honestly,' Elom replied.

'It's Sunday today: just cook a big pot of stew – tomatoes, onions, add some aubergine, you can get chicken drumsticks and add some too – you've seen me do it. And you can freeze it for the week.'

'Ah, woman, he knows.' Kodzo laughed, and Elom smiled for the first time during the call.

'I'll be fine, Mum. Thanks though.'

Abena gave up. Dzifa had got the hang of cooking now, and now that Elom was living on his own again, she hoped he would start to make the effort.

'What are you guys up to anyway?'

'Your dad is just looking at houses.'

'Oh yeah?' Elom asked. 'In Ghana?'

Abena looked at Kodzo, watching as he found the right words, slightly less casually than usual. 'We'll still go, but we'll buy here first.'

Elom nodded, silent for a moment. 'When are you going?'

'I'm not sure,' Abena replied.

'Hm.' Elom paused in thought. 'Let's all go together,' he said, quietly.

'All of us?' Abena asked. 'You and Dzifa?'

'Yeah. Tell us when works for you and we can figure out leave.' He looked more animated now to Abena, and she was excited that he might be excited about coming to Ghana with her.

'Do you want to?'

'Yeah, I want to see it. Think I need to get out of London too, to be honest.'

'We can organise something, I'm sure,' Kodzo said.

'Yeah.' Elom sat up again slightly from the slump he had slid into on his bed. 'Yeah. Though you're retiring and you're turning sixty. I'll talk to Dzifa; we owe you something.'

'Ho, you don't have to do that,' Abena replied, blushing, but grateful at the thought. They had never gone before as a family because it was simply too expensive, then once the kids started working, it had seemed impossible to pin everyone down at the same time.

'Ha. Okay, maybe not everything – let us have a look at how much it is first. But it'd be nice to see what home looks like.'

The surprise was still with Abena an hour later. Elom had been distant for a while, and she loved that he was coming back. She wondered if it was a coincidence that he'd decided to come to Ghana so soon after he and Ben had broken up. She'd mistrusted Ben. She'd been uneasy with the thought that Elom had so suddenly started a relationship with a man when he'd moved to London, and had never understood his influence over her son. After Elom's initial reveal, and him skipping Christmas, he had never really asked Abena or Kodzo to meet Ben, and she had never pushed. She hadn't wanted to cause an argument, but she also hadn't known if Ben had been the one pulling Elom away. She was relieved they had broken up, and that now she might get to go back home with her family because of it. As she stirred a thickening pot of powdered fufu on the stove, she smiled, wondering what it would be like to eat it pounded in a pestle outside, splitting off four soft, starchy balls at a table on a verandah somewhere.

*   *   *

Two months later, Abena squeezed her gloved hands in her pockets as she and Kodzo strolled down Byres Road, looking in shop windows obscured by white spray-painted 'snow'. Kodzo's cholesterol level at his last check had been borderline high, so they'd walked from home, underestimating the bite of the cold on their way to get a coffee. Since the phone call with Elom, they had all agreed a trip for some vague time after Kodzo's retirement. Dzifa had looked at flights and thought she and Elom could split the cost, but since then the subject hadn't been mentioned, and Abena felt like she wasn't supposed to bring it up. The cold sliced through her patience as she thought about warmer places.

'I think we should go to Ghana as soon as you retire – we can skip the winter and just stay until it gets warmer. I don't want to do this ice and snow again!' She chuckled to hide her exasperation.

'Maybe,' Kodzo replied, distracted by a display of electric razors in a pharmacy window, 'but that's a good time to buy houses, too – in January things go up for sale.'

'We can just look when we come back, no?'

'I don't think so.' He spoke casually, looking both ways as they crossed the street, and Abena felt he was looking everywhere but at her. Her impatience grew with the volume of her voice.

'What are you talking about?' She stopped in front of the coffee shop they had walked an hour to get to, and Kodzo only noticed when he held the door open for her and saw she was a few paces behind him.

'Abena, come inside.' He shuffled as a couple awkwardly passed between them.

'Why are you being like this about Ghana?' Abena was suddenly scared, and she didn't want to walk through the door with Kodzo until he explained.

'It's not a big deal, things take time.' He looked weary, but Abena stood her ground.

'Kodzo, do you want your children to go to Ghana or not?'

'Yes. Yes, of course. They need to see it, of course.'

Abena stepped towards the door which Kodzo was still holding, to the annoyance of the customers inside whose warm air was being stolen. He walked in ahead of her, letting the door fall back into her outstretched hand. As it landed, and she saw him in the warmth, something clicked. 'Kodzo, do you not want to go back?'

He turned. 'Come inside, you're letting the heat out.'

'Do you?'

'Yes, of course.' He gestured at her to come through, looking around, embarrassed by the scene they were creating. Abena looked at him, and at how he was still avoiding her eyes, and for the first time she felt confused by him. Kodzo had always been totally transparent – his intentions were always written in his face, and Abena always knew how to read them, and it had made her feel safe. Now, she couldn't tell if he was hiding something, or if he was just confused himself, and she didn't know what to do.

She joined him and sat down while he ordered. Being in Ghana with Kodzo had felt restorative. She could tell he'd found the changes in the village affronting, but change was expected. She hadn't expected him to have changed his mind about staying – it had always been the plan to go back home. It had been everyone's plan.

He came back with the coffees, but she remained silent. There were other things to plan: Christmas with the kids, the retirement party, her birthday – and, she conceded, moving house – but looking beyond that scared her. If it hadn't been Aunty Esther's chores, it had been Abla, and if it hadn't been Abla, it had been Elom, and now, it was Kodzo. She refused to see her family as a burden, but managing their lives always seemed incompatible with having control over hers. She had thought she was finally about to get control, but now it was like Kodzo had painted over the finish line, and she no longer knew what she had been running towards all this time.

Chapter Twenty-Six

Kodzo – April 2018

Kodzo met Mensah and Peter at the pub by the canal to watch the football. Peter arrived later than the others and sat down with a sigh.

'You're looking tired, brother,' Kodzo said after shaking his hand with a click.

'Hm.' Peter took a sip. 'I had to go in last night. Complicated labour – the registrar needed help.'

'You are too old for this, now,' Mensah chided. 'You should have retired long ago.'

'I did.' Peter shrugged, and Kodzo laughed. Peter had retired from obstetrics two years earlier, but took locum posts in his old hospitals, working, as far as Kodzo could tell, full-time or more.

'Ah, I mean actually retire,' Mensah replied.

Peter shrugged again. 'And do what?'

Peter's question was short, but Kodzo recognised the boredom and fear dammed behind it: retirement could look like an empty stretch to death. Peter had lasted a few months at home before picking up shifts again, and Kodzo didn't blame him. Mensah had carefully kept Ghana all these years, flying back and forth, so his retirement was a natural slide home. Peter had work. Kodzo was glad that he himself had learned how to relax, and that having days to read new books and go on trips with Abena made his heart beat more calmly.

That new pace of life included an eventual trip back to Ghana with his kids. The details were yet to be confirmed, but everyone was on board for fresh coconut on the beach, in the sun, all together. Abena hadn't brought up moving in a while, as they had been busy planning for other things, including looking for a cottage to downsize to in the countryside, and Kodzo was glad that they were finally on the same page. All of their friends agreed: Ghana was for holidays, maybe longer trips, but not for living in, not at their age.

'How's everyone?' Peter asked, munching on some salted peanuts he had placed in the middle of the table.

'Everyone is fine,' Mensah answered. 'Maria is in Ghana for Easter – I'll be joining her next week. Mawusi, too, she is fine. She's trying to buy a flat with her boyfriend in Shawlands, so, yeah, they are doing well.' He nodded, as if to seal the still-open sentence. Kodzo felt the awkwardness of the word 'boyfriend' in his elderly Ghanaian friend's mouth, even though Mawusi and her boyfriend had been together for almost a decade. 'What about Abena and the kids?'

Kodzo told his friends that they were well. Abena had been preparing for his retirement party. Dzifa and Elom were working hard. He had last seen them both at Christmas and was looking forward to reuniting with them at the party.

'Are they going to stay in London?' Peter asked.

'I'm not sure,' Kodzo replied honestly. 'They don't have anything tying them down, really.'

'Okay,' Peter replied. 'I was thinking, my cousin's daughter arrives in London in a couple of months to study. It would be good to put them in touch.' He smiled.

Kodzo nodded. 'Sure, that would be nice.'

'She's a lovely girl. I'll let them know at the party.'

The suggestion was straightforward, but Kodzo felt like he was lying by omission by not explaining about Elom. It was silly: Peter just wanted some familiar faces to show a relative around, like they all used to do in the old days. Besides, anything Kodzo might say was Elom's business and not his. Kodzo wasn't like the old guard – his children could speak for themselves. It had been difficult for him to learn, but he was proud that he had.

'*Ɛyi* – matchmakers, please,' Mensah interrupted with a smirk, his eyes still on the screen, 'let's watch the match we are here for.' Peter and Kodzo rolled their eyes, turning to the TV.

Dzifa and Elom arrived on the day before the party. They left their things in their old bedrooms and immediately went to the fridge, pulling out leftovers while Abena cut and topped bits of filo pastry and dipped things in breadcrumbs. Kodzo was surprised to see them put their dishes in the dishwasher without protest, then join him outside to set up the marquee he had bought from the middle aisle in Lidl. He brought a wireless radio out into the back garden as they worked, while Dzifa told them about her most recent rotation.

'I looked after this old Ghanaian lady recently,' Dzifa said as she pinned down the plastic windows. 'She was super sweet, and she asked me what church I went to. It was a bit awkward when I said that I don't.'

Kodzo agreed. 'For many Ghanaians it's not really an option.'

'Yeah, I was wondering, like, why did you guys stop?'

'I'm sure we've told you already,' Kodzo said as he picked up the leftover packaging. 'It just wasn't really serving us anymore.' It was the truth, but not the detailed truth. Kodzo liked talking about religion generally, but talking about why he had changed course was awkward – it was a story about his mistakes.

'You've said that, but I don't quite get it,' Dzifa replied. 'I was thinking about tomorrow, too, like seeing Uncle Peter and all of them. Was it not awkward leaving? Didn't you miss them?'

'Ah ah, who do you guys think is coming tomorrow?' Kodzo said. Dzifa rolled her eyes. Kodzo knew he was being evasive. 'Look, let me tell you something. Leaving the church was really difficult. But if you think I was lonely when I left – because I think that's what you're trying to say?' he asked, and they nodded awkwardly. 'Mm-hmm, if you're wondering about that, I wasn't lonely when I left the church. I was lonely when I was in the church.' He gave them a moment to process as he fixed some pegs.

'What do you mean?' Elom asked.

'I mean I was surrounded by people every Sunday, but I couldn't get the help from them that I needed. And even God – the whole point of the thing, I mean, come on – even God, I couldn't approach Him for the help I needed.'

Kodzo had never spoken to Elom and Dzifa about what help he had needed. He wasn't ashamed anymore, but he also didn't want sympathy from his children. He didn't know how to tell them how low he had been, and he didn't want to dwell on it himself either. They were smart kids, though, and he was confident they could see from the books he read, and the way he spoke, that he wanted them to live life on their own terms, and he could see that they did. Dzifa had always been happily bold. Elom had once been uninterested to the point of insolence, with flashes of anger, but he had since moved to London, started a new career. He was a man far from God, in a good way. Kodzo didn't understand Elom's sexuality, but he appreciated that it meant that Elom was a man living without the yoke of Christianity, and Kodzo was glad Elom had that freedom, despite Kodzo's hopes – once upon a time – of having him join the fold.

Kodzo had only recently stopped taking anti-depressants, and he'd found mindfulness to be a helpful companion for controlling his anxiety. He hadn't had a panic attack – he knew what they were, now – in years. He was calmer: church had been a rollercoaster of ecstasy and failure. The worship was great, but he could never be a good enough father, husband, man or Christian. No one could, and the only way to get better was to pray harder. If nothing changed, it was somehow his own fault for not praying hard enough, or believing enough. The church was supposed to have given him control of his life, through God, but instead he had felt powerless. Now he felt he had the power to fix things in his life, and the grace to accept some of the things that he couldn't.

'It's more personal. And I still have good relationships with my friends. Religion's better without all the ceremony and rules, if that makes sense.'

'Yes, totally – I get it, Dad,' Dzifa replied. 'It's brave. I'm proud of you, not many people can do that.'

Elom simply nodded in agreement. Kodzo smiled and sipped his tea, proud of himself too.

The day itself went as smoothly as Kodzo could have hoped. It started with quiet sex – Kodzo hadn't realised how creaky the bed had got since the kids had moved. Elom and Dzifa helped lay out the food and blow up some balloons. Abena looked great in a tailored dress of deep blue batik and a new curly wig, and Kodzo was enchanted by her ability to stir four pots on the stove whilst looking like a ten. There was only a spit of rain around noon, when the guests were due to arrive, though of course none of the Ghanaians arrived until after 2 p.m. Kodzo and Abena took their time, sharing drinks with the kids and taking photos in their new clothes for their WhatsApp profile photos. Elom and Dzifa helped keep the first arrivals – colleagues and neighbours – entertained during the awkward early stages.

By the evening, the house was full, plates were empty, and those with good enough knees were on their feet to the Daddy Lumba or Sarkodie, tumbling out of the kitchen door into the back garden. The kids' present was a welcome surprise: tickets for a family trip to Ghana ('Date TBC') and Kodzo was touched not by the expense, but by the fact that Elom and Dzifa had done it together, for him and Abena. It felt like the years of grounding and shouting and parental stress had paid off. Although they lived in different cities, they were together. He remembered once feeling embarrassed that he was a nurse, and not a doctor. But when he looked at his home, and his family, and the adventures they still had ahead of them, he thought himself blessed. Peter was a doctor, and he was still slogging away in the hospital, barely seeing his one granddaughter because his work had been his life. When Kodzo went to bed, his legs were tired from dancing, his cheeks from laughing, and his throat from talking all day. Abena joined him after wiping off her makeup, and they fell asleep in each other's arms.

The four of them sat down to lunch after the morning clean-up.

'I'm so glad Mawusi came,' Abena said as she stripped a leftover piece of chicken from the bone with one hand. 'I forgot how funny she is!'

'Yes!' Dzifa agreed. 'It's so weird we never hung out as kids. She was just a couple of years older, which seemed like such a big deal.'

'Next time you visit we can all do dinner together or something,' Abena suggested, 'the parents and the kids too.'

Elom nodded. 'Yeah. I spoke to Uncle Peter too last night.' He scooped a fork of jollof and kept his eye on his plate as he spoke. 'Hadn't talked to him in ages. I forgot I used to call him Uncle Magic.'

Kodzo laughed. 'He used to pull fifty-pence coins from your ear. You loved that one so much.'

Elom nodded again. 'He said he has a family friend in London he wants me to meet. Gave me her number.'

'Oh?' Kodzo asked. He had forgotten about the suggestion.

'I took it, so no worries.'

'That's fine – you don't have to get in touch, only if you feel like it,' Kodzo said.

'Yeah, I know,' Elom said tightly. 'It was just a bit of an awkward . . . I mean, it was actually quite annoying.'

'Why annoying?' Abena asked.

Elom didn't reply, and Dzifa answered, 'Elom, I don't think he meant anything by it.'

'You live in London too and he didn't ask you.'

'Elom . . .' Kodzo was confused, and suddenly reminded of a much younger Elom, reserved, terse, always battling with something. 'Did he say something bad or what?'

'It's not that big a deal, it's just . . . it's like I have to keep coming out all the time? I hate pretending that I didn't have a boyfriend, or that I'm looking for a girlfriend.'

'You don't have to do anything, Elom,' Abena said, and Kodzo could hear that she was also seeing the sixteen-year-old they thought they had left behind.

'Have you told him I'm gay?' He looked directly at Kodzo.

'No,' Kodzo answered truthfully.

'Yeah,' Elom replied.

'It's nothing to do with them – why would I go around telling them that you're straight or gay?' Kodzo didn't understand Elom's frustration – he didn't talk to them about who Dzifa slept with. In fact, he didn't know himself.

'I was with Ben for years and it never came up? It's just avoiding it then, surely?'

'I haven't avoided anything. Ghanaians don't talk about . . . sexuality like that.' Kodzo saw no obligation to talk about intimate things that were nobody else's business but his son's.

'It's not in our culture,' Abena added.

'I don't buy it. Any time you mention your wife, or husband, or Peter talks about Mawusi and her boyfriend, they're talking about sexuality. I just think you've chosen to leave me out.' Elom took a breath, and it looked like the anger left with it, or was at least diluted. He seemed flatter, more tired. 'Have you told any of your friends I'm gay? Would you?'

Kodzo was becoming exasperated. 'It's not my business. If you want to tell people, you should tell people; if you don't, then don't. Why is it my job?' It didn't make sense to take ownership of something so personal, and so contentious. He didn't want to be responsible for opening Elom up to the judgement of others. His job was to support him if he made that decision, and he felt like he had done. He couldn't understand why he was being attacked.

'It's fine, you're right, it isn't your job,' Elom replied, eyes back on his rice.

'Do you want to hand me your plates?' Abena asked, standing up. Dzifa joined her in the kitchen, and Kodzo heard the clinks of the dishwasher being filled.

'Want some juice?' Elom asked Kodzo.

'Yes, please.'

Elom came back a couple of minutes later with a glass. Something scandalous came on the news, Dzifa popped in to ask Elom how he wanted to get to the station, and Abena shared some pictures of the party she had just been sent. The equilibrium reset, as often happens with family, so that things were at least no longer terse when Kodzo dropped Elom and Dzifa off. On his way back home, he thought about Elom sitting back, small and disappointed, on the sofa. Elom had resigned himself to the fact that Kodzo was hiding him, rather than protecting him – that he was embarrassed, or maybe even ashamed of his son. The idea was ludicrous to Kodzo – as ludicrous as when Elom thought his grounding for exams was punishment rather than protection: Kodzo only ever had his best interests at heart. It hurt him to think that after so much time, Elom could still think so poorly of him, and could understand him so little. He couldn't comprehend why his own child would be so disappointed in him. It felt like a wilful misunderstanding. Even if Elom wanted to talk to him, Kodzo simply stating that he cared wouldn't change his son's mind. With the tiniest of pops, Kodzo felt his little balloon of pride puncture.

Chapter Twenty-Seven

Elom – May 2018

Please mind the gap.

Elom sighed at the part-robotic, part-human voice: a person stripped of humanity, or a computer program attempting to emulate it. It felt more like the latter, and it was funny to Elom that TFL wanted the software to sound more human. To convince him that the robot-person would feel sad if he were to stumble forward and clamp himself between the train and the platform. As if he wasn't crossing the yellow line as a favour to her.

It was Monday, which meant a jostle through the Underground, then another in the office. Elom disliked pitch meetings: he had woken early to scour Google Trends and listen to the *Today* programme, but judging by the tweets liked by his colleagues, he was already behind. He read articles about the same wars, elections, referendums and sports stars he read every morning, reconnecting to the Underground Wi-Fi every few stations to load a new report. His Spotify playlist was downloaded and cycled smoothly from Little Simz to Laura

Mvula, the opening bells of 'She' sounding like a train from a dreamscape.

Elom accidentally pushed the standby button as he turned up the volume on his phone. It went momentarily black, and he saw his reflection, run through by a thick, shiny smear on the screen. It was a trail from the lube he had used to jack off the night before, whilst swiping through video after video. He wiped it away with his thumb and turned up the music, then reconnected to the Wi-Fi at the next stop.

His phone buzzed with a message from Pippy, which he swiped away too. He hadn't seen her, or Freya, in weeks. He felt guilty, but it felt worse to see them. The last time they had met for dinner, every item on the menu had had an ingredient he had never heard of. He ordered confidently, laughed through anecdotes, and even shared his frustrations about Kodzo from the party. But he felt like he was acting – at understanding the food, and at understanding their friendship. He didn't know what they saw in him, and he used to be able to ignore it, but it scared him now. At school, he had acted to fit in with friends he thought liked him, and then he realised that they didn't even respect him. He had thought he understood Ben, until he didn't. He hadn't replied to messages from Kodzo or Dzifa either. Elom was tired of feeling small and confused.

Eight journalists sat around a table chequered with paper cups. The meeting was a frenzy of Elom's colleagues trying to convince their editor Mark that they had the best idea for a story, often based on access to contacts. Rebecca successfully pitched a feature on the care-home crisis (labour shortages were the cause),

Tom, an interview about mid-life crisis (with a famous author) and Polly an investigation into the climate crisis (honey was the secret to solving it).

'Elom, what've you got?' Mark asked.

Elom scrolled through his crisis Rolodex, falling on 'G'. 'It's almost a year since Grenfell. We're due a follow-up on the survivors, and those lost. Life after rehousing, current housing policy, what's changed, maybe some profiles on some of those who died?' There were some nods in agreement. Elom got the detached feeling he often got in these meetings, particularly when he was tired. It felt like his main processor had gone on standby, but his back-up drive whirred efficiently, knowing what cues to follow, and what vague sentences were required of him. It was shameful. Everyone else around the table was engaged – their pitches had been well researched; at the very least they remembered what they had scrolled past this morning whilst sweating on the Tube. Elom knew how brutally the people of Grenfell had been treated, and that they deserved champions. He knew he'd had a river of empathy for them when he first reported on it a year ago. But something was different now, and it made him feel disgusted with himself. He felt like his empathy had been dammed up behind concrete. He was hammering away, dying of thirst, but he couldn't break through, and it left him struggling to remember how to care.

Fast train approaching.

Elom stood on the yellow line, his toes gently pushed up by the rippled slabs lining the platform edge. His saliva tasted sweet and thick after four scrumpies at post-work Wednesday drinks.

At five thirty, Elom had signalled to his colleagues that it was time to leave the office by packing up his laptop. People were ready – the office was already abuzz with conversation as they wound down from work. Elom even stood idly for a minute, willing people to move. But it wasn't until Tom – charming, jocular, well dressed, always somehow so visible – definitively signalled his readiness by swinging his bag onto his shoulder, that the flock followed. Elom's invisibility continued at the pub. He always felt a tension between being cool enough to leave, or cool enough to be the last one standing. The outcome was never satisfactory: either he left and everyone stayed to have fun without him, or he stayed and felt weak, envying those who had the confidence to call it a night when they felt like it – regardless, his actions never set the pace. Tonight, he had chosen to stay, and already regretted the coming hangover.

A man stood a few metres to his left, just in front of the yellow line. Elom looked around, but nobody seemed to have noticed him. Earlier on, the robot-voice had said that a service was delayed due to 'a person on the track', and Elom wondered exactly what that looked like. He looked at the man again, fighting the eternal internal battle about whether to speak to a stranger on the Underground.

A whistle rose to a screech in Elom's right ear, and with a shudder the billboard in front of him was replaced by a racket of metal and glass. He could feel the wind on his face, and on the whites of his eyes, and as soon as it had arrived it was gone. The silence throbbed, as if the noise had been sucked from his ears with the train, and the vacuum left behind tugged at his body. The man still stood to the left of him, and Elom thought about the distance between them, and how little it would have taken to reach out and touch him. He thought about the distance between himself and the train, and how little it would have taken for him to step forward.

At home he cooked pasta and ate it in bed. He suddenly felt the need to trawl through his unread WhatsApp messages, finally opening the videos, music links, pictures and memes from friends, family and old hookups, replying to them one by one, apologising for hiding himself and letting them know they had been seen. He had mostly stayed in group chats while Ben had left, but as he trawled, he realised that they weren't that active anymore anyway. He imagined new groups had been set up, welcoming Ben back with a fanfare of emojis.

When he got to the family chat, he wondered how his mum and dad were doing, and what they had congratulated Dzifa for in a message preview he had seen yesterday, but opening it felt burdensome. So he plugged in his phone and opened his laptop; Netflix turned to YouTube, and at midnight he found himself logging on to xHamster again.

Mark liked Elom's Grenfell story, and asked him to meet the podcast editor, Mel. Two days later they sat together in a studio, dialling in Karim who was living in a bedsit in Whitechapel. He sat framed by a double bed and two identical bedside tables topped by two identical lamps. Karim's story was brutal, life continued to be difficult, and he was clear about what he needed in order to be able to make it work. He spoke with intelligence and clarity, and they had to pause several times to allow him to wipe away tears.

After recording, Mel took a deep breath, let out a 'Woo!' and fanned her eyes. She said it had been 'a powerful interview'. Elom thought of the last time he had cried: Ben had bought them tickets to the Laura Mvula concert, and had held Elom from behind as they swayed to 'She'. Usually, Elom bristled at being held like that, as if Ben were claiming him, but for a moment he relaxed into it. It was a song about loneliness, and love; about what we give up to someone in our desperation to belong, to be saved, but how hard it is to believe we've been found.

Laura's voice had soared over the swelling strings and driving snare. The calls of the backing singers filled every space left, and Elom had been reminded of Abena. His eyes got hot, and he had squeezed his eyelids, trying to stem the feeling. Suddenly, everything had fallen away at its peak, leaving only Laura and a mournful cello. The song ended with the opening verse. *She* was looking again: she would never stop.

A tear had fallen from Elom's left eye, and trickled down the curve of his nostril, tickling it as it passed. For a brief second, the release felt euphoric, and Elom was surprised by the pride he felt at such a simple act. By the time he had raised his hand to quietly wipe the tear away, the feeling had passed and, like the moment immediately post-orgasm, he felt no impulse to go back. He was even slightly embarrassed by the display, which felt so alien. By the end of the song, he had moved to stand side by side with Ben, and he never told him what had happened.

Now, Elom lay in bed with the lights off, plugged in his headphones and pressed play on *Sing to the Moon*. His nerves rose as 'She' approached, and intensified as the opening chimes started. He put it on repeat and closed his eyes, willing himself to feel something. His eyes stayed dry. All he felt were his nerves, which fell with each repetition of the song, until he pressed pause half an hour later, pulled out his headphones and rolled over to sleep.

The next day, Elom asked Mark if he could leave London.

'Just temporarily. Family reasons, but I think it could also help us build a readership in Scotland. Grow into a more UK-wide publication.' Mark looked at Elom, confused. Elom was aware of the contradiction of such a drastic request with such a feeble argument. He avoided looking out of the floor-to-ceiling windows, which gave him the thrilling urge to jump. He couldn't explain that he wanted to leave because he couldn't face working in an office any longer with people he felt nothing for; that he felt an overwhelming impulse to run.

'We don't have a Glasgow office.'

'That's kind of the point. But I could work remotely and come down when I need to. If I'm doing stories across Scotland, maybe I'll be further north for fair amounts of time anyway.'

Mark was unconvinced, but Elom persisted. After a few more meetings, Mark agreed to keep him on a six-month retainer, with Elom working freelance from Glasgow. A month later his colleagues threw him a surprise leaving do – cake and drinks in the office after a 4 p.m. finish on Friday.

'It's a shame to see you go, Elom,' said Tom, patting Elom on the back and passing him cava in a plastic glass. Elom drank the sour fizz and smiled, promising to join them at the pub when he was visiting London.

He finished his glass too quickly and refilled it from the warm bottle. Elom wanted them to like him: he'd felt small when they didn't follow him to the pub, and he felt good today as they celebrated him, but he was surprised that they would miss him. He couldn't call them friends: fortnightly drinks and the occasional lunch seemed too shallow a basis for that. But he also knew that they called each other friends and meant it. He picked a pretzel from a Styrofoam bowl and chewed on it, drying out his mouth. Either they were lying, or friendship was something different to how he understood it – or maybe he didn't understand it at all.

Elom thought of Chris and Del, the many Guys, Pippy, Freya, Luc. He thought of the constant itch with them, searching for a connection that could settle his restlessness, and comfort him. He thought of Ben, and how hard it had been to be loved by him, and how little he had been able to give him back. On the rare times he was lucky enough to understand his emotions, or desires, he hid them. He was always alone, no matter how hard he tried, or how hard others did. With a certainty usually alien to him, he realised that he was the problem.

Chapter Twenty-Eight

Elom – August 2018

Elom woke up in his childhood bed and reached for his phone. Kodzo and Abena had used Kodzo's retirement pot to buy a bungalow in a village outside of the city, and had planned to renovate and rent out the family home. Elom moved back before they had called the builders, and they suggested he just move in to save money for his six months in Scotland. He hadn't always been happy in Glasgow, but his life there had felt real, and he wanted to feel real again. Moving back to the home that had made him felt like a way to root himself.

He had snoozed three times already, which had eaten into his eating, shitting and showering time, so he got up, brushed his teeth and dialled in to his morning meeting. The thick cloud and heavy rain darkened the sky outside, so he felt like he was calling from a different time zone when he saw his colleagues framed by their clean, English late-summer light. Mark pushed him again for stories about the Scottish government, independence and the north–south divide. Elom had never enjoyed political reporting, but it had been the price of his move to Scotland. After the meeting he made some tea and went back to bed, leaving the cup to cool on the bedside table beside three others of varying emptiness. His current piece – a rare non-political article that Mark had conceded to – required interviews with families around Glasgow, investigating the effects of prison on women and their families. He had sent a few emails to a local prison, and called a charity based in Drumchapel, but he felt happier in bed. The fear of missing his deadlines was becoming less motivating.

Elom opened Grindr. In the months he had been back, the grid had become familiar. There were more faceless profiles than in London, but he hadn't blocked them in case one messaged, and happened to be hot. After confirming nothing had changed, he opened WhatsApp. There were fourteen unread messages, mostly from group chats from friends in London. He hadn't told any of his old friends from Glasgow that he was back. There was a message from an unsaved number which Elom had ignored for a couple of days, and he finally tapped it open, feeling a little surge of adrenaline.

Hey Elom, I'm Anj. I hope you don't mind, I got your number from Ben . . .

She was an ex-colleague of Ben's who had just moved to Glasgow and was *'up for grabbing drinks / checking out some music / would love a gym or swimming buddy!!'* Elom hadn't spoken to Ben in over a year, though he regularly checked his Facebook, Instagram and Twitter feeds for updates. He presumed Pippy had mentioned that he had moved, and the thought that their friendship was continuing without him came with a flash of jealousy. He wondered if Ben had given Anj his number willingly, or begrudgingly. It could have been an olive branch, or maybe a way of binding Elom closer to him. He wasn't sure how to respond.

Elom lay back on his pillow and stared at the Artex ceiling. He noticed that the line where the ceiling met the wall was uneven, and that there were a few bits where a wisp of blue spun onto the white ceiling border. There were still four oily marks on the wall from the 50 Cent poster he'd put up when he was thirteen. He closed his eyes and dozed off again, waking up an hour later to pale sunlight filtering through the window.

He left the bed unmade and went downstairs to make a pot of coffee, passing the shut door to his parents' old room on the landing. He had been sleeping in the single bed in his childhood bedroom rather than his parents' old king: the thought of wanking there, or having a hookup round on their bed felt illicit.

Everything in the house was almost the same. The only difference was the use that clung to everything. As he closed the cupboard, he saw the exposed wood around the handle where the paint had been rubbed away and the wood stained. The brown tinge of sweat, sebum and skin that had built up over decades made him feel sick, and he tried not to touch it. He wiped his hand on a dishcloth and headed to the living room to start working.

His desk faced the wall, with the windows on his left and a coffee table in the corner on his right, with the sofa lining the perpendicular wall beside it. The desk stood where the television had once been – his parents had taken that and left no replacement. The rest of the morning was somewhat productive,

SELALI FIAMANYA

and he arranged an interview for the following day. His laptop beeped its low battery alert as he half-heartedly copy and pasted references into his draft document without reading them. His charger cable had fallen, and he had to reach under the coffee table to try to extract it. It was tight, and so he moved the sofa, then the table, revealing the cable, surrounded by fluffy clumps of dust. As he reached down to pick it up, he saw a stained corner of wallpaper, peeling from the yellow wall underneath.

Elom recoiled. He thought of himself as a child, playing hide-and-seek under that table, nestled in that corner. He couldn't remember if it had been that dusty then; if the piss-colour stains had rubbed off on his clothes. He felt dirty and nauseated. He turned back to his laptop and saved the document before closing it, turning up the stairs and switching on the shower.

Over the next few days, Elom was equally repelled and obsessed by the corners in the house. He kept checking if the black mould in the bathroom was growing, and hoovering up the dust under the sofas didn't make him feel any more comfortable sitting on them. Everywhere he looked, there was grime, creeping towards him. He wanted to spend more time outside, but as soon as he left, he was scared again, of who he might see lurking in corners to remind him of his past. On the night he submitted his latest article to his editor, he got another text from Anj.

Hi Elom, no worries if it's not your thing but I've got a membership to the Baths in the West End. I'm going tomorrow at 3pm for a swim. if you fancy joining I can sign in a guest! In the past week, he had spoken only to ex-prisoners, a prison warden, children of prisoners and his editor. He also hadn't swum in years. He opened his underwear drawer. Stuffed at the back was a pair of bright orange, almost knee-length swimming trunks – he had barely worn them since the trip to Magaluf a decade earlier, when he had tried to impress Chris, only to need Chris to rescue him. He'd been scared of the sea since then, and thinking about that holiday gave him a hot flash of shame and humiliation. But remembering Chris calmly swimming beside him, he chastised himself: he never remembered the kindness. He was always so morose – even the step to free himself of London had left him putrefying in an old house.

Elom thought about Ben again, and the guilt came back. He still felt like he had been wrong, or had overreacted, or misinterpreted the things that had made him so sad; he had repeatedly shown himself that he didn't understand relationships. And here he was again, rejecting a nice thing for no other reason than his awkwardness. He wondered if Ben would be disappointed that he hadn't seen his friend yet. He took out his phone and replied, *Hey Anj sorry for the late reply, been busy with a deadline. Sure, I haven't gone swimming in ages but would be good to meet you. Can be there for 3!*

Elom cycled to the pool the next day, proud of getting out, but nervous too – he was no better a swimmer than he had been ten years ago. Anj met him in the lobby with a big smile and a hug, wearing a mix of expensive corduroy, denim and knitwear. With her shimmering confidence Elom could instantly place her amongst the London set of Freyas and Bens, and the familiarity was comforting. They changed and met by the poolside. Elom had already slid into the shallow end when she arrived.

'It's gorgeous in here, isn't it?' Anj said. The pool was Victorian, with high windows and original tiling. There were a dozen other swimmers in, and Anj spoke loudly, her voice reverberating against the cathedral-like ceiling. Despite her volume, which made Elom feel more conspicuous than he wanted to be as the only people of colour in a members-only baths, Anj made him feel surprisingly at ease, and they chatted as their bodies warmed up. She made it easy, talking freely about herself, but also asking easy questions.

'So, what brought you back to Glasgow?'

Elom answered with his stock responses about family, affordability and nature, and she replied similarly. 'I'm keen to do some more wild swimming. There's some great lochs not too far from here.' She pronounced it 'locks', rather than 'lochs' with a soft, throaty ending.

'Wild swimming?'

'Yeah, just out in nature. Have you done much before?'

'I can barely swim in a pool, to be honest.' Elom laughed off the embarrassment.

'Lol,' Anj smiled, 'it's amazing. Can be fucking cold but honestly it just makes it better – you just feel . . . it's hard to explain, but you just feel amazing. I'll tell you next time I go.' She lowered her goggles, somehow signalling the conversation was over without any awkwardness, a skill that Elom was immediately jealous of. 'Shall we?'

Anj pushed off, emerging a few feet ahead with a powerful front crawl. Elom followed, with Anj passing him a while later on her way back. Elom stopped to catch his breath after the first, and every subsequent length, with Anj joining every few lengths for a shorter break before pushing off again. The pauses were embarrassing, but each time he pushed off he enjoyed the tightness in his shoulders and thighs as his muscles worked to propel him forward. He hadn't been this out of breath in a long time, and the new sensation paused his usual thoughts. He stopped worrying about what the other swimmers thought of his glacial pace, or what Anj might tell Ben about him.

Anj joined him at the shallow end, taking off her goggles to show a red imprint underneath her eyes. 'Break?' she half asked, half stated, while reaching for her water bottle at the edge of the pool. Elom agreed, whilst being surprised at his surprise that you could get thirsty even whilst immersed in water. He made a note to bring a bottle next time. Anj ducked under the divider into the open swimming area, which now had a few kids splashing and dunking themselves in it. They slowly made their way to the middle as they spoke, where Anj began to tread water. Elom joined in as she drifted further away, his already tired muscles becoming painful with each second. Anj talked about her colleagues, and how she hadn't yet sussed them out as they were yet to go on a night out together, and Elom breathlessly mentioned that he similarly hadn't made any work friends as there was no office here.

After a minute of flailing his legs and arms underwater, Elom drifted back to where he could firmly plant his feet on the tiles, pulling him just out of conversation distance so Anj had to swim over to join him.

'Sorry, just getting a bit tired again.'

'No worries. I might just float for a bit,' she said, lying back and stilling her limbs. She closed her eyes, bobbing as the ripples from swimmers in the adjacent lanes reached them.

'I've never been able to float like that,' Elom said.

Anj looked up. 'Really? Just lie back.'

'Nah, seriously, I can't.' He avoided saying that kids used to tease him, saying it was because Black people's bones were denser.

'Try it,' Anj said, dropping her legs. Elom lay back and brought his legs up, swirling his arms in an attempt to stop them falling down through the water. He lasted a few seconds before he was back to treading.

'You need to stick your head back a bit.' Elom tried again. 'No, like, right back in the water. Watch.' Anj brought herself back to the surface and dipped her head into the water, so her ears were submerged. It looked serene and effortless to Elom. He tried once more, and as he dipped his head below the surface, the sounds of the pool disappeared then reappeared as the water splashed around his head. He lost his focus on the ceiling and sank into the water, the burn of chlorine filling his nostrils.

'Yeah, I can't,' he said, flashing Anj a smile and wiping the water from his face before putting his goggles back on.

Anj laughed. 'Okay, we can try again next time.'

Elom wanted to ask about Ben – he wanted to know if she had seen him recently, if he had spoken about Elom and who they were to each other, or why they'd broken up. He wanted to know if Ben was seeing anyone else, if anyone else had fucked him, and if he had found someone able to bottom for him. He started to ask just as Anj righted herself again and lowered her goggles, pressing the lenses to seal them around her eyes. 'Cooldown lengths and then coffee?'

*　*　*

Afterwards, Elom waited in the lobby for Anj.

'Hey!' she called as she came up the stairs. 'Know any good cafés?' Her voice was clear and loud, and Elom instinctively looked around the room apologetically. As he did, a man at reception turned in their direction. It was Chris, ten years older. His stubble had evened out, and he filled his gym-issued polo shirt much better than he had his school uniform. An intense fear rose in Elom, and he immediately looked back to Anj. It felt like his lungs had stopped working, and his limbs trembled.

He hadn't answered her question and didn't know how long he had been staring at her. 'Yeah, let's go,' he managed breathlessly. Elom strode across the lobby, avoiding Chris's gaze and making a show of how comfortable he was with Anj, staying a few inches closer to her than he had all day. He placed his hand on her back as he held the door open for her, ashamed at himself for playing a straight charade he thought he had left behind years before. He was glad for the water dripping from his hair that could be blamed for the sweat that was forming on his forehead. In the split second their eyes had met, Chris had given him a look of recognition. Elom wasn't sure if it would become an awkward nod, a broad smile or a snort of laughter, and he didn't look back to check.

Elom cycled home an hour later, his cortado adding an anxious edge to his ruminations. His memories of Ben and Chris were cluttered: every time he tried to categorise one – good, bad, my fault, his fault, serious, insignificant – he was distracted by ever more images and feelings. Ben had hurt him in ways he was only

just beginning to understand, but Elom knew he had also hurt
Ben. Sometimes he wondered which had come first, and other
times he wondered if it mattered. Chris reminded him of total
confusion; boggy and endless, though at times thrilling.

He kept cycling down Great Western Road, missing his
turning as his legs pushed on. He wasn't ready to stop, despite
not having eaten since breakfast. He tired as he approached a
retail park with signs for fast-food restaurants. Turning in, he
saw a B & Q; he had gone there as a child with Kodzo, picking
up what felt like random objects which would sit in the damp
hut at the bottom of the garden for years. Elom locked up
his bike and passed through automatic sliding doors into the
cavernous room.

After roaming for a few minutes, he found himself in an
aisle of ropes. There were balls of tightly wound cotton or
jute twine, and loops of thicker, colourful polypropylene or
bungee cord sold by the metre. One of the red loops had a max
load capacity of 1650kg, with a breaking force of 1980kg. He
felt it. It was smooth. As he ran his hand along it, he noticed
the scar under his knuckle, which he'd got from a broken
mirror a decade earlier. He remembered the anger, shame, fear
and guilt he had felt back then, and which had been reflected
back at him. Trapped in Glasgow, trapped at home and forced
to study, trapped in a group of friends that didn't seem to
care, trapped in the closet, and about to be sent to a Christian
camp. He had seen his reflection trapped in the mirror, too,
and couldn't find the words to set himself free. Now, he still
felt trapped. Those emotions were still there, but blunted: he
didn't feel them jostling inside of him, desperate for release.

Instead, things felt less urgent now – like there was less at stake, after all.

He let the rope fall back and turned down the aisle again. On the rack directly in front of him were tubs of paint stacked five shelves high. At eye level stood a tub with the words *Caramelised Mountain Ochre* on it. The sample swatch showed a colour as clean as yellow, as warm as orange, and as vibrant as both. Elom smiled just looking at it, and he picked up two tubs.

The wire handles dug into his hands as he walked to the bus stop, leaving his bike chained to the barrier outside the store. At home, Elom opened the shed, which his parents had yet to clear out, and found a putty knife, a paint tray and an old, stiff roller with hardened spikes of dried paint. He tapped play on *Channel Orange* as the sun set, and moved his desk, the coffee table and couch away from the back wall. Starting from the peeled edge in the corner he pulled, tore and scraped, then stopped to google for advice before wetting sections with a soaked sponge and scraping more. When he was done, he rolled the paint on in great streaks, and it dripped down plug sockets and onto the layers of newspaper and old wallpaper lining the floor. In the morning he lay on the couch with his feet facing his newly completed wall, bright and wet, rippled with patches of lining paper and unsanded glue, and fell asleep smiling.

Chapter Twenty-Nine

Elom – October 2018

Elom turned on the windscreen wipers, and they moved with the music for a few beats before disentangling themselves. *nostalgia, ULTRA* was playing loudly enough that he could barely hear his own voice, and so could convince himself that his runs on 'Novacane' matched Ocean's note for note. He was driving back from the Highlands after some interviews for a piece on rural healthcare. It was twee and lazy, but he had stopped caring. He wasn't sure if he would move back to London when his retainer ended in a few months.

The rain picked up, and Elom turned up the wipers and further slowed his already sluggish pace. He had barely driven since he passed his test, years before, and felt uneasy on country roads. He got the same nervous thrill every time a car passed on his right that he got when standing on a high balcony. As he turned a corner, a strong gust of wind rocked the car, and Elom held the steering wheel firm to stop himself veering into a passing van. It was a few more miles before his heart settled, and when he saw a turning for a car park by a sea loch, he took it.

He stopped the engine and pulled out his store-bought sandwich. His coffee was already cold, but he drained the last grainy drops from the paper cup. The falling rain filled the silence left by the stereo turning off. It sounded like a constant sizzle; a fading firework. He couldn't see the loch in front of him and so he turned the key in the ignition, restarting the wipers and the music along with it. The loch disappeared between swipes, but he could see a couple of overturned wooden boats on a short, rocky beach. The wind pushed dark grey water into white, frothy waves, slapping against seaweed-covered stones.

Elom remembered Anj's love of wild swimming. He hadn't seen her since the day at the baths. He couldn't go back and risk seeing Chris, but he also didn't feel like he could tell her that – partially out of embarrassment, but also out of anxiety over what she might tell Ben – so he had made excuses whenever she had asked him to join her for another swim, and then ignored her last message to meet for a coffee. He felt guilty, but now too much time had passed, and he thought she might already have told Ben that he had ghosted her, which embarrassed Elom even more. In many ways, Ben knew Elom more than anyone else had, yet had still loved him. Despite himself, Elom still cared what Ben thought about him, and he didn't want that opinion to change.

He watched the waves on the shore and the boats rocking slightly in the wind, and looked around at the surrounding treeline: he figured he was completely alone. He wondered how the wild swimmers were able to get in the water – whether it was bravery, recklessness or masochism that allowed them to swallow the cold. Elom could barely cope in a swimming pool, and the last time he had stepped into a sun-drenched sea, he almost hadn't made it out. He wondered how cold it really felt. He had read that dunking yourself in ice water, like the Finns did, was good for your brain. There was a pause between songs where he heard the sizzle again, warm and comforting. 'Swim Good' started, and Elom smiled, rolling his eyes. He knew what he was supposed to do, and he dared himself to do it - to try being bold again - but instead he stayed sitting in his car, watching.

The longer he waited, the less silly it seemed. What was stopping him? The song felt like a countdown. If he stayed to the end, he would be stuck there – alone, undecided, always scared and angry with himself. Frank's falsetto drifted off at the end of the bridge. There was a split second where Elom's ears re-focused on the sound of the rain, and his thoughts came back to the car, and to his body. The beat dropped into the chorus an instant later, and Elom pushed open the car door with it, kicking off his shoes.

The sound of rain on metal became a whistle of wind against his ears. He stepped out, squinting his eyes against the water and pulling up his hood. The jagged shale pressed into his feet. He walked against the wind for 20 metres towards the shore. In seconds, his feet met an advancing wave. All he felt was a pulse of cold – they were already wet and numb. The wave retreated and he followed it, wading into the water until it reached his ankles. The cold became an ache in his joints, and his skin started to tingle as the rain pelted his face and the wind pushed him backwards. His feet pressed into the rocky sand, and it yielded, gently, welcoming him in. Despite the storm around him, Elom felt rooted and calm. He looked around and laughed at his own absurdity. He shouted into the wind: it was totally thrilling.

A heavy gust threw a surge of water at him, knocking him back a few steps. Once again, he was pulled back into himself, and the absurdity seemed less benign. He turned quickly, running back with heavy footsteps. He crashed into his car, took off his wet jacket and turned the heating on full before driving home barefoot, shivering with cold and adrenaline.

Over the next few days, Elom found himself checking the loch on Google Maps when he was supposed to be writing. He would drop the little man on the spot to see the beach, calm, with clear skies and a family picnicking on the shore. He started watching wild swimming videos on YouTube, falling asleep to them rather than xHamster. Some had trim, middle-aged men giving tips on the best £600 wetsuits to buy for a triathlon, others younger, carefree women extolling how free and at one with nature it made them feel, and others still talked about neurochemicals and depression. Wild swimming seemed to lie somewhere between extreme sport and meditation. None of the videos captured what he'd felt, though, when he'd planted his feet in the sand and felt the waves ebbing around him.

On the following Sunday afternoon, he visited Kodzo and Abena in their new house for Kodzo's birthday. Each time Elom saw him, Kodzo looked smaller than he remembered. Abena made banku and they ate in the living room with the television on in the background. The idea that his parents would grow old and frail in a strange, memoryless house saddened him, but he was surprised at how quickly it felt like home just by them being in it. They phoned Dzifa, who was on call that weekend, and spoke about how excited they were for the trip to Ghana, booked for Easter the following year, and Elom felt the slight pang of jealousy he sometimes had on these calls at how easy and open the conversation was between Dzifa and their parents. After lunch, Elom helped Abena put the plates away, then put on his jacket. 'I think I should get going now before it gets dark.'

'Already?' Abena asked.

'Sorry – I'm just not ready to drive on those roads late at night yet.'

'Okay,' Kodzo replied lightly. 'Maybe next time you can stay over if you want.'

'Yeah, sure.' Elom had enjoyed their lunch together, but it was still an effort to leave his bed, and he was looking forward to crawling back into it. Looking at his dad, balder, rounder, smaller, sitting on the faux-leather sofa, awkwardly placed in this new house, Elom felt a pang of regret for something yet to happen. 'I can try to come down more weekends, too. I'll be doing some wild swimming near here as the weather gets better.' Elom said this to let them know he would try to see more of them, and partially to imply he wasn't spending all of his free time in bed.

'What's that?' Abena asked.

'It's just swimming in, like, lakes and the sea. Like, open water so not swimming pools.'

'That sounds dangerous. Do you go alone?' Abena asked.

'Well, it's not that bad. Just don't go in during a storm, obviously,' Elom replied. He hadn't actually done any wild swimming yet, but he didn't want to seem too naive.

Kodzo laughed. 'Not for me, son. You'll freeze in this here Scottish water.'

'Apparently it's not too bad with a wetsuit,' Elom said, smiling. 'They say it's good for your mental health.'

'That's good,' Kodzo nodded.

'Please be careful,' Abena chided. Elom smiled again, zipped up his jacket and hugged them goodbye before driving home with a bag full of leftovers in Tupperware. He was frustrated that Kodzo and Abena hadn't shown more curiosity about his new hobby, but not surprised. He was also aware that they couldn't know more about him if he didn't lead the way, but turning the conversation to things that were important to him felt too hard, given how long he had spent trying to keep them secret. He wondered if Dzifa had ever felt the same.

Elom felt they reacted to any discussion of mental health in the same way they did his sexuality – a compassionate avoidance, but avoidance nonetheless. Pushing for an overt display of sympathy felt whiny and self-obsessed, like he was asking to be coddled when, in fact, they were already there for him, in their own way. They had never cast him out, they had worked endless hours to feed him, and now he was living in their house rent-free when they could have been landlords, filling up their retirement pot. Yet, to his shame, he still couldn't manage staying overnight with them.

The first weekend after his wetsuit arrived, Elom packed it along with some sandwiches, a towel, a swimming cap, a flask of tea and some goggles, and drove north. He pulled into the same sea loch, though this time he wasn't alone: a couple

of cars and a van were in the small car park, but there was
nobody on the beach or in the water. He presumed they were
walking in the surrounding hills, though he kept an eye out as
he approached. The water was calmer than before, and as he
stood at the shoreline, he could see through it to the murky
seabed below.

The water felt like an ice pack pressing against his wetsuit
boots. As he stepped further in, there was a sharp cold around
his ankles as it filtered between his boot and the bottom of his
wetsuit leg. By the time the water reached his neck, he was
shivering from the freezing layer which had trickled into his suit
through the zip along his spine. He trod water, building up the
courage to lower his head under the surface. Every time he took
a deep breath to ready himself, he would let it out again, partly
from nerves and partly from the cold working his chest. After
a few more attempts, he started a countdown from three. He
breathed deep, lifted his legs to his chest and allowed himself to
fall, like a slow-motion cannonball dive. He lasted a few seconds
before reaching up with a gasp.

The laugh came back to him, the same one from when he'd
stood in the water a few weeks prior. He had less breath to
manage it, but it was there, and it felt good. He was proud of
himself for getting into the water; for staying in and immersing
himself. He turned to swim, parallel with the shore as he was still
nervous. He had forgotten his goggles in the car, and awkwardly
held his head above the bobbing waves as he haphazardly
switched between breaststroke and front crawl. He was no longer
shivering, and at times felt a splash of warmth as the water in his
suit picked up his body heat.

Soon, his shoulders started to ache and he was finding it harder to maintain his breath. He had barely swum 100 metres back and forth across the beach, but he pulled himself out of the water onto the shore. He was exhausted, and still felt the undulation of the water in his body as he steadied himself; the receding tide pulling him back in a somatic illusion. He smiled all the way to his car – a panting, open-mouthed smile as he looked back at the water that had carried him. Peeling off the wetsuit took longer than the swim had: his numb fingers were metal rods attached to his hands. He wrapped himself in his towel and sat in the driver's seat with the heating on, enjoying the last of the menthol tingle the cold water left on his skin.

Elom began wild swimming every weekend, occasionally staying overnight in B & Bs, or in his car, bathed by stars. During the week he'd do lengths at the local leisure centre. He became one of the men in the pool with long Lycra shorts. His body changed. He was wanking less; waking up early to get to the pool and falling asleep more quickly at night. The water cooled his mind. He started driving past the turning to his parents' house after swims, not wanting to interrupt them.

Work had become arduous. All Elom wanted to do was get back into the water. It was new to him, this feeling of longing. Everything else had been confusion, in part defined by not knowing what he actually wanted, like with Chris, or how to express it, like with his family, or Ben. He had felt as though everyone around him had been drawn, then neatly coloured in: a body full of substance and desire. In his case the whole page had been filled with bright greens and reds and blues and blacks, but his outline remained an empty, negative space, only defined – if defined at all – by what it wasn't. Now, for the first time, he wanted something, and wanted it so strongly it almost scared him – the quiet, the solitude, the sound of water splashing in his ears.

A month before his contract ended, Mark told him they would not be extending: Elom just felt relief, like taking off a hat that was too tight. He read the email on his phone in bed, then rolled over and started searching for holiday lets. He would have to write a few more pieces, but he didn't need to stay in Glasgow. In any case, any motivation to deliver his best work had faded.

He found a place for a couple of weeks on Mull, which promised clear blue water. When he texted Dzifa, she said she'd love to join for a weekend, and that she would check her shifts. Elom wanted her to come, and for them to share the sea together, but he knew she would be too busy, despite her excitement. He told Abena and Kodzo the following week at their house, and said he would be working there for a week and then taking a week off. He didn't say he wouldn't be going back to work afterwards. They seemed happy that he was going exploring, and when she found out it was self-catered, Abena sent him home with a few tins from her cupboard and a bag of rice. Elom felt guilty as he pulled out of their driveway with them waving at him through the open front door. It felt like he was abandoning them, but he couldn't say that he just wanted to be alone. It wasn't that he couldn't be himself around other people, or that he was himself in the water. It was that in the water he was no one: nothing. He was the sound of his breath, and the cold on his skin, and the pain in his shoulders, and nothing more. When the day came, Elom emptied the fridge and filled a couple of bags with food he wouldn't be able to get on the island, then packed his suitcase, locked up the house, and left.

His bed and breakfast in Tobermory overlooked the quaint, pastel-coloured houses in the harbour. On the first morning he drove to Calgary Bay, a green, hilly horseshoe of land with a white shell beach. It was just after 9 a.m., but there were a handful of people already there, some in wetsuits like his, some just in Lycra; one had a large jellyfish tattooed down her leg. Others were in raincoats and scarves, walking their dogs.

Elom felt graceless as he walked across the beach, his wetsuit sticking to the folds of his body. He was still the only Black person he had seen on the island. He wasn't sure if he should be wearing a swimsuit, or a wetsuit, or if it mattered either way. But as he stepped into the water, he felt the familiar attention shift. He focused on his legs as they waded into deeper water, navigating the sand underfoot. Each step came with a pleasant slurp as the water moved around his thighs, trunk, then arms, until he lowered himself under the surface and heard only high-pitched tinkles.

He swam along the arm of the horseshoe, mentally calibrating the point at which he was halfway to exhaustion. He could still only manage a couple of hundred metres, and stopped after a hundred to attempt to float on his back. The saltwater and wetsuit helped, but he still had to flail his limbs to stay at the surface. Onshore, the calmness faded again. He walked towards his car, hoping no one had noticed how short his swim had been.

'You're braver than me!' a dog-walker called. She was middle-aged, hurling a ball with a big plastic ice-cream scoop. Elom shrugged as if to say, 'Not really,' and continued walking.

'My sister-in-law does triathlons, but it sounds too much like hard work,' she laughed. 'Are you staying on Mull?' She stopped in front of him, and Elom reluctantly stopped too, realising she wanted more than a passing hello.

'Yeah,' he nodded, 'a B & B in Tobermory.'

'Aye, I can't imagine a tent's very warm to go back to after a swim in the sea.' She chuckled, and Elom relaxed: she was friendly, and it felt nice to be welcomed onto the beach. 'I've a wee holiday home in Bunessan.' Her dog – a wet Jack Russell with long, grey muzzle hairs – dropped the ball at her feet and waited impatiently for another toss.

'Where's that?' Elom asked. He had started shivering despite wanting to appear hardy, but he felt he needed to ask at least one question.

'Down on the Ross of Mull, on the way to Iona. Have you been over to Iona yet?'

Elom shook his head.

'It's stunning.' She said this bluntly, suddenly very serious. 'Stunning. And lots of great places to swim, too.' The Jack Russell barked, and she bent down with the scoop. 'I'll let you get on. Have a nice trip.' The ball swung in another arc across the beach, followed by the dog.

'Thanks, you too,' he said.

She had asked more questions than his parents had about his holiday.

The week went by very simply: Elom swam, drove, ate and slept. He kept work to a minimum, and instead looked for more secluded swimming spots. His car was loaded with cans of tuna, tea and chocolates, and he ate the leftovers Abena had given him for dinner. When he went to the shop to restock a few days later, he realised that the last person he had spoken to was the woman on the beach. He no longer felt the shame he did when this happened in Glasgow after a day in bed.

He took her advice and visited Iona. The ferry port was tiny, facing a mile-long stretch of water to the island, with a correspondingly tiny ferry already shuttling people back and forth between them. Elom immediately felt a pull – a serenity diffusing over from the sliver of green between the deep blue of the water and light blue of the sky. Once on Iona, he felt a similar peace to that which he normally felt in water, like the small island was a jewel, calmly twinkling, mesmerising him. He turned left and walked along the coast until he found a beach to swim from. The water was perfectly clear, like molten glass, or tears, and he exhausted himself in it before lying back and stretching out his legs, attempting, unsuccessfully, to float for a few seconds before swimming back to shore.

He returned over the next few days, making the long drive back and forth from Tobermory through the rain. On his last day on Mull, his anxiety rose, as he imagined unlocking the door to the house in Glasgow, seeing his unmade bed and tired laminate floors. He opened his phone and found another low-season let, this time on Iona. He fell asleep, warm and content, to the sound of a storm against his windows.

Every morning on Iona, Elom swam further, making it across the Sound to Mull and back in a day. He learned how to sit with the pain in his joints, focus on his breath, and thought about one day swimming completely around Iona. He started by going from bay to bay, climbing out of the water to rest, or walking back home when he was tired. The weather was changeable, but despite the cold, his wetsuit was becoming warm and ungainly with the longer distances and he had switched to Lycra with boots and gloves in the water.

Two weeks into his stay on Iona, Elom went for an evening walk across the island. He bought a beer and sat outdoors in the grounds of a fancy hotel and looked out at Mull across the water, watching the birds move together in the sky. He took a selfie in the evening light and sent it to the family WhatsApp. He had been away for a month and was finally due back tomorrow.

Iona has been so sick!

Abena responded with *looks lush* and Kodzo with *well deserved relaxation. Have a beer for me and see you soon.* Dzifa said she was gutted she wasn't able to join this time but was hoping she could soon. Elom finished his beer and hurried back to his B & B, escaping the bursting rainclouds.

The next day, Elom rose early, before his alarm. There was plenty of time before checkout, and he had a small bowl of porridge and jam before heading out to the beach. He started towards the north of the island this time. The water was icy cold, and the weather in the Highland mode of bright sun and light drizzle at the same time. He swam west, away from the ferry, which would soon be bringing tourists over. He had swum this route before, getting out at Port Ban Beach, but when he reached it this time, he felt he had more in him. He looked right at the expanse: the next land mass in his path was Canada. He turned towards it, not quite ready for land, or people, and with the pain in his shoulders bearable. It was so quiet; there were only splashes – of his feet on water, his hands on water, of the gentle rain on the water, and his own breath in bubbles and gasps. It didn't take long for his gasps to become harsher and less rhythmic. He slowed, then turned and trod water for a minute, catching his breath as he looked back at the island. The moment felt serene.

The first time Elom had swum in the sea, Chris had saved him. On that trip, he had shown Elom kindness and cruelty. Ben and his own family had, too. And so had the sea itself. Now he didn't see either, or he saw both, whipped into waves and folding into each other, or crashing onto the shore. The sea soothed as it numbed, the saltwater stung as it cleansed. It pushed, and it pulled. It held the promise of floating and the threat of drowning. It was all kindness and cruelty, as far as the eye could see.

Elom thought about his people, and wondered what could have been different if he had been able to speak his mind, and if they had understood. He wondered what might have changed if he had known how to accept the love they had tried to give him. He realised he wasn't angry at Chris anymore. He thought about himself back then, totally governed by fear. Elom had learned

since then that people don't keep you in their lives unless they
want to, and Chris had tried, despite the number of texts Elom
had ignored after moving. It seemed pointless, but he allowed
himself to imagine for a moment what could have been had
he been less defensive; what secrets of his own Chris might
have been keeping, and what questions Elom never asked. He
thought of Dzifa, too, accepting the jealousy that came with
his pride for her. She had been able to do it all – move through
life with determination and grace, and make the connections he
never could. He was glad, at least, that he hadn't held her back:
that she didn't look up to him in a way that meant she learned
his bad habits.

Tears blurred his vision as he pictured his mum and dad on
their leather couch at home. It was unfair that between Ghana
and Scotland, a language had been lost. There was something
they never understood about him, and things he was never able
to tell them; ways of loving they couldn't agree on, though he
knew the love was there. He had never been taught how to talk
about his feelings. He had only recently started learning how
to understand them. Ben had tried to give him a language to
love in when Elom didn't have one of his own. But just looking
in Ben's eyes, hungry with love – with wanting to be loved –
felt like falling, and so Elom would look away before he hit the
ground. Apportioning blame seemed futile: he could see now
that Ben had been controlling, and that he himself had been
unreadable. Ben had built him the confidence to live the queer
life he had wanted, but he had also crushed him. It wasn't clear
what stood out more from the relationship – the hurt, or the
love. Elom couldn't tease them apart.

Elom could never make sense of love. The people who loved him, who he had idolised, or wanted to impress, had all shown him kindness. But they had also hurt him, had thought of him as disposable, or worthy of ridicule, or someone to manipulate, or be ashamed of. They had shown him that love was a tightrope between freedom and control. He didn't know how others seemed to walk it with ease.

He bobbed in the current, shivering and exhausted. He had never had control, or he had always given it to someone else. He was ready to take it back. Maybe loving himself and giving himself control were the same thing. Maybe it would help him love others.

Elom lay back and rested his head in the water, blocking out the sounds of the waves and the birds. The silence was almost total, and he smiled. He lifted his legs towards the surface, breathed in deep, slow breaths, and floated, for the first, and final time.

Acknowledgements

This book exists because people gave opportunities to underrepresented writers. Troy Fairclough of *Black Gay Ink*, and Olumide Popoola of *The Future Is Back*, I speak for scores of queer people-of-colour when I thank you for your workshops, which gave us space, knowledge, resources and your time. Thanks, too, to Spread the Word and Arts Council England for supporting them. Curtis Brown Creative's *Breakthrough Novel-Writing Course for Black Writers* was a gamechanger. To the entire team – and particularly Jacob Ross – you treated my writing seriously, and I'm so grateful: it helped me take it seriously too. These workshops also built supportive, talented communities of writers – thank you all for the feedback, commiserations, congratulations, and the sharing of opportunities. My writing fam is a model of generosity and abundance. This is a win for us all, and I can't wait to celebrate your wins together, too. Special thanks to Nick Ishmael-Perkins and Dale Taylor-Gentles of *Help a Brother Out,* and to Kim Squirrell for holding *the creatives' room* together.

Anna Soler-Pont, Maria Cardona Serra and JJ Bola, I'm indebted to you for launching a prize to help writers like me. You saw my potential, took me on at PONTAS, and showed kindness when navigating my entry into publishing. I'm still flummoxed at The Borough Press for taking a punt on an unfinished short story collection, and seeing what it could become. Special thanks to my first editor Margot Gray for your belief (and hand holding), and to my final editor Jabin Ali for understanding what I wanted to say, and helping me say it.

I started writing through zines. Big up Anu Henriques and *Skin Deep* for first showing me I could work with words. Love to zine collective *People of Content,* and Tara Montrei of *whut?* for indulging me when I wanted to make my own. To all the friends who kept asking about the book, and insisted I send the pre-order link; who celebrated with me and made me feel like I was doing something of value, your support carried me through. Thanks Mark Simpson for telling me to dream big. Cheers, Tom Chetwode-Barton and Caoláin Power for making me take breaks. Thanks too, to Dave Bath, for always being in my corner.

For help with the text, particular thanks to Mercy Fiamanya (aka Mum) for all things Fante, Ga, Twi, and food; Eric Fiamanya (aka Dad) for the Ewe; Emily Bootle, Memuna Konteh, Ena Miller and Rob Powell for your advice on journalism; Anna Ploszajski for reading sections on wild swimming; and Natasha Heliotis for the Greek names. May Anderson, I can't believe you read that entire bloated second draft – you showed me it was possible for someone to actually read a book I wrote, and enjoy it. Yara Rodrigues Fowler and Mendez, your sage advice as formerly debut authors calmed my nerves.

Finally, my family. Mum and Dad, you are determined and uncomplaining, and you built a home in which I never – not even for a single second – felt unloved. Edem, I've always looked up to you, and I'm so proud of the man, and dad, you've become. Danielle, despite my envy of your talent, your laser-focused commitment to your craft is exemplary, and I can only try to emulate you. Each of you have taught me what hard work looks like, and what we do it for. You've taught me the importance of thinking deeply about everything that matters (and in the process given me infinite stamina for a debate); and that we all have capacity for great change, and to embrace it. But most importantly, you taught me about love, and for that I thank you.